Prai… :

'Atmospheric, engaging and sublimely satisfying'
Veronica Henry

'M…-watering and mysterious. A compelling read'

'A sizzling forbidden love story'
Heat

'Delightful and delicious: a must read'
Nina George

'If you are a fan of Kate Morton or Kate Mosse you will enjoy this book. I think this is her best book yet'
Over the Rainbow

'A truly stunning story that will captivate you'
Kraftireader

'I know I will return to read again and again'
The Very Pink Notebook

'Heartbreaking. A must read'
Jera's Jamboree

'An incredible story and certainly one for the keeper shelf'
Shaz's Book Blog

'A story about love, loss and finding your way . . . This book will transport you'
Our First Year Here

'A complex and mesmerising read'
Alba in Bookland

www.penguin.co.uk

After a childhood spent acting professionally and training at a theatre school, Laura Madeleine changed her mind and went to study English Literature at Newnham College, Cambridge. She now writes fiction, as well as recipes, and was formerly the resident cake baker for Domestic Sluttery. She lives in Bristol, but can often be found visiting her family in Devon, eating cheese and getting up to mischief with her sister, fantasy author Lucy Hounsom.

You can find her on Twitter @lauramadeleine

Also by Laura Madeleine

The Confectioner's Tale
Where the Wild Cherries Grow
The Secrets Between Us

and published by Black Swan

AN ECHO OF SCANDAL

Laura Madeleine

BLACK SWAN

TRANSWORLD PUBLISHERS
61–63 Uxbridge Road, London W5 5SA
www.penguin.co.uk

Transworld is part of the Penguin Random House group of companies
whose addresses can be found at global.penguinrandomhouse.com

Penguin
Random House
UK

First published in Great Britain in 2019 by Black Swan
an imprint of Transworld Publishers

A CIP catalogue record for this book
is available from the British Library.

ISBN
9781784162542

Typeset in 11.5/14pt Bembo
by Integra Software Services Pvt. Ltd, Pondicherry

Printed and bound in Great Britain by Clays Ltd, Elcograf S.p.A.

1 3 5 7 9 10 8 6 4 2

To absent friends

I will mix me a drink of stars,—
Large stars with polychrome needles,
Small stars jetting maroon and crimson,
Cool, quiet, green stars.
I will tear them out of the sky,
And squeeze them over an old silver cup,
And I will pour the cold scorn of my Beloved into it,
So that my drink shall be bubbled with ice.

– 'Vintage', Amy Lowell, 1914

Part One

BLOOD AND SAND

Take a pony of fresh blood orange juice and another of good Scotch whisky. Add into this the same of Cherry Heering and sweet Italian vermouth. Shake violently enough to break a sweat and strain into a coupe glass. An experience rarely repeated.

Blood and Sand.

It's the name that haunts me. It takes me straight back to that night. Every time I read the recipe, I can't help but imagine another one, written in its place:

Take one girl as ripe as fruit and one man as hard as liqueur. Throw them together with sweet words turned rotten and fill them with alcohol until the result is inescapable.

It's the Scotch that does it. After that night, whenever I opened a bottle – however expensive – all I could ever smell was blood.

The Señor was the source of it. The blood had run down the sides of his neck on to the pink flowered rug that had been his gift from Madrid, glistening on the creamy roses before sinking into the pile, as if into sand. His gaze was fixed on the corner of the room. That's where she stood, with her pretty dress spattered and the broken neck of the bottle still clutched in her hand, the jagged edge dark with his blood. Droplets of it fell into the Scotch that had pooled around her feet, like vinegar into oil.

I should have spun on my heel and screamed, should have bellowed murder down into the courtyard below. But I didn't. And that was the start of all the trouble for me. It's what brought me here.

I've always suffered because of blood. Right from the start, I was told that the two bloods that made me, rich and poor, shouldn't have been mixed: that they had no business being shaken together and even less business resulting in a child. Some of our customers – like the Señor Ramón Vélez del Olmo who bled out on the rug – called me a mongrel. Most of the girls called me that too, though never to my face.

It was all right for them. They were *of* somewhere. I was of nowhere, except for the inn. Which is why, I suppose, I eventually named myself for the place. *Del Potro.*

The Hostería del Potro stood on one side of a small plaza, where the city had once held horse fairs, back before anyone could remember. It was the centre of my world, the plaza, with its fountain topped by a crumbling stone horse, and its tiled rooftops that butted and jostled one another, a cat's highway down to the river. I knew those roofs and streets as well as my own body, and nowhere better than the hostería, the oldest inn in Córdoba.

I believe I was born there, or at least, was left there soon after. The hostería's flaking plaster walls absorbed the sound of my first cries. The draught through its cracked windows was the breath that soothed my fevers, the groan of its floorboards was a grandmother's voice murmuring a lullaby, the clanking of bedposts and the snores of countless men were the familiar sounds of my childhood years.

I had been at the inn longer than anyone, except for Mama Morales. Once, I made the mistake of asking whether *she* was my mama. She had looked at me with such contempt that I knew the truth immediately: I did not belong to people, to mother or father or family. I belonged to the inn, like the cats born in the stable that lived and died too soon amongst the hay.

I sometimes worry it could still get me into trouble, this talk about the inn. But it seems so small now, so distant, after everything else. I'll never go back to Córdoba, and anyway, you already know that *I* didn't kill the man.

It's the rest of it that could be dangerous for me; what came after. The only other person who knew it all is dead and gone. Perhaps – at last – I have kept his secret for long enough. I drowned it at the bottom of cocktail glasses and buried it beneath the scrapings left on silver platters. I tied it with white silk and hid it in plain sight. I held my tongue, kept fifty years of silence. Even he could not have asked me for more.

Of course, if he had, I might have given it. But he is not here, is he?

Perhaps silence is no longer the answer. Perhaps this is a story that should finally be told.

And after all, I have already begun.

Tangier

July 1978

'Are you sure there's nothing else? There's rien? Pour Hackett. H – A – C –'

Metronome steady, the man shook his head.

'Non.'

'You're certain? Vous êtes sur?'

'Oui, monsieur.'

Sam dropped his chin, staring at the scuffed wooden countertop. The room was dim and sweltering, a fug of cigarettes and the more pungent smoke from joints of kif. It made it hard to concentrate, hard to do the mental arithmetic required. He couldn't afford a bribe, and anyway, shouldn't need to give one. He never had before, not for a letter. He stared at his hands. They were not exactly clean, veins standing out from the heat. One of the cuffs was stained with tar from some boat or beach or railing.

'S'il vous plaît,' he said again to the man at the counter, 'could you double-check? Hackett, Samuel? There should be something.'

The man gave him a look, between irritated and perplexed. He called over his shoulder into the main postal office, beyond the honeycomb of wooden pigeonholes. Sam waited. The official turned to the next customer, and was soon arguing over a handful of papers. The post office was full, as always. There never seemed to be enough time during opening hours for the workers to be anything other than harassed. He leaned on the counter, feeling sweat trickle down his neck. An electric fan whirred above, doing nothing to cool the air. On the other side of him, a man wearing a long striped djellaba began to roll a cigarette.

'Aquete?'

The word was repeated several times until he realized it was his name, the consonants strange and full of angles. A postal worker was holding something small and pale blue.

'Yes.' He moved so quickly the man in the djellaba flinched. 'Yes, Hackett, over here.'

The letter was thin, flimsy as carbon paper. A miracle it had made it across a vast ocean in one piece. He moved aside and tore at the red-and-blue chevron edges, opening it carefully to catch . . .

Nothing. Just one sheet of airmail paper and his mother's handwriting in thick ballpoint.

'Monsieur,' he called. 'Are you sure there is not . . . ?'

His eyes caught a word, the shape of an *s* followed by a tightness of *r*'s and a blunt-tailed *y*.

Sorry.

He closed his mouth. No one had heard him anyway.

The post office was in the new town, all dust and fumes from motorbikes and restaurant kitchens, the light coming off the buildings in a flat slap. He ducked into the shade of a doorway.

Your father and I have agreed. Your return fare will be covered. We will pay for a one-way ticket home and arrange for you to collect it from a reputable travel bureau. But there will be no more money. *I'm sorry, Sam, this is for the best. We've been more than fair.*

He didn't take in the rest of the letter. Something about a vacation in Cape Cod and Steven moving to a new office, and the prospect of a job for him in a local printing firm. He could see his mother now, sitting at her dressing table, slippered feet neatly crossed, pressing each letter deliberately into the thin paper, while the TV warbled distantly through the rug, and his father sucked and sucked at his pipe. He crumpled the letter carelessly and shoved it into his shirt pocket, alongside the empty packet of cigarettes.

When he stepped out on to the pavement, the sun hit him like a sheet of aluminium. Not eleven a.m. and already baking. He kept his head down. The shades he'd bought in London were gone, pawned to Abdelhamid to help pay last week's rent. He squinted, feeling a headache coming. Probably dehydration and heat and noise and the knowledge he was one hundred per cent screwed.

He swore and kicked at an empty can. It spewed out something sticky as it clattered away, soaking the toe of his espadrille. He swore again, only for a passing woman to give him a faintly disgusted look and pull her scarf a little higher over her face.

He turned and headed up the Avenue Pasteur. It was a main artery of the city, where life teemed hot, pushing itself up from the docks, hurtling around the Grand Socco before breaking off and draining through the thread veins of the casbah, back into the bay. There, ships floated, like torn white paper on a poster of livid blue.

His headache would only grow worse in the sun. At the top of the avenue, he made a dash between vehicles, leaping the last few feet to avoid a taxi that was pulling away from the kerb. He stepped beneath the awning of Gran Café de Paris with relief.

Something soothing about the Gran Café. Perhaps because it looked as though it hadn't changed for fifty years, with its cork-tiled walls and vinyl banquettes, all in shades of brown. Sam slid into a seat opposite the mirrored wall, where he could watch the café come and go. It was cooler inside, a little, the air soft with the hum of talk and coffee and cigarettes. He breathed deeply, trying to pull some of the nicotine into his own lungs. The waiters moved from table to table, wearing their old burgundy jackets, despite the heat.

'Café, shukran,' he ordered automatically, before immediately thinking better of it. The coffee would hit his empty stomach like acid, and wouldn't help his headache any. But the waiter was already gone. What he wouldn't give for a cold beer. Not likely. The bars that sold it wouldn't be open yet and anyway . . .

He pulled the remaining dirhams from his pockets and counted them out on to the table. Twenty-nine. And his rent for the week was twenty-five. It had seemed cheap when he first arrived. Now he could barely pay it and eat.

The coffee arrived. Another dirham he didn't have any longer. He gulped down the glass of water that came with it, and began to stir sugar into the coffee. Three lumps, four. Might as well get his money's worth.

No more money. And twenty-nine dirhams. He'd have to avoid Madame Sarah, whatever happened. She was already suspicious of him, after last week. He stirred mechanically, running through an inventory of his belongings. Another shirt, in a worse state. Underpants, the jeans he was wearing. A couple of dog-eared pulp novels, too cheap to fetch anything. His boots: sturdy leather, a gift from his parents several years back, they could be pawned . . . No, one of them had been lost in Cádiz, in a scramble on the beach. He returned to stirring. There was only one thing of value left, and the idea of seeing it disappear into the depths of the medina was too painful to contemplate. Yet it was that, or home. And he was not ready for home.

He took a sip of the coffee. It was disgustingly sweet.

Across from him, two well-dressed elderly men were eating pastries. They unfolded the paper bags with care, exclaiming over the flaky, buttery goods. Sam couldn't help but smile. He'd seen them in here before. It was a daily ritual of theirs: coffee and pastries and talk of the old days at the Gran Café de Paris.

He stopped trying to drink the coffee and sat back. As far as he could tell, he was the only American. He stared into the mirror, taking in the occupied tables, the backs of people's heads, but apart from the two elderly ex-pats, everyone looked Moroccan, or at least was speaking French or Darija. When he'd imagined Tangier, he'd pictured groups of people like him, talking in the cafés by day, watching life hustle past, drinking by night and smoking kif on the rooftop of some riad, making love and art fuelled by cheap living and the distance from home. He'd heard stories of how it had been for others, not so many years ago: how they'd slept peacefully on the streets of the casbah wrapped in berber blankets, cooking tagines on gas stoves and washing in the fountains, all for free.

Not any more. Picking up the glass, he downed the rest of the coffee with a grimace, and rose to leave. Twenty-eight dirhams. Perhaps Madame Sarah would let him pay for half a week, until he could figure something out. He was almost out of the door and bracing himself for the heat when he heard a voice, the words snatching at his attention:

'Mais, look, c'est suffit, no? There!'

The speaker sounded British, with a terrible French accent. Looking back into the café, he saw one of the younger waiters standing over a man in the far corner, someone with a blur of reddish-blond hair. Sam couldn't help himself. He stepped back into the café, trying to look casual.

'. . . simply refuse to believe,' the agitated voice continued, 'that this is not enough money. I demand to see the manager!'

Rounding the central island of banquettes, Sam was able to see the person at last. Young and filmed with sweat, in a beige checked jacket and a tie. *New arrival*, the pale face and shiny leather shoes screamed. A moment later, the young man caught his eye.

'Oh,' he half rose out of his chair, 'excuse me, do you speak English?'

Sam managed to keep most of a smile from his face. 'Sure do,' he said, glancing at the waiter. 'What's up?'

The two of them began speaking at once, the waiter pointing to the young man's empty coffee cup in frustration and exclaiming in Darija, and the young man holding up his wallet.

'It's not on!' he said loudly. 'I refuse to believe that a cup of coffee is more than fifty dirhams, he's trying to stiff me!'

Sam couldn't help but stare. The young man's wallet was stuffed with banknotes. And he was waving fifty dirhams around as if it were a handkerchief. No wonder the waiter was looking pained.

'He isn't trying to stiff you,' Sam said, holding a hand up to the waiter to show that he would explain. 'It's just that a coffee is *one* dirham.' He pointed to the note. 'He's telling you he doesn't have change for that. Haven't you got anything smaller?'

The young man flushed, right up to his eyes. 'Oh.' He stared at the note in his hand. 'Well then, why didn't he say? I know a bit of French. He could have told me. I thought they all spoke it here?'

Sam shrugged. 'Spanish, more likely. Do you have anything smaller?'

'What? Oh. No, I don't. This is it. Just came from the bank, you see.' He stared down into the wallet, as if it would magically sprout small change. 'I don't suppose he'd accept pounds?'

Sam grimaced. He already regretted coming over, but then again, there was that wallet . . .

'Here,' he said, pulling a few santimat from his pocket. 'Let me.'

'I couldn't possibly . . .' the young man began to protest, but Sam had already dropped the coins on to the waiter's tray. The waiter nodded to him before walking off, rolling his eyes and shouting to a co-worker near the kitchens.

'That was very decent of you,' the young man said, collecting a leather briefcase. It seemed he wanted to be out of the café as fast as possible. 'I can pay you back.'

'It's only a dirham,' Sam murmured. *Twenty-seven*, he thought bleakly.

'Nonsense. I'll pay you back right now, if you come with me to my hotel. It's just down the road. Surely *they* will have change.'

Stepping out of the café was like diving into a pool of colour and smell and noise. Sam sometimes felt as if he was swimming, when he walked the streets during the day, coming up for air when he stepped into a café or a bar or up to a rooftop. It was different at night, of course. But in the day, the city seethed. He watched the young Englishman sweating in his suit as they walked. The man's eyes kept darting everywhere, from the stray cat that washed itself at the edge of the kerb, to the old woman crouched in a doorway, her hands pushed out to them, her face creased by the world.

Did I look like him? Sam wondered. *That mix of panic and concentration, all out of rhythm with the street?* Probably, he thought. Amazing what a couple of months could do.

'I'm Ellis, by the way.' The young man was holding out a hand. 'Ellis Norton.'

'Sam Hackett.' He shook quickly, conscious of the dirt beneath his nails. 'You're British?'

'Yes.' The man sounded breathless. 'Arrived from London last night. You're American?'

'Got it in one.'

'You seem to know your way around,' Norton said, ducking past a group of women laden with shopping. 'How long have you been in this hellhole?'

'Here? A few months. Two, nearly three, I guess. I've lost track.'

'I hope I get used to it.' Norton stopped on the street, where two potted palms flanked a recessed door. 'Well, this is me. Come in and I'll get you that change.' He glanced inside. 'Actually, there's a bar here too. Let me buy you something stronger, to say thanks.'

Sam stared at him, then beyond into the dark lobby, where a uniformed bellhop waited. The El Minzah was one of the good hotels. He shifted in the sticky espadrilles.

'I'm not exactly dressed for it.'

For the first time, Norton seemed to look at him properly, eyes roaming from the tangled hair brushing his shoulders, to his jeans. 'I'm sure that won't matter,' he said uncertainly. Then his eyes brightened. 'Here,' he said, loosening his tie and passing it over. 'They won't say a thing if you're wearing that.'

Sam dropped the loop of fabric over his head, feeling stupid, knowing that he looked it too. *The man must be desperate for company*, he thought. *About as desperate as I am for a proper drink.*

He followed Norton into the lobby, trying not to duck his head. Inside, it was quiet, marble-cool. A record was playing somewhere, soft jazz. For a second the lobby and the streets seemed to curdle around him, like milk and orange. Norton was sighing in what sounded like relief, walking up a short flight of steps, and Sam had to follow.

He'd heard of the bar at the El Minzah, but had never been in. Too expensive. Not his scene. Ahead, he saw a cavernous space, where red carpets made the air drowsy with dust, barely disturbed by a breeze, despite the open windows. It was empty, except for a pair of older women who sat stiffly on a sofa, small glasses before them. It wasn't yet noon.

'God,' said Norton, dropping into a chair. 'What a day.'

Sam followed suit. He had the odd feeling that he had tripped, somewhere on his way up the Avenue Pasteur, and had fallen into a different reality. It was all too strange; Norton and his fat wallet, the stuffy bar with its promise of booze. What if the man was a fake and wanted something from him? He watched as Norton craned around to summon a waiter, and decided that he didn't have the energy to care, not for an hour. Perhaps in that time, he'd work up the courage to ask about borrowing a few dirhams.

'What'll you have?' Norton said, shucking off his jacket.

'I don't know.' Sam's head felt light from the coffee and the sugar and the lack of nicotine. 'Are the beers cold here?'

'No idea, but I'm having a whisky soda. Want one of those?'

Sam nodded. He'd never have ordered one himself.

'Two whisky sodas,' Norton told the waiter.

The waiter nodded blandly, and went away. Sam was just beginning to feel uncomfortable when Norton took out a packet of cigarettes. He accepted one eagerly.

'So,' Norton asked, settling back in his chair. 'What brings you to Tangiers?'

His manner had changed entirely. Gone was the flustered youth, the anxiety. Here, he was at home. *Old money*, Sam thought. You could hear it in the way he said *Tangiers* the old-fashioned way, with an s, as if the city was more than itself, as if it was somehow plural. He took a drag on the cigarette, wondering how to answer Norton's question. To someone else he might have said: 'Just to be', or 'Just the road', but those kinds of answers would sound ridiculous, here.

'I'm a writer,' he said cautiously.

The man's eyes widened. 'No, really? But so am I.' He reached for his jacket, and pulled out a card.

ELLIS NORTON
JUNIOR FOREIGN CORRESPONDENT
INTERPRESS

'This is my first job out,' he said, watching with obvious pride as Sam read the card. 'I wanted one of the bureaux in Paris or Rome, but then everybody does. A year in the trenches, they said, and I can move on to somewhere more civilized.'

Sam made a vague noise and offered the card back.

'Keep it –' Norton waved '– in case you want to get in touch.'

Sam pocketed it. He couldn't imagine a world where he and Norton were regular drinking buddies, but then, being an ex-pat did strange things to people.

The whiskies and sodas arrived. Norton took a sip of his, then downed it, almost before the waiter had finished laying a napkin before Sam. 'Bring another couple, would you?' he said.

Unperturbed, the waiter nodded. He was obviously used to such behaviour. Sam took a sip of the drink. The whisky was strong, almost shocking, softened by the mineral dash of soda. There was something illicit about it, drunk on an empty stomach. A shiver ran down the back of his neck. It felt wonderful.

'What do you write then?' Norton was asking. 'Don't say you're a journo too.'

'No, I was never quick enough for that.' He spun the ashtray a few times. 'I'm writing a novel,' he admitted.

'A novel! A Great American one?'

Sam laughed. 'I doubt it.'

'Are you published?'

'A few short stories.' He concentrated on his cigarette. He wasn't about to confess that the last time he'd sold anything was more than a year ago, and for a pittance. 'I've been travelling, mostly. France, Spain, England. As research.'

That got Norton talking about his travels in Italy and Switzerland, the summer he'd spent in the south of France. Sam nodded along, finishing the first drink and starting work on the second, which disappeared far too quickly. He was starting to feel quite drunk.

'One more?' Norton asked, checking his watch. 'I've got to find my way to the damn office, but that can wait until this afternoon. I'm told everyone lunches like the French, here.'

'All right,' Sam said, accepting another cigarette. He was beginning to like Norton more. It was easy to let the chatter wash over him.

'Must say, I'm glad I bumped into you,' Norton said, when the third glasses were empty. 'This has done me the world of good. I was feeling wretched in that café. But you can give me the lay of the land here, can't you? Be my Dante through the inferno?'

'Sure,' Sam said, feeling a warm glow of booze and superiority. 'There's a little bar where ex-pats meet, I can take you there.'

'You're a pal.' Norton pushed back his chair and fished the wallet from his jacket. 'Must use the gents. Here, pay the waiter if he comes by.' He handed over the fifty dirhams. 'Shouldn't be a problem this time, eh?'

Sam held the note in front of him as Norton hurried off towards the lavatories. The man was crazy, he had to be. There was nothing to stop Sam from pocketing the money and walking nonchalantly out of the door, never to be seen again. That much money would buy him another two weeks. His hand twitched towards his shirt pocket. If he was careful . . .

His hand fell back to the table. Norton might be an idiot, but he was a generous idiot. And Tangier was a small place. He sighed, and called the waiter over.

HAVE A HEART

Take a jigger of gin and a pony each of Swedish Punsch, fresh lime juice and imported grenadine. Shake the ingredients together in a well-iced glass, before straining. A drink of sharpness and spice.

Ifrahim used to have a phrase, for whenever I was cowardly or hesitant about something. 'Ale,' he would say – for he knew I preferred to be called that, rather than Alejandra – 'Ale, hacer de tripas corazón.'

Ale, make a heart out of your guts.

I first remember him saying it when I was little, perhaps six or seven. I had tripped over in the yard and was crying to see blood on my knee. He sat me on the kitchen table, washed it off and told me solemnly to make a heart out of my guts. I didn't understand him fully, and had wondered at the idea of my guts squirming up through my body to wrap around my heart. My heart must be too soft, I thought. That's why it needed the guts to protect it. It was good advice to a child growing up in that place.

Ifrahim was the inn's cook, and he had been there almost as long as I. Mama Morales hired him after she found out that María, the old cook, had been cheating her on prices and pocketing the difference. I don't know what happened to María. People said that Morales paid a man to break her hands, but that might just be rumour.

Ifrahim was as different to María as could be. Where she was loud and sour he was quiet and gentle. He wore a faded red shirt and never opened his eyes too wide, as if it hurt to look at things. No one was sure where he came from, with his deep brown skin that seemed almost silver beneath, and his wiry, pepper-black beard. I once heard him say that his father was from Zanzibar, and was a sailor. One of the girls told me that his mother had been a fine French lady from Réunion Island, but that he had been given up, and raised by a 'grandmother' in Lisbon. Any of that was enough to make people at the inn sneer at him, especially Morales. For all her defiance of others, she was a fierce Spaniard, and a proud cordobesa, and that was why she despised me, I think, for my aimless blood.

Everyone wondered why she had hired Ifrahim, until we tasted his food. I was just a child, but I still remember it, that first meal. He served salmorejo; poor man's food, made from bread too hard and tomatoes too soft to be of use. But Ifrahim's salmorejo tasted different. Beneath the hot blue sky, that cool soup calmed and kindled at once; it bit with acid and licked with oil, rewarded us with salty little stars of ham. We wiped the bowls of every last trace, and all the while Ifrahim sat at the door of the kitchen, smiling quietly and shelling hard-boiled eggs. There was never any question of his employment, after that.

Later, I found out that Ifrahim had a bad heart and had been thrown out of the Foreign Legion on account of it. Sometimes, in the night he'd cry out and we would rush to where he slept in the storeroom to find him sweating and clutching at his chest. We would steady him, and spoon him oil and milk of magnesia until the racing began to slow, until his heart stopped trying to escape through his ribs. Perhaps it was an ill fit, too big or tender to last in our world.

Anything good I took from the inn, I took from Ifrahim. I wouldn't be here now, speaking, if not for him. It was he who spoke for me, when not another soul would have.

I should explain. There are things you must be wondering about me, about the inn. You must have already guessed, with the little you know about her, that Mama Morales would not have kept me there for free.

Morales took guests and served meals and charged peasants and farmers to water and stable their mules while they were in town. She also kept girls, and that was where most of the inn's money came from. About half a dozen year-round, who had to double up and share their beds with newcomers during the busy months. Most didn't last too long, a year perhaps, or two. There were only five people who were constant: the old groom called Antonio who barely spoke, Ifrahim, when he came, Mama Morales and Elena and me.

Elena was Morales' daughter.

People said she had hidden herself in Morales' belly until it was too late to be rid of her, that even when Morales tried, the little thing wouldn't be budged. She was a year older than me. Morales told me that if she hadn't still been paying a woman to breastfeed Elena when I came along, I would've starved and died, for *she* certainly would not have fed me.

That was Morales for you.

The girls looked after Elena and me, and when we were old enough Morales sent us to school in the mornings, saying that she didn't want ignorant lumps in her house who couldn't figure a bill or read a name. The rest of the time we skivvied. Elena got an easier time of it, because she had fairer skin than me, and nice hands, and Morales didn't want them spoiled by too much sun or hard work. It wouldn't make a difference to mine, she observed.

I didn't mind. Kitchen and stable, courtyard and storeroom, those were my domain. I didn't like to venture up the stairs too often, on to the wooden balcony that surrounded the central yard, where the rooms were. If I did, it was only to collect chamber pots or laundry. I wasn't fond of the sickly stab of violet perfume, covering the reek of men's sweat and cologne, or the way they always forgot that the inn leaked sound like a sieve and we could all hear their noises, even through a closed door. I thought they were foolish, the men. Still, I couldn't help but watch as they strolled uncaring along the corridor, their trousers half-buttoned and their jackets over their shoulders. Something made me want to follow them, to walk as they did, out into the night. There was a power in their lifted chins, in the way they paused at the edge of the street to light a cigarette, and though I imitated them in secret, I knew it was a power that could never be mine.

Elena spent more time upstairs than me, especially during the day, before business started. Then, she would let the girls fuss over her and make her up with waxy lipstick and powder, while I played with the kittens in the warm stink of the stables, or helped Ifrahim among the old cooking fat and fresh peelings of the kitchen. But at night, the pair of us shared a bed, in the smallest wedge-shaped room under the eaves, lulled to sleep by the creaking of the gate, the snorting of horses and the noises of the girl working the room next door.

It went on like that, slow winters and busy summers, morning lessons and chores and the smell of Elena's hair against my nose at night, until my thirteenth year. That was when everything changed.

It happened during the feria, the festival of our Señora de la Salud: Our Lady of Health. Morales always laughed and said we should rename her Our Lady of the Health Inspector. It was May, our busiest month, and the city was overrun. People came in from all over to drink and dance at the festival; farmers, miners, factory workers, even people from as far away as Extremadura.

As a child, I'd been excited by the feria. Elena and I would run to the river to see the old, striped canvas tents go up, to watch the gitanos arrive to entertain the crowds with their wailing, roaring songs and their feverish guitars and clacking heels.

We'd have performances at the inn too, whether we wanted them or not. Motorcars from Granada and Seville would bring the swells, slumming it in fine clothes that they would ruin with sweat and wine. They'd drink and weep and turn their starveling eyes on the girls and the gitanos, and the air would become raw with smoke and lust and gut on wood, and by the end of the first evening, the whole of Córdoba would have lost its mind.

On the night it happened, there were four of them; four men determined to drink the deep wells of each other's pockets dry. They were from Jaén, and I wondered why they should have come all the way to Córdoba, when they had their own feria at home. If I'd looked closer, I would've found the answer in their indifferent laughter, in their loosened clothes, in the way they sucked on their cigars and put their boots on the chairs and never once lowered their voices. They were here precisely because this was not their home; here, they had the freedom to act how they pleased.

The four of them had already spent a great deal of money when they asked to see Morales. Their request, whatever it was, did not take long to convey, for she soon came weaving through the crowded courtyard towards the kitchen door, where Elena and I were shirking our table-clearing duties, laughing as we watched a large gitano woman try to sing her throat right out of her mouth. We jumped up when Morales approached.

'Go and wash and put your Sunday clothes on,' she told us.

We stared at her. Elena was silent. I was the one to ask why.

'Because I say so.' She turned and beckoned over one of the older girls, 'Caterina!' I did not hear what Morales murmured in her ear.

Was it the heat of the night that made Caterina's hand so slick in mine? 'Why must we wash?' I asked her, as she pulled us up the stairs. 'No one is looking at us.'

'Someone's always looking,' she said, and gave us both a push into our room. We did as we were told, with a cloth and pitcher of water. Grumbling, I scrubbed my face and neck, my underarms, and did Elena's while she shrugged into her blouse. She had breasts now, mostly, whereas I only had vague swellings that sometimes hurt in the night.

'If I have to clear tables, I'll get this blouse dirty and Morales will beat me for it on Sunday,' I complained. Elena said nothing. Her face, always paler than mine, was paler than ever.

Caterina eyed us critically as she led us along the corridor. 'Be good,' she said, and her grip was hard. 'Don't talk back.' She stopped outside the parlour. 'Don't cry.'

She pushed open the door. Inside were the four gentlemen from downstairs, almost done with a bottle of sherry. Abruptly, I realized what they wanted us for.

I couldn't move. I had always known that I would have to do this one day, but Caterina and the others were older, fifteen or sixteen at least. Elena grabbed my hand, dragging me with her into the room as the door swung shut behind us.

I forgot how to do anything but breathe. One of the gentlemen was saying something, gesturing to a pair of chairs at the table. He was smiling, his whiskers damp with sweat and spirits. Another man eyed us, mouth occupied with his cigar, another blinked rapidly, as if he could not see us through the smoke.

'Señoritas,' greeted the first, 'have a drink with us. Do you like sherry?'

Elena's face was red to the eyes as she nodded, looking down at the tablecloth. I gripped her hand and stared into the corner. At the edge of my vision, I saw a little glass, brimming with sherry, pushed in my direction.

'We have ordered some pasteles from the kitchen,' the blinking man said, 'and we have these for you. Sweet things, for sweet girls.'

He pushed a box across the table. It looked expensive, creamy pink cardboard decorated with golden swirls and the words *Delicia Turca*.

Elena was still staring at the cloth. 'Gracias,' she whispered.

'Well,' the first man said, 'salud.'

I watched as Elena reached out and took hold of the glass before her. Her hands were trembling, and the sherry slipped over the rim on to her fingers. As she raised it, she glanced at me. *Please*, her look said, *don't leave me alone.* That's what made me copy her. I picked up my own glass and raised it to my lips and drank the sherry down in one.

It was disgustingly sweet.

The men were laughing at something. I looked up at last and found that it was me they were mocking. At my side, Elena still held her sherry. She had only sipped it.

'That one might be dull but she's got fire,' the man with the cigar observed. 'That's how they make them on the streets: slow in every way but one.'

His lip curled at me. My stomach gave a lurch and a shudder, as if my guts were creeping upwards. I couldn't take my eyes from his starched white collar, from his beautiful suit. I kept wondering what he'd done to get those fine clothes.

'Come here,' he said.

I wouldn't have moved if Elena hadn't let go of my hand, so abruptly that I swayed. It was as if she was backing into a corner without moving an inch, leaving me exposed. I stood, cold sweat on my back and a strange, bitter taste in my mouth. If I ran, could I reach the door? If I did, where would I go? My guts squirmed, climbing higher, making their way towards my heart, to wrap it, to shield it, to keep it from being crushed by the world.

When I stood before him, the man stared at me critically, chin to toe. 'How old are you?' he asked.

I opened my mouth to tell him 'thirteen', but what came out was not sound. Instead, a sudden rush of vomit surged from the guts that were now in my chest, hot and furious, all over the man's beautiful shirt front.

Through my stinging eyes, I saw his face and almost laughed. Then he was shouting in disgust and kicking me away from him, screaming that I was diseased. I fell back against the table, and something shattered, but I couldn't see what; all I could think about was the nausea and my roiling guts as I vomited again. I heard voices, Morales' voice, saying that I wasn't diseased, just a stupid girl who wasn't used to drink, and that if the gentlemen came with her, she would have the girls arrange baths for them, and another bottle of Tío Pepe, on the house.

When the scraping of chairs and curses finally stopped, I looked up, my lips shaking, my nose and eyes streaming. Only Morales remained, and Ifrahim, who must have arrived amidst the chaos, the tray of pasteles forgotten in his hand.

Morales hit me then, harder than she ever had before. It made me bite my tongue, but the wash of blood tasted clean, after the sherry and the sick.

'You disgusting maggot,' she said, wiping her hand on the tablecloth. 'I always knew you'd cost me.'

I risked a glance at her face. The anger was gone, or trampled down deep where it didn't show.

'Out,' she said.

I tried to speak, and choked. She didn't mean out of the room, but the inn. It was impossible. The men, the clients, they might simply get up and leave, walk out of the gates and into the world, but I wasn't like them. I had no money, no family, no name or friends to call upon. There wasn't anywhere else for me.

'Please,' I said. 'Please, I'll work.'

'You think they'll want you after that?' She looked at me, still revolted. 'What use do I have for a thing like you anyway? Your youth is the only thing of value, and if I can't sell that . . .' She turned towards the door. 'Ifrahim, make sure she—'

'Camila.'

For all my pain and terror and sickness, I remember being stunned by that. I had never heard *anyone* call Morales by her first name. She stopped moving. I couldn't see her face from where I stood, but I could tell her eyes were fixed on Ifrahim's.

'I'll use her in the kitchen,' he said, softly, the way he always spoke. 'God knows I could do with the help.' He winced and shifted his chest, and I knew his heart was paining him. Morales knew it too, because I saw her lower her head a fraction, as if to look through his ribs. 'If she doesn't work,' he said, 'I'll throw her out myself.'

I don't know what passed between them in that silence. I could only see Ifrahim's face, his brown eyes betraying nothing as he held Morales' gaze.

She never agreed. Never disagreed either, just turned her head and walked from the room.

It was Ifrahim's heart that caused him to speak for me that day, I am sure of it. In the kitchen, he helped me clean my face and gave me a lump of precious ice from the box to soothe my tongue, and let me sleep in front of the stove, so that I wouldn't have to tread the corridors of the inn, where the men might still be at their business.

The next morning, early, he set me to chopping onions and peeling potatoes, while he went to the plaza to argue for meat. Vegetable tears stung my eyes as I worked, and I wished that they were tears of love, so I could give them to Ifrahim.

That day, we made tortilla. We used eggs from the market and oil from the huge canister by the stove and my own cut onions and potatoes. And when I saw the gusto with which the guests greeted those plates of tortilla, when I saw them cramming it down with bread and beer, a strange realization crept into my mind.

Without us, those people would have gone hungry. Ifrahim and I kept them in their seats; *we* held them there spellbound with only a few humble ingredients. It was a kind of magic – slender but potent – and I understood for the first time that Ifrahim lived by it. Being a cook gave him authority; he wasn't like the men upstairs, with their clean shirts and their deep pockets, but he had a control they didn't, and he could wield it in ways they never would have imagined.

Later, my hands cracked from scrubbing soap and blistered from the kitchen knife, I moved my things out of the room I had shared with Elena. I can't say exactly what made me do it, only the knowledge that something had shifted for us both. She did not look at me while I collected my few clothes, only sat on the edge of the bed, holding the hem of a beautiful white lace mantilla between her fingers. I supposed it was a gift from the señor with the cigar.

The box of Turkish Delight was there too, open beside her. They were untouched save for one, chewed and glistening, spat out amongst the others.

'Take them away,' she said, when she saw me looking, 'I don't want them.'

I didn't want them either but I picked them up, chewed lump and all. I thought about giving them to Ifrahim, in thanks, but I knew it wouldn't be right. I burned them instead, in their pretty box, until the whole kitchen smelled of animal bones and roses.

I slept in the kitchen every night after that, on an ancient truckle bed wedged next to the stove. On colder nights, I'd wake to find the inn's cats tailoring themselves to my body, beneath my arms, against my neck, in the gap between my knees, purring for warmth. I didn't mind them. They had fleas, but they kept the rats away. With them, and Ifrahim in his storeroom near by, I felt safe.

I told him that one night, a few weeks after he'd spoken for me. We had finished our labours in the kitchen, the inn gates were closed, and everyone else had moved upstairs, to sleep or entertain. He'd nodded slowly.

'There's safety here,' he agreed. 'Cooking saved my life.' He took a drag on his pipe then, and looked at me through the stove light. 'Feed them, Ale,' he said softly. 'Feed them well and they will want you, they will need you. Make them forget you're a girl and think of you instead as a kitchen-thing, a duende, a stove-spirit. Then, they will want you for your usefulness, and leave you be.'

We looked at each other in the silence. The memory of Morales' words hung between us, and I shifted, hunching further beneath the kitchen smock, willing my growing breasts to remain flat, to stay away. In that moment I wished I was Ifrahim's son; I wished we truly were kitchen-spirits, untouchable and free. But I wasn't, and we weren't. Ifrahim closed his eyes, and I could tell he too was thinking about his body, his heart made of guts. He was thinking about the day it would unravel, and take his life with it.

But before that day, he taught me everything he could. He taught me how to make a batter and coat chunks of aubergine and drop them into hot oil. I got burns from that – my forearms and hands speckled with red marks – but it was worth it. Because when the platters went out, drizzled with molasses, I smiled to see people gobbling the morsels, burning their tongues and saying *hoh hoh* and reaching for their wine. *I* had done that. *I* had burned them, as surely as if I'd walked up and singed their tongues with a coal. The thought made me almost savage with delight.

I didn't realize it fully at the time, but by teaching me to cook, Ifrahim was also teaching me how to live, how to carve a space for myself in a world that didn't want me. He taught me how to bewitch people; how to change the course of their thoughts – if only for an evening. Our ingredients were humble; salt and fruit, meat and oil and wine. But Ifrahim could spin them into a hundred different pleasing shapes.

'Watch them close, and they will tell you what they want, Ale,' he whispered, as we stood together at the kitchen door, watching a hard-faced English merchant in the courtyard, who sweated and fidgeted in his pressed suit, eyeing the girls with a nervous scowl. 'They won't even know they're doing it, but watch them and they'll spill all.' He smiled down at me. 'We'll be their confessors.'

That was the day he taught me to make sangria; a drink as old and false as rouge. He set me to chopping leftover fruit, the peaches that had burst from their skins at the market, slices of bitter orange and shrivelled grapes that no one wanted. I watched as he glugged Málaga over the lot, so that the fruit began to drink, sucking the sweet wine into withered flesh until it seemed full and luscious once more.

'Now, how much brandy?' he asked, nodding at the stern Englishman who sat in the courtyard, fretfully breaking toothpicks into shards.

'A cup,' I said slowly. 'No, two cups.'

Ifrahim smiled. 'For a fish as cold as that, I believe we will need three.'

The brandy was followed by red wine – cheap stuff from the cooking cask that would leave a headache, but no matter – and seltzer from the glass dispenser. Finally, Ifrahim stirred in his secret: a pinch of pepper, 'to warm the heart'.

That jug of drink turned the Englishman's sour face pink, made his narrowed eyes big and bright. It undid his cravat and sent his hat flying across the dusty ground of the inn. It sent him upstairs with a girl on one arm and a second jug clutched to his chest. Most importantly, that drink reached into his pocket and emptied his wallet a note at a time with its sticky, red fingers.

All of Ifrahim's lessons were like that, two-faced as a conjuror's coin. He taught me how to gild bad fish with pimentón, how to hammer horsemeat and soak it in wine until the stallion-loving bastards who slummed it at the inn would have made their own mothers swear it was beef. He taught me how to pilfer more than I paid for at the market, how to protest my innocence if I was ever caught being light-fingered and swear that it was a mistake, that it was only 'the sun in my eyes'.

Four years of those lessons. Milk puddings and how to cheat at Nap. Fish 'à la française' and how to tell a person's wealth by what they ordered to drink.

'Watch what comes out of their mouths, as well as what goes in,' he told me, 'and you will know them for what they are.'

One January day, Ifrahim's heart finally came loose, and he died. It left me terrified; I was seventeen, and that alone would surely be enough to make Morales rethink her decision – to give me the choice once more of a room upstairs, or the road.

I would choose the road, I told myself fiercely in the night, as the cats whirred against my belly. I would take my chances outside the inn. But in reality, the prospect was unthinkable. The world was not kind to girls like me, with no money and no name. Even taking what Morales offered might be better than being forced into the same thing miles away, where no one, not even the cats knew me.

So I tried to do what Ifrahim had instructed. I tried to make everyone forget that I was a young woman and become instead a kitchen-thing, a witch of cook-smoke and cleaver, of red face and blistered fingers and saffron-stained nails: desirable to no one, useful to everyone.

I hid beneath the kitchen smock, wore Ifrahim's rough work trousers and kept my hair tight beneath a scarf, so that if anyone did look at me, they might see a sullen, grubby boy, rather than a woman to be bought.

It was the same with Morales. Whenever she saw me, I made sure my hands were full of something, red to the wrist with blood and gristle or slick with fish tripe and scales. I kept the kitchen ledger as regular as Ifrahim had, the columns of numbers neat. I blagged and bartered and stole more from the market than ever, to make her see that I could be economical, that I could run the kitchen better than anyone else.

I asked for nothing, and Morales seemed to accept my presence. So long as I was more valuable at the stove than I was on my back, so long as I charmed and conned the clients with food and drink and kept the accounts straight, I would be safe.

At least, that was what I told myself. In truth, I knew my safety wouldn't last, just as Ifrahim had always known that the knots of his heart would slip and tumble back into guts in the end.

I just never imagined it would happen the way it did. I never imagined that everything – myself included – would change, so unrecognizably, for ever.

Tangier

July 1978

It was the call to prayer that woke him. For a bewildering moment, he thought it was morning. But the air smelled wrong for that; it still held the heat and the dust scuffed up by the day's passage.

Seven in the evening, then. He opened an eye. He was lying on his hard, narrow bed, still fully dressed. The muezzin's chant crackled and echoed from a loudspeaker on the nearby rooftop and for a long moment he kept still, just listening. It was all drifting back to him. Norton, with his whisky and sodas and smokes in the El Minzah, shuffling home in a careless haze, managing to avoid Madame Sarah for long enough to get into his room. There was something he didn't want to do, he remembered that. Whatever it was, he'd thought a nap would help.

Blinking hard, he sat up. His tongue was powdered with the lingering taste of cigarettes, stomach a tight ball of wax. After a moment, he made himself stand and open his door a crack, peering along the corridor and out on to the roof terrace. Madame Sarah sometimes sat up here and smoked when she thought no one was watching, but now it was deserted. He stepped out beneath the sky.

A haze hung over the city, ochre-blue with evening. The call had finished, and from somewhere near by came the sound of a radio playing a French pop song. He took the lid off the water container, dipped the bowl and drank. It was warm and stale and a little plasticky, but it washed the sandpaper from his tongue, made his headache retreat a few paces. Another bowlful went over his neck and head. He used another to wash his hands, and felt better.

The second he stepped back into his room, a reminder of the thing he had to do – the thing he didn't *want* to do – was sitting there, waiting for him. He stared. Orange and white, the keys a little dirty, a sheet of paper flopping back. His Hermes Baby. The only thing of value he had left.

The page in it was half covered in type, abandoned mid-sentence. He ripped it out and let it fall to the floor, on to a pile of other sheets. *You're not writing anyway*, he thought as he extricated the cover from under the bed. *So what the hell use is a typewriter?*

Madame Sarah was in the kitchen, clattering a tray, preparing tea for herself and for Pierre, the other lodger. Pierre was a teacher, always prompt with his rent, always neatly dressed. Madame Sarah treated him like another son. As Sam crept past, Aziz – Madame Sarah's youngest – looked up and caught his eye. Sam had bought his loyalty early on with an old football shirt. The child was wearing it now as he sat eating a peach, CONNECTICUT HUSKIES emblazoned in white across the worn blue cotton. Sam put his finger to his lips as he edged towards the door. Aziz nodded solemnly.

Then he was out, ducking down the nearest alleyway. It was cooler here among the shadowed streets of the casbah. He took a right, through a passage that looked like a dead end but which led to a set of steps that would spit him out near the old, crumbling city gate. He'd been lost in the casbah more times than he could count, and even now, if he wasn't concentrating he'd find himself facing a blind, peeling wall which he could have sworn was a gate the week before.

He ducked past a tendril of some climbing vine and emerged on to a tiny square with a fountain in the middle, surrounded by children and women with buckets. It smelled of wastewater and drying dirt and ripe garbage from the pile in the corner. Some of the kids yelled when they saw him and rushed over, trying out *monsieur* and *señor, are you lost? Follow me!*

He shook his head and brandished the typewriter in its case, but a few still ran ahead of him, staring back over their shoulders and calling: 'Follow, follow, you are French? American? This way!'

'I know the way,' he said. 'I'm going to see Abdelhamid in his shop.'

'Abdelhamid?' one boy persisted. He had no shoes, his shorts torn at the hem. 'He is sick today, not there, come, I will take you to his home.'

Sam shook his head and pressed on. The boy tried a few more times, but eventually, one of the other children called to him and he wheeled around, disappearing down another passage. Sam sighed and tried to blink his headache away. The typewriter was growing heavy, the handle slick with sweat.

The smell of the casbah changed, the lower he went. Smoke and cooking, the thick fug of diesel from generators and the waft of fish innards, left out for the cats. He passed the weavers, their looms stretched into the middle of the passage, their hands crooked and swift, their legs sinewy from years of working the pedals. A few doors down rugs were spread over the uneven stones. The shops grew in number, spilling out from closet-like spaces, every inch a basket or drawer. In one, clocks and watches and alarms. In another, rounds of buttery msemen. He faltered at the sight of them.

Cash first. Then food.

Abdelhamid was just inside the entrance of his shop, wearing his fine old djellaba and brocade hat, as always.

'I heard you were sick,' Sam called, stepping a few inches out of the thoroughfare.

Abdelhamid looked up in surprise. 'I am never sick, monsieur, and even if I was, you would find me here.' He smiled, and laid the kif workings to one side. Sam smiled back, and shook his hand. Abdelhamid cleared a space for him to perch at the edge of the shop. Usually, it filled Sam with pleasure to sit like this, watching the street, especially when he could catch the eye of bewildered tourists.

'How are you?' he asked.

'Labas, Monsieur Hackett.' Abdelhamid's eyes flicked to the typewriter case. He had clocked it the moment Sam approached, but he didn't mention it, only continued rolling.

They talked a little, as the evening flowed by. The dust hung in the air, making everything hazy, almost dreamy. People called to Abdelhamid as they passed, exchanged words, jokes, news. They glanced at Sam and sometimes smiled. Everyone knew why foreigners became so well acquainted with Abdelhamid.

'What can I help you with, my friend?' the man himself asked, finally. He raised his eyebrows. 'Hash, kif?'

'In a minute,' Sam said, trying to sound offhand. 'I was wondering . . . what would you give me for this?' He opened the case. The typewriter sat within, its orange body glossy in the evening light, the keys a little discoloured from years of his fingertips. 'I'm tired of lugging it around.'

Abdelhamid lifted the case on to his lap. 'No money from America yet?' he asked, testing a few keys.

Sam rubbed at his head. It was the reason he had given last week, after selling the shades.

'No.' He tried to think up some excuse, but couldn't. He was tired and his head hurt. It would probably cost him. 'No more money,' he sighed. 'A ticket home, but no more money.'

Abdel made a noise. 'For you, there is always more.'

'Not this time. Not from my parents. They mean it.'

'But you have other family?'

'They won't help. My sister refused last time. My brother's never given me a cent and he won't start now. I told them all that I have nothing and this was their answer. No more.'

Abdelhamid shook his head, and peered into the case. 'I do not know if I can sell this here. There are not many people who would buy it, only foreigners, and they will want one that is new—'

Sam shoved himself to his feet. Abruptly, it was too much. He couldn't sit there while the Hermes was torpedoed, couldn't be told that it was a worthless thing and nod in agreement.

'Forget it,' he said, holding out his hand. 'Forget I brought it, it was a stupid idea, I . . .'

The world began to fuzz, turning blue and yellow before his eyes. His head squeezed and his ears rang, as though he'd dived underwater. He heard a clatter and the next thing he knew he was sitting on Abdelhamid's step again, blinking hard. There was bustle around him; he'd knocked over a stack of brass bowls. Abdelhamid's neighbour was helping to retrieve them, before they rolled away into the socco.

'Sorry,' Sam mumbled. 'My head.'

Abdelhamid just waved a hand, smiling a little. He yelled to a passing boy, and pointed up the road.

'You Americans,' he said then, sitting down. 'You smoke and you drink and you forget to eat.'

Sam managed a husk of a laugh.

'How much money do you have?' Abdelhamid demanded.

'Twenty-seven dirhams.' It felt pointless to lie. 'And I owe twenty-five to Madame Sarah for the rent.'

Abdelhamid picked up his workings. His fingers moved calmly, but with every movement back and forth Sam knew he would be calculating exactly how much money Sam would need to buy kif, and pay the rent, and eat besides.

He'd met Abdelhamid in the Petit Socco soon after he'd arrived in the city. A young man had approached him in one of the cafés and sold him a pouch of kif, which turned out to be just tea dust and dried weeds. Abdelhamid had been sitting a few tables away, watching the whole exchange. He had burst out laughing at the look on Sam's face when he realized the con, and told him not to take it to heart, that Yassine hooked every new American the same way. They'd talked a little, and after sharing a few of Sam's cigarettes, Abdelhamid had slapped him on the shoulder, and told him to follow. They'd found Yassine in one of the other cafés, illicitly drinking a bottle of brandy with a friend. After a bit of shouting, he'd handed Sam most of his money back, which Abdelhamid then appropriated, plus a finder's fee of course, in exchange for some real and excellent kif. Over the weeks, Sam had come to think of him as a friend; if he was going to be fleeced by anyone, he'd prefer it to be Abdel.

'OK.' Abdelhamid finished his roll-up. 'I can give you sixty dirhams for the machine.'

Sam's eyes felt hot. He couldn't complain about the low offer. He was desperate, and he'd shown it.

'I won't take anything under two hundred.'

'Bzzaf.' Abdelhamid looked disappointed in him. 'No one will buy it for that.' He held out the cigarette, laced with kif. 'Perhaps one hundred.'

'Come on, have a heart. One fifty at least.'

'Impossible, my friend.' A moment later Abdel's face brightened at the sound of a shout.

The boy from earlier had returned with two bowls in his hands, and a chunk of bread stuffed in each pocket. Abdelhamid gave him a few coins.

'Here,' he said, passing Sam a bowl. 'You need to eat.'

Sam looked down into the soup. Harira; the smell of tomatoes and sweet onion and spices told him so. There was chopped hard-boiled egg on top, its pale surface sprinkled with salt and cumin. He was so hungry he could have unhinged his jaw and swallowed the bowl in one.

'How much do I owe you?' he mumbled.

Abdelhamid shook his head, already starting on the soup. Sam followed suit. He scooped up half of the egg with the bread and for a minute or two, he forgot everything else.

'Maybe,' Abdelhamid said when Sam was mopping up the remaining lentils with the last mouthful of bread, 'maybe I could offer you one hundred and ten.'

Sam swallowed. It was less than he needed, far less. And yet, what choice did he have?

'One thirty,' he said, wiping his mouth.

Abdelhamid gave him a look. 'One fifteen.'

The bowl was empty. Sam sighed.

'OK. One fifteen.'

To celebrate their deal, they smoked kif and talked, until it grew dark and the street's vendors began to pack away, ravelling their wares into the tiny, cave-like shops that lined the Rue de Commerce. Sam helped, lazily handing in old beaten brass lanterns and jugs, paintings dark with time and baskets of metal ornaments that were mostly just shiny new ones scuffed up with boot polish until they looked suitably aged. He watched as the Hermes was tucked on to a shelf.

Abdelhamid caught the look and smiled in sympathy. 'You are thinking of the great book this machine would write.'

Sam shrugged. 'In someone else's hands maybe.'

'Inshallah. But now you have kif, you have money, you will write again?'

'Inshallah,' Sam said, and Abdelhamid laughed. 'Though I'll have to write in pencil, or on my walls in charcoal. Madame Sarah would like that.'

'In years to come she will open your room as a museum. Here is where the great writer Hackett did his work.' Abdel patted his shoulder, then stopped, holding up a hand. 'Wait a moment.'

He stepped back into the shop, and began to root through the stacks of old suitcases and cracked trays and framed photographs, blooming with age spots.

'Ah!' He straightened his back with a wince. 'Yes.'

In his hands was a small leather case, not much bigger than a document wallet. The corners were battered, and the clasp that held it shut was thick with rust. 'Here,' he said, placing it into Sam's hands. 'Look.'

Obediently, he peered down at the case in the fading light. He could make out the indentations of initials tooled into the leather.

A. L.

The kif made everything seem warm and unhurried. He turned the case over and heard something clunk inside. 'What is it?'

Abdel steadied it in his hands, working at the rusty clasp. A few flakes came away on his fingers, but then it released and the lid creaked open.

A smell wafted out, pungent leather and musty paper. For a brief moment, it reminded him of the attic at his grandparents' house; a warm-cold cinnamon smell of dust and objects long forgotten. He peered inside.

It was a writing case. At the bottom was a blotter, the corners holding a sheaf of blank pages, yellowed with age. In the lid there was a leather pouch for envelopes, another for cards, and a tiny paper calendar that told him the year was 1928. Alongside the blotter was space for ink, a pencil and a pen. The ink was dry in its glass bottle, the pen crusted with it, like old blood. But it was all there, as if someone had scrawled out a last letter fifty years ago and hastily packed away, intending to return and clean up later.

'Where did it come from?'

Abdelhamid shrugged. 'It has been here a long time, that's all I know. Mouad found it, I think.'

'Mouad?'

'My second brother. He used to work the docks. He lives in Casablanca now.'

Sam touched the sheets of paper. *This* was how people used to write, for themselves, for each other. Not relying on springs or keys or ribbon, not sending brief biro messages on cheap airmail paper. They wrote tangibly, personally; putting themselves into every curl and dot and line.

'It's beautiful,' he said.

Abdelhamid smiled. 'It has been lying here waiting for a writer. For someone like you. If you want, I could let you have it for maybe twenty dirhams . . .'

BULL SHOT

Take a jigger of imported vodka and a gill of homemade beef bouillon. Add half a pony of lemon juice and three dashes of Worcestershire sauce. Season with salt, pepper and hot Spanish paprika. Shake well and serve over cracked ice.

Not for the faint of heart.

I knew from the beginning there was something wrong about that day.

Put it down to intuition, to a thief's gut instinct, if you like, although it was undeniable that the morning started badly. Not long after breakfast a horse had gone wild in the stable – for no discernible reason – and trampled one of the cats. I didn't blame the horse. They say animals know things, and I believe the creature had opened his nostrils and snuffed in the scent of a city on the edge of hysteria. Anyone would have gone wild, smelling that.

It was the final day of the feria, the night when anything could happen. The heat of the past three days had been unbearable, too hot for the season, and people had taken to drinking themselves to sleep, only to wake an hour later tangled in their clothes, sweating sherry. Sore heads, parched throats, minds all too aware that after the feria came the heat of summer, merciless as the cracked mud of the yard.

I'd not yet recovered from the chaos of the stable when I came face to face with Morales. Her dark hair was already damp with perspiration, her blouse giving up its starch to the heat.

'We've received a request for tonight's meal,' she said.

I nodded. It was not unusual for a group of swells to think highly enough of themselves to order something special. 'What do they want?' I asked.

Morales shifted her neck in the taut collar. For a heart-beat, I thought she looked uncertain. 'They have asked for rabo de toro.'

I frowned. Stewed bull's tail. It was rich and meaty and thick, and not at all suited to a summer night, to stomachs full of sherry.

'I don't have the ingredients,' I told her. 'And anyway, it's too hot.'

I don't know what made me speak like that. Perhaps it was the blackened end of my temper, or the animal shrieks and frenzied hooves that lingered in my mind.

Morales' face hardened, her lip curled as she leaned towards me.

'They have asked for rabo de toro, and that is what you will make.'

The words were plain, but there was a viciousness in her tone that made me step back.

'Of course,' I murmured, dropping my eyes. 'I'll make it. For how many?'

'For four,' she said. 'The Señor, and his friends.'

My guts flinched at that. We had many señors visit us, genuine or otherwise. I disliked most, and envied them their freedom, but Morales knew which señor I truly despised, the one I kept the greatest distance from, the one who seemed to take pleasure in my discomfort.

'Don't skimp on the sherry,' she said, watching my face.

There were few things she could have said to make my day worse.

Although it was barely ten o'clock in the morning, the Plaza de la Corredera was already awake. The plaza itself, a slab of hot stone, was empty. Life was taking place in the shade of the colonnades, in the cave-like bars.

The market smelled of bruised tomatoes and fermenting vegetables, fish turning pungent in their trays, perspiring cheeses. The stalls had already been picked over. With all the extra mouths to feed in the city, other cooks would have arrived at dawn, perhaps even waylaid the farmers on the road into town to buy what was best. I jostled through, wishing I could wear Ifrahim's old, roomy work trousers out here without being sneered at, instead of the too-thick skirt that made my thighs chafe.

The butcher looked at me as if I was mad when I asked for bull's tail, and I had to bite my tongue rather than roll my eyes and remind him that we always catered to clients' whims. He was a church man and didn't like us. The second butcher was friendlier. His stall was smaller, dirtier, and sold what the other had turned down.

'Try the slaughterhouse,' he said, palsied hands laying down the cleaver. 'Heard they had a bull in today. If not, they might give you cow, or a bit of ox. Those drunk bastards won't know the difference.'

Outside the slaughterhouse, the cobbles were tacky with bloodstained water. When I stepped across the threshold into the dim, reeking shed, I found the place in a frenzy. The butcher was right, they had just slaughtered a bull, but it had gone badly. The creature had worked loose and tried to escape, crushing a boy's chest in the process. When I asked, the man in charge skinned the tail and gave it to me for free, saying that the beast had been possessed by the devil, and if I wanted to cook with its meat, that was between god and myself.

The bull's tail was so fresh that it dripped through the newspaper. I paired it with some old, ropey ox-tails and thought it lucky that the slaughterman was such a fool. I imagined telling Ifrahim about it. He would have winked at me and said that idle fears never did put food on the table. That thought was enough to dilute some of the anxiety I'd felt since speaking to Morales.

I had to hurry, for there was the noon meal to prepare and the girls to feed. All week I'd served ajo blanco for lunch, soaking the previous day's bread in milk and water and pounding it into a silky soup, as cold as I could get it. People scooped it down, sitting on stools in the shade of the balconies, and I was glad to see them eat – glad to see them sigh, soothed by the simple flavours, for a little garlic and bread does wonders for stomachs wretched with wine.

That day, the siesta hour felt strange. Heads fell on to arms, shutters were pulled closed, and hardened drinkers shrank into the darkness of the wine cellars as usual, but there was something fretful about it all; like a breath being held.

No rest for me, not with a rabo de toro to make along with everything else. In the kitchen, I changed into Ifrahim's old trousers and hid my hair under a scarf once more. Then, slowly, I unwrapped the bull's tail. The animal had killed someone today, for all I knew. When they ate it, the señors would have the blood of the bull's victim in their stomachs.

Watch what comes out of their mouths, as well as what goes in, and you will know them for what they are . . .

I had never liked those men.

I smiled as I portioned the tails and plunged them into water. I smiled as I cut onions and burst ripe tomatoes into fleshy pieces, and smashed cloves of garlic with the heel of my hand. I smiled as I rolled up my sleeves to get the stove going, though I feared I might keel over from the heat of it. By the time I tipped the tails into the stew pot, threw in bay and peppercorns, I felt like a true witch, brewing strong magic while the rest of the world slumbered away the afternoon.

Though it sounds superstitious, ridiculous, I still can't help but wonder whether what happened next was my fault. How do we know the slaughterman wasn't right about the bull; that its meat carried a bloody violence, which *I* brought to life?

A good rabo de toro takes at least three hours to cook. Mine stewed quietly at the back of the stove, its powerful scent of meat and bone filling the kitchen. I tried to ignore it and work on other things; wafers of sweet-salt jamón and dishes of toasted almonds, platters of tiny fish ready to fry in oil, and bread to soak up wine. But the stew kept catching my attention. It was as if there was another person in the room, who disappeared every time I turned to look.

All too soon, the sun was sliding towards evening, the church bells were tolling nine and the first guests were arriving, demanding to be served. Aside from sangria, Ifrahim had never shown much interest in drink. After a lifetime within the inn's walls, I felt differently. Beer was like fuel to some men, wine like blood. Brandy could make them lose their heads and break down crying, sherry could corrupt like a slow poison. Gin was what the girls often drank when alone in their rooms, hard and clear as tears. Drink was a potion, as much as food, and if I could control it, I could control them, the men who came here to satisfy themselves.

It became almost a game to me: how to keep them drunk enough to sing and empty their wallets, but not so drunk they would grow violent or collapse. I diluted wine with lemon soda, to make them drink slower, longer. A canny merchant from Jerez taught me how to make a Rebujito – sherry and soda and a sprig of mint, cool enough for any hot head. In one of Elena's discarded fashion magazines I even found a recipe for a cocktail, called a Marianito, which I longed to try. But it belonged to another world, to inconceivable places like New York or Paris. It could never exist at the inn. Nevertheless, I kept the torn-out page next to my bed so I could daydream the impossible: that one day I might sit in a bar, in a city far away and order myself a drink, as easily as breathing.

I thought of my dream that evening, as customers hollered for wine, more wine, more raciones, more sherry and I ran to and from the kitchen, trying my best to give them what they wanted, to control them before they went crashing into the night. I was so busy, I almost forgot about the strange, bloody day and the rabo de toro seething on the stove. Until *he* arrived.

The moment I heard his voice the hairs on my neck rose despite a layer of sweat. My guts turned cold and kinked themselves once, twice as the Señor and his friends sauntered into the inn.

I stopped in the kitchen doorway, waiting for them to pass, to fill their eyes with the sight of the girls in their tight dresses and crowns of flowers and lace. But the Señor didn't look at them. He looked straight towards me, and smiled.

It was then I understood: he had not ordered the rabo because he wanted it, but because *I* would have to make it. *I* would have to pour time and sweat into the pan. *I* would have to serve him at the table with my own hands. I had thought that cooking was a sort of freedom, a way to gain an ounce of control over the people who dominated my world. But I was wrong. I was not Ifrahim, able to drift and charm and cook my way across a continent. I was a woman, and the Señor only had to flex his will to remind me – to remind the world – what that meant. I would never be free.

By the time I returned to the kitchen my palms were clammy with fury and nerves. I swiped them down the apron, trying to think, my mind cloudy as old fat. He might have ordered the rabo but he didn't know about the bull, about the blood. Did that make it my weapon, or his? I wasn't sure. All I knew in that moment was that it *was* a weapon, and that it was dangerous.

I busied myself with whisking oil and garlic, with dredging fish in flour. I didn't want to think about him, but I couldn't stop, the smell of the stew kept getting in my nostrils. Before, the Señor had been content to eat and drink like anyone else, to grasp Elena's waist and throw the occasional leer my way as I crossed the patio. Why did he now . . . ?

My hands stilled. This was the first feria without Ifrahim; the first year without his quiet presence, filling the kitchen.

Perhaps he had spoken for me, all these years, in more ways than one.

I took a breath. I would serve the rabo de toro. I would leave them to their drinking. I would be the cook, nothing more. I told myself all of that, but I also picked up one of the kitchen knives and dropped it into the pocket of my apron. I was no longer a child. I'd do more than vomit on the man if he tried to touch me.

A flicker of movement in the doorway made me start. It was Elena. She was wearing the pale flowered silk dress that the Señor had given her, the year before. It was girlish, but then, that was how he liked her. The lace mantilla, his first gift, fell around her face, over her shoulders and down her back. It made her look like she was on her way to communion. Morales wanted her to seem that way for him, the man who paid to have her clean and to himself for the feria.

We stared at each other, Elena with her soap-scrubbed skin, me soaked in sweat and reeking of the stove. For a moment, the kitchen seemed to fill with the smell of gelatine and roses.

'Mama sent me to check on the rabo,' she said. 'Is it ready?'

I pulled the stew pot towards me and gave it a stir. Rich, viscous and silky with marrow. A piece of the bull's tail rose, tender around its star of bone.

'Almost.'

'Well, hurry up,' she said. 'They are drinking imported whisky. It's making them impatient.'

I glanced over at her. There was something odd about her manner, something furtive. She was worrying at the web of skin between her thumb and forefinger, worrying it red.

'The Señor seems different tonight,' I said.

Her round face flushed. 'What do you mean?'

I could hear the nervousness in her voice, barely held back. I left the stew and took a step towards her, my eyes on the door.

'What's going on?' I whispered.

She looked at me for one shallow breath, two.

'I'm leaving.' Her voice was so quiet I could barely hear it over the din coming from the courtyard. 'He's going to take me with him, after tonight. He said . . . he told me that when I turned eighteen he'd take me away from here, set me up in my own apartment.' She pinched at the skin of her hands. 'I'm eighteen now. So he's got to take me with him tonight.'

The lace mantilla, the sherry, the Turkish Delight, they weren't what had made her bow her head and follow him into a bedroom, four years ago.

'Elena—'

'He has to.' There was a tremble of panic in her voice. 'He swore he would.'

'But you hate him.'

She looked up at me. In that moment, I saw Mama Morales in her, in the defiance that coloured her cheeks and made her lips compress, in the rigid stare that said *there is no way but this*.

'I hate this place more,' she said.

And so I set the stew in front of them. I watched from the shadows as they ate, as their mouths and moustaches became coated with juice from meat and bone, as they mopped the thick, brown sauce with bread and washed it down with glasses of their expensive, foreign spirit. When the Señor lifted a piece of meat on a spoon and held it to Elena's lips, I wanted to rush out and tell her about the blood and the bull, tell her not to eat. But I couldn't. I could only watch, and wait.

Trouble was brewing. As I crossed the yard to clear the table I could hear it in the music, in every cracked-throat cry and feverish guitar note, in the hands that beat *slap slap slap* against each other. I collected the dishes. The Señor's eyes crawled over the nape of my neck.

'A fine rabo de toro,' he said, as I loaded the tray. 'Though a little forceful for my liking.'

I couldn't help it. I looked at him. He was drunk, his face reddened from sun and alcohol, the brash smell of whisky all about him. His friends had been diluting theirs with seltzer, but I watched as he tipped some into his glass, neat, spilling it on the tablecloth. Beside him Elena sat, pale and sweating. He caught my glance towards her.

'Poor little Elena, your rabo was too much for her.' He drank his whisky. 'Perhaps the two of us should take her up to bed.'

'Be my guest,' I retorted and walked away before I could see the consequence.

I didn't have to wait long. Morales stepped into the kitchen a few minutes later, where I was hacking the bread to crumbs.

'He wants ice, upstairs,' she said. 'Take it to him.'

I stopped my sawing and met her gaze. My lips were shaking with rage. *I did what you wanted*, I told her silently, *I made what he asked for. Now leave me be.*

'I'm busy,' I said.

'You are not too busy for this.'

'Get one of the girls to do it.'

'No.' Her face didn't change. 'He wants you to take the ice.'

In that moment, I remembered the knife in my pocket.

You know the rest. You know what I found, when I carried that bowl of ice upstairs and opened the door.

Blood and sand. Whisky and violence. Elena with the bottle in her grip – sharp as a freshly broken promise – and the Señor, his throat slashed, bleeding all her hope out on to the rug.

Tangier

July 1978

By the time Sam reached Madame Sarah's again, it was dark. He'd drifted through the evening streets of the casbah on a wave of good feeling, had even smiled at the kids who nearly hit him in the face with a football.

He was still smiling as he opened the door of the house. Madame Sarah was in the kitchen. It was warm and yellow in there, filled with the crackling sound of the radio, the smell of gas from the stove and fish frying in spices. For a moment, he wished Madame Sarah would smile at him the way she smiled at Pierre, wished she would ask him to sit down and eat with her and Aziz. But her face soured when she saw him.

'You owe me rent,' she said, pointing a fork at him. 'Now.'

He nodded humbly and stepped into the kitchen to count out the money. He didn't blame her for being angry. He felt awful about it. Impulsively, he added an extra few dirhams on to what he owed. Her eyes narrowed when she saw that. No doubt she was wondering what he'd done to get the money, but he gave her his best smile.

'Here it is.'

She gave a sniff, and folded it into her apron.

Behind her, next to the gas burner sat a stack of msemen. He could already taste them, the thick, chewy layers, rich with clarified butter, like the best pancake ever made.

'Could I . . . ?' he heard himself asking, pointing to them, already knowing what the answer would be.

But to his surprise, she sighed, shook her head a little and picked a couple up.

'No more late money,' she said, handing them over.

He knew he must have looked like a fool, grinning and nodding at her, but he didn't care. He ran up the stairs two at a time, already chewing. His room was cool and blue with its open shutters. A breeze was blowing in from the strait, and he could see the lights from ships, port and starboard stars in the darkness. On a rooftop somewhere near by, a man and a woman were talking softly. Sam smiled to himself and lay back on the narrow bed. In that moment, all of Tangier was the taste of warm flatbread and cumin and sweet mint and smoke, the musk of old leather and the worn, fine presence of the past.

The first thing he saw when he awoke the next morning was the writing case.

He groaned, remembering what it had cost him, on top of a supply of kif. How had he spent almost a week's rent on a piece of junk? His parents were right, he didn't deserve money. But at the time it had seemed so . . . right. He'd believed that the writing case had been waiting for him. He sighed and pushed himself upright. Perhaps Abdelhamid would take it back.

It was good leather, must have been expensive, once. How had it washed up here? It looked tattier than he remembered, the leather gouged on one side, peeling on the other, the initials *A. L.* almost bare of gilt. The calendar inside was English, he remembered. Did that make *A. L.* British, or American?

When he turned it over, it rattled, something tumbling inside. Perhaps he hadn't replaced the pen properly. He swore and balanced it on his knee. Abdelhamid would never take it back if something was damaged. He worked at the rusty catch, and eased it open.

The smell came first; fusty paper and brittle leather. He opened it wider. The paper was there, yellowed but clean, the pen and pencil and ink snug in their holders. What made the noise, then?

He shook it. There *was* something loose, sliding and rattling about. He looked more closely. The blotter wasn't set all the way into the case; there was an inch of space beneath.

He tried to work his fingers under the edge. It was difficult, the thing fit perfectly, and he almost gave up, thinking it was too much work for what was probably a nub of pencil.

What else do you have to do? Stare at the space where the Hermes used to be?

Finally, by holding the case upside down and poking one edge of the blotter, he was able to work it free. Gravity did the rest, sending two small objects tumbling out on to the sheet. One of them glinted silver, like sunlight on water.

He leaned forward, wondering whether he'd finally smoked too much kif. But no, his fingers touched metal, tarnished and real. It was a key, a small one, the type that might open a bag or a chest or a bureau. Automatically, he looked to the front of the case, but there was no lock there, just the rusted clasp. *Stray key*, he thought in delight, *what do you open?*

Abruptly, he was wide awake. It was as if the silver of the key had shone into his brain and illuminated a corner he had forgotten about. It brought a shiver of excitement, the crackling sensation that came with a new idea, with the urge to write something down. The seed of a story, a mystery. He'd always been a sucker for those, for cheap paperbacks filled with secrets and thrilling adventures, much to the disapproval of his literature professors.

Eagerly, he looked at the other item. It was dull and brown, an offcut of leather, curled like a leaf. *Don't get excited*, it seemed to mumble, *dead things, that's all we are*. He picked it up anyway, and turned it in his fingers.

It wasn't an offcut at all, he found, but a rectangle, like a luggage tag. Smoothing it out, he saw a design embossed in gold, a stylized lion's head. And beneath it, stamped into the leather, was a number:

15

*

Noon found him hurrying through the streets of the medina, the writing case clasped to his chest. In his haste, he stepped in a pile of fish heads left out for the cats and almost slipped, but he carried on, not thinking about his shoes, just trying to reach the shop before it closed for lunch . . .

'Abdelhamid!'

He caught him just as he was turning the key in the lock.

'Monsieur Hackett,' Abdel greeted. 'Good afternoon. You have not run out already?'

'Not yet.' He tried to catch his breath. 'I was looking at the case, and I found something inside.'

'Oh?' Abdelhamid squinted. 'What did you find?'

'A key –' Sam dug into his pocket '– a key for something, like a chest. Did the case come with anything else? From the same set of luggage maybe? And I found this too. Do you know what it's for?'

He held them out, the key and the crumpled leather tag. A second later, he felt a stab of uncertainty. What if Abdelhamid thought they were important and wanted to take the case back? Sam gripped the handle tighter.

But Abdel just shook his head, turning the little silver key in his fingers. 'No, no, it was always alone, always just . . .' He looked down at the label, and shrugged. 'Why? You think they are something?'

Yes, he wanted to insist, *they are*. But of course, they were probably not. Whatever the key opened – suitcase or travelling trunk – it was no doubt long gone, crushed in some dumpster back in the States or mouldering in an attic in an English village. Whoever A. L. was, they probably owned a dozen keys far more important than this one. And yet, here was a piece of someone's life, a sliver of it, from fifty years ago; perhaps, if he tried, he could find out more.

'Could you talk to your brother Mouad?' he asked. 'See if he remembers where the case came from?'

Abdel's frown transformed into a smile. 'You are inspired by this,' he declared, patting the case. 'You see? I told you. Much better than a typewriter!'

Sam laughed with him. It was true, he *felt* inspired. The case, the key – they itched at his brain. He found himself speculating, imagining, eager for more. He could get a story out of it: a mystery of the casbah, beginning with a young man who finds a key . . . Either that, or he was just desperate for something to do. He shoved the thought aside.

'So you'll ask Mouad?'

Abdel jerked his head. 'I will try. Come.'

Sam sat at the back of the café for twenty minutes, his feet twitching in his shoes, listening to Abdelhamid's phone call, not able to understand more than a few words.

'Mouad does not remember the case,' Abdel said finally, hanging up the phone. 'He says, if he sees it, maybe he will.' He shook his head, seeing Sam's disappointment. 'He will visit soon, before Ramadan. Then we can ask him.'

'When is Ramadan?' Sam followed him out of the café.

'August. The first days. You will still be here, then? You shouldn't miss it.'

Sam tried to smile. He had enough money for another two weeks, but then . . . 'I hope so,' he said.

After saying goodbye to Abdelhamid, he wandered out into the heat of the Grand Socco. It was busy and baking, café tables crammed beneath awnings and faded umbrellas, all occupied by people trying to cool themselves with tea or Coca-Cola. He hadn't eaten since the msemen Madame Sarah had given him the night before; had been filled instead with kif and excitement. Now, he found himself ravenous.

He bought a couple of crispy briwats, no idea what was in them. Shredded chicken and cinnamon, it turned out. A water seller ambled past, bent-backed beneath his plastic drum, brass cups clinking on the bandolier across his chest. Sam stopped him, and after a few long swallows of water, he began to feel better, more cheerful than he had for days.

An idea was forming. He'd write to his parents again; write to them properly this time, not scrawled on airmail paper, or dashed out on the Hermes. He would sit and put pen to paper and try to make them understand what he couldn't fully explain, even to himself: that he couldn't come home, not yet.

At a stationer's shop he bought a bottle of ink, and asked the owner – in mangled Spanish and worse French – about a new nib for the ink pen. The man seemed surprised, but after a few minutes of rooting through drawers, he produced a box of nibs. They tried them out in the pen until they found one that fit.

Armed, Sam made his way to the Gran Café de Paris and chose a quiet table in the corner. He took out the ink, the new nib, and centred the leather case before him.

When his coffee arrived, he leafed through the paper to find the least yellowed sheet, and set it on the top. His hands were trembling slightly as he dipped the pen into the ink and held it poised. It felt egotistical to stain one of those old pages with his writing, but at the same time, the case had sat idle for fifty years, hadn't it? Surely it was time for it to break its silence? He smiled, touched the nib to the paper, and began to write.

1928. That's what the calendar in the lid said. The clink and chatter of the café faded around him. If only he held the pen tightly enough, wrote fast enough, he might look up and find himself back there, when living was wild and Tangier was filled to the seams with people like him; people who didn't fit anywhere else, who had chased themselves across Europe to this city in order to turn themselves inside out with drugs and glamour and mistakes . . .

'Monsieur?'

A waiter stood above him, looking expectant. Sam blinked hard. For an absurd moment, he thought an old-fashioned motorcar might drift past the window, thought he'd hear jazz on the radio and see people in the clothes of half a century before.

'Yes?' he asked, rubbing at his forehead, trying to pull his mind back into the present.

'Another?' the waiter asked, pointing at the long-emptied coffee cup.

'Yes, yes, thanks,' Sam mumbled. He didn't really want another one, but neither did he want to leave the cocoon he'd created around himself. It reminded him of the few times he'd written something good; when whole hours had been lost to the act of creating a world, spinning it into existence using nothing but the words inside his head. It had been like that, before the waiter interrupted.

He sighed and sat back. Before him, two sheets of the thick letter paper were covered with writing, awkward and scratchy at first, but growing more fluid as he got used to the pen. He picked up the first sheet, to read it back from the beginning.

Dear A,

He stared, feeling odd. He'd intended to write to his mother, his father, but that wasn't what had happened.

Dear A,
I have your case.

What followed was almost a confession, about how he came to buy the case at the expense of his Hermes, about his failure as a writer, a traveller, a son, as anything really. He felt the heat rising to his face, alarmed by his own honesty. He'd written about Tangier as it was now and how he imagined it then. He'd written to A. L. wondering whether they were similar people, wishing he could post the letter back through time and space, and receive a reply from the past.

The letter broke off mid-sentence. He stared at the pages, thrilled and uneasy. As a piece of writing it was next to useless; it wasn't a plea to his parents, or even a story he could sell to a magazine to make some money. And yet, it felt like a start, the beginning of something new.

It was as he was reading the letter for a second time that his neck began to prickle, as if he was being watched. He looked up into the mirror that reflected back the café: a few tables away, someone was staring straight at him.

It was an old man, his eyes concealed by semi-opaque spectacles, and by a fedora hat that would have been stylish in another decade. Slowly, the man's mouth twitched and he nodded.

Sam turned in surprise, only to catch sight of his own face. There was a huge dark smear across his forehead; he'd managed to cover himself with ink.

What an idiot. No wonder the old man was staring. Too embarrassed to look up again, Sam pushed himself from the table and headed for the bathroom. In the dim light, he scrubbed the ink from his skin, staring critically at his half-open shirt, his straggling, sun-licked hair and dirty tan.

If he'd lived fifty years before, he would have been dressed smartly, elegantly.

Lost in thought, he made his way back to the table. He'd bring the letter to a close; sign it off with his name. A first chapter, maybe . . .

He sat down and reached for the pen, only to stop. Everything was just as he had left it, except for the letter.

The letter was gone.

ALABAZAM

Take one teaspoonful of Angostura bitters and half a pony of orange Curaçao. Add to it one teaspoonful of white sugar and one teaspoonful of lemon juice. Then pour in half a wine glass of brandy. Shake up well and strain in a claret glass.

Brief, dark and bitter.

We once had a conjurer visit the inn during the feria. He was a shabby-looking man with drooping moustaches and a threadbare velvet cloak. I wasn't very impressed; no one was, until we saw his trick. He took a duck from a cage, and wrenched its head clean from its neck. The girls shrieked to see it, and flinched as he paraded around the courtyard, the body in one hand, the little feathered head in the other. Then, he put his hands beneath a red silk handkerchief, said a word and *whisk!* the duck was back, whole and quacking and pedalling its legs in protest.

That's how I felt as I stood in the doorway, looking at the Señor as the life flowed out of him. I kept expecting someone to say a word and wave a cloth, for him to stop his empty gulping, open his bloodstained mouth and grin. But no one said anything. Neither of us moved until the soft, wet gasping sounds finally ceased.

Then, Elena staggered. The broken bottle fell from her hand, the bowl of ice from mine as I stepped forward to catch her.

'I didn't,' she gasped, clinging to my apron, her eyes bulging and frantic. 'I didn't . . .'

She looked down at the Señor, his blank eyes fixed upon the ceiling. 'Ramón!' she screamed and dropped to her knees beside him.

She was gripping his face, trying to lift his head, but he was gone, the wound at his neck bleeding sluggishly. That's when I heard footsteps on the stairs, and the echo of voices. I turned to meet Morales' gaze.

I didn't know that a life could change so drastically in the space between one heartbeat and another. For one trembling breath everything hung suspended, like alcohol in water: Elena holding the Señor's head, me with blood on my apron, the dropped ice, the broken bottle. Morales' eyes flicked to her daughter, before settling on me.

'Murder,' she said softly.

I started to cry out, to explain, but my voice was lost in hers as she shouted the word. The doorway behind her was filling with the reddened, sweating faces of the Señor's friends, on their way to the parlour. I saw their redness curdle, their mouths fall open, and still I stood paralysed. Then Elena looked up. Her pretty face was tear-streaked, her fingers slippery with blood as she pointed at me.

It was enough. The world descended into hands grabbing, clawing, wrenching my arms behind my back as Morales shouted murder. I struggled and threw myself sideways, trying to see Elena. We locked eyes and I knew, in that moment, what she and her mother had agreed, without words.

I screamed at her, spittle flying from my mouth as I called her a lying bitch. It didn't help my cause. One of the gentlemen hit me with his fist, a blow that folded me over in shock, made my eyes flood. A few drops of blood splattered from my nose on to my smock as they hauled me towards the stairs.

Morales was calling for help, calling for someone to fetch the guardia, to find Capitán Davila and tell him there had been a murder at the inn, tell him to bring men and a car to arrest the murderess.

Her voice slapped me into wakefulness. Capitán Davila – who came to the inn every month to inspect the premises and claim his 'commission'. Capitán Davila who had known Morales for years, who at her word would throw me into a cell and shrug and call it a night's work.

'Elena,' I choked, as they pulled me down the stairs. 'It was her, he promised to take her away from here, he promised and she found out the lie—'

One of the gentlemen beside me faltered and glanced at the others. I recognized him from the night in the parlour. He was the one who had offered the Turkish Delight. 'Please!' I begged him. 'Please, you know it's true! Tell them!'

He flinched away, and I saw something in his eyes, a shred of belief. The Señor must have bragged of his nights with Elena, must have laughed over how he could make her do anything, for a handful of promises.

But the man was shaking his head, his grip weak. 'I can't have my name in this,' he said breathlessly, 'if my customers discovered, my wife—'

'Does she know our names?' Another man was interrupting, shaking me. 'What if she talks?'

He was addressing Morales, who stood at the foot of the stairs. She looked at me, her eyes hard.

'If she talks, who will listen?'

My strength faded when she said that. She was right. No one would listen. *Bad blood*, they would say, *rotten whore*, and they would be believed. The girls would be silent. Antonio the groom would be silent. Only Morales would speak out, to send me to be garrotted for murder in Elena's place.

The thought made my head cloud, and I half fainted. They lifted me underneath each arm. My feet dragged uselessly, my hands brushing at my apron.

That was when I felt the weight of the knife.

We'd reached the bottom of the stairs. Through burning eyes, I could see the courtyard to my left, with its press of guests and tables. To my right, the open gate and the street, crowded with people, all drinking, shouting, making their way towards the river.

One chance.

I collapsed again with as much force as I could. This time I made it to the floor, slipping from the grip of one of the men. It was the one with the blinking eyes, the one who might have spoken for me. Doubled over, I managed to work my hand into the apron's pocket before he renewed his grip beneath my armpit and hauled me to my feet.

I didn't wait, I didn't even breathe. I flailed out with the knife, stabbing at him. He let me go and I whirled, slashing at the other man. Blood spurted, a voice yelled in pain and for a split second, no one held me.

I threw myself towards the gate. Someone made a grab for my legs, and had I been wearing a skirt rather than Ifrahim's old work trousers they would have brought me down. But their fingers slipped from the fabric, and whoever it was hit the ground. I darted into the street, barging my way through the crowd.

There were shouts behind me and booted feet and Morales' yelling for someone to stop me, but there were horns too, and tambourines and bells and I ran like a wild thing from the Plaza del Potro.

Get to the river. That was my only thought: the river where it was dark and where there were tents teeming with people. As I reached the far side of the square, I glanced back and saw one of the gentlemen staring through the crowd, conspicuous in his fine, black jacket. I ducked down, pulled off the stained apron and bundled it in my arms, wiping the blood from my nose. Keeping my head down, I slipped into a large group of people who were jostling, hootingly drunk, towards the river, and vanished.

At least, that is what the newspapers said. According to them I disappeared into thin air, evading capture by calling upon a network of gitano thieves and bandits, who smuggled me past the tireless guardia.

They said other things: that Señor Ramón Vélez del Olmo was a great man, a philanthropist who had donated thousands to the Church and its reformatory. They said that I had tried to extort money from him, and had become enraged when he refused. They said he had only been at the inn to seek out a friend, in order to dissuade him from sinning. About Elena, they said nothing. Why should they? Men just like the Señor ran the newspapers, and they all had Elenas of their own. So, Señor Vélez del Olmo was a great man, and I was the venal whore who murdered him. That was the story they told themselves at their card tables and racing parties.

The truth is always less glamorous.

The truth is that I passed the hours following the Señor's murder in terror, trying to lose myself in amongst the feria. I had no one, nothing but a knife and the clothes I stood up in – old trousers and a blouse and stained apron – unsuited to the world. My nose throbbed like the devil. When I explored it with my fingers, it felt hot and swollen but thankfully unbroken. Behind some of the tents were barrels of water for the mules where I rinsed the dried blood from my face.

In the light of the fireworks, I saw myself reflected; hair wild and straggling from the scarf, nose swollen, face gaunt with shock. By the time the second shower of light came, I had pulled the scarf from my hair and wet it so that it lay neater, I had turned the apron back to front and tied it around my waist, so that it looked almost like a skirt. While people were still distracted by the lights, I stole into the back of a tent and swiped an embroidered shawl that had been abandoned on a chair.

I crept through the people clutching drinks, staring upwards, their eyes and teeth reflecting red and orange. I sought out the most boisterous crowds, at the end of the river where the rich folk did not go. I tried to blend in by pasting a smile on to my face and clapping my hands to the music like a toy monkey.

But all the while, my mind was racing. I had to get out of Córdoba, I thought as I grinned and clapped, I had to get out before morning. It seemed impossible. I had never left the city before. My only knowledge of the world came from Ifrahim's stories, of French jails and Portuguese shipyards, English enclaves and African souks, and they were just that: stories. Even if I did know where to go, I had no money for a bus or train ticket, no papers, no proper clothes even.

Only the knife.

Tangier

July 1978

'I'm telling you, it just vanished.'

From the corner of his eye, Sam saw Norton shake his head.

'Are you sure you didn't imagine the whole thing? Maybe you never even wrote a letter, just sat there daydreaming after a bit too much –' Norton mimed smoking a joint.

'Of course I didn't imagine it,' Sam snapped. 'I wrote the damn letter. How else did I get ink on my face?'

Even so, he felt a prickle of uncertainty. It was true, he'd lost himself in the act of writing, had scrawled out a confession to an unknown person without meaning to. But he *had* written. Hadn't he? 'Anyway,' he said, rubbing his neck. 'I didn't smoke much this morning.'

'But you did afterwards?'

'Sure. I was freaked out.'

Norton sighed. He looked more relaxed today, in chinos and a shirt and some sort of cravat, a jacket slung over his shoulder despite the temperature. The sun had set but the streets still held their late orange heat. 'This letter,' he said, 'did it have anything important in it? About you?'

Yes, Sam wanted to say. But he knew what Norton meant: name, address, social security number. He shook his head.

'Then why are you worrying?' Norton stopped. 'Look, it was probably nicked by someone who thought they could pull one over on you, extortion or whatnot. I'd put my money on one of the waiters.'

'There *was* this old man. I thought he was watching me but . . .' There was every possibility he'd imagined that too.

'Well there you go,' Norton said. 'I'll bet he was just some loony who liked the look of you. And he didn't take that.' Norton poked the writing case under Sam's arm. 'So no harm done.'

'I guess not.'

'Good. Let's get a drink and forget about it.'

They set off down a narrow street that led towards the beach. Sam took the roll-up from behind his ear and lit it, before offering it over to Norton. He watched the Englishman's face crease at the taste of the kif.

'Too much of this stuff will make you paranoid,' Norton said, smacking it away from his tongue.

'You know what they say, "A pipe of kif in the evening is worth a dozen camels in the courtyard."'

'Who says *that*?'

Sam laughed at Norton's expression, feeling his shoulders ease for the first time since the morning.

The Hold was open. Sam could tell, because the dark rectangle in the white, salt-damp wall was slightly darker than usual, and music was spilling out, the scratchy, warbly jazz the old-timers liked to play. At the threshold, Norton faltered and glanced at the peeling, hand-painted sign.

'Hackett. Where are we?'

Sam smiled. 'We can't drink at the El Minzah every day, old chum,' he said, mimicking Norton. 'And anyway, you said you wanted to meet other ex-pats.'

'I meant Peruvian oil barons and Russian heiresses,' Norton muttered, 'not ex-cons.'

'What's the difference?'

A shallow set of stairs led down to the bar, where it was cooler, away from the fierce heat. As Sam stood blinking, with Norton at his back and the bright streets in his eyes, he heard someone exclaim:

'I'll be damned. Is that Samuel Hackett?'

Squinting, he took a few steps across the uneven floor. Slowly, the bar resolved itself from the gloom. A padded bench ran around the edge of the cellar, low tables before it. A record player sat at the end of the bar, next to a crate of records, where Roger, the owner, could keep a watchful eye. Leaning next to it was a woman. She was smiling at Sam, her blue eyes startlingly bright against skin that was as tanned and creased as hide. There was a cigar in her hand, unlit.

'We'd given you up for dead,' she said, her lips forming a smile. 'Some of us before others.'

'I don't owe you money too, do I?'

She snorted. 'Well, *I* never did expect to get it back.' Her eyes settled on Norton, lingering at the bottom of the stairs. 'But what have you brought us?'

'A compatriot of yours,' Sam said, enjoying Norton's expression. 'This is Ellis Norton, he's here with Interpress, fresh off the boat.'

'How dreadful for you.' The woman smiled at Norton with all her teeth. A great many of them were gold. 'I'll bet you wanted Rome.'

Norton flushed, extending a hand. 'I'm determined to make the best of it, Mrs . . . ?'

Sam winced and leaned over the bar to call Roger from the back room.

The woman was staring Norton down. 'Mrs Nothing,' she said. 'It's Captain. Captain Elizabeth Lowe.'

'Bet used to have a ship,' Sam murmured over his shoulder.

Norton seemed at a loss, before clapping a hand to his jacket pocket. 'Ah, perhaps a drink?'

'Now, young man,' Bet said, biting off the end of the cigar, 'you are speaking our language.'

Roger appeared, limping and gruff as always, and got them a round of beers. He'd grown even hairier since Sam had last seen him. No one really knew how the Welshman had ended up in Tangier, running a hole in the wall. There were a dozen stories about him. Someone said he'd been in a secret desert task force during the war, and couldn't bring himself to go back to Swansea with all the blood on his hands. Others said he'd been in the Merchant Navy, and had gone AWOL one night only to wake up in the casbah two weeks later with the keys to a bar in his pocket.

And you, Sam asked himself, draining the glass of beer, *what great story can you tell? A dropout, begging from his parents?* The writing case sat beside him, bringing back a memory of the letter; a first chapter of something new. *Perhaps not*, he thought.

The bar soon began to fill up with regulars, many of whom had been coming for so long they'd worn the grooves of their arses into the bench. Sam knew better than to try and sit in their places. Bet sat at her table, next to the record player, nearest to the bar. Next to her sat Dr Halligan who taught at the American school and usually had a few college students in tow – undergrads who'd lost the sheen of home. Giles from the British Embassy, sipping his Benedictine; Kline from – nobody knew where Kline was from. Germany, perhaps. Or Switzerland. Anyway, he had something to do with shipping, and was perpetually murmuring to Bet about tide times and anchorage. Wizened Derek Bluff and his glamorous wife Lina. Sam couldn't help but blush when she leaned in to kiss him on both cheeks, filling his nose with powder and perfume. Roger once told him that Lina was a White Russian who had been a spy, and that Bluff was the British Service man who had unmasked her one fateful night in Gibraltar, only to fall unaccountably in love.

Sam exchanged pleasantries with them, brushing off questions about his writing, about where he had been. He wasn't sure why he'd stopped coming to The Hold. He'd begun to feel as if it was a strange hinterland, a twilight zone between the denouement of a story and a coda that never came. *Everyone* there had a past; a wild, dangerous, murky past, yet now they lingered, the crescendo behind them. He felt so blank in comparison. High school, college, summer work, bumming around England and France and Spain. In Connecticut, that made him adventurous, but here . . .

He glanced over at Norton, who was holding forth to Giles about his golf handicap. Sighing, he called to Roger for another couple of beers.

Over at her table, Bet was peering down at a map that Kline had spread before her, and was marking things in pencil, talking softly. When he appeared, they both looked up abruptly.

'Here,' he said, passing her the beer. 'Am I interrupting?'

'No, no.' Kline folded the map away. 'I am picking only Bet's knowledge. Please.' He vacated his seat, indicating Sam should take it.

He did, and took a sip of the lukewarm beer. In the background, one of Halligan's students was trying to replace the jazz record with David Bowie. Sam glanced over at Bet. He'd never been able to guess her age. Anywhere from fifty-five to seventy-five. It was impossible to tell.

'Remind me, how long have you been in Tangier, Bet?' he asked in the end, raising his voice over the start of the Bowie record, with its trumpets and squelchy notes. She looked at him steadily, and in the dimness of the bar, in the pungent cloud of cigar smoke, the voice from the record player seemed to be coming out of her blue eyes, singing of dead-end streets.

'Long time,' she said, tapping the cigar into the tray.

'But how long?' he pressed. 'What year?'

She frowned at him. Information was a currency, in Tangier.

'1951, or thereabouts,' she said eventually. 'After I was demobbed from the Wrens and nearly went out of my mind with boredom in Plymouth. A girlfriend got a job on a pleasure boat here, serving drinks, said I should join her.' Bet puffed on her cigar. 'It was the International Zone then. Anyone and everyone came here. You couldn't move for embassies and freight companies, French, Spanish, American, Dutch, Italian, it didn't matter. I wanted to sail so it worked for me.' She showed a few gold teeth.

'All those charts and radar plotting during the war, I could've sailed from here to Gib with my eyes closed. Fat lot of good it did. No one willing to hire a female pilot, in those days. But eventually I met . . . a person who ran an import-export concern.' She slid a glance at Sam. 'They gave me a job. Said I was the best they'd ever seen. We worked together for years after that.'

Sam smiled, trying not to let his disappointment show, but Bet caught it anyway. She laughed, blew out smoke. 'Not what you wanted to hear?'

'Yes, I did,' he hurried. 'It's just, I found something the other day, from the late 1920s . . .'

As the bar grew more crowded, he found himself telling her about his trade with Abdelhamid, about the Hermes and the old writing case, the calendar in it and the letter he'd written, which – he was sure – had been taken at the café.

'There was an old man,' he said, over the sound of a few young Moroccan guys calling greetings to Roger from the stairs. 'He was watching me in the mirror.'

Unlike Norton, Bet didn't roll her eyes. She only frowned. 'Old man,' she repeated. 'How old? What did he look like?'

'Hard to say. Seventy, maybe? He was wearing dark glasses, big ones, and an old-fashioned hat. Western clothes, a suit, I think.'

Bet tapped her empty glass on the table. 'Done something you shouldn't have, Sam?'

The ease with which she asked it shocked him. *Another reminder I'm not from her world*, he thought.

'No. I've not been doing anything. Apart from smoking kif.'

She snorted. 'Well then. You'll just have to wait until you see him again, won't you?'

'Yeah.' A moment later, Sam dug into his pocket, pulling out the piece of leather. 'Listen, I don't suppose you know what—'

Before he could finish, Norton stepped up to the table. He held a sticky glass, and the scent of Benedictine, herby and boozy, hung around him.

'Captain Lowe,' he said, pulling up one of the stools, 'I've just been hearing the most marvellous stories from Giles. He said you were a *smuggler*! Is that true?'

Norton's necktie was loosened, his face flushed. At another time, Sam might have said that he was drunk, but just the day before he'd seen the man dispatch three double whiskies, and barely blink. Perhaps the heat was getting to him. He glanced over at Bet. Everyone knew the rumours about her, but there was something uncouth about saying it aloud, to her face. He shifted in his seat, but she only laughed.

'All ancient history.' She put out the cigar. Without it, she seemed smaller, older. She gave Norton a little smile. 'How about another drink, dear boy?'

'Of course.' He was on his feet. 'Beer was it? Back in a tick.'

Sam watched him move towards the bar, belching out a loud 'excuse me' to the Moroccan guys. He looked back to find Bet's eyes fixed on Norton.

'Hmm,' she murmured, before levering herself to her feet. 'I must have a word with Giles. Bring my drink over when it arrives, Sammy, there's a love.' Her eyes fell on the scrap of leather that lay forgotten on the table. 'Where d'you get that old thing?'

'This—' He stared at her, before grabbing it up. 'You know what this is?'

She gave him a pitying look. 'You young people. I will admit though, most places use paper these days.'

'Bet, what *is* this?'

She was searching through her handbag for something. 'It's a cloakroom tag, from the Continental. I'd recognize that old tomcat design anywhere. The manager used to write me the most obscene love notes on the hotel stationery. "Elizabetta, Pirate Queen", he called me – where are you going?'

He had grabbed the writing case and was pushing his way towards the stairs, the tag clutched in his hand, not caring whose feet he stepped on. As he reached the doorway, Norton turned from the bar, his hands full of drinks, eyes fixed sharply on Bet. A second later, he saw Sam and his expression changed, melting into a wide smile. 'Hey!' he yelled.

But Sam couldn't think about Norton now, he couldn't think about anything except Bet's words: *Cloakroom tag, Continental*. Thanks to the case, he had written, truly written for the first time in months. And now, here was something else, a clue to the mystery. It might lead to a second chapter, and that chapter might lead to a third . . . This could finally be what he had been searching for through the streets of London and Paris and Barcelona, across the beaches of Málaga and the Strait of Gibraltar: a story, one that would make him want to write and write and never stop.

BLOODHOUND

Take three quarters of a pony of French vermouth and the same of Italian vermouth. Add a jigger of dry English gin. Crush two or three ripe strawberries in your hand, and shake until truly muddled.

It was the silence that woke me, abrupt and strange. Groggily, I moved my hand, expecting to find one of the inn's cats whirring and kneading my legs. Instead, I found metal and wood resting in my lap. The knife.

I opened my eyes. Before me was a grime-encrusted windscreen and through it I saw the sky pink with dawn, like blood beneath the skin. Day would be breaking in Córdoba too, illuminating the mess of the night I had left behind; the stains on Elena's rug, the Señor's eyes, weighted down by coins. In a rush, it all came back: my flight into the feria, the darkness and the knife in my hand, my escape from Córdoba in this van, driven by an old man heading south, with his cargo of empty wine casks.

I had told him that I lived near Ronda – a name I pulled from my memory – and that my purse had been stolen during the feria and with it my bus fare home. He knew I was lying. He knew it from my bruised nose and shaking hands, from my strange, jumbled attire. But he had eyed my chest and laughed and said he would be happy to help a nice girl like me.

As soon as I had shut the door, he'd tried to take his payment, his hands pushing at my legs, groping my chest. But I had been ready and shoved him back, saying I was a good Catholic girl. He'd laughed again, as if at some great joke, and might have continued had I not taken the knife from my waistband and showed it to him. He left off then, and was sour as he started the engine and drove into the night. Still, from the glances he cast my way, I knew he had not given up on the idea.

I blinked hard, trying to see where and why we had stopped. My mouth felt dry and sour, limbs stiff and aching from the long drive. As I sat up, I caught movement in the van's mirror: my own reflection. A girl was staring back at me, her hair a tangled mess, a bruise seeping across her cheeks from a swollen nose. I touched it, and she winced.

I was about to lean forwards, rub at my eyes and push at my hair when I saw something else in the mirror behind me. A man was emerging from a shed. I slumped down, pretending to sleep, and watched through lowered eyes as he stared at the van, scratching at his crotch through a pair of overalls. Only when he moved away, when a door squealed open, did I open my eyes again and look around.

We were parked outside a shack, wooden-walled and tin-roofed and covered in advertisements for oil and shellac and cigarettes. The driver of the van was inside the shack, then, with the man in overalls. Cold fear and nausea washed through me. One old man I could handle, but two . . .

Stowing the knife in my belt, I opened the door as quietly as I could. Beyond the gasoline pumps I could see no other buildings; there would be no one to hear if I screamed. Instead, the land rolled away into greyness. In the distance were the smudges of mountains. I had no idea where I was.

I slipped to the ground. Out here, I could hear the murmur of the men's voices, could smell gasoline and cigarette smoke and road dust on the dawn air. I crawled around the back of the van, and peered out.

On the other side of the road was a slope. If I could make it that far, I might be able to get out of sight. But the distance between the shack and the road's edge seemed impossible. Everything else was still and silent; even if I crept, they would surely hear my footsteps . . .

A bark of laughter, a cough and the shifting of furniture made my decision. I took off. Four paces, five, and the door clattered open behind me. At any moment, I thought I'd hear someone pursuing, feel someone grab at my shoulder, but there was the edge of the road, and the slope beyond. Throwing myself over it, I lost my footing and fell, tumbling over and over down a steep slope, until my shoulder collided with something hard and I slid to a stop, the knife clattering from my grip.

For long moments I didn't move, the wind knocked out of me, dust filling my mouth. Grey shapes loomed all around, pale and twisted. Olive trees.

There was a yell from the top of the slope. The driver – shouting that I was a puta and that they'd find me. A handful of stones came raining down amongst the trees. I didn't make a sound, not even when one of them caught me on the leg. Finally, he swore to himself and hurried back towards the shack. I didn't wait around to see whether he'd return.

⋆

It makes no difference what I did or said to get myself away from that place. Just as it matters not at all whether the men I eventually persuaded to pick me up by the roadside were carrying tomatoes or grapes or eggs on the back of their van. What matters is that it happened, that they took me as far as their destination.

Gibraltar.

I had heard of the place from Ifrahim's tales; a rock in the ocean, a great lion rearing and turned to stone. The first time I saw it, I thought it was a trick of the afternoon heat. But we drew closer and I knew that it was real: a mountain at the edge of the sea.

And the sea . . . I had never seen it before. Can you imagine that? The only water I knew was that of the Guadalquivir river, sluggish and brown and clogged with reeds and run-off from the city. I had seen pictures of the sea, on postcards painted in garish blues, but I didn't think they were real, just as lips are never truly carmine.

I was wrong. As we emerged from the foothills, I heard a cry above the truck and looked up. A great white bird had built her nest at the top of a pole. Elegantly, she stepped from the edge and opened her wings. I followed the path of her flight, her legs trailing, and suddenly my eyes were flooded with blue.

It hit me like flash powder: vast blue, potent blue. Even now, I find the sensation hard to describe. If colour were a taste, the sky would be powdered sugar, but the sea – that would be molasses.

I never believed in love at first sight. Fascination, yes, lust, certainly. I saw those things many times at the inn. But the moment I saw the sea, I was lost. It was love, and I never wanted to stop looking. Even today, I gaze upon it every morning like a new lover.

But of course, on that day it soon dropped from my view, replaced by a rail track and shabby houses and the start of a town. I fidgeted, wanting to keep it in my sight.

'What's the matter, sister?' I remember one of the men taunting. 'Lice biting?'

I didn't care. I didn't want to think about anything except the sea. Finally, the van began to slow, Gibraltar looming monstrous beyond a sandy wasteland and a fence, guarded by . . .

Sentry huts, men in uniform, guns at their hips. They were stopping every person who tried to cross, men with mules and wagons, women on foot, even children.

'What's this?' I croaked, my throat thick with road dust.

'Border,' one of the sunburned men in the back yawned. 'They're checking papers.'

Papers. I had none. But worse than that: what if the news from Córdoba had arrived ahead of me? What if the soldiers had been ordered to keep watch for a young woman of my description? The driver released the brake on the van, and it began to roll forwards.

'Gracias,' I gabbled, and the next thing I knew I was jumping from the back of the van. I landed badly, half-sprawling in the grit on my knee. I got up immediately and began to walk without looking back, though the men behind me called out, 'Sister!'

I didn't know where I was going. I just wanted to be away from the soldiers and the uniforms, and their sharp eyes. And so, I made for the sea, for my new love, washing at the edge of the beach like the brightest silk coverlet ever sewn.

The sand beneath my boots made me start but it did not slow me down. When I reached the shallows, I dipped my hands and brought them to my face. The water was fierce, it stung my sunburned skin and bruised nose and it burned my tongue. It made my eyes stream, as if the salt in my body wanted to greet its long-lost cousin.

When I straightened, I found that I could barely stand, could barely keep my eyes open in the heat. It was exhaustion that made me lie down in a strip of shade, concealed between two fishing boats. There, surrounded by the strange mineral reek of drying seaweed and crusted barnacles, I slept.

Tangier

July 1978

Sam hurried along the Rue Dar-el Baroud, his throat raw from running. A wind had picked up, scudding across the city, bearing its load of grit and sand towards the Mediterranean. The night sky was tinged pink, bloody at the edges and in his sudden fever he felt as though some djinn was whirling around him. *A night for wild schemes*, he thought.

He'd passed the Hotel Continental many times but, like the El Minzah, had never been in. It stood at the very edge of the casbah, past the Grand Mosque, built out of the old city walls, staring seaward like a grand dame decked in jewels, her face turned away from the shabby city at her heel.

Sam stopped on the steps that led up to the terrace, beer thudding in his head, the writing case stuck to his hand. If this place was anything like the El Minzah he couldn't just fling himself in to the reception, crumpled and breathless, and present them with a fifty-year-old cloakroom tag. They'd look at him as if he was mad.

I am mad, he thought. Whatever item the tag belonged to was probably long gone. A shiver ran across his skin as he pulled the scrap of leather from his pocket and stared at it in the green and red light of the hotel's illuminated sign. What did he expect to find here, except disappointment? He turned it in his fingers. Perhaps finding wasn't the point . . .

Swallowing some moisture back into his throat, he tucked the writing case beneath his arm, and walked up the steps, trying to look dignified.

But the Hotel Continental was not like the El Minzah. Instead of dark wood and stern marble, he found himself among a riot of coloured tiles, kaleidoscopic from floor to ceiling. For a moment, it was dazzling. Then he blinked and saw that many of the tiles were cracked or missing, the velvet drapes threadbare and sun-stained, the brocade sofas worn bald with use.

The empty reception smelled of ancient rose petals and hot dust. There was no one at the desk. He rang a bell and the noise wandered away into the hotel's interior, in search of a reply that never came.

Hesitantly, he walked into a hallway hung with portraits, darkness creeping from their corners. There were grand stairs, the gilded banisters chipped and flaking. He followed them up, towards a clinking sound, and found himself at the entrance of a long gallery, with huge arched windows that overlooked the bay. For a moment, he thought the clinking would be nothing but a curtain tie, stirring in the breeze, but then he heard voices, and a figure materialized from the gloom: a young man in an old-fashioned green uniform.

'Bonsoir, monsieur,' he said softly. 'A table?'

He looked so hopeful that Sam almost considered saying yes, taking a strange, quiet meal alone there in the glittering carcass of the hotel.

'No,' he forced himself to say, 'no, I'm sorry. I was looking for someone at reception. I wanted to ask about . . . I wanted to ask a question.'

The young man's eyes were wide. 'Please, wait, I will fetch the manager.'

'No, don't disturb—'

But the young man was already gone, his footsteps echoing away. Sam had no choice but to wait, surrounded by the quiet murmurings of the few diners at the far end of the room. He allowed his eyes to blur, his imagination to run. Had A. L., the owner of the case, once sat here in solitary splendour, penning a letter before departing Tangier, never to return? Perhaps the dining room had been full of guests back then, champagne and brandy and music from a piano, chatter in French, English, Arabic, cigar smoke swirling like secret code.

'Monsieur?' He looked up. A middle-aged man was standing before him. 'I am Farouk, the manager here,' he smiled. 'How may I help? You are interested in a room? I am sorry for your wait, we do not have many staff tonight.'

'That's, ah, OK.' Sam shifted in his espadrilles. 'I'm not here about a room. I wanted to ask about your . . . cloakroom. It sounds crazy, but I have this.' He pulled the tag from his pocket. 'I think it came from here?'

The manager frowned, holding out his hand. In the dim light, the leather tag looked older than ever.

'Oui,' he said at last. 'Oui, oui, this belonged to the Continental.' He looked at Sam over his spectacles. 'How did you come by it, monsieur?'

'I found it,' Sam said, before immediately regretting the words. He needed some reason to explain his being there, to make it less strange. *I'm trying to write a book* wouldn't cut it. 'That is, I found it among my late uncle's possessions. This was his too,' he said quickly, showing them the case.

The manager looked no less confused. 'Your uncle was a guest with us?' He held up the tag. 'But this is very old. I have never seen one like it, and I have worked here for twenty years.'

'Yes, I think he was a guest.' Sam could feel himself turning red. 'Perhaps some time around nineteen twenty-eight?'

'That is fifty years ago, monsieur!'

'I know, I know, I just—' He groped for some rational argument, but there wasn't one. 'I just wondered why he kept it,' he muttered. 'Whether he left any belongings here, unclaimed, for some reason. I'm sorry. It was a stupid idea.'

The manager was smiling now, polite but pitying. 'It is true we sometimes store items for guests, but for this long?' He handed back the tag. 'I do not know.'

'Store? Then you do have a storage room?'

'Of course, monsieur.'

'Could . . .' His curiosity was too much. What might be lurking in the storeroom of a hotel like this? 'Could I perhaps have a look?'

The manager's eyebrows rose. 'We do not allow guests to enter the storeroom. It is untidy. Too many old things.'

'But I'm not a guest. I'm a writer. I'm writing a book about this place,' he bluffed, hoping to sound convincing. 'About this hotel, about the past in Tangier. That's why I've been going through my uncle's things. It would be great to have a quick look. Even if my uncle's belongings aren't there.'

The manager gave a little sigh. Sam scrabbled in the pocket of his jeans.

'Please,' he said again, reaching for the manager's hand. 'It's important to me. I'd be very grateful.'

The ten-dirham note felt crumpled against his fingers, and for a moment, he thought the manager might drop it in disgust. But then the man was straightening his jacket, and the money was gone, as if it had never been there at all.

'Very well, monsieur. I do not see the harm. I will send Mohamed with you. He will assist.' *Keep an eye on you*, in other words.

The storeroom was low down in the hotel, a semi-subterranean room that looked as if it had once been carved from the coastal rock itself. When the metal door swung open, it released a waft of air, cool with stone-must. Perhaps this cave had once been used to house barrels of wine, crates of tobacco and contraband rowed in from creaking ships. Perhaps Bet had even used it, back in her smuggling days, bribing the manager with charm and French cigarettes, stowing boxes and suitcases in the dead of night, conducting shady business from the hotel terrace.

An overhead bulb flickered on, sickly yellow, illuminating the space.

The manager was right. There was no romance of the past here, no buccaneer's hoard, only the detritus of decades, washed up against the sides of the room. A broken hat stand listed from a vast pile of newspapers and periodicals, a lidless toilet yawned mournfully. There were empty metal drums that had once held oil, rusted gas canisters, a mattress from another era, sporting the stains of its many occupants. Nevertheless, junk could hide treasure . . .

'You see, monsieur,' Mohamed said, 'there is nothing—'

'It's great,' Sam interrupted. 'It's perfect. The mess doesn't matter.' He squinted upwards. 'Is that the only light?'

'I am afraid so.'

'Do you have a torch or something?'

He saw the young man hesitate, no doubt worrying what the manager would say if he found out that the strange foreigner had been left alone in the storeroom, to lay his hands on god knows what.

'I'll stay right here until you're back,' Sam said. 'I wouldn't want to trip over anything.'

That seemed to do the trick. Mohamed nodded. 'I will get a torch. But please, do not touch.'

Sam stood completely still, letting the fusty air of the storeroom surround him. He wasn't sure why he wanted to be alone, but now that he was, he could feel anticipation prickling beneath his skin, like the surface of water just before it boils.

He took one step forward, then another. The smell of salt-damp and rust grew stronger. His eyes traced the forms of shelves crammed with objects; frayed electric cords, glass seltzer dispensers clouded by time, miscellaneous fabrics long-folded, stiffened into parchment. There was something thrilling about all those things, left to decay. He felt like an archaeologist, unravelling the secrets of lost decades, of countless lives, one ordinary object at a time. Was it a lie, to say he was writing a book about Tangier, about the past? For all he knew he was: that's what the letter had been. An arrow, shot back through the centuries.

The space grew cramped, shelves closing in. He had to turn sideways to squeeze between them. One was stacked high with squarish objects. The light from the bulb barely stroked the darkness here, and Sam wished Mohamed would hurry back with the torch, while simultaneously hoping he would not. Against one wall, a broken mirror was propped, shards of glass clinging to a frame. Carefully, he worked one of them loose and crouched down. Sure enough, when he angled it this way and that, a few inches of light flashed across the shelves, illuminating leather, rusted metal, paper.

Luggage. He was looking at a huge shelf full of luggage; suitcases and valises, trunks and hatboxes. He stared, opening his eyes wide, trying to see more in the gloom. What if A. L. *had* left his belongings, all those years ago, through absentmindedness or misadventure?

He began to move the beam of light back and forth across the shelves. He tried to be methodical, but there were so many cases, stacked floor to ceiling, and he didn't even know what he was looking for.

Gold flashed in the darkness and he stopped. Hardly daring to breathe, he inched the beam of light back across a shelf until it caught on something. There, on the front of a leather suitcase, two gold initials were glinting, half obscured by grime:

A. L.

CONTINENTAL SOUR

Take a bar glass and fill with shaved ice. Into this add a teaspoon of sugar dissolved in water and the juice of half a lemon. Add a jigger of whisky, shake and strain into a sour glass. Dash with claret. A marriage of two worlds.

When I awoke on that beach, I became aware of three things, above all others. First was the smell: baked seaweed and tarred rope and sun-scorched wood. Second was the feel of sand, in my hair, clinging to the sweat on my skin. And third was hunger, like I had never felt before.

No matter how bad things were at the inn, I rarely went hungry. Perhaps that was why I didn't entertain thoughts of leaving, until there was no other choice. Ifrahim and I would often keep back the best for ourselves, sneaking slivers of the choicest cuts of meat, corners of fresh cheese, glasses of wine. When the rest of the inn was replete, we would take our cook's reward in the kitchen. It was a habit I continued after Ifrahim died. Sometimes, I'd even use one of the best crystal glasses for my stolen wine, and recline by the stove, pretending there was someone to wait on me, to turn down my bed at the ring of a bell.

Full belly, happy heart, the saying goes. Mine had never been so empty as that evening on the beach, the end of my first day as a fugitive. My belly wrung itself out, and my guts lay leaden, unable to stir themselves to help my heart.

I staggered to my feet, thinking only of food. From along the beach came the sound of shouting and the smell of cigarette smoke. I made my way across the sand towards it. There, I saw a small boat rolling in the shallows, men swarming around it. They had formed a chain, over a dozen of them, and were passing goods from the boat to the beach, to a wagon that stood, half-loaded.

Before another minute was up they were done, pushing the boat back out to sea. In a daze, I drifted forwards. Hunger and thirst drove the fear of being recognized as a wanted woman right out of my mind.

By now, the men were crowding about someone, exclaiming and stretching out their hands. In the middle of the group, a huge man was paying the workers, counting coins into their palms. Beside him stood a man in a black hat, wearing a starched collar despite the heat. Money – the thought crossed my brain, slug-like – that was what I needed. Money for food and drink and a safe place to spend the night.

Finally, the last men were paid. They dispersed, laughing together, weighing their wages in their hands. One of them caught me staring.

'Hola chica,' he said, rolling a coin.

I ignored him, watching the man in the black hat instead, the one who was undoubtedly in charge. But he was already walking away, the leather bag held tight. Abruptly the beach looked deserted.

'Wait!' I heard myself calling. The worker who had spoken to me turned back.

'Changed your mind?' he leered.

'Please. Can you spare a céntimo? I haven't eaten for days.'

He laughed at that, showing the dark gaps of missing teeth. 'You and me both, sister.'

His friends were catcalling, telling him to hurry up and not to bother talking to a perra.

'Please,' I said, following him as he walked. 'I'll pay you back when I find work. I'm a good cook, I just need to eat. Please.'

The man's smile sank into irritation. 'You want work, go do it on the Calle Mirimar, like all the other whores.'

I watched him go, biting back tears of shame and anger. Except for the Señor, it had been a long time since any man had spoken to me like that. They didn't dare; even the truly insolent ones usually held their tongues when they realized that I was in charge of the kitchen, and could easily drop something foul into their food, or worse.

But that world was gone. Out here, I was nothing. These people didn't know that I could take offcuts of meat and stew them into spiced softness or make a man sick to the guts with a few pinches of powder in his soup; that I could mix a drink to empty a purse or cook a rabo de toro that could lead a girl to murder. All they saw was a woman in stained clothes with a bruised, sunburned face. I truly understood then, for the first time, how the girls at the inn must have felt. Long hair and a skirt and a pair of open legs, that was all men saw of them. It was all men would see of me now. I had *wanted* to disappear into a wash of humanity, but not like that. Never like that.

My wandering steps took me into a town; La Atunara, I saw it was called. It began as a stretch of shanties beyond the beach, makeshift structures of wood and tin, tar-smeared cloth and whatever else could be found to plug the holes.

Children played naked in the dust, dogs roamed, vines and small trees sprang in yards, where chickens scratched hopefully. Amongst it all, I went entirely unnoticed.

Eventually, the street widened and the houses became bars, gaudy with tacked-up advertisements. On one corner, a woman was cooking fish over a brazier. Sardines, whole, skewered four to a stick, grilled in nothing but salt and their skin. The scent of food made me stagger with longing, and I reeled out of the thoroughfare to lean against a wall.

It can't have been more than a minute or two before I heard someone addressing me. I opened my eyes. It was a girl, her lips rouged, her blouse worn sheer, showing the frayed lace of her chemise.

'What?' I murmured.

'I said that's Concetta's spot. She'll beat you if you stay there.'

I blinked at her, but the street seemed to be lurching forwards and backwards. All I could do was steady myself on the wooden wall, and close my eyes again.

She swore and walked away. I willed myself not to faint. If I collapsed, no one would lift me up, and if they did, it would not be in kindness.

'Here,' I heard the girl's voice again, up close now. 'These are mine but you can have a few.'

She was holding out a newspaper bundle. The smell hit me, fish oil, chargrilled flesh, warm paper. It was filled with scraps of sardines, the bits that had fallen off into the brazier.

'She lets us have these for cheap,' the girl said, jerking her head at the fish-woman. 'Knows we don't have time to eat a whole stick. I tried once. Made me sick, eating them that fast.' She picked out a chunk of blackened fish, and ate it. 'Well?' she asked, chewing.

I reached towards the paper, took a piece and put the whole thing in my mouth. It was glorious, burnt salt, sweet flesh that tasted just how the sea had smelled. We never had fish that fresh at the inn. Often I had to spice it with a heavy hand, redden it with paprika and pepper to disguise the fact it was bad. But this . . . I reached for another piece.

We ate like that, chewing and spitting out the sharp bones, until the fish was all gone, and only the oily paper remained.

'Thank you,' I told her, my mouth tingling with salt. 'I was about to die of hunger.'

She dropped the paper to the ground. 'You just get here?'

I nodded. 'From inland. Looking for work.'

She laughed and looked me over, her eyes flicking from my bruised nose to the dirt beneath my nails. 'No offence but you might have to wait till it gets late, there's that many girls working here. Most of us got regulars.'

'I didn't mean—' I stopped.

She looked at me, her lips twisted. 'You mean you didn't come here to whore? None of us did, chica. Most of us came looking to be domestics, over there.' She jerked her head in the direction of the rock. 'Course no one tells you before you leave home that there isn't any work, that the Brits bring their own lot in.'

'What about the men on the shore?' I asked. 'They had work, carrying cargo from a boat. There was a man who paid them. In a black hat.'

The girl smiled. 'Black hat, beard like a mule's ass?'

That made me smile too, despite myself, and I nodded.

'That's Bautista. He's got the biggest racket round here. Runs the show. Usually pays well.' She glanced about the street. 'If he had them working tonight, I might have some luck after all.' She tugged at her blouse, pushed a few hairs back from her face. 'Wait till they've had a few. They're less picky then.' With that she began to walk away.

'Wait,' I called. 'I . . . don't have anywhere to sleep. Do you know a place?'

She turned. In the light of a flickering electric bulb that hung outside a bar, I saw that beneath the kohl and the weariness, she was younger than I'd thought. 'You got any money?' she asked.

I shook my head.

She sighed. 'There's an empty warehouse, border end of the beach. People sleep there, sometimes. Anything worth nicking?'

'Only a knife.'

She gave me a sort-of smile. 'Watch your back, chica.'

I wandered, no idea of where to go, or what to do with myself. The girl was right about other women, there were two to every corner of the main street. I saw the tell-tale signs of their profession everywhere; a chair sitting empty outside a house, a bit of bright rag tied to a window, the smell of violet perfume, liberally doused. Finally, at the end of a quiet street, I found a water pump, and stuck my head beneath it, rinsing the salt spray and sweat from my face, drinking until the pieces of fish swam in my belly.

When I looked up, the streets were dark. I began to feel afraid. The water had washed away a film of grogginess and reminded me of the truth: that I would have to spend the night in the open. It struck me then just how protected I had been at the inn, despite Morales' threats. Road or room, that had been her offer in the past. Now I knew for certain what I had only suspected before: that she knew first-hand the realities of both and had once made the choice herself. Perhaps her fierceness came from the knowledge of what lay beyond the gates for a woman like her. Like me.

As I pushed the hair back from my face, I became aware of someone watching me. A man, leaning heavily on a wall in the shadows, his lips slack, his eyes fixed on my chest, where the water had soaked through my blouse. I didn't smile, though I knew what the girls would have done. I knew the tricks and bits of business they used, to secure their clients.

'Like what you see?' I asked, my voice hardly audible. The man looked on without moving. Remembering the Señor's dog-like stare, I almost turned and ran, but then the man was grunting and lurching forward. When he got within a few feet of me I realized he was sopping drunk. In a dark corner of my mind, an idea began to form.

'How much?' he slurred. I don't believe he could see me properly, for his eyes were drifting out of focus. *All the better*, I told myself, before I swallowed hard, and answered with a price.

He began to fumble with his belt.

'Not here.' He turned his vacant gaze on me. 'There,' I pointed to a dark alley.

It was a dead end. In that moment, exhausted and half-feral with fear, I don't believe I had much notion of what I was about to do. I could hear the man behind me breathing harder. We reached the wall and he stepped close, his hands going to his belt again. My own hands went to my waist, to where my guts were coming to life, trying to protect me, to give me strength.

'All right,' the man said, his trousers loose, 'you—'

I turned, and drove my knee into his groin. The air went out of him, and he made a strangled noise of pain as he fell, choking and retching. Before I could think twice, I began to wrestle the trousers from his legs.

When he felt that, he kicked and flailed. I took the knife from my belt and held it against his thigh.

'Stop,' I hissed. 'Take the jacket off.' When he hesitated, I pressed the blade closer. He yelped as blood began to well. After that, he did as I said. In a matter of seconds, I grabbed up the jacket, and the trousers and his cloth cap for good measure. Before he could utter another word, I fled into the night.

Tangier

July 1978

The suitcase banged against his leg as he hurried through the dark streets of the casbah, the writing case tucked under his arm. He felt like a fugitive, fleeing with his possessions, convinced that a figure would step out of the shadows into his path, that footsteps would echo after him, that a voice would shout and torchlight dazzle him into blindness. He took the most twisting way he knew back to Madame Sarah's – a sharp left, a sudden right – as if trying to shake off a pursuer who didn't exist.

Mohamed had helped him pull out the case from under a stack of six others. It had come free in a cloud of grit and decaying leather, and for one second, they had both held the handle. Then, Sam was swinging it away.

'My uncle's luggage!' he'd exclaimed. 'And look, it matches the writing case he left me. Who'd have believed it? How lucky, thank you . . .'

He'd talked his way out of the storeroom, gabbling about his uncle and the possessions. Mohamed had tried to interrupt, said he should go and fetch the manager, but Sam had just clapped him on the shoulder and hurried out of the hotel, breaking into a half-run as he fled down the steps and into the shadows of the casbah.

What was he doing? *This is theft*, he told himself, heart beating faster than his footsteps, *this is stealing*. All the same, he was reeling with excitement. This was the feeling he'd come halfway across the world for. *This*, he thought, *is brilliant*.

By the time he reached Madame Sarah's he was sweating, despite the sudden gusts of wind that had propelled him along. He let himself in as furtively as he could, and crept up the stairs. Only when the door of his room was locked behind him did he sink down to catch his breath, and allow himself to look closer at the suitcase.

It sat on the floor in front of him, real and aged and impossible. He stared, fearing he'd made a mistake, that in the strange, dim atmosphere of the storeroom he'd misread the initials. But there they were, in the same faded gold as the writing case.

A. L.

A corresponding leather cloakroom tag hung from the handle, looped on by someone who would never have dreamed that, half a century later, it would still be there, curled and crusted with salt-damp.

Sam reached for the writing case, for the key that was inside, before stopping. He couldn't just go rushing into this; he had to document every moment, every detail. He rolled a cigarette, making a bad job of it, before taking out a sheet of paper. Scrappily, he wrote down everything that had happened that evening: talking with Bet at The Hold, running through the casbah chased by the wind, the smell of the Hotel Continental, a piece of luggage that had lain forgotten for fifty long years . . .

His eyes drifted to the suitcase. Its presence filled the room. He could feel it, even smell it beneath the pungent smoke of his cigarette, burning down in the ashtray. Finally, he let the pencil drop, and reached for the small silver key. *Please work*, he asked silently, as he fitted it to the lock, and closed his eyes.

It grated, before turning with a gentle *thunk*. He held his breath and, slowly, lifted the lid.

Decay, that was what he smelled. Dank and oddly organic, as if the objects inside – glass and paper and fabrics – had reverted back to bone and sand and flesh. He peered down. The inside of the case looked orderly, despite his run from the hotel. Clothes, neatly folded, small glass bottles clipped in place by leather straps. He leaned in closer and the stink of age seemed to lessen, giving way to other scents: a faint trace of sandalwood and something he wanted to call ambergris without any idea of what ambergris might be. He let his fingers trail over the bottles, before reaching in, and lifting out the top layer of cloth.

It was a jacket, a man's suit jacket, which clung to its folds. It was made of linen, fawn brown, tailored for another era. Mould bloomed in its creases. Gingerly, he checked the pockets, but found nothing.

Matching trousers came next, mutated by long-storage, shirts fine but yellowed, and collars, their starch turned to crusted powder. Underwear and silk socks lay curled like strange boneless fish in the darkness of the case. So far there was nothing to tell him anything about A. L. except that he was a man – someone who could afford personalized cases and silk and scent. As he lifted out the last bundle of socks and handkerchiefs, he saw an extra pocket, half-concealed down one side. Immediately, he reached in.

Heavy paper met his fingers. With a stab of excitement, he pulled it free, expecting a letter, or perhaps money, but it was neither. Instead, he was holding a rectangle of green card.

PASAPORTE
Consulado de España de Tánger
Certifico de Don: Alejandro del Potro
Profesión: Secretario
Natural de: Sevilla, España
Edad: 21 años

Sam frowned. Alejandro *del Potro*? But the suitcase said A. L. He looked eagerly at the face on the passport. It showed a young man – younger than he'd expected, with dark hair and eyes and a wary, scowling expression, at odds with the stylish hat pulled down over his forehead. He didn't look wealthy enough to own personalized luggage. So then, who was he? Someone who had bought the case second-hand, like himself? Someone who was borrowing it? Or – Sam's fingers tightened on the passport – a thief?

He began to search the case again, convinced he'd missed something. Finally, tangled amongst the socks, he found another object. A book, pocket-sized. At first he thought it might be a diary or a journal, until he saw a title printed on its worn blue cover.

THE GENTLEMAN'S GUIDE

If anything, it was even stranger than the passport. Why would someone pack a book on etiquette when they were obviously travelling light? Still frowning, he flicked the book open and saw a scrawl of handwriting. A dedication, written in English:

If you're going to play the game, you have to learn the rules.

The hairs on the back of Sam's neck stood up. No initials, no date, just that sentence, almost a warning . . . He turned the page, hoping to find more writing, but there was nothing, only chapters of advice on dressing and deportment, luncheon menus and which type of hat was appropriate for a picnic. Occasionally, words and phrases had been underlined in pencil, as if the book had been diligently studied. Sam kept turning the pages. About a quarter of the way through, the spine felt looser, the leaves coming away from the binding, as if the section had been read many times. It contained recipes for cocktails, for punches and sodas, and – left to itself – fell open on one particular entry.

BLOOD AND SAND

Take a quarter glass of fresh blood orange juice and the same of good Scotch whisky. Add into this a quarter glass of Cherry Heering and half a glass of sweet Italian vermouth. Shake violently enough to break a sweat and strain into a coupe glass.

Blood and Sand. He'd never heard of it before. It was probably the kind of thing people had drunk long ago, when spirits were plentiful and a pocketful of dollars could take a person across a continent in luxury. Not like now. He traced the title. Was this A. L.'s favourite drink? Or del Potro's? Fifty years ago, would he have ordered one at a party, among a crowd of ex-pats and wanderers, all searching, drinking, writing music and painting and pouring out work that was considered new and vital . . . ?

Sam dropped the book, and stared into the case once again. What had happened to A. L., to make him leave a suitcase behind, to make him lose a writing case? And who the hell was Alejandro del Potro? Sam's hands began to twitch. He wished he still had the Hermes. Ideas were jostling at the ends of his fingertips. A. L. could have been a rich British gentleman or a poor young man from America. Alejandro del Potro could have been a friend, a colleague, a lover, a criminal.

I'll write them, Sam thought, looking at the passport, the book, the clothes. *If I can't find out who they were, I'll write them into life. A. L. and Alejandro del Potro, they can be characters in my story, one that starts in the casbah, with the sale of a typewriter . . .*

AFFINITY

Take a pony of French vermouth, a pony of Italian vermouth and a pony of good Scotch. Stir into this two dashes of Angostura Aromatic Bitters. Strain into a chilled glass with some lemon peel. A drink of brine and smoke.

I ran until I reached the darkness of the beach, the stolen clothes clasped in my arms. They were grimy and badly needed washing, but I didn't care. My whole body was fizzing with a cocktail of fear and elation about what I'd done. Another crime, to add to the one I didn't commit. A murderess, now a thief.

No use thinking about it, I told myself, as I crouched in the shadows to search the pockets of the jacket. Three battered cigarettes, a box of matches, a length of string and nothing else. I spat out the saliva that clogged my throat. So that was why the man had been roaming the alleyways; no doubt the other whores, who could tell a good mark from a bad, had already rejected him. He wouldn't have been able to pay me at all.

Still, the clothes were more valuable to me. They offered the safety I had once found in Ifrahim's old trousers and the apron that shielded my body. Hopefully, they would make men's eyes slide across me without seeing, tell them I was just another grubby lad, and not a young woman with a body that could be bought. Not a young woman who was wanted for murder.

There, hidden amongst the boats on the dark beach, with the sea as my only witness, I began to shed who I had been. I used the knife to hack the stained kitchen apron into strips, and then pulled the blouse and chemise over my head to bare my chest. I could barely see myself as I wrapped the fabric tight over my breasts, cinching it, knotting it firm. The blouse had a scrap of lace at the collar. I hacked it off. Without that, it looked enough like a man's shirt. The old work trousers would serve as drawers, and to bulk out the stolen pair. Next the jacket, too big, but all the better to hide in.

Finally, in the darkness, I dragged the scarf from my head and shook out my tangled mass of hair. At the edge of the shore I knelt, and sawed through handfuls of it, letting it fall like black weed into the surf. *Take her away*, I told the waves, *the woman they're looking for, take her away.*

My head felt light, my neck naked and prickling in the sea breeze. I ran a hand across the uneven tufts, then knotted the scarf around my neck, for comfort, as much as anything. Last came the man's cap. It was just as well it was dark, or I might have lost courage and wept to see those scraps of myself, hair and lace, being washed out to sea.

The beach was silent, but from what I'd seen that evening, there was no guarantee it would stay that way. I didn't want to be caught up in the darkness by a gang of smugglers, wanted nothing more than shelter.

At the border end of the beach, a campfire trembled in the night. With one hand on the knife in my pocket, I walked towards it. The light from the flames illuminated the edge of an empty warehouse where shadows moved and people muttered and coughed. No one said a word as I crouched down before the fire, though some looked. Mostly men, one woman, her face lined too young. She began to speak to me but when I glanced at her from beneath the hat's brim, her gaze was vague, her speech a meandering string of English and Spanish that made no sense at all. Some boys, perhaps only ten or eleven, laughed at her and eyed me appraisingly before going back to scraping at crab shells with their teeth when they saw I had nothing to steal.

Inside, the warehouse smelled of unwashed flesh and old urine, the stench of stale alcohol seeping from pores, and a sweetness that I recognized as cheap opium. Crumpled shapes lay here and there in the darkness. I found a corner that didn't smell too bad, where the earth seemed dry, and lay down.

I don't believe I slept, at least not for more than a few moments, waking again with a lurch of fear every time I drifted off. I thought about the kitchen at the inn, the food I had once made, rich with oil and wine and spices, the smell of Ifrahim's pipe and the cats that would purr against my belly, and I had to stifle my face in the rank collar of the jacket, so that the sound of tears did not give me away.

At one point, startled by footsteps, I opened my eyes to find a figure leaning over me. Without a word, I drew the knife. The figure stopped then, and moved away. I passed the rest of the night with the knife in my hand, glinting in response to the eyes I was certain were watching.

By the time dawn came I felt even weaker than the day before. Hunger and weariness made my ears ring, my eyes glaze, turned my thoughts into a mass of tangled threads. I knew I had to do *something*, but I couldn't fathom what. If I could only get a meal, if I could only fill my belly, I might be able to think.

When I stepped out of the warehouse, the rising sun nearly felled me. It was so bright, so generous, spilling radiance over the sea. I wanted to drink that light. It would taste of pomegranates and cold butter, strawberries wet with dew and honey dripping from a comb. I followed the light down to the water's edge, dipped my hands into the surf, deliciously cool, and drank.

Of course, it made me sick, and the dream faded, leaving me shivering and wretched. I suppose it must have cleared my head a bit though, for when a shadow fell across me, I was able to look up.

An old man – or a man who had been made old – was side-eyeing me as he rinsed a shirt in the water. His ribs stuck clear of his chest like a dog's, and there were scars across his abdomen. He might have been the one who had come near me in the night. I didn't know.

'Tap's behind the boats,' he said, jerking his head.

I muttered thanks to him, before remembering the crumpled cigarettes in my jacket. When I took one out the man's face turned almost as bright as the sun. I held it out to him and we smoked it together, crouched at the shore.

'Border's good picking, around breakfast time,' he said, after a while. 'Show you if you want.'

With that, he pulled the wet shirt over his head, and set off up the beach.

The rock towered above us as we walked, white gulls circling the crags. In the clear morning light, I could see buildings; stark military defences and white villas, steep rows of houses and before it all, a dusty strip of no-man's-land.

When we reached the border I understood what the man meant about pickings, for there was a queue of motor vans, rumbling and spluttering, waiting to cross into Gibraltar. They were being held, I saw, while British soldiers checked papers. I shrank back at the sight of those uniforms, but the old man quickened his pace, joining the half-dozen beggars already there. By the time the next vehicle pulled up, they were at its side, jostling to reach the windows.

I watched, unable to take in more than one thing at a time. It seemed an unlikely way to get anything, especially beneath the glare of the soldiers, who occasionally shouted and kicked stones at the beggars' ankles. I kept my head low, afraid to be seen, until I realized I was making myself more conspicuous by standing on my own. I stepped into the shelter of the group.

Before long, I was jostled forwards amongst them. I copied them, holding out my hands and saying *por el amor de Dios, por favor señor, my children are starving, please señora, please help us, my mother cannot feed my brothers and sisters, I lost my job, Dios te bendecirá.*

From the first few vehicles I got nothing except elbows and shoves from the other beggars. I flinched and clasped at my cap, afraid that it would be knocked off, that I would be discovered. Perhaps it was that cringing posture which made a deliveryman throw a céntimo and his half-smoked cigarette towards me. I snatched up both like a wolf, and smoked the cigarette in quick, hungry drags. It was cheap and acrid but the nicotine filled me with a fizzing sort of spice, pushed the haziness at the edge of my vision back a few inches. I gave the end of it to the old man who had told me about the tap, and then passed my second crumpled cigarette around the group, which earned me a little more currency with them, and fewer elbows.

It was endless, thirsty work, but it held the possibility of money, and anyway, I did not know what else to do. As the sun began to dazzle overhead, my voice grew hoarse and cracked from pleading. The cars grew less frequent, for no one, not even the British, were fools enough to venture out on the roads at noon. Eventually, the other beggars began to wander off, to pass the rest of the day asleep in the shade. I would have done the same, had I known where to go. Walking away would mean abandoning myself to the streets of La Atunara once again, where someone might recognize my stolen clothes.

One more car, I told myself, as the sweat trickled from beneath my cap, *one more.*

I was the only beggar left, apart from a pair of boys who were more interested in taunting the soldiers. Every time I blinked the stinging brightness of the road from my eyes, it became harder to open them. When I fought my eyelids up for what must have been the tenth time, I thought that I must have been dreaming.

An automobile was roaring towards me, flashing silver in the sun, like nothing I had ever seen. Through the dust and the dazzle of the windscreen I saw a face; white teeth shining, a slick of dark hair, a bright eye, peering over smoked lenses. It was the face of an altar saint, surrounded by brilliant gold.

To this day, I can't say what made me do it. Was it the glamour of that car, the heat and my hunger? Was it desperation? Or was it the pull of the future, a bolt of electricity lighting up all that was to come?

I don't know. All I know is that when the beautiful, shining car came within ten feet of me, I met the eyes of the driver, and stepped into its path.

Part Two

Tangier

July 1978

Sam wrote for hours, by the light of the cheap little bedside lamp. Around him, he heard the house settle; stairs creaking, bedroom doors closing, lights being switched off. Outside the open window, night began to bloom. It seeped through the plaster walls, fluttered in the form of the tiny moths that found him, wedged in the corner of the room, the pen scratching at sheets of paper, the edge of his hand ink-stained a deep, ocean blue.

Eventually, he squeezed his burning eyes closed, easing out a crick in his neck. He had no idea what time it was. Not morning, but not far off either. Outside, the streets seemed utterly still, as if the hustlers and grifters had finally given up, and night had rolled down the hill to the beach, to disappear into the cool, grey sand.

Sam picked up the papers, covered on both sides with his spiky writing, and shuffled them into some kind of order. He smiled as he did it; how long had it been since he'd written a stack of pages like this? A year, two years. Not since college.

The stolen letter was the first chapter – he'd have to try and remember it at some point. This second chapter of . . .

whatever it was he was writing, began with a heading, with the words *Blood and Sand*.

He put the pages to one side. Though he was tired, he didn't want to stop. If he stopped, he might start thinking too hard about what he'd done, taking a stranger's possessions from the Hotel Continental, pawing through them, writing about them, like a voyeur.

Inspiration, he told himself, *that's all this is. And anyway, A. L.'s long gone.* Rubbing his face, he dipped the ink pen again, and turned over the sheet of paper he'd been writing on.

Pencil marks caught his eye, silvery in the dim light, like veins beneath skin. He blinked hard. Was he seeing things?

Words. There were words, scrawled across the page at a hasty angle, in pencil so faint it didn't show on the other side of the paper. A drop of ink splattered from the pen and he swore. What if he'd ruined the page by writing on the other side, made it illegible? He dropped the pen into the ink bottle and held the page directly under the lamp to see.

Sure enough, blue ink had seeped through, making the letters difficult to decipher. Why hadn't he been more careful? This page had been in the writing case the whole time, waiting for him, if he'd only been patient enough to look for it.

He turned the page this way and that, peering at the shining lead letters. Only when he brought it closer to his face did he see the top line:

A,

A what? An initial, an address? Was this a letter to A. L. – just like the one he had written in the café?

He sat back, eyeing the paper. He was burning with curiosity and yet this page – whatever it was – had never been intended for him. What if it contained something deeply personal?

Almost unintentionally, his eyes strayed back to the paper. It was no use; he had to know.

D Portuna, 28.7.28

A,
I am sorry.
One day, I hope you'll understand.

★

He woke in a sweat at noon and pushed back the shutters, feeling as if he'd been running all night. Outside, the city was alive. He breathed it deep, tasting the bustle of the day, the tang of the sea, burning rubber, wet dust from washing. Leaving the window open, he went back to the tangled sheets and looked down at the writing case, open on the floor, surrounded by ink-scrawled papers. The pencil-written page lay on the top now. Rubbing his eyes, he picked up the stub of pencil from the case, wondering if it was the same one which had written that feverish note.

After a while, he fished around for a scrap piece of paper. *Not* the stuff from the writing case, he wasn't making that mistake again. Instead, he found the airmail letter from his parents, clumsily folded. *Such a grateful son*, he thought as he smoothed it out and wrote on the back:

A. L. = A?
Alejandro del Potro?
Game – rules?
28.7.1928?
Continental?
Blood and Sand?
Sorry?

There was something else, some word that had prickled at him. Going back to the beginning of the letter, he saw it:

D Portuna.

D Portuna. An unfamiliar word. Someone's name? He scrawled it down, followed by another infuriating question mark.

By mid-afternoon, he was wandering up the Rue Anoual, turning it all over in his mind. A writing case lost to the casbah, a letter never sent, a suitcase never collected, all fifty years ago. A strange passport and now this name: *Portuna.*

It was like eavesdropping on a conversation, without being able to hear the whole thing. He'd fill in the gaps using his imagination; weave these fragments together into characters, events, into a story that made sense.

If you're going to play the game, you have to learn the rules.

Smiling, he pushed open the door of the Gran Café de Paris. He hesitated for a moment, feeling the waft of warm air from the ceiling fans. He shouldn't waste money, not even on coffee. Even with the small flush of cash from Abdel-hamid, things would soon begin to look threadbare again. There was nothing else to sell, no one else to ask, except maybe Norton . . . The idea made him grimace. But what the hell, he decided, he couldn't stay in his room all day, and it was only a dirham. He sat down in the corner, and placed the writing case in front of him. His head was bubbling over with ideas, just waiting to be brought to life in scratchy ink.

'Café, shukran,' he said to the waiter who appeared on the other side of the table.

'Excusez-moi, vous êtes appelé Hackett?'

He looked up in shock. He'd never told anyone at the café his name.

'Yes.' He half stood from the chair. 'Is everything all right?'

The waiter signalled for him to sit down again. 'Oui, oui, pas de problème. Mais . . . I have something for you.'

Did he mean the letter? Maybe one of the waiters *had* taken it after all, and here was the manager, giving it back. Sure enough, the man was reaching into the pocket of his apron and pulling out an envelope. He laid it on top of the writing case.

'Is that my—'

Sam stopped abruptly. The envelope was addressed with one word:

HACKETT

For a second, he couldn't speak.

'Where – did you get this?' he spluttered to the waiter.

'It was left here,' the man said in broken English, 'for you.'

'Who?' Sam was up from his seat again. '*Who* left it? How did they know who I was?'

The waiter was shaking his head, as if he wanted to deny any involvement. 'Je ne sais pas, I do not know his name.'

'He? Was it an old man? With a hat, glasses?'

The waiter nodded, looking uncomfortable.

'Did the man—' Sam stopped, forcing himself to speak more calmly. 'L'homme, the old man, he knew my name?'

'Oui.' The waiter was looking around, wanting to take his leave. 'Oui, he said you are an American, and I will know you by this.' He tapped the writing case.

Sam stared. He'd written a letter to the past, and now here was a reply. What the hell was going on?

'Wait.' He caught the waiter's arm as he turned away. 'This man, have you seen him before? Does he come here regularly?'

The waiter shrugged, freeing himself. *He's been paid*, Sam realized, watching the man hurry away towards the kitchens. *He's been paid to stay quiet.*

Stunned, he turned back to the table, to the impossible letter. *HACKETT*. Hardly daring to touch it, in case it crumbled into nothing, he eased open the envelope and peered inside.

A single sheet of paper. Not *his* letter at all. This paper was clean, new, covered in neat black writing.

Dear Mr Hackett,

You have something of mine. I would like it back.

Please reply, outlining how much you will take for the case. Leave your response with Khalid, the manager here. Do not try to contact me by any other mean.

Regards,

A

WHITE LION

Take one teaspoonful of white sugar, and the juice of half a lime, dropping the spent rind into the glass. Add one wine glass of Santa Cruz rum, one teaspoonful of Curaçao and one teaspoonful of imported grenadine. Shake well with ice, and strain. Cool and deceptively sharp.

Why do certain individuals have the power to change a person's life, above all others? To anyone else, they might be a face in the crowd, the tip of a hat at an open door, but to that one person . . .

They are the branch that falls on to the track and derails the train; they are the cigarette that starts the house fire, the one drink too many that pushes a night into chaos.

That's what he was to me. I knew it the second we locked eyes, the second before I was hit by the car.

Not badly. He was too fast for that. Our eyes met, I knew, and he acted, sending the car veering away from where I stood. Still, the running board clipped my leg and sent me spinning to the ground.

For a moment, everything was a fog of dust, the world reeling around me. The car's wheel was five feet from my head, and in its mirror-bright hubcap, I saw a face.

A boy was looking back at me. He had ragged dark hair and a fading bruise across his nose. There were purple rings beneath his eyes and blood on his lip. I spluttered out a breath and the boy did the same, droplets spattering the ground. Blood and sand . . .

All around, voices were shouting, feet scuffing. My English wasn't as good then, but nevertheless I picked up some of what was being said. The British soldiers were angry, pointing at me and shouting, their candy-coloured faces redder than usual. I heard the words *beggar* and *lying*, more than once. I was afraid they would punish me for getting in the way of the car, and tried to rise, only to feel a stab of pain in my leg. I cried out, and fell back to the dust.

That's when he appeared. Leather shoes like browned butter, the hem of linen trousers as pale as the car itself, silver flashing from his cuffs, and finally his face: his saint's face, brought down from its altar.

It wasn't flawless; nothing truly beautiful is. It was tanned, not the rough, burned tan of the British soldiers, but bronzed – that's the word, bronzed – as though burnished by an artisan. As he took off his hat I saw brown hair, slicked gold by sun and pomade. Finally, I looked into his eyes, peering over the dark lenses. They were brown as well-worn wood, like the butt of a gun, like the handle of a knife.

'Boy,' he said in English. 'Are you hurt?'

Above the dust I caught his scent, musk and soap and something rich I couldn't name, and when he reached out a hand to me, I flinched away, ashamed of my grime. The movement made me cough, and in utter horror, I saw a droplet of blood from my lip land on his shoe.

Though I didn't know it at the time, the blood is what did it. You see, when he saw it staining my lips and teeth, he was afraid that my insides had been damaged, that I might die then and there on the road, and he might be held accountable.

'He's badly hurt,' he told the soldiers. 'I am taking him to a doctor, and I don't care to be held up about it.'

'Sir, with all respect he's just as likely acting,' one of them answered. 'He's been here all morning, begging—'

'Be that as it may, I won't be easy until I've had a doctor look at him.'

'There are doctors in La Atunara.'

'Over there? Quacks and butchers. No, I have to insist. An English doctor.'

'Has he any identification with him? Any passport?'

Even in my state, I heard that word well enough. *Passport.* They meant papers, and of course, I had none. I couldn't let them search me. If they found out I was a woman, they would be suspicious. Who knew if they'd heard about the murder in Córdoba? The next time their voices turned in my direction, I coughed and gave a terrible groan of agony.

It must have been convincing, because I heard a woman's voice, exclaiming. I opened one watering eye a fraction and saw her, hanging over the side of the car. I hadn't noticed her at first; she must have been the person the man was laughing with as he drove. She was just as fine-looking as he, in a peach-coloured hat, hair the colour of custard waving below its brim.

Her rouged mouth was open. I didn't catch exactly what she said, though she sounded hurt on my behalf. Amongst the words there was one in particular that found its way through the ringing in my ears.

Arthur.

I don't know how he did it; a mix of stolid English insistence and righteous indignation perhaps, but soon I was being pulled to my feet by the soldiers and deposited into the back seat of the car, beside the woman. The soldiers looked unhappy about it and made the man take a piece of stamped paper. A temporary pass, I found out later, issued on the condition that I left Gibraltar as soon as a doctor had seen to me.

The woman made me lie on the back seat with my head on her lap. It made me nervous, because although my disguise might have fooled men easily enough, women were another matter. So I screwed up my face and tried not to look into her grey eyes.

'Oh it's too awful, Arthur,' she said, as the man got into the car. 'He's so young, barely more than a boy.'

'We'll get him seen to, Hilde,' the man said, slamming the door. 'Well?' he shouted to the soldiers. 'Are you going to let us through at last?'

Then came the clacking of the barrier, and the great, warm car was purring into life, speeding forwards, taking us into Gibraltar.

That day was one of many firsts for me. I had been in a motor before, but never one so luxurious or fine. I had been close to wealthy patrons at the inn, but never this close: had never rested my head on legs covered with silk, never smelled perfume that didn't reek or cloy, but soothed, like the gloved hand that stroked my forehead. I had never wanted so badly to disappear, or to plunge myself into a bath and emerge gleaming new, to match those people.

But there are some things that soap cannot wash away. I could scrub and scrub and still I would be different. Beneath my skin was the past, my bad blood: the inn, the Señor and the threat of the garrotte if I was caught. They – bright creatures – knew none of that. Scorn rose in me to war with admiration, mistrust of those gloved hands and amused faces. I had grown up watching their kind; I knew how their interest could disappear in a finger-snap. I had seen them drop people back into the dirt and drive away, leaving all the damage behind them. That's what I would be to them, I thought as we drove, a temporary diversion, nothing more. In which case, I had to be smart. I had to get what I could.

Even so, it was all I could do to keep up my pretended groans as we entered the streets of Gibraltar. A different world to La Atunara, just across the border. Here were motorcars and gleaming shop fronts, fussily dressed matrons next to sailors and soldiers and beyond them all boats – so many boats, jostling white on the sea like gulls.

The hotel they took me to was set high on the rock, above the tangle of narrow streets. The Grand, it was called. I had never set foot anywhere like The Grand.

Where the inn was straw and stone and old wood tough as iron, The Grand was marble and white gravel and shining polish. I did not belong there, in my grimy suit. Even the doormen, who were paid not to notice, looked at me as if I were a bird dropping on a scrubbed step.

But the lady was helping me out of the car; she was insisting I put my arm about her shoulder. The man was calling for a chair. One was brought, a wicker thing on wheels, and I was taken through a lobby that smelled of flowers into an elevator – another first for me – and from there along a corridor with a patterned wooden floor, into a room.

Doctor, the Englishman was saying, and I felt a stab of panic. A doctor was a thing that could not be fooled: the girls at the inn had never been successful in concealing their ailments from the health inspector. If the gentleman and the lady discovered I was a woman, what would they do? Question me? They would undoubtedly think I was no good, a whore on hard times perhaps, and tell the hotel to take me back to the border, once they were satisfied I would not die. I might have time to get away, if the Spanish authorities had not alerted the British about the murder, but if they had . . .

My mind racing, I began to look around the room for a way to escape. It was like the car: wide and cool and very clean, with thin curtains that billowed like sails. At any other time I would have sighed to be there, but all I could think about was my lie, and how to maintain it, and how soon these people would lose interest, and leave me to my fate.

The lady appeared with a wet cloth in her hands. I smelled her perfume again as she pushed me back into the cushions of a sofa.

'You must stay calm, the doctor will be here soon.' When she tried to wipe gently at my face, at the blood on my lip, I flinched away. No one had ever touched me like that before.

If anything, she looked sorry. 'We should see about your chest,' she murmured. 'Let me—' Before I knew what was happening, she had slid her hand inside the jacket, dangerously close to the strips of cloth that bound my breasts. I cried out, cringing away from her.

'Leave him be, Hilde.' A voice came to my rescue. 'He's clearly frightened. And in shock, I would guess.' The man was standing at a sideboard. When he turned, he held two glasses, filled with brown liquid. He seemed to belong in that room the way a painting would, or a statue.

'Here.' He held out one of the glasses towards me.

I took it, unable to look at either of them, and sipped the liquid.

Scotch. It was Scotch. The smell of it ambushed me and I was back at the inn, breathing in spilled liqueur and the stink of blood that rushed from the Señor's throat. I choked and the glass tipped in my hand. The lady plucked it from my fingers.

'Arthur, really. The poor boy's probably never had a drink of whisky in his life. Go and get some brandy instead, that's better for shock.'

Soon I found a big, bulbous glass pressed into my hands, filled with brandy. Exceptionally good brandy. I gulped it, gasped as it stung my lip and gulped the rest.

'Bueno,' the man said. '¿Cómo estás? ¿Dónde estás herido?'

I looked at him sharply. I hadn't expected him to speak Spanish. In English, I could hide, I could play dumb, but in Spanish it would be harder.

'Mi pierna,' I said, nodding at my leg. 'Sólo mi pierna.' I didn't want anyone prodding at my chest. 'Y mi labio,' I muttered, pulling down my lip to show where it was hot and swollen.

'Gracias a Dios,' he said, his eyes creasing in a smile. 'I was worried you were bleeding from your guts or something.'

I shook my head, though my empty guts were smarting from the brandy, squirming at the memory of blood and Scotch. I glanced at the man again, as he spoke to the lady in English, and she made a noise of relief. When I looked back, it was into his eyes once more.

'What in god's name were you doing, stepping in front of my car like that?'

He said it lightly, and looked amused, tolerant, but still I was wary.

'I did not mean to,' I said. 'The sun was in my eyes.' Ifrahim's old excuse; the answer of a petty thief.

The man was watching me, his own eyes unfathomable. 'Mine too,' he said.

'¿Cómo te llamas?' That was the lady, interrupting in clumsy-sounding Spanish.

My swollen lip twitched. 'Del Potro,' I told her, without breaking the man's gaze. 'Alejandro del Potro.'

Tangier

July 1978

Tangier, 12.7.78

Dear A,

I would be happy to return your case. However, I would like to do so in person. I have a lot of questions. One to start: did you take my letter?

Best,
Sam Hackett

*

12.7.78

Dear Mr Hackett,

To answer your question: yes. I apologize. I can only say that I acted in shock, seeing something again I had long thought lost.

I am afraid it is impossible to meet. I ask you again to consider my request. I am prepared to offer a substantial reward for the return of the writing case. Forgive me for saying so, but it appears you could make use of the money.

Regards,
A

★

Tangier, 13.7.78

Dear A,

Forgive me *for saying so, but my financial situation is my own business. The fact of the matter is this: I have something else of yours too, something I believe you will want more than the writing case. What if I said 'Hotel Continental' and '15' to you?*

Best,
Sam

★

'What does he mean, "impossible to meet"?' Sam held the letter away from the sticky bar. 'It can't be literally impossible.'

'Maybe he's house bound,' said Roger, pouring out a gin and tonic.

'Maybe he prefers to remain incognito,' Bet winked, tapping her cigar.

Roger laughed, and went to deliver the drinks. Sam shifted on the bar stool and took another long gulp of beer. He couldn't escape a nagging feeling of guilt, telling other people about the suitcase, about A, whoever he was. A fifty-year secret wasn't something to be thrown about a bar like tittle-tattle. And yet, he'd felt off balance ever since he'd received the first note. It was as if the fiction he'd been writing had come to life; as if he'd conjured 'A' into being using only his imagination. He *had* to tell someone, if only to make sure it was all real, that he wasn't going insane.

'He must live in Tangier,' he said, after a silence. 'Or the notes wouldn't arrive so fast.'

'They all come through Khalid, at the Gran Café?' Bet asked.

Sam nodded. 'There was another one waiting when I went in yesterday. I tried to grill Khalid, but he's not saying a word. I sat there for three hours, waiting to see if anyone came to collect my response. Nothing.'

Bet gave a half-laugh and sucked on her cigar.

'Then there's the passport I found in the suitcase, belonging to this del Potro character.' Sam kept his voice low. For some reason, saying the name aloud made his neck prickle. 'Do you think he stole A. L.'s case? Maybe—' He swallowed. A person rarely abandoned an entire suitcase, especially one containing their passport. 'Maybe something happened to this del Potro. Maybe he *was* a thief and he was arrested, or died, and that's why he never returned?'

He looked up hopefully, only to find Bet staring at him, a strange expression on her face.

'What did you say that name was?' she asked, her voice husky.

'Del Potro. Alejandro del Potro.' He sat up straighter. 'Why? Have you heard of him?'

Bet was silent, working her lips. Finally, she shook her head. 'Before my time. It sounded familiar, that's all.'

He looked over at Roger, but the bartender just turned away, depositing some empty glasses in the sink.

'Are there *any* people left here from that time?' Sam asked, frustrated. 'There was a date I found in the writing case, July nineteen twenty-eight. Is there anyone who might remember what Tangier was like back then? If nothing else, it'd be great to get some more material. I think I might be on to something with this . . . whatever it is I'm writing.'

Roger smiled. 'Good for you, lad.' He rubbed at his beard thoughtfully. 'There are a few. But you have to understand, a lot of stuff happened when Tangier was the International Zone. Not much of it legal. Folk tend to keep their pasts to themselves, even now. Only person I can think of who might talk is old Lil Simcox. What d'you reckon, Bet?'

Sam couldn't read the expression on her face. 'Lil was born here,' she said. 'Die here too, if she's got any say in it.'

'Do you think I could talk to her?'

Roger and Bet exchanged a look.

'You can talk,' Roger said eventually, 'as long as you don't expect much of a response. Poor old girl is losing it.'

'Hardly surprising, after her life,' Bet muttered, and pointed to Sam's glass. 'Another?'

Norton didn't turn up at The Hold that night, something Sam was strangely thankful for. He'd already spilled A's secrets to two people; any more and it would be halfway around Tangier before he made it home to bed. Anyway, it was *his* story. Telling Roger and Bet was one thing, but confiding in a journalist was quite another.

He was up and out early the next day, despite having written until late. Yawning, he hurried down the Rue d'Italie with the writing case in hand. The Gran Café de

Paris smelled of bleach and stale smoke and the coolness of night, punctured by the first hot coffees of the day. Khalid was there, setting out chairs. He rolled his eyes when he saw Sam and reached into his apron.

Another envelope.

'When did this arrive?' Sam demanded, tearing at the paper. The café had been open all of ten minutes. Whoever delivered the letters had beaten him to it. 'Was it him again, the old man?'

Khalid shrugged. 'I cannot say, Monsieur Hackett. I was in the kitchen.'

14.7.78

I do not care for evasiveness. If you are trying to blackmail or bribe me, then get on and do it.

A

Sam stared at the letter, stunned. What had he written to cause that kind of reaction? He thought back to his previous note.

What if I said 'Hotel Continental' and '15' to you?

His face flared with embarrassment. Of course. He thought he'd been clever, witty, dangling what he knew in front of A without an explanation. But he'd misjudged the situation, caught up as he was in his writing. The case belonged to A's past, his real past, not Sam's fantasy. No wonder the man was pissed off.

But still – blackmail? It seemed extreme. Why would A bring that up, apropos of nothing? Unless he had something to hide . . . Sam smoothed out one of the last sheets of the old paper, and began to scrawl a reply.

14.7.78

Dear A,

I'm sorry. I didn't mean to insinuate anything, and I promise, I have no interest in blackmail or bribes. I'm a writer, that's all, and I find myself writing about you, or at least, the things that once belonged to you. You see, in the bottom of this writing case, I found a key and a tag, with a number.

It was the longest letter he had written to date, describing how he'd discovered that the tag belonged to the Hotel Continental, and how he'd searched the storeroom there, and everything that came after.

There was a passport in the suitcase, belonging to a man named Alejandro del Potro. Was he someone you knew? Please believe me when I say I don't want to get anyone into trouble. I just want to know a little more about you, who you are, your life here. It must sound strange, but you've caught my imagination in a way nothing else has.

He paused. Was it too much? Maybe, but he wanted to be honest. The only thing he hadn't mentioned was the strange, pencil-written letter.

Please write back. I have so many questions.

Sam

He sealed the letter, scrawled *A* on the front and went to the counter to find Khalid.

'I'll be back this afternoon,' he said loudly.

Khalid nodded, and tucked the letter into his apron. He obviously didn't relish his role as go-between, no matter what A was paying him. Sam walked out of the café and turned, making sure Khalid saw him pass the windows. As soon as he was out of sight, he stopped and turned. If Khalid wouldn't tell him who A was, he'd have to find out another way.

The French Embassy stood across from the café, with its stern, clipped hedge and stone pillars, entirely at odds with the grime and hustle of the street. Trying to be casual, he stepped through the gates and looked for an unobtrusive place to wait. He found that by standing in the shadow of one of the hedges, he could see the terrace of the Gran Café de Paris without being seen himself.

All right, he thought, taking the rolling papers from his pocket. *Let's see who you are.*

One cigarette became two as the morning grew warmer. Before too long the sun drove the shade away, beating down on the back of his neck. He tried to keep his eyes fixed on the café as it filled up with men in suits and sports jackets and djellabas. A couple of girls went in, American or British students possibly, and he almost gave up on the stake-out. *Another twenty minutes*, he told himself, *another ten*.

His scalp was prickling in the heat, feet swollen in the sloppy espadrilles. It must have been nearing eleven. When a man walked past the embassy pushing a cart full of melon, hacked into slices, he couldn't stand it any more, and ducked out of the gate to buy some.

He ate it with the writing case tucked under one arm, and his eyes on the café, the juice running down the backs of his hands, dripping from his wrists. He almost expected it to hiss when it hit the gravel below. It was lukewarm and honey-sweet, washing the taste of nicotine from his mouth, filling his head with a rush of sugar.

A uniformed guard found him just as he was spitting the pips into the hedge.

'Qu'est-ce que vous faites?' the man barked.

'I'm, ah, waiting for someone,' Sam said unconvincingly. 'I'm American and I—'

Something flashed across the street; the glass door of the Gran Café de Paris, reflecting the sun. A figure was hurrying out, looking down, sliding something small and rectangular and white into a shoulder bag, something like an envelope . . .

Without thinking, Sam broke into a run, though the guard shouted angrily and made a grab for him. He barged through people on the pavement, almost tripping head-first into a roadside stall filled with broken watches and old shoes. More people shouted at him, he didn't care. He blinked hard, staring down the street.

There, the figure was walking away, one hand gripping the bag. Whoever it was, they were swathed in a brown djellaba, the hood pulled up against the heat. Sam jogged, trying to close the distance between them, but the person was already nearing the corner of the Rue de la Liberté.

'Hey!' he shouted.

The figure paused and half turned towards him. He caught a glimpse of dark hair before they whirled around and disappeared between two taxis.

'Hey!' Sam yelled again and lunged to follow, only to almost be knocked down by a moped, the driver screaming at him. Heart hammering, swiping sweat from his eyes, he looked down the street and caught a glimpse of the figure, rounding a corner. He raced to follow. Beyond, the road curved left towards the Place de France and the English Church, right towards the tarpaulined chaos of the medina. He had no idea which way the person had gone. Gasping in a lungful of hot air, he took a gamble, and turned right.

It couldn't have been a worse time. Late morning, and the narrow paths between the market stalls were swimming with people, crowded with breath and voices and the smell of wet dirt and meat, pungent fish, crushed spices. He fought down one passage, turned left and battled past the stall that sold live chickens and ducks, squawking in their cages. Blood and water ran across the cobbles from the butcher's stalls, making his shoes stick to the ground. Almost every person there was wearing a djellaba, it would be impossible to . . .

A flash of movement, the strap of a shoulder bag, a figure elbowing through the crowd towards the Grand Socco. Sam had no breath to shout, could only fight his way to the edge of the market, clinging to the writing case. *I'll never smoke again*, he swore as he staggered into a run, lungs heaving. The figure was nearing the edge of the socco and the old city gates, the entrances to the maze of the casbah. If whoever it was stepped through there, he'd be screwed, he'd never find them.

At the mouth of the Bab el-Fahs the figure glanced back over their shoulder. Sam had no breath to call out, but he raised his hand, and the case in it, holding it up like a plea. He must have looked absurd, but for a moment, the figure seemed to hesitate—

'Hackett!'

Hands were slapping his arms, a face filling his view, white and red and shiny with sweat. Norton.

'What a lucky meet,' the journalist was saying, 'I'm just on my way to lunch. Care to join?'

Sam shrugged out of Norton's grip and stepped around him, peering into the crowd; too late. The space by the gate was empty. The figure was gone.

FEDORA

Take a pony each of brandy and Curaçao. Add to this half a pony of good Jamaica rum and half a pony of Bourbon. Stir into this half a teaspoon of powdered sugar and a slice of lemon. Shake with ice and serve ornamented.

The devil knows how I fell asleep. Perhaps it was the exhaustion or the pain, the heat of the brandy in my empty belly or the assault of so many new things upon my senses that made my mind close the shutters for a while, sending me into nothingness.

When I opened my eyes, the first thing I saw was the hat. It was sitting upon the table before me, quiet and elegant, the colour of cream with a dark brown band. A piece of paper was resting beneath.

I hoisted myself on to an elbow. Only then did I realize that the room was empty. For a moment, I stayed very still. Someone had half closed the shutters to keep out the heat. A clock ticked, a fly droned and the *tock* of croquet balls floated up from the hotel's lawn.

They were gone, the gentleman and the lady. There was nothing in the room to suggest that anyone would return, no suitcases or valises, no kicked-off shoes or robes hanging on doors. Even more worrying, I found that my trouser leg had been rolled up; the cut on my shin had been washed with livid yellow iodine and dressed with a bandage.

When had that happened? Uneasy, I felt at my chest, but everything seemed the same, the bindings in place. Had they found me out? Were they keeping me here while they called for the police? I listened again, and heard nothing. For a minute or two I became convinced that if I went outside, I would find the world deserted, every motor-car abandoned, the dining room full of half-eaten plates and no one but me left to wander through it all.

Hands a little unsteady, I took up the note, to reassure myself that this was not a dream:

This should keep the sun from your eyes.
With compliments,

A

A. Arthur. The man with the saint's face and the cryptic smile was giving me one of his hats? It seemed too much, a strange, personal gift. I lifted it gently to touch the inside band, which must have rested against his forehead and lapped the sweat of his brow, only to stop, as another piece of paper fluttered into my lap.

A twenty-five peseta note. I could only stare. Twenty-five pesetas . . . it was more money than I had ever held in my life. It would buy me a room in La Atunara for weeks, even a good one. It would buy me fifty meals, a hundred drinks. I touched the corner of the note, afraid that I would turn it over and find it one-sided and false. But it was real. What did it mean? Had the man tucked the money into his hatband and forgotten it there? Who would forget twenty-five pesetas? The man must be richer than I thought.

I picked up the note again. *With compliments.*

It was hush money, I realized, like Morales used to pay to the guardia and the city inspectors. It was a reward for my silence, a request for me to leave Gibraltar quietly and without fuss. I shoved the note into the wrappings around my chest, blinking hard. It was more than I'd anticipated getting from this encounter. Far more. So why was I disappointed?

Carefully, I picked up the hat and pushed myself to my feet. There was a mirror on the wall near by, large and gilded. The reflection in it was still a shock. A boy, that was what I saw. A moody gitano boy who'd been in a scuffle. I placed the hat upon my head. It was bigger on me than it had been on the man, but it fitted. The cream colour suited my skin, but combined with the grubby suit, it looked absurd. I felt a pulse of envy for the man who had left it, for his wardrobe of beautiful, pristine clothes, for the way he had carried himself without a care. And at the same time, something rushed through me that I couldn't name, something like excitement, a shiver of possibility that made me raise my chin just a fraction . . .

There was a noise at the door. I swiped the hat from my head and held it tight.

'Who's there?' I called.

It was a hotel man in a dinner jacket, a stiff collar around his turkey neck. His mouth was tight with distaste, and I dropped my chin, not wanting him to look too closely.

'I see you are awake,' he said. 'In that case, we will have you taken back to the border.'

'To the policía?' I backed a pace into the room. 'I have done nothing wrong.'

'You are not in trouble,' he said, irritable. 'But neither can you stay in Gibraltar.' His eyes flicked to the hat in my hand, and he frowned.

'Where are they?' I asked, gripping the hat's brim. 'The man and the lady? I'd like to thank them.' Really, I didn't want to do anything of the sort. I only wanted to know who they were, whether they were still in the hotel.

The man's face hardened. 'Mr Langham and Lady de Luca Bailey departed after luncheon. You are very lucky. There are not many who would have treated you so well.'

Langham. The word caught my attention, like a thorn snagging cloth. Arthur Langham.

'What do you mean "departed"?' I asked, forgetting any pretence at manners. 'Departed where? Will they be back?'

The man's face was turning sourer by the second. I saw now that he held the piece of stamped paper in his hand, the one that had been issued by the soldiers at the border.

'They took the afternoon boat for Tangiers,' he snapped. 'Whether they will be back is their own business, and none of yours.' He held out an arm, to funnel me towards the door. 'Now, I must insist . . .'

Thirty minutes later, I found myself ejected from Gibraltar, back into the dust of La Atunara. Thankfully, the British soldiers didn't ask any questions, only ripped up the temporary pass, pleased to see me back where I belonged. I stared up at the great, gnarled rock from the wrong side of the checkpoint. I wanted to walk freely there, among the stiff English men and ladies, wanted to feel the power of a suit that smelled of starch and cologne, that didn't bag and chafe, that wasn't ingrained with dirt. I wanted to plant a cane into that ground that was neither England nor Spain and stare out to sea, the way the man – Arthur Langham – had done.

Tangiers, the hotel man said. Tangiers. The name was familiar. Was it from one of Ifrahim's stories? I squinted in the late afternoon sun, trying to find the dark shape of land on the horizon. The name brought an idea of hot sun, of a port full of ships from every country of the world, of money and spices and danger, where anything was possible, where a person might pull a brand-new name out of the air.

Tangiers. Beneath the bindings, my heart began to quicken. I turned towards the town, the peseta note crinkling against my skin.

Money can buy many things. In La Atunara it was possible to find a suit of passable quality amongst the clothes stalls of the market, a tailor to shorten the trousers, to unpick the initials of the person it had once belonged to. It was possible to find a pair of second-hand shoes, a bundle of men's socks and linens, a roll of bandage stolen from a military hospital. It was possible to find a barber who would trim uneven clumps of hair into better shape, without commenting on a young man's lack of stubble. It was possible for a person to transform themselves over a couple of days, all for the cost of ten pesetas.

I bundled up the stolen clothes, the torn apron, everything that remained of my old existence. The only thing I kept was the knife, its handle worn smooth by years of use. I did not want to walk the streets of La Atunara without it, in case someone saw through my disguise.

Langham's hat was the final piece. Holding it before my face, I caught a wisp of his scent. Wax from rose-scented hair pomade, musk from cologne and a faint, elusive note I recognized as sweat. I settled it upon my head, and looked at myself.

I looked young, too young, almost a boy still. The suit hung loose on my frame, the hat looming over my lean cheeks and the fading bruise. And yet, I might pass in a crowd for a semi-respectable young man. The suit, the leather shoes, and most importantly, Langham's fine hat, would hopefully be enough to fool people. In a stuffy, locked room of a cheap hotel, I began to knot Alejandro del Potro and myself together, tooth by tooth, eyelash by eyelash.

'Señor Langham,' I murmured, dropping my voice a few tones lower, 'I am delighted to see you again.'

I put the remaining pesetas into the pocket of my jacket. There was one last thing I needed, and it would be the hardest to obtain, even in a place like this. I could declare that my name was Alejandro del Potro until I was blue in the face, but no one would believe me. What I needed was proof; a piece of paper to vouch for my existence.

I had an idea of where to go, though it made me nervous. I waited until dusk to leave the hotel. Even so, the second I stepped from the door, I felt a surge of fear. My head was clearer now than it had been when I had slept among the beggars. People in La Atunara were sharp-eyed; what if they saw through my suit to the truth beneath? What if they could tell by the way I walked, how I held myself? I kept my head lowered beneath the hat, my hands in my pockets, and slouched along, my guts twitching, my heart squeezing itself against my ribs. A few times, people called to me, women from their corners or bartenders but I didn't stop, not even when I became out of breath thanks to the tight bindings. From a kiosk near the beach, I bought a newspaper, and a packet of cigarettes. Props, to occupy my trembling hands.

Sure enough, groups of men were beginning to loiter near the shore, where the smuggling boats put in, cracking their necks in preparation for the work to come. I sat on an upturned boat, a little way from the activity, and opened the newspaper.

Of course, I didn't read it. I kept half an eye on the beach beyond, on the milling groups of men waiting for something to happen, for a ship's horn or a yell or a flashing light in the bay. I turned the pages mechanically, headlines washing over me until:

BUSINESSMAN SLAIN AT CÓRDOBAN INN
MURDERESS STILL AT LARGE

The suspect, a prostitute and thief named ALEJANDRA EXPÓSITA, remains a fugitive, and should be considered dangerous. She was last seen three days ago in the region of RONDA. The Vélez del Olmo family are offering a reward of TWO HUNDRED pesetas for information leading to her capture.

I couldn't breathe; the air was too thick with tar and salt and panic. Alejandra Expósita. It was a surname they gave to foundlings, to orphans, to abandoned children. It wasn't my name: I'd never truly had one. Morales must have given it to the authorities as proof of my illegitimacy, my baseless existence.

She's not you, I told myself, fumbling open the packet of cigarettes. *Not any more.* And yet, I'd chosen del Potro, named myself for the very place I was trying to escape. I could have picked anything: Moreno, Gómez, Ávila . . . I put one of the cigarettes in my mouth, only to realize that I didn't have any matches. I forced myself to breathe as if I was smoking anyway, to slow the racing in my chest. No. For better or worse, the inn had shaped me. It was mine: the only thing I had ever known. I wouldn't let them take that from me, too.

When I looked up again, the beach was all activity. A boat had appeared and men were striding towards the waves, away from a figure in black, who stood overseeing everything. I tucked the cigarette into my jacket pocket, keeping my eyes on that man.

I waited until the work was done. Only when all the contraband had been stacked on a wagon and hauled away, when all men had been paid and the man in black had closed his satchel did I stand and walk towards him.

'Señor Bautista,' I called. He turned. His eyes were blank as they took in my suit and my hat. I hid my trembling hands in my pockets.

'Who wants him?' the large man who dealt with the men said, stepping up beside Bautista. A brute, a boot and fist man. I'd seen his kind before.

'I—' My mouth lost all its moisture. 'I lost my papers. I heard you might be able to help.'

'Get lost,' the brute said.

Bautista continued to stare. I knotted my guts about my heart.

'I can pay.' I wrenched the ten-peseta note from my pocket. After all my expenses, I had fifteen left; five would be enough to survive another week or so, if I was frugal. 'I can pay well for the papers.'

Bautista smiled. His face was ordinary, forgettable with its donkey-grey beard, but in that moment I was afraid, for there was something about his expression that reminded me of Morales. The money fluttered in my outstretched hand.

'Where are you from, chico?' he asked, after a while.

'North.'

'And you have no papers?'

'They were stolen.'

'They were stolen,' Bautista repeated, holding my gaze. 'Well –' he beckoned for the money. I let him take it, but kept hold of the other end. 'Chico,' he chided mockingly.

I let go. In that moment, I truly did not know what he would do; whether he would agree to my request, or whether he would have his man beat me bloody. Had I been wearing the stolen suit, poor and stained, he might have done just that.

After what felt like an age, he nodded. 'Bueno,' he said, folding the note into his pocket. 'Let's talk in my office.'

The girl I had met on the street was right: Bautista ran the show in La Atunara. He could give me what I wanted, knew the people who could make it happen.

By midnight, I was sat in his warehouse office, watching as a forger with stained fingers and beautiful handwriting inked my new self on to a blank passport.

'Name?' he asked, stilling his shaking hands with nips of liqueur from a flask. In the corner, another man fiddled with a camera, setting up a pair of hissing electric lamps.

'Alejandro del Potro.'

'That your real name?'

'Of course.'

The man snorted. I watched as he wrote the name neatly.

'Profession?'

That made me hesitate. *Cook*, I wanted to tell him, but it might give me away.

'We'll put "secretary",' the forger said, into my silence. 'Gives you options.' The pen scratched softly. 'Age?'

The older I was, the more distance there would be between my former self and this new, suited stranger. 'Twenty-five,' I said. But that only made the man laugh.

'You're not more than sixteen. Look at that chin. Smooth as an egg.'

I felt myself turning red. 'Twenty-two?'

'Twenty-one,' he said firmly. 'Got to be convincing.'

'Stand there,' the photographer yawned, pulling down a roll of paper on the wall.

By mid-morning the next day, Alejandro del Potro had been born.

'Scuff it up a bit,' Bautista said, looking critically at the document in his hand. 'Don't want it looking too new.'

I nodded. My mind was swimming, body buzzing with nicotine. I hadn't slept much. I had been too nervous to stretch out on one of the wooden benches along the edge of the warehouse, in case I murmured in my sleep and blew my disguise. I had tried to leave once, saying that I would return when the papers were ready, but his brute had blocked the door. The message was clear. I could leave when Bautista told me to. Not before.

'So, chico,' Bautista said, tapping the passport on the desk. 'Where are you going to go?'

'That's my business.' I stood up and held out my hand for the papers, wanting out of that place. 'Gracias, señor.'

Bautista only laughed. 'Sit down, del Potro. This is not a charity. I am a businessman. And business between us is not yet concluded.'

'Why?' I made my voice rougher. 'You have your money.'

He smiled. 'Ten pesetas is not enough for a set of papers of this quality. Not nearly enough. Did you think it was?'

My guts began to squeeze themselves together. What if he had seen through me? 'What do you want?'

He was watching me closely. 'I want to know where you are running off to. France? Gibraltar? South America?'

'Tangiers,' I said, tense. He had control of the port. He would know if I lied.

'Tangiers.' He rubbed at his donkey beard. 'What's there for you?'

'Nothing. A fresh start.'

He was silent for a moment. 'Tangiers,' he said. 'Bueno. You'll wait until this evening to take the boat. I'll have a little job for you by then.'

'What kind of job?' My skin was prickling. I thought about the knife, hidden deep in my jacket.

'Relax. You will take something to a friend of mine, that's all.'

'What?'

He tutted me. 'Too many questions. Just take what I give you, deliver it and don't peek. My friend will know if you have, and he's not so nice as me.' Bautista picked up the passport again. 'If you are caught, you do not know my name. If you talk, we will find you. Otherwise, our business will be done. That's fair, no? A small favour, compared to what I offer.' He waved the document. 'You can have this when you board the boat later. Not before.'

Crime upon crime. Smuggling, forged papers. If I were to be caught . . .

The hat rested on my lap, the gift from Mr Langham. I pictured him once again, at the wheel of that bright car, remembered the smell of his cologne and the way he'd glanced at the shape of land on the horizon, the way he'd commanded the respect of the hotel staff and the look on his face when I told him the sun was in my eyes. The way he'd said, *mine too.*

'Well?' Bautista said. 'Are we agreed?'

Tangier

July 1978

'Whoever it was, you shouldn't have chased after them, old man, those kind of antics can get you into trouble here.' Norton wiped his mouth with the paper napkin and grimaced down at the dry chicken on his plate. He'd insisted on eating in a dismal little hotel at the edge of the new town, partly, Sam suspected, because they served alcohol. 'Too much bother to eat in these temperatures, don't you think?' he said, reaching for his wine glass.

'I wasn't chasing the person, I was . . .' Sam pushed his plate away with a sigh. 'I was just trying to find out who they were, where this A person lives.'

Norton made a doubtful noise. 'The whole business sounds shady to me. Next thing you know you'll be waiting at a rendezvous with your passport in hand, primed and ready to be mugged.'

'But A thought *I* was trying to blackmail him! As soon as I mentioned the case—' Sam stopped himself abruptly. Through sheer frustration, he'd told Norton about the notes, sent back and forth between himself and A, but the rest? He glanced over at the Englishman, to find him emptying the rest of the bottle into his glass.

'He what?' Norton asked.

'He clammed up. I got a two-line response.'

'I'm not surprised. He's probably worried you're on to whatever scam he's trying to run.'

'I don't think there's a scam,' Sam said. He groped for an explanation, when of course, there wasn't one. He didn't know what A was up to; he didn't even know who the man was. A character, inexplicably come to life, a mystery to be pursued on the page, but in reality . . . 'Do you know,' he said, changing the subject, 'I've written more in the past three days than I have in six months? Pages of it. I've lost count. I think I'm on to something. A story about Tangier.' He drained his glass. 'Of course it had to happen now, when I'm counting how many days I might have left here.'

'Say it isn't so!' Norton put down his glass. 'Why would you leave? Visa? Money troubles?'

'Trouble's the word. Another week and I'll be out on my ass.'

'Well, if you smoked less kif . . .'

Sam laughed, a little. 'I haven't been. At least not as much as usual.' Running out of kif would mean a visit to Abdelhamid, which would mean telling him about the Hotel Continental, and the suitcase. He didn't feel ready to share the whole truth with anyone yet, not with Abdelhamid, not with Norton, not even with Bet and Roger. It felt private, like something that might disappear if he talked about it too much, that might wither in the hard light of reality.

'Well, if this chap's serious about getting his old writing case back, doesn't that solve your problem?' Norton said.

'Flog it back to him for a princely sum and stay as long as you like.'

'True.'

Norton was right; it would solve a problem. And he did want to stay. But he also wanted to keep writing. Something told him that if he handed over the case and took the money with no questions asked, A would vanish into the streets of Tangier, taking the story, and all Sam's inspiration, with him.

'Tell you what.' Norton slapped the table, interrupting Sam's thoughts. 'If you do find anything interesting about this old guy, let me know. A sordid past, sob story, whatever. The city editor might be interested in it, nice bit of local colour for the mid-section. I could write it up for you, and we'll split the commission. That'd keep you in kif for another week, wouldn't it?'

Sam nodded, irritated by the offer for some reason. 'Sure. Thanks.'

Norton checked his watch. 'Must get back. I'm working on a juicy piece right now. Paris papers will *definitely* want it, mark my words.'

The heat and colour and brightness of the streets was a relief after the drab hotel dining room. Sam said goodbye to Norton and wandered towards the old town. Here, he could lose himself; he could be just another tourist, another nameless drifter with a few dirhams in his pocket. In the old town, he didn't have to think about his past. He didn't have to have a future beyond tomorrow.

He found himself at the edge of the Grand Socco, where he'd lost the mystery letter carrier. Norton was right, he shouldn't have run after the person, whoever it was. It seemed absurd, thinking of it now, made his guts squirm a little in their bath of lunchtime wine. He didn't even know for sure that they *had* collected the letter. But there was something in the way they had looked back, as if they knew him, and had considered speaking to him, just for a moment.

A truck sped past, its tyres flinging up grit. He stepped out of the way. Behind him was a flower stall, where blooms were beginning to wilt in their plastic buckets. The woman who sold them was tiny and old and wrinkled beneath a wide straw hat of the country farmers. How long had she been coming to Tangier, to sell her flowers by the road? Twenty years? Thirty? Had she been here as a girl, when A strode through the streets? Had he once stopped to buy a bloom for his lapel? Before Sam was fully aware of what he was doing, he was pulling some coins from his pocket and pointing to a bucket of wild-looking pink roses and to another of tiny star-white flowers. The woman told him a price in Darija. He wasn't entirely sure how much it was, but he didn't bother to haggle, just gave her a handful of small coins. She nodded, picked out a few, and handed the rest back.

He set off, taking the road that led towards the beach. In the writing case beneath his arm was an address for Lillian Simcox, the woman Roger said had been in Tangier in the old days, and who might talk.

The address was for a private hospital, located in one of the tall modern buildings that overlooked the bay. Tangier had begun to stretch itself along the coast, and everywhere Sam looked there was steel and scaffolding, concrete and tinted glass. By the time he reached the building, the wine was wearing off; his reflection in the glass doors of the hospital looked scrubby and tired.

He sighed and rubbed his face on his sleeve. He shouldn't be disturbing an old woman just to ask questions, but still, her memories could be invaluable. She could bring the city of the past to life for him; help him turn the Tangier of now into the Tangiers of then, from black and white to Technicolor. Was that selfish? He stared down at the bouquet in his hand. Probably. But then, perhaps she'd be pleased to have a visitor.

'Bonjour,' Sam murmured to the man at the front desk of the hospital. 'I'm here to see Lillian Simcox.'

'Your name?' The receptionist didn't seem too interested.

'Samuel Hackett.'

'She is expecting you?'

'No. Well, sort of. Someone telephoned to say I might be coming.'

The man just gave a listless nod. Perhaps he was used to eccentric foreigners visiting unannounced. 'Take the elevator to the third floor,' he said, lifting the telephone. 'Wait there. Someone will come.'

In the closed space of the elevator, the scent of the flowers was suddenly overwhelming. The roses smelled drunk with the sun, the tiny white flowers heady and unruly in that disinfected place, carrying the dust of the medina on their petals. He felt the same, with the wine growing stale on his breath and his sunburned cheeks and the grime of the markets on his shoes. He shouldn't be here, dragging the city in with him. The elevator bounced to a stop on the third floor. He was about to turn around and press the down button when the doors slid open. A nurse in a white uniform and blue headscarf was waiting.

'Monsieur Hackett?' she asked.

He had no choice but to nod and step out of the elevator, trailing the feral scent of flowers behind him.

'You are a relative?' she asked, in near perfect English.

'No, I'm, ah, an acquaintance. A friend of a friend. I've never actually met Ms Simcox before.' He half hoped she'd tell him to leave.

But the nurse only smiled. 'Madame does not receive many visitors. She will be pleased to see you.' They stopped outside a door. 'You know of her condition?'

He nodded. Roger had mentioned it.

'Don't worry if she seems confused. I will stay.'

'Thanks,' he murmured.

The room was bright and somehow cooler than the rest of the hospital. Two big windows were open, a breeze from the sea blowing the net curtains. He couldn't see the street below, with its traffic and construction, only the dazzling blue water of the strait, and the dark shadow of Spain on the horizon.

'Madame,' the nurse said clearly, stepping towards a high-backed chair by the window, 'this is Monsieur Hackett. He has come to visit you.'

Lillian Simcox was frail, a fine cloud of white hair about her face, one of her eyes milky. The other was blue, as bright as the sea outside the window. The deep tan of her skin spoke of a life spent outdoors, beneath Morocco's fierce sun.

'Hello ma'am,' he said, sitting opposite her, holding the flowers and the writing case awkwardly. 'I'm sorry to disturb you. Roger gave me your address.'

She frowned slightly, her bright eye fixed on him. 'Roger?'

'Roger Jones, who runs The Hold, down near the beach.'

She just looked at him. He felt his cheeks begin to turn as pink as the roses.

'Yes,' she said at last. 'Dear Roger. He telephoned. He said something about an American.'

Her voice was soft, impeccably British. It was the kind of voice Sam had only ever heard in old black and white films.

'That's me,' he said, feeling scruffier than ever. 'I'm a writer. I'm writing a book about Tangier, in the old days, the nineteen twenties. Trying to, at least. Roger thought you might be able to remember what it was like back then.'

As soon as the words were out of his mouth, he wanted to unsay them. *Remember*, what a stupid thing to say to an elderly lady in her condition. But she was smiling, her eyes half-closed.

'Dear Roger,' she murmured, as if she hadn't heard him. 'The number of times I fell out of that place three sheets to the wind.' Her eyes drifted open again. 'Are those for me?' she asked.

'Yes,' Sam stuttered. In the cool, sterile room, the flowers looked even more ragged than before.

'How lovely.' Her thin hands gathered up the stems and raised the bouquet to her face. Abruptly, her expression changed, the vague smile fading. 'Jasmine,' she said, 'jasmine in the dark, and wet roses.' Her good eye found his. 'How did you know?'

His neck prickled. 'Know what?'

'Lost,' she said, her voice thick, her hands among the petals. 'Lost souls, all of them.'

'Who?' He leaned forwards. 'Who do you mean?'

She didn't answer. After a long moment, the nurse appeared at his elbow.

'I'm sorry, monsieur,' she whispered, 'this doesn't seem to be a good time for her. Perhaps you could come back tomorrow?'

'Of course.' He was ashamed of himself, causing an old lady distress, purely for the sake of his writing. 'Of course, it doesn't matter.'

He rose, tucking the case under his arm. Opposite Lillian he felt as huge and clumsy as an ox. 'Thanks for your time, ma'am. I'll be going now.'

She didn't answer him, only stared ahead.

He was almost at the door when she spoke again, her voice barely audible over the sound of the curtains flapping.

'July, nineteen twenty-eight.'

Sam stopped. 'What was that?'

'Roger, on the telephone, said something about July nineteen twenty-eight. Did he mean that night at Dar Portuna? But he was never there.'

Sam stopped, his mouth half open. *D* Portuna – *Dar* Portuna. Of course, *dar* meant house in Darija, he'd seen it written on signs all over the casbah. How could he have been so stupid? D Portuna was a place, not a person. A place where something had obviously happened . . .

Before the nurse could stop him, he took a step back towards Lillian.

'Dar Portuna,' he asked, 'where is it? Do you remember?'

Her eyes creased. 'I remember such nights there. We drank until dawn, watched the sun rise through the old sea gate. Half of Tangiers was sick with love for him.'

'Who?' Sam knelt beside her chair. 'Who are you talking about?'

She didn't reply, only stared into the distance, a smile trembling on her lips, as if she was back at that party once more.

'Who?' he pressed.

The smile fell from her face. 'Arthur. Poor man.'

'Why poor man? Did something happen?'

Slowly, she nodded. 'I was there the night it happened. I saw him.' She met Sam's eyes. 'I saw them both.'

BARBARY COAST

Take a pony of gin, a pony of Scotch whisky and a pony of Crème de Cacao. Add to this a pony of fresh cream. Shake together with cracked ice and strain into a chilled glass. Strange, sweet and dangerous in quantity.

I'll never forget the moment I saw Tangiers.

From the deck of the ship, the white walls of the city gleamed, like a milky eye in the darkness. The bay was a phosphorescence of boats and lights, red and purple and green stars. I willed them closer. The moment I reached that shore, I would be a step further away from the murder charge that waited back in Spain; a step closer to freedom.

I watched the dock approach, my palm slick with sweat on the handle of the suitcase. It was surprisingly light. I didn't know what was inside, and neither did I want to. I just wanted to hand it over and be done.

A small price to pay for freedom. On the darkened docks, I could see the shapes of men, catching ropes, waiting to unload cargo. I swallowed dryly. Somewhere down there, Bautista's 'friend' was waiting for me.

The French official didn't give the suitcase or my papers a second glance, just stamped them and motioned me on with an impatient flick. My blood seemed to stall and waver and flow again in the other direction as I took my first step on to African soil.

Voices, voices, breath, tar, pungent smoke and men all around trying to take the suitcase, assuring me that they knew the best guesthouse, the best girls, the best hashish, trying words in French, Spanish, English. I held the case to my chest and didn't say a word, just walked, following the crowd. How was I supposed to find anyone, here? I didn't even know what the man I was to meet looked like. *He'll know you*, was the only instruction I'd been given.

Finally, I broke free of the pack of hustlers and stopped, staring up at the city. On the hill above the port was a huge building, sparkling with lights, red and green bulbs surrounding a sign that declared HOTEL CONTINENTAL.

A shadow loomed and I flinched as a man stepped close to me. I couldn't make out a face beneath his hat, only the glint of small spectacles.

'Del Potro?' he asked, voice low.

'Sí.' I gripped the suitcase. 'Are you . . . ?'

'Márquez.' A false name if ever there was one. He glanced towards the ship, towards the officials who were lounging, exchanging gossip. 'Let's go.'

He began to walk purposefully. I hurried after him, holding out the case. 'Wait! Here, take it.'

The man snorted. 'It's not me you need to give it to.'

'Then who?'

'Stop talking, will you?'

He moved like a stray cat, head lowered and watchful, snaking along. We passed the edge of a huge beach, on to a promenade lined with bars, shack-like things strung with feeble lights, tables scattered before them. Motorcars were rolling to and fro, spitting dust. I tried not to stare at it all, smelling hot rubber and grilling fish, a wave of perfume as a well-dressed woman fell laughing from a car. Maybe we were heading to one of the bars, I thought hopefully, watching the man in front.

But he stalked past it all into the alleyways beyond, which were darker and smelled of excrement, rotting vegetable matter and singed butter from kitchens. My hands were trembling as I followed him into a sort of courtyard, a tight chimney of space between buildings. Something scuttled over my shoe and I let out a noise of disgust.

'Quiet,' he barked. Before us was a rusted metal door. The man tapped on it in a distinctive rhythm. Then a bolt was grating and light was spilling out, sending the creatures on the ground fleeing.

'Inside,' he said.

In hindsight, I know I was a fool to do it. A silly, trusting fool. If I could go back, I would grab myself by the lapels and shake myself. But at the time, I thought I was tough enough, with my forged papers and my knife. I stepped inside.

Immediately, Márquez slammed the door behind me. We were in a sort of storage room, long and low and dim, stacked with crates and boxes. A table was pushed against one wall, a creased tide map hidden beneath papers. Before it sat a man. He was younger than Bautista, his cheeks and chin covered in a dark stubble that merged with the rest of his close-cropped hair.

'Any problems?' he asked Márquez, without looking at me.

In the corner, two Moroccan men were slouched, smoking and watching closely.

'No problems, señor,' Márquez answered. 'But this one's green all right.'

The boss man looked at me then. He had odd, tawny eyes, like a goat or a cat; eyes that saw too much.

All at once, the room felt stifling. The bindings made it hard to breathe. I ran a finger beneath my collar, releasing the sweat trapped there, sending it trickling down my chest. If these men found out what I was . . . The strange man's eyes went to the suitcase.

'Did you look inside?'

He was well-spoken, more refined than his surroundings.

'No.' I kept my voice gruff. The less I said, the better.

The boss man barked something in a language I didn't know. One of the Moroccan men clambered to his feet and came to take the suitcase from me. The moment it left my grip, I realized I shouldn't have let it go, that empty-handed was a bad thing to be, in that place.

'Give me your papers,' the boss said.

My heart gave a sick thud. 'Why?'

'Don't ask questions,' Márquez snapped. His breath stank of old garlic. When I took the passport from my pocket, he snatched it and handed it over.

The goat-eyed man began to look through the document, peering at it beneath the lamp. 'Decent work,' he murmured. 'What happened to your real ones?'

'They were stolen,' I said. The side of my face was prickling. One of the Moroccan men was staring at me, as the other jimmied a knife back and forth in the lock of the suitcase.

The boss scratched at the ink with a fingernail. 'Why've you come over here?' he demanded. 'Got an offer of work? Trouble back home?'

'No,' I lied. 'Just a fresh start.'

In that grim, seedy room it sounded ridiculous, and the man laughed.

From the corner, there came a clicking sound. The Moroccan man called something, and pushed the lid of the case open. He shoved aside a bundle of old clothes to reveal what looked like cardboard, dull green files stamped with red. Márquez lifted one out, riffling through the papers. A moment later, he nodded over his shoulder.

The boss man tossed my passport on to the desk. I stared at it, that little rectangle of card, so precious to me. *Let me go*, I begged silently, *please just let me go.*

'What did Bautista pay you?' the boss was saying. I dragged my eyes back.

'He didn't. He gave me the passport. That was the bargain.'

The man snorted. 'Here.' He held a peseta coin towards me. 'A tip. Take it.'

There was no way to refuse. 'Gracias, señor.'

He picked up my passport and handed it over. 'Go get yourself a drink,' he said. 'And a girl. Not the ones on the beach, though, if you know what's good for you.' He fixed me with those yellow eyes. 'Keep your mouth shut.'

I nodded. I knew he could see the terror on my face, and that it satisfied him. Then, Márquez was unbolting the door, giving me a shove into the thick night. The moment it clanged behind me, I took off.

My back was crawling with sweat, with the feeling that I'd been standing in the hot maw of a lion, and had – by chance – slipped free. I ran until I reached the sandy promenade, with its brash lights.

Alone in Tangiers. What was I doing? I didn't know anything about the place, other than the fact it was somehow international territory, belonging to many countries and none. My only thought had been to get out of Spain, out of danger. But I had been here only a moment and danger had found me once again. If Márquez and his boss were to discover that I had lied, that I was not the young man I appeared to be . . .

No. I walked briskly up the promenade. No, I had to be smart. Something had drawn me here, across the strait. Someone. The way Langham had looked at me, despite the presence of the woman at his side. Had I imagined that? My lips twitched a little, an almost smile. We'd been all women at the inn, but I knew what some men liked, and though I'd never met anyone like Arthur Langham before, so cool, so refined, I'd met plenty of other wealthy men. I was clever, I was quick; I could get what I wanted from him, through sympathy or persuasion.

But what did I want? I watched as two men ran from one of the bars on to the beach, whooping drunkenly, their polished shoes filling with sand. Their carelessness made my bound chest contract, made me ball my hands into fists in my pockets. I knew what I wanted well enough, but it was impossible for someone like me. Security, I told myself severely. Safety. That was what I *needed*.

I followed the flow of people up a steep street into a tightness of buildings. All my plans involving Langham would be useless if I couldn't first find him. In Córdoba, the Plaza de la Corredera was where life happened. It must be the same in any city, surely: there would be a central place, where people lingered and talked and talked.

When I'd imagined Tangiers I'd pictured palm trees and gleaming ships, grand villas that looked like the Mezquita back home. But here, the plaster walls were pocked and crumbling, revealing layers of colour beneath. Pigeons shuffled in crevices, gulls wheeled hungrily overhead, like flashing eyes in the dark.

Soon, the streets grew more crowded. Modern buildings sprang up amongst the old, their signs bellowing for my attention: HOTEL DETROIT, CAFÉ-BAR POSTO, BOUCHERIE BENSIMON. Donkeys idled on corners beneath signs for *Marlboro* and *Coca-Cola* and *Cinzano*. From a rusted basement window, a child's face looked up at me, gaunt and solemn. I was shoved by passers-by whenever I stopped on the narrow street, but I couldn't help it. I couldn't stop looking, for here – it seemed – was everything.

Brightness and misery, rope sandals and gleaming shoes, animal dung and French perfume, music and screamed insults. A boy elbowed past, newspapers bristling on his arms like the feathers of city pigeons. *Edición noche!* he bawled at a group of men who sat smoking on a step. *Edition soir! Evening paper, sir! Abendausgabe!*

From above, I heard a shriek and jumped to the side just as a splash of liquid came cascading down. Every orifice of every building seemed to be spilling, oozing with life.

A few steps on, the street seemed to take pity and expand a few paces, leaving room to breathe. Here it was brighter, café awnings marching down the sides of a small square. I took a step towards one of the bars, my heart squeezing at the thought of fulfilling my dream: of sitting down on my own and ordering a drink, like any young man in a hot foreign city.

But after a moment, I felt someone watching me. It was a woman at a table near by, an unlit cigarette in her hand. Her red hair was tightly curled, eyelashes black with mascara, smudged beneath. She smiled and raised an eyebrow. No one had ever looked at me that way before. Face burning, I turned away, too late.

'Do you have a light?' she called in English.

Her accent was strange. American, I realized, looking from her to the two men at her table. I'd never met Americans before. All three of them were young, and deeply tanned, yet the skin of their faces looked waxy and one of the young men had bloodshot eyes. *Too much*, those faces said, *too much*.

'Well?' she asked again, waving her cigarette.

'No, señora,' I muttered. 'I am sorry.'

'Señorita, please,' she said. She looked up at me again through her lashes. 'And no matter. Are you lost?'

'No.' I kept my face lowered.

'Well, you sure look it. You *must* be new in town?'

I nodded, glancing over my shoulder, wondering how to escape.

'I always can tell.' She began to search through a tiny bag on her lap. 'Looking for anyone?'

I took a step away, only to hesitate. The Americans looked wealthy enough. And I had to start somewhere. 'Excuse me,' I said. 'I am looking for someone. His name is Arthur Langham.'

They looked blank. I repeated my question in broken French, until the blond man made a noise of recognition.

'Langham? Is that what you're saying? Langham?'

'Sí, Langham,' I tried to swallow the sound as he did. 'You know him?'

'Sure. He lives up on the hill.' He jerked his hand vaguely. 'Big place, huh, Dolores?'

'Langham?' The woman frowned. 'Oh, *him*! Yes, what's his place called? Like a ship, or a goddess.'

'Dar Portuna,' the third man said moodily.

'That's it! Dar Portuna.' She looked at me. 'Why? Do you actually *know* the man?'

I faltered. I had known that Langham was rich, and upper class; the woman with him had been a Lady after all, but these people spoke about him as if he were a king. My suit, which had felt so respectable in La Atunara, seemed to be unravelling as I stood there, revealing me for what I was. A stray dog, trailing along after a scrap of kindness. I firmed my chin.

'Yes, I know Langham,' I said, with as much confidence as I could. 'We were in Gibraltar together. I was going to call on him, but I lost his address. Perhaps you would be kind, and show me the way?'

The woman's eyes kept landing on parts of my face, my lip, my cheek, the corner of my eye. This close, I could smell the gin she had been drinking, her powder and perfume.

'Why certainly,' she said. 'I'd be delighted to. Join us, won't you?'

The men seemed none too pleased when she said that, but they shifted their chairs to make room for me.

'Dolores Moberly.' She gave me her hand, and I brushed my lips across it. 'That's Bobby Tallerton and Jim Clough.' She gestured at the two men.

'Glad to meet you,' I said, not caring which was which. 'My name is del Potro. Alejandro del Potro.'

'Well, isn't this *something*?' Dolores was leaning towards me. 'To meet a friend of Mr Langham's down here in the socco. I confess I've only been up to the house once, so far. It's the devil's work to get an invitation. I'm sure we won't have any trouble, though, with you being a personal friend.'

I almost laughed when I heard her tone. She thought *I* was her ticket into Langham's house, when in fact she was mine.

'Do you know,' I asked, doing my best impersonation of a gentleman's bored voice, 'if Lady de Luca Bailey is here with him?'

Dolores' eyes grew round. 'You know Lady Bailey too?'

'Sí, señorita. I saw her only a few days ago.'

'I believe she is here, yes. I must say, though, she isn't what I would call a good hostess. She didn't do a scrap of entertaining when I was there last, not one introduction—'

'That's because she isn't the hostess,' one of the men said lazily. 'She's just a guest up there.'

'What trash,' Dolores laughed. 'Everyone knows she and Langham are special friends.'

'Not what I heard,' the other man said, with a strange, leering smile. 'I heard he's one of *them*.'

'But the two of them have been seen together,' Dolores persisted. 'And people say he was engaged to a Russian heiress, after the war.'

'Smoke and mirrors, darling,' the man said, taking a cigarette. 'It always is.'

Dolores turned her bright eyes on me. 'Well, which is it? Surely you know whether Langham and Lady Bailey are . . . *au fait*.'

'I—' I stammered. I had no idea whether Langham and Lady Bailey were a couple. They had certainly seemed close. But I remembered the feel of Langham's eyes on me, his expression. *One of them*. My face began to burn.

I was saved from answering by the appearance of a waiter.

'What'll we have?' Dolores asked.

'Scotch?' the moody man suggested.

I swallowed. Blood and ice and liqueur, pooling on the floorboards . . .

'Not Scotch,' I said, trying to sound casual. 'Something else.'

'Mr del Potro is quite right. Brandy is better. Fundador!' she said to the waiter. 'Fundador and a bottle of Apollinaris! Vite!'

She looked back at me and laughed, her knee touching mine beneath the table. And though my guts were kinked with nerves, I smiled back and tried to do the things any young man might, until I could convince her to take me to Dar Portuna, and to Langham.

Tangier

July 1978

Sam stepped out on to the street. Only then did he realize he was trembling. Taking a deep breath, he found a doorway and sat down, resting the writing case on his knees.

What had just happened? He started to roll a cigarette. An old lady, her mind wandering and confused at the end of her years; that was all. But even as he struck a match, the strange shudder returned at the back of his neck.

I was there the night it happened. I saw him. I saw them both.

He took a drag. Who was she talking about, and what did she mean, *that night at Dar Portuna*? Abruptly, he remembered the pencil-written note, and its words: *A, I am sorry. One day, I hope you'll understand.*

She'd mentioned the name Arthur. Was he A, or was Alejandro? And in either case, who had written it? He blew out smoke, and rubbed at his face with one hand. What was wrong with him? He didn't need to know this stuff in order to write.

And yet, something whispered to him that here was a story, more brilliant than anything he could invent, just waiting to be uncovered. He had all the ingredients: the writing case and the letters, the old book, Alejandro del Potro and now this mysterious Arthur, the scent of those damn flowers and the unshakable certainty that something wild had happened, all those years ago.

Jasmine in the dark and wet roses . . .

If only he could step back into Lillian Simcox's memories; if only he could stand beside her fifty years ago, a drink in his hand, and turn to find A – Arthur or Alejandro – watching him, smiling as dawn broke across the jumbled rooftops of Tangier, as the sun rose through the old sea gate.

He stopped, the cigarette halfway to his mouth.

The old sea gate. That's what Lillian had said. Did she mean one of the old city gates in the wall that surrounded the casbah? He knew the Bab el-Fahs was the medina gate, the Bab al-Assa the gate of sinners, but the sea gate? He wracked his brain. He had a hazy memory of stumbling across an ancient archway on one of his kif-fuelled night walks, and seeing the bay through it, sparkling with lights . . . He threw the cigarette into the gutter, grabbed the case and began to stride down the road, towards the beach, towards the old town.

He was gasping by the time he took the steep road that led up to the edge of the casbah, where the Hotel Continental presided high above the bay. The writing case was sticking to his hand again. He should have left it in his room with the suitcase. And yet, it felt like a talisman, an enchanted object with the power to lead him onwards. It was what had started this whole thing; he knew it would help him find the way.

He sucked in air, sun-hot, stone-cold, scented with human lives, and dived into the casbah. Ordinarily he would hurry through, trying to outmarch the kids who ran after him, begging for change, or the stares that followed. Now he walked slowly, peering at every wall, every doorway. It had seemed a simple idea, in the new town, to look at all the houses near the city walls for that one name, *Dar Portuna*, but soon, the casbah streets began to play their confounding tricks.

Sam ran his fingers down the walls, tried every dead end, no matter how private it looked. He did find names, more than he could have imagined: *Dar Nour, Villa Katerina, Dar Esperanza*, but never the one he wanted. He found corners of the casbah he never knew existed: a huge, old chimney oven where the neighbourhood was baking bread. A door that he had only ever seen closed thrown open to reveal the bright, intricate beauty of a mosque courtyard. The smell of soap and wet dust coming from a dark recess that turned out to be a hammam, a bath house, its opening hours for men and women chalked on the wall.

Finally, at the very top of the casbah, he found himself in the spot he remembered: the crumbling archway that looked out over the strait. *Bab al-Bahr*, a painted sign told him. *Gate of the Sea*. Heart thumping, he began to search the streets around it, striding up and down once, twice. Only on a third pass did he begin to consider that what he was searching for might no longer exist. Dar Portuna could have been demolished, or renamed, or swallowed into the casbah. After fifty years, it was ridiculous to think A might still be there.

He slumped against the Bab al-Bahr, defeated. Somewhere near by, a loudspeaker gave a high-pitched whistle and the call to prayer began, the low, tinny chant that even now made him raise his head in wonder and awe, reminding him how many thousands of miles he had come from home. His eyes stung. He didn't want to leave all of this. The story he was writing wasn't only a piece of fiction, he knew then. It was his reason to stay.

Slowly, he walked away, alongside the old city wall, back towards Madame Sarah's. He'd find a way to remain here. Even if that meant selling the writing case to A, he'd do it, and hope for the best. He walked blindly, and didn't notice the puddle until it had already splashed up his jeans, soaking his shoe.

Swearing, he stepped back. Thankfully, the water looked clean enough, emerging from a hole in the white wall beside him. He stopped, shaking his foot, only to catch a scent on the air. Water yes, and dust, but something else, sweet and heady in the evening: *jasmine and wet roses.*

The wall was high, twelve feet at least, vegetation straggling over the top. He followed it around a corner and the scent grew stronger, until he came to . . .

Nothing. The white wall ended in a rocky outcrop, a pile of rubble from the old fortifications. No gate, nothing, just trash blown into a corner. A great wave of jasmine was growing over the wall here, like a thick velvet curtain studded with flowers. They were just beginning to release their evening scent. He breathed it in, thinking of Lillian Simcox.

He'd take a bunch for Madame Sarah, he decided. If he wanted to stay, he'd probably have to persuade her to overlook more late rent. He was about to break off a stem when something caught his eye, deep in the tangle of vegetation. A curl of metal.

Dropping the case, he shoved the branches aside. They caught at his hair as he tugged old stems away from the ironwork affixed to the wall, uncovering a *D*, then an *a* and an *r* until at last he stood, his nails green with crushed jasmine flowers, staring at the rusted letters:

Dar Portuna

HOP TOAD

Take one jigger of Hungarian apricot eau-de-vie, the juice of half a lime and two dashes of Peychaud's bitters. Shake well and drink very cold to make the heart leap and the tongue jump.

In Tangiers, there is always a way in. Whether it's a soft word or a wink, a jackboot or a silver dollar in the palm, there is always something that will open the door.

I thought Dolores Moberly would be my key, and so I let her drag me through the night, let her waft brandy and broken French and Spanish into my face. I didn't hear a word. I was too busy looking around, as we stepped heavily from the taxi.

We had pulled up alongside an ancient stone archway. From up here, I could see the lights of ships, glinting on the strait.

'Where are we?' I asked impatiently. I'd expected us to pull into a driveway, or alongside a grand entrance. Here, I could see nothing but a high, white wall, running away into darkness.

'We're here, darling.' Dolores took my arm. 'That's Dar Portuna, look!' She pointed to the wall, the tiny bag swinging on her wrist. 'Funny name, isn't it? Wait!' She stopped dead on the dark road, listening.

Noises were drifting over the top of the wall: a treble of laughter, a splashing sound, a squalling jazz horn that broke the night open. I forgot the woman who held my arm and walked forwards, my nose to the air, because now I could smell cigar smoke and jasmine, heady in the night. The sounds and scents led us around the corner to a gate, where double wooden doors barred the way and an ornate, curling sign announced:

Dar Portuna

'If I'd known we were coming to a party, I would've worn my silk,' Dolores was murmuring, dabbing at her face.

Her two friends had trailed behind us, sullen and smoking. I tried the handle of the gate. It was locked. There was a bell, buffed bronze, and I jabbed at it without a second thought. Too late I realized that my suit was dusty, that the tie was loose around my collar, the woman beside me undeniably drunk. The door swung open.

'Señor Langham—'

Not Langham. A Moroccan man in a pristine brocade robe was staring at me.

'Hello,' I tried in my best English. 'I am looking for Señor Langham?'

'Have you an invitation?' he replied in French.

'I,' I stuttered. 'No, but I know him—'

'Yes, and we've been before,' the woman interrupted, leaning on my arm. 'Miss Dolores Moberly and friends. Your master is sure to remember.'

The man's face didn't change. Beyond him I saw lights twinkling through trees, windows shining. I stepped forwards.

'No admittance without an invitation,' the man said.

'Wait!'

The door slammed, a bolt slid, and we were out in the dust of the street once more.

'How rude!' Dolores slurred. 'To send a *servant* to lock us out.'

'You said yourself it was the devil's work to get in,' the blond man muttered, lighting a cigarette. 'Let's go to The Grand instead.'

I said nothing. I *had* to get in. I had to see Langham. If I could talk to him, just for a second . . . I took a step back.

'Alejandro?' Dolores asked.

I ran for the wall, leaping for the wooden trellis that supported the jasmine. Stems broke under my weight, the smell of flowers and crushed greenery swamping me as I hauled myself upwards, shoes scraping at the whitewash. With a burst of effort I managed to sling one arm over the top, then the other, then a leg. I caught a glimpse of Dolores, her mouth hanging open, before the branches sagged under my weight, sending me tumbling ten feet to the ground the other side.

For a few seconds I lay stunned, lungs flattened by the fall, hat knocked askew. When the air rushed back into my chest, it brought the scent of a garden, ferns and lilies and the sweetness of mint, crushed beneath me. Wincing, I pushed myself to my feet.

'Alejandro?' I heard Dolores calling beyond the gate. 'Are you all right?'

I never answered her.

The house stood surrounded by its gardens, softly white and draped in shadows. Windows looked down from the highest floors like half-closed eyes, their wooden shutters carved with stars. Below, doors were thrown wide, muslin curtains swept back, lights creeping on tiles until I couldn't tell what was inside and what was out. From the other side of the house came the sound of the party, piano notes drifting in the lantern-lit trees.

Brushing off the hat, I moved forwards, the brandy making me bold. At a pair of open doors I paused, peering inside. I saw a lounge, empty of people, flickering with candlelight. The remains of a buffet littered a sideboard and before I knew it I was rushing inside, seizing a bread roll from a basket and cramming it into my mouth, glancing over my shoulder. I couldn't remember the last time I had eaten properly and on seeing that food, the flash and fire of the brandy disappeared, leaving my belly as empty as a cavern.

I had no idea what most of it was. Eggs sprinkled with red powder, I stuffed one of those down, and a strange thing in a pastry case that tasted like fish. After the opulence of the house and the gardens, I had expected the food to be the same. It wasn't. The fish was on the turn, the eggs chalky. I seized a cutlet next, which sat in a pool of congealed cream sauce. It was not much better. I licked my fingers and turned to find the next dish.

'I say.'

A woman was standing in the door. I froze, hoping the dim light would hide any green stains on my clothes.

'Don't s'pose you've seen Claude?' she asked.

She was drunk, I realized, her eyes unfocused. I shook my head and fled through another set of doors on to a veranda. There were more people here, reclining on cushions that had been thrown on the marble tiles with no regard for dust or dirt. The music and noise and conversation was louder than before. On a low table beside me, a drink had been abandoned. I picked it up and took a gulp only to cough and grimace at the sting of raw liqueur. I held it to the light. It glowed grenadine-red, but like the food, it didn't taste right, left a sticky burning in my throat.

I kept hold of it anyway, trying to look as if I belonged, even though I was sweating, my hands clammy and trembling. Now that I was here, I had no idea how to go about my plan. *Find Langham,* I told myself, *ask to speak to him in private.* I swallowed hard. What happened next would depend on his reaction.

Ahead, a string of electric bulbs illuminated a path to a raised terrace, where the party was in full swing. Around a small swimming pool, people sat drinking, talking, their shoes flung off, their teeth and eyes catching the light. There was a splash: a woman in a silver dress had leapt fully clothed into the pool. She emerged to applause, the jewels around her neck sparkling with water.

Beneath an arbour, a gramophone was warbling out a record, and there beside it stood Langham, just as I remembered him, with his saint's face and his hair slicked bright. He looked so easy there, so in control, I felt my conviction sputter and die. I'd been thinking about him as if he was one of the gentlemen at the inn; rich, indolent, predictable. But as soon as I saw him, I knew I was wrong. He might have been rich, but he was as sharp as glass.

I took a step back, turned rapidly, only to come face to face with the man from the front gate.

'You.' His mouth was tight with anger. 'How did you get in?'

He seized hold of my arm. I jerked away, the glass flying from my grip, shattering on the tiles.

There was a lull in talk and laughter as people turned to look. Beneath their flat, intoxicated gazes I felt as if every ugly thing I had ever been or done was laid bare. Vomit and burning Turkish Delight, the Señor's blood and the hot breath of the man I'd robbed in La Atunara, Bautista's sneer, the goat-eyed man's hostile stare. Worst of all, I felt Alejandro del Potro begin to fade. I clung on to him as I looked up, into Langham's eyes.

'What's going on?' he called. 'Bouzid?'

'Rien, monsieur.' The man increased his grip on my arm. 'An intruder. I will remove him.'

Langham was coming forwards, frowning. 'I know you,' he said slowly. 'You're that boy, from Gibraltar. Del Potro, isn't it?'

Behind him, I saw a figure stand. It was the woman, Lady Bailey. She looked incredulous, her mouth open.

'Sí, señor,' I said, my face on fire.

'What the devil are you doing here?' He didn't sound angry, but when I looked into his face I thought I saw the ghost of something else. Suspicion, perhaps even fear. 'How did you find out where I live?'

'Some people I met in the Café Central told me.' I answered in Spanish, as if that would protect me from his glittering, scornful guests. 'Some Americans. I am, señor, I am here . . .' Beneath Langham's gaze, all of my careful, calculated words seemed ridiculous. He would see straight through them. And that only left the truth. 'I am here to see you.'

'Who is this boy, Arthur?' I heard someone call. 'What does he want?'

'He's the lad I knocked down in Gibraltar,' Langham called back, his eyes fixed on mine. 'He says he has come all this way to see me. Isn't that extraordinary?'

He was mocking me. An easy thing to do, to make his guests laugh. I felt anger flicker in my chest, but kept my gaze steady.

'What do you want?' Langham asked. He raised his eyebrows at the hat on my head. 'I thought we parted on good terms.'

I knotted my guts. Bribery wouldn't work now, I knew. Nor would pleading or begging. He'd sneer and throw me out for that. I needed to do something else, something surprising, that he wasn't expecting. Rich people were always bored. I took a breath.

'We did, señor. You were kind to me, and I have not forgotten it. So, being alone in the world, I have come to ask if you might consider allowing me to work for you, in exchange for room and board.'

There was a pause. 'Work for me?' Langham said. 'Doing what exactly?'

He laughed, but his voice was careful. Looking into his eyes I felt it again, the jostling of unsaid words between us. I raised my voice.

'I will be your private chef, señor, I will work in your kitchen and serve you and your guests. I will make anything you want. I am a good cook. You will not be disappointed.'

I couldn't look at the party guests, though I heard exclamations from the ones who spoke Spanish, their mirth at my expense.

'I hire in a chef when I need one, del Potro.' Langham's lip twitched. 'Why should I employ you?'

'Because your chef is bad. And a crook too, I'll wager.'

That made his eyes narrow, his lips pinch a fraction.

'What makes you say that?'

My heart was thumping beneath the bindings. 'Because the fish I tasted tonight is half rotten,' I said, with as much authority as I could. 'Whoever cooked it has tried to hide the taste with too much dill. The cutlets were not much better. The butter used to make the sauce was rancid, the wine cheap. The grenadine in your drinks –' I nodded towards a glass '– is fake. It's just sugar and cochineal. I'll bet whoever cooks for you takes your money, buys the cheapest he can get, and pockets the difference. Probably thinks you'll all be too drunk to notice –' I swallowed '– señor.'

The guests around the pool had fallen silent. I could feel the man who held my arm staring at me hard. I hadn't meant to speak so freely, had lapsed into my old inn talk without even realizing. If I'd gone too far . . . Langham's face revealed nothing. Slowly, he half turned his head to address the people behind him.

'The lad claims the food I've served tonight is rotten,' he called. 'Is that true? Or is he having me on?'

There were coughs and mumbles as people took hasty sips of their drinks. *Come on, you bastards*, I told them silently, *one of you must have noticed*.

'Well, I didn't like to say,' came a voice, crisp and clear in the night, 'but that fish was rather ghastly.'

It was the woman in the pool, who stood peering up at us, her chin on her hands, hair dripping. She caught my gaze and her dark-stained lips curved into a smile.

'Thank you, Lillian,' said Langham. 'Bouzid, what do you have to say about all this?'

The man who held my arm shrugged a little. 'I do not know, monsieur.' He hesitated. 'It is true Monsieur Hubert arranged his own food delivery.'

'Well,' Langham said to his guests. 'I'd be a poor host if I let you all go hungry. Shall it be trial by fire? Shall we give the boy a chance? Shall he cook us a midnight feast?'

Glasses were raised, people cheering in agreement. At the edge of the crowd I saw Lady Bailey, frowning at us. When I looked back, it was straight into Langham's eyes as he smiled.

Tangier

July 1978

'Hello?'

Sam stopped, one hand resting on a peeling wooden gate. It was open, which he hadn't expected. Derelict buildings were usually boarded up. Unless it wasn't derelict . . . But there were no signs of life, and the entrance had been overgrown. Still, he hesitated, staring at the curling iron name. Dar Portuna.

Once he stepped through the gate, he would be walking into reality, rather than the world of his imagination. *Isn't this what you wanted*, he asked himself, looking down at the cracked stone threshold, where A might once have stood. *The true story?*

He snatched up the writing case from the dust, and stepped inside.

Green filled his eyes, a wilderness of green. He took a step forwards and smelled mint, crushed beneath his shoe. Weeds swarmed over a once-white path. Sun-baked grass hissed around old lavender plants. He pushed through them, past a fountain that stood, dry and silent.

He stopped to listen to the brief, questioning notes of birdsong, the drone of insects. It felt a thousand miles from the hot, dust-clogged streets of Tangier, and yet the casbah was just beyond the wall; if he listened carefully, he could hear the faint buzz of a moped, the blast of a ship's horn, down in the harbour.

Pushing beneath the branch of an old, drooping lemon tree, he came face to face with the house.

It stood amongst the wilderness, surrounded and protected by it. Vines draped the doorframes, a rose bush had exploded from its bed to reach the windows. On one side, trees grew higher than the roof, shielding the house from any who might look over the walls. It must have been beautiful once, and to Sam, it still was, the perfection of the past in every line.

He walked on to a stone veranda. French doors stood closed, their glass miraculously unbroken, paint peeling from the lead frames. He couldn't see inside; the early evening sun was painting every surface with light. Idly, he tried the handle, only for it to move. He snatched his hand back. It *couldn't* be open. No one would leave a house like this open, for anybody to walk into. Carefully, he pressed the handle again. It grated, stiff in its casing, until finally the latch released and the door drifted towards him.

His intended call of *Hello?* died as the scent of the house billowed out, filling his mouth with must and old perfume and sweet, decaying leather.

He was looking into a lounge. A huge Moroccan rug stretched across the floor, its ornate patterns faded by the sun. Sofas stood around an empty fireplace, their satin cushions dulled by time, the lining sagging. In a corner stood a grand piano, furred with dust. Mesmerized, he stepped through the door. The rug absorbed his slow footsteps as he crossed the room, so that he might have been a ghost, drifting through the past.

Was there anyone here? He stopped, listening carefully, but heard nothing. Heavy velvet curtains, blooming with mould, were drawn over the opposite windows. Carefully, Sam drew them back, the brass rings sliding like bangles on a wrist. Light flooded the room, orange-pink with evening. Beyond was another garden, he could see tangles of roses, blood-red and flesh-pink, dripping colour, stone benches, fountains, and a path, leading into a wilderness . . .

Dar Portuna. Was this where A lived fifty years ago, where someone else must have lived, until recently? Ears straining for any sound, he crept over to the bookcase, looking for clues as to whether the house was inhabited. The books he found were disappointingly dull; volumes on fishing and a leather-bound encyclopaedia set, the red spines faded to pink. At one end of the shelf sat a small silver cup, tarnished and rimed with dust. Gingerly, he picked it up and wiped his thumb across the engraved letters.

TANGIERS BLUE BLAZER
ANNUAL SAILING RACE
1927 WINNER
ARTHUR LANGHAM

Arthur, poor man, Lillian had said. A. L. Arthur Langham.

So this was *his house*, Sam thought, staring at the trophy. *Or* – his neck prickled – *it still is* . . .

A noise made him leap, the trophy clattering back on to the shelf. He listened, eyes wide, to a faint repetitive thudding that echoed through the house, to a squeal and clank that sounded like antique plumbing. His eyes began to sting with panic. There was someone here.

Carefully, he turned around, as if any movement might give him away. The sounds were coming from the other side of a thick, wooden door. What if someone discovered him, and called the police? The argument that he was only there to write a book probably wouldn't cut it. *I should get out*, he thought feverishly, *I should go back to the front gate and ring the bell, I could send a letter instead, like a normal person.*

But none of that would work. There *was* no bell on the gate, and no postman in Tangier, no matter how experienced, would be able to find this place. He stopped, one foot out of the glass door, even as every sensible thought yelled for him to hurry.

But who *was* in the house? A man with dark glasses and an old-fashioned hat? A man who signed his name only *A*, but was truly Arthur Langham, the owner of a lost writing case, a forgotten suitcase? And if so, who on earth was del Potro? Before he lost courage, Sam crossed the room and opened the door.

Beyond was a long hallway, cool and dim and tiled. Sounds were coming from the other end: the rattle and clank of metal, the splutter of water, a scraping noise. As he stood there with every nerve bristling, a scent drifted to him, sharp above the must.

Onions. Someone was frying onions. The smell reached for his belly and dragged him forward, one step at a time. He passed a half-open door and glimpsed a book-lined room, but he didn't stop, he kept walking towards the sound, towards the smell, towards whoever was there, cooking and clanging and whistling a tune from another era.

Noiselessly, he pushed open a door.

It was a kitchen. Although faded like the rest of the house, it seemed lived-in, welcoming. Copper pans glowed against the peeling walls, bunches of herbs stood in jam jars on the windowsill. In the centre of the room, an enormous wooden table was littered with baskets, plates and open books, and amongst it all a chopping board, where something oozed red.

He took a step further and a figure before the stove came into view; a tall, slim figure with messily cropped black hair, and cool olive skin, who tapped the pan with a wooden spoon and began to call out in Spanish—

'I,' he blurted, stepping forwards, 'I'm sorry . . .'

The pan of onions clattered to the floor.

A young woman was staring at him, her eyes huge. A second later he held up his hands, because she had snatched a meat cleaver from the table.

'Sorry,' he stuttered again, 'I didn't mean – I didn't know there was anyone here.'

'What are you doing?'

She asked it in English, her voice rough with shock. She wore a stained apron, jeans, bare feet. She looked furious.

I heard about this place in a letter. I wanted to return the writing case to Mr Langham. I have his things. I have to meet him. I'm writing a book.

'I . . . I found the gate. It was open.'

'No.' She was shaking her head, coming towards him with the cleaver. 'No, there is nothing for you here. You have to leave.'

She knows who I am, Sam realized. The next second she had grabbed him by the wrist and was dragging him towards a back door that gave on to the gardens.

'You don't understand,' he said, trying to free his arm. She had a strong grip, her fingers bloodied from meat, sticky from the onions. 'I've got to see him, please.'

'What are you talking about?'

'The old man who sent me the letters. A. Arthur Langham!'

The woman stopped. Her expression changed, anger and confusion giving way to fear. 'No,' she said, shoving him forwards. 'No, you must go now.'

'It was you, wasn't it?' He was babbling. 'It was you who I chased earlier, *you* collected the letters. Why won't you talk to me?'

'Please, please, just go, before—'

'What is going on?'

The young woman froze. Sam felt her fingers tighten on his forearm. Together, they turned.

Someone was standing in the doorway. Through the floating dust, he saw grey streaked hair, a cream linen suit, a cigarette held in one sinewy hand. Deep brown eyes met his.

'Samuel Hackett.' A husky voice filled the kitchen. 'You have your wish. It seems I shall have to introduce myself after all.'

Part Three

THIRD DEGREE

Take a jigger of Plymouth gin and a pony of French vermouth. Into this add four dashes of absinthe. Shake and strain into an old-fashioned whisky glass. Of a challenging and potent nature.

I would love to say that once I found Langham, my life ran smoothly on its tracks. I would love to say that after I arrived at Dar Portuna, all my hillsides were oregano, all my dishes were flowers and whipped cream.

But that's not how it was.

I remember so well the smell of the kitchen that night: boiling milk and old lard, half-rancid fish offcuts and discarded onion skin. I remember too the mess that the hired chef – who had scarpered as soon as dinner was served – had left behind for some poor servant to clear. Bad workmanship. I observed as much to Langham's man, Bouzid, who had showed me to the kitchen.

He only grunted. 'You have what you need?'

In that moment, the audacity of what I was doing struck me, hard. It was almost eleven and Langham had ordered food for midnight; I had a single hour and an unfamiliar kitchen with which to secure my future. I was not cooking for half-drunk townsmen at the inn, unfussy and distracted by the girls. I was cooking for *Langham*, for a saint and his exalted guests. I was cooking for my life. Every trick

Ifrahim had taught me to please the teeth and charm the tongue, I would need now.

'Yes,' I told Bouzid. My hands hesitated on the lapels of my jacket. I didn't want to take it off; it was my protection, a shield between my bound chest and the world. I'd already caught his sharp, sober eyes watching me. 'Is there an apron?' I asked gruffly.

The garment he returned with was a huge, canvas thing, stiff from laundering. With my back to him, I shucked off the jacket, and ducked beneath the apron's cover. As soon as it was tied around my waist, I began to feel better. I bared my wrists to wash my hands at the sink, and became aware of the familiar tingle in my fingertips, the itch to spice and shape the world.

'You can leave me now,' I said, over my shoulder.

My kitchen self and Alejandro had not yet met each other. If I was to introduce them, if I was to stir them together until they were blended, inseparably, I needed to do it alone. Bouzid watched me a moment longer, his dark eyes sceptical. Then he turned and disappeared into the garden.

Thankfully, the stove wasn't a fancy gas contraption, but a huge old blackened thing with a glow of embers deep in its belly. I rattled them up hot, fed it more wood, and went to search out the raw ingredients of my future.

I was right about Monsieur Hubert, the cook. It takes a thief to know a thief, and the hired chef was a lazy one. Almost everything I found was cut-rate or half-bad. The milk skimmed and skimmed again, the cooking wine no better than vinegar. How had it not been noticed? Perhaps Langham and Lady Bailey did not often eat at home. A smile found the edge of my lips. I could change that.

Almonds, my hands moved across the shelves. *Garlic. Olive oil.* Ifrahim's voice was with me. *Herbs from the garden. Lemons. Bones. If in doubt, serve the best things whole and let them speak. Let them be barefaced*.

I tumbled what I had found on to the table and freed the kitchen knife from my jacket. It had come with me all this way, it had blistered my childish hand and tasted men's blood to aid my escape. Now, it would help me win my freedom.

Outside the back door, the gardens were warm, fanned by a breeze that smelled of brine and sea fog. The noise of the party reached me as I knelt among the dark plants. The scent of herbs rose up; must from oregano, the tough greenness of parsley, bright, clean rosemary. *Rocío del mar*, Ifrahim had always called rosemary; *the dew of the sea*. That was what I needed.

It was not until I returned to the kitchen that I realized how tired I was. Luckily, my hands remembered the work. The guests outside were drunk, for the most part, so they'd want strong tastes, guilty, heady morsels. And salt. It was the easiest charm to work upon a tongue, especially ones drenched in liqueur.

I found potatoes and onions in the pantry, a shrivelled chilli pepper, the end of a chorizo sausage that I guessed the chef had been gnawing on. It would do for a patatas a lo pobre. The onions hissed like laughter; I'd serve poor man's potatoes to those rich beasts and they would wolf them down like caviar. Soon the onions were joined by spicy sausage, turning the oil crimson.

What else? Anchovies, freed from their coffin and plunged into a pool of olive oil and lemon and garlic. More garlic for an aioli, another trick, a way to dazzle the mouth. No matter that it would linger long after it was welcome; what mattered was approval, here and now.

Watch what comes out of their mouths, as well as what goes in, and you will know them for what they are.

Leaning out of the back door, I listened to the party. It was raucous still, but the voices were growing languid. Somewhere near by, foliage rustled and two people hushed each other's laughter. I smiled. Sweetness was what I needed to add, and decadence. There was a lump of hard cheese on one of the shelves, which I sliced finely to disguise its age. Next came a pot of honey, which I drizzled all over, followed by a scattering of rosemary flowers. It wasn't subtle; it was blatant and heady. That honey would linger tantalizingly on fingers, shine on lips, and the guests would praise me silently for helping them in their seductions.

I hadn't noticed the time racing by. Suddenly, Bouzid was back, looking dubiously at the dishes on the table. I didn't blame him. It wasn't food to be eaten with silver cutlery and linen, but with hands. It was a gamble on my part, a guess that Langham's guests hadn't come to this hot, dazzling city for luxury alone. They were here because they were *hungry*, famished for what they couldn't get in their own countries. They wanted to crush the world to their mouths and sink their teeth into its flesh, they wanted to suck at the juice and fling the rinds away and never think about the cost. *I can see you*, I wanted my dishes to say; *I can give you what you want.*

Bouzid and I carried the platters between us, two on each arm, like I used to at the inn. The guests were waiting on the veranda, a pack of bright, wild things, their beautiful clothes splashed and crumpled and pushed askew. I saw Lady Bailey amongst the cushions, leaning forwards over a pipe, her pale hair sliding across her cheek. And in the middle of them all was Langham, the head of that lost troupe, his face smooth, his mouth full of secrets.

We locked eyes. 'Supper is served,' I said.

'Very well, del Potro,' he smiled. 'We'll taste your petition. With what do you make your case?'

'With patatas a lo pobre,' I told him quietly. 'And aioli. Sardinas en salsa de limón. Queso con miel y romero.'

'Peasant food,' he murmured. 'You've given yourself away, boy.'

'Bon appétit,' I said. It was a challenge.

I stood in the shadows, watching as Langham's guests fell upon the food, as they laughed at the novelty of scooping aioli straight from the bowl, picking up salt-scattered potatoes with their fingers, their lips flushed and tingling with chilli. I watched as the woman from the pool fed a slice of honey-slicked cheese to a man, following it up with her lips. I watched as another man, his waistcoat hanging open, dropped a whole sardine into his mouth, imitating a gull. It was grotesque, it was glorious, and I was torn. Half of me wanted to fling myself into that revelry, drink until I was like them, until I could no longer taste the bitterness of the world. The other half of me held back, an outsider, thrilled by the power of what I had done, how I could affect people's behaviour, with nothing more than kitchen scraps.

I looked for Langham. I tried to see him eating, tried to guess at his face, but every time I thought he was about to bend towards a dish I lost sight of him. Eventually, the platters were emptied down to scrapings and skin, and people began to drift off, towards pools of light or quiet shadows. Only then did I come forwards to clear the plates, relieved and frustrated. For all his words, I had never once seen Langham eat my food.

On the cushions, Lady Bailey lay insensible with her head in the lap of another man. The long, slim pipe hung loose in her hand. If she and Langham truly were together, then where was he at such a moment?

'Leave that,' a low voice told me. I turned and found Bouzid. 'Monsieur wants to see you. In the study.' He pointed to the farthest end of the veranda, where I could just see a pair of glass doors, open to the darkness.

My body gave a thud of anticipation. 'All right,' I muttered. Bouzid was holding out his hand for the apron. It obviously wouldn't do to wear it in there. Gritting my teeth, I took it off, hunching my chest. I wanted to go back to the kitchen and fetch my jacket, but Bouzid blocked my way.

'You should not keep him waiting.'

I had no choice but to walk into the shadows, trying surreptitiously to check that the bindings were still tight around my chest, praying they hadn't slipped in all of my activity. Too soon, I came to the glass doors. I was sick with nerves, all my arrogance, my kitchen magic seeping away. Had I fooled Langham? Would he actually consider hiring me? The others had eaten my food; I had bewitched them, in whatever small measure, but him . . .

'Del Potro?' His voice drifted from the darkness. 'Come in.'

I stepped through the doors. Beyond was a large room, lit by a single oil lamp that rested on a desk. Its flickering light caught varnished wood, papers, the corner of a leather writing case, where two initials glinted gold. A flare of orange in the darkness made me look up. Langham was leaning there, barely visible save for the end of his cigarette.

Abruptly, I became aware of the cooking smells that clung about me; hot oil and onions, garlic and lemon sharp on my fingers.

'You wanted to see me?'

Another flare of the cigarette. 'I did.' He moved forward to sit on the corner of the desk before me. He was so close that his own scent began to mingle with mine. I breathed waxy pomade and sweat-damp silk, tobacco and roses, the blunt sting of liqueur. His voice was as quiet as the smoke. 'I want to know what you're doing here.'

The scant light caught the side of his neck, his cheekbone, the very edge of his mouth. I sensed that we were playing some game and that I had to tread carefully, because I didn't know the rules.

'I came here to find you,' I said, gambling that the truth would be more potent than a lie.

'Why?' The smoke from his cigarette was filling the space between us. 'Why me?'

'Because . . .' The truth ran out. It was something that didn't exist in words, yet, only in the stab of my heartbeat, the singing of my blood, the yearning in my constricted chest. *Because you have everything I want.*

He didn't ask me to continue. Instead, our breathing filled the silence until he moved abruptly, reaching along the desk.

'Where did you get this?' he asked.

It was my passport. Bouzid must have gone through the pockets of my jacket. I tried to see Langham's face, but it was lost in shadow and his voice gave away nothing.

'From the consulate.' I tried to keep my voice steady.

'The consulate here in Tangiers?'

'Yes.'

'Then you've been here before?'

'No. I lost my papers. A friend helped me to replace them.'

'A friend,' Langham said softly. He opened the passport, to where my face stared up sullenly. 'Del Potro,' he read, and half laughed, 'what a name.'

'It's the only name I have,' I told him.

He looked at me, and I could tell he knew everything; that the name was false, that I was here because I was desperate, because I was running from something. *Almost everything*, I thought, as the bindings squeezed my chest.

After what felt like an age, he nodded. 'Very well, del Potro. I will consider your request, if you can assure me of two things. First, that you will not bring trouble to my house.'

I shook my head rapidly.

'I will not, monsieur.'

'Second –' Langham paused '– that you will give me one thing, without question or condition.'

I swallowed, feeling a pulse beat in my throat. 'Which is?'

He closed the passport and held it towards me.

'Your loyalty.'

Tangier

July 1978

'A drink?'

Sam looked up, trying to bring his thoughts back into some kind of order. He'd been staring, trying to take everything in: the expensive rug on the floor, the varnished desk, the bookshelves lined with ledgers, the small, curved bar built into one corner of the room, and the person who stood behind it . . .

'Yes.' The word stuck in his throat, and he coughed. 'Yes, thanks.'

He watched as the man confidently took up spirit bottles and a measure, scooped ice from a bucket and shook droplets of who knew what into a measuring glass. Only when the clinking of the stirrer stopped could Sam bring himself to speak.

'Who are you?'

It wasn't the sort of question he should have asked, but he couldn't help it; his thoughts were a mess of what he'd imagined and what he'd written, what he'd heard from Lillian Simcox and what he'd read in the strange exchange of notes.

There was a grunt of laughter from the bar.

'Who do you think I am?'

He's playing with me. Sam gripped the case. 'You're A. L. Arthur Langham. You're the person who owned this case, and the suitcase I found. You're the one who wrote—' He stopped. He hadn't yet said anything about the discovery of that short, desperate, pencil-written plea. The old man at the bar was watching him closely.

'Wrote?'

'The notes to me, at the Gran Café de Paris. And stole my letter?'

The man smiled a little, pouring the drinks. 'Yes. I am sorry. I was rather surprised, you see. I had not seen *that* –' he pointed to the writing case '– for fifty years. I could not believe my eyes.' He stepped out from behind the bar. 'I had to know who you were, why you had it.'

'You could've just asked me.' The man didn't reply. Sam felt as though he'd said something stupid. 'You could've agreed to meet me at the café,' he ploughed on. 'Then I wouldn't have tried to find this place.'

The man crossed the room slowly, as if one hip was paining him. 'Mr Hackett, I have my reasons for acting as I have. Just as you, no doubt, have yours.' He held out a glass. In the twilight it glowed ochre-gold, beaded with ice.

Sam took the glass. 'Thanks,' he said, groping after some kind of normality in the charged room. 'I'm sure all of this can be explained easily enough—'

'Why on earth would you think that?' The man raised his eyebrows. 'It cannot be easily explained and you would not have come here if you wanted it to be. You're a writer, Mr Hackett, I know that much. You don't *want* something easy and plain. You want something tricky and tangled.' He smiled. 'You want a story.'

'That's not,' Sam stammered, 'I mean, I don't want to pry—'

'But you do. You want to pull up the surface of the world and see what's underneath.' The man took a sip of his drink. 'You've come to the right place to do it. Tangiers is nothing but layers. Pull off the paper and you'll find a dozen stories. Scratch the plaster and you'll end up with a saga beneath your fingernails.' The man lowered himself into a chair. 'This city is built on stories. And right now, there is a new one being written. By you.'

'Yes,' Sam murmured, as if at confession.

'And to write your story, you have to hear mine? Isn't that so?'

'Yes,' he said again.

'Then you must promise to listen carefully, and to hear it whole, beginning to end, for I'll only tell it the once.'

Sam looked up in surprise. 'I will, I mean, of course.'

The man gestured at the glass. 'Drink to it.'

He drank. Brandy stung his tongue, followed by sharp herbs and bitter citrus. It was strong. When he swallowed, the liqueur seemed to fill him from gullet to gut.

'What is this?' he asked, into the quiet. Beyond the door he could hear faint evening birdsong, the clatter of kitchen pans.

The stranger smiled. 'The beginning.'

TWIN SIX

Take a dash of imported grenadine and four dashes of fresh orange juice. Add the white of one egg, half a pony of Italian vermouth and a jigger of dry English gin. Shake well together and strain. Smooth, and very deceptive.

I awoke abruptly, with sweat-drenched limbs and a thundering heart. For a minute, I didn't know where I was.

Light was filtering in through a carved window screen, illuminating a small room, pristine white sheets that were tangled about my legs. Then I remembered: the party. The food and the encounter with Langham. Afterwards, Bouzid had shown me here, and I'd been too tired to do anything except lock the door, struggle out of my suit, and fall face first on to the bed.

Sitting up, I looked about the room. There was a bureau, a silver lamp, a patterned woollen rug. I stared at it all, thrilled and terrified in equal measure. I had never had my own room before. Slowly, the sense of wonder faded. This would not come free. Nothing did. Langham wanted something in return.

I swung my legs to the floor. Loyalty, that's what he'd demanded last night. I had agreed; of course I had. Did he know I was lying? I'd never been loyal to anything or anyone before, except, perhaps, to Ifrahim.

The suit I'd bought in La Atunara was crumpled on the chair. The sight of it made me hesitate. It was stained in places, and the length of bandage I had been using to bind my chest was beginning to yellow with sweat. I tightened it reluctantly. I wanted cool, clean linen. I wanted to wander out into the garden dressed in a morning robe and slippers, with no one to answer to or decide what the day held but myself.

Of course, I couldn't do that. I could only dress again in the suit, wash my face and wet my hair to make it presentable, and step outside the door, to see what was waiting.

I hadn't seen much of the house last night. I only knew that my bedroom was on the ground floor. I crept down a short corridor into a kind of courtyard, open to the sky. Everything was quiet, only the sound of birds and a clock ticking somewhere. Was Langham sleeping now? Did he wear fine, satin pyjamas? Was he brought his breakfast on a delicate tray? A staircase wound up to a balcony, where the bedrooms must be. I wanted to walk up there, explore dressing rooms and bathrooms and lounges. Instead, I turned, and found my way back to the kitchen.

It had been cleaned, scrubbed of the previous night's mess and debris. A basket of fruit stood on the table, as though just delivered; apricots and melons, prickly pears and yellow plums. There was no one around to see, so I helped myself. The plums were mottled like the gold of a church altar; they had a drowsy sweetness which filled my mouth. I took another.

Outside, the sun was burning through the freshness of dawn. All around was gentle birdsong, the sound of water. I stepped on to the path, examining the place in daylight.

High white walls surrounded the garden of Dar Portuna. The house was perched on the very edge of the city: on one side were the narrow streets, on the other the remains of old crumbling fortifications, and a steep slope, running all the way down to the port. Citrus trees lined the walls, their dusty leaves hiding orbs of yellow. An old fig tree stood, bent-backed, in one corner. The paths had been swept, last night's revels tidied away. I came to a stone bench next to a star-shaped fountain, where lilies grew, water caught in their throats. Here, in this garden, the sharp edges of the world were held at bay. Something only the rich could afford: such peace in the heart of a city.

'Del Potro.'

I spun around, like a guilty thing.

Lady Bailey stood watching me, her pale hair ruffled above her chin, a blue embroidered robe dragging on the ground. I met her gaze. The last time I'd seen her, she had been lying on a pile of cushions with a silver pipe in her hand.

'You stayed,' she said.

I remembered some manners, and dropped my gaze. 'Excuse me?'

'I said, you stayed.' She came towards me, to sit on the bench.

'Yes.' I backed up a few paces. 'Monsieur Langham has given me a room, near the kitchens. I am to be the new cook.'

She looked at me, her grey eyes hard. 'He never lets people stay. They can drink until the sun comes up, so long as they go home at the end. Why is it different for you?'

I remembered Langham's face, close to mine in the darkness of the study – the strange tension between us as he asked for my loyalty.

'I am not a guest,' I murmured. 'I am here to work.'

She said nothing, only frowned at me, sucking in her lower lip. Were they lovers, after all? Was she jealous? Her piercing gaze made me nervous.

'Please excuse me,' I said. 'I must go and see if Monsieur Langham would like breakfast.'

'You won't find him. He's already gone. Never sleeps much.'

I stopped. I had thought of Langham as a man of leisure. 'Gone where?'

'Business.' She took a handkerchief out of her sleeve. 'Always business.'

I wanted to ask, *What business?* but instead I dropped my head. I had to learn this role of the polite, disinterested cook. I had to disappear behind my apron again, to be safe. 'Will you be wanting breakfast, mademoiselle?'

She sighed and sat back. 'No, I couldn't possibly. And it's madame, not mademoiselle.' She looked down at her hand. It was tanned, save for a pale line that encircled her wedding finger. 'I suppose you weren't to know that.'

I hurried back towards the house, adding another mystery to the hoard that seemed to dwell in Dar Portuna.

I was prowling the kitchen, poking into every corner, searching through the cupboards when Bouzid found me.

'There will be six guests for dinner tonight,' he told me in Spanish. 'They will take an aperitif at eight, followed by dinner at eight thirty. Monsieur Langham wishes to impress upon you that his guests will be using cutlery. Not their hands.'

I gave him a polite smile. 'Of course.'

'Do you wish me to send out for the food?' The man was looking at me curiously, as if trying to gather information, now that he saw me in the daylight. 'Monsieur Hubert, the previous chef, had his own supplier. A French importer.'

'That'll explain why it was all so bad,' I said. 'It was probably half-rotten by the time it left Marseille.' Was that a glimmer of amusement on Bouzid's face? 'I would prefer to buy my own supplies from the market, thank you.'

'You mean the medina?'

'Yes,' I said, pouring myself a glass of water, as if that was what I had meant all along. 'Perhaps you could point me in the right direction?'

When I turned back, I found Bouzid stony-faced. 'If you truly wish to buy your own ingredients, it will be best if I show you. The medina can be . . . confusing, for foreigners.'

I watched him over the rim of the glass, wondering at his motives. I decided to be gracious. I needed every scrap of help I could get in this place.

'Merci, Bouzid,' I said.

'Also, Monsieur Langham has asked me to give you this.' He took something from the pocket of his robe. 'He believes it might be of some help, with regard to menus.'

It was a small parcel, wrapped in brown paper. A gift from Langham? Hurriedly, I turned my back on Bouzid to open it, afraid that my face would give me away.

Inside was a book, not a new one. It was well worn, the cover bent and scratched, the gilding half rubbed from an English title.

The Gentleman's Guide.

I frowned. Why should Langham have this, why was it so well-thumbed and studied, when he was already a gentleman? I opened the cover, searching for a name or a stamp, something that might hint at the book's past. Instead I saw fresh ink, where someone – Langham – had written:

If you're going to play the game, you have to learn the rules.

I snapped the book shut.

I turned back to find Bouzid studying me hard. 'Bueno,' I said, dropping the book into the pocket of my jacket, as if it was of no consequence. 'I am ready when you are.'

If I had thought the streets around the Café Central were confusing, they were nothing compared to the ones Bouzid steered me down. This was the casbah, he told me, as we turned left and right and back upon ourselves until I gave up trying to keep track of our direction.

I am not too proud to say that without Bouzid, I would have been hopelessly lost. It was all I could do to keep my mouth closed. I had thought our market in Córdoba was plentiful enough, but here it seemed as if the whole countryside was laid out at the edge of the pavement. Women shaded by huge straw hats sat behind piles of tomatoes, the stones around them already littered with flesh and seeds. Aubergines groaned purple, onions hung with soil still clinging to beards. Barrows of melons, heavy as heads, engulfed us in their honey-vegetable sweetness as we passed.

Bouzid kept glancing at me. I think he was enjoying my astonishment. We came up for air in a large open space, only to plunge into yet another covered market. It was loud beneath the tin roof, packed with voices. Women in robes and headscarves were inspecting, rejecting, haggling with the sellers, who pleaded as if they were in court. There were mountains of eggs, white cheeses spread on palm leaves. The smell grew stronger until I realized we were approaching a meat market: fish and fowl, old and bloodied and new. The dirt floor grew clogged beneath our feet; a skinned sheep's head leered down at me from a hook as if it were about to leap on to my shoulder and whisper a tale into my ear.

I'd never seen so much flesh before. Cracked skulls revealing brains, dishes heaped with lungs, tongues, guts and hearts: the ingredients of life, ready to be remade into something new.

The spectre of the meat market released us, only for another to swallow us up, one of perfumed breath and rattling chillies and shivering dried husks. I had to stop myself from plunging my fingers into a basket of rosebuds, had to resist licking my finger and touching it to a pyramid of powder the colour of the sun.

'Down here are olives,' Bouzid said, but I had to stop him in order to catch my breath.

He tutted at me impatiently. Still, he looked a little gratified. 'Do you know what you will need for tonight's dinner?' he asked.

I nodded, and closed my eyes to buy time. In truth I had no idea. The scents and sights were overwhelming. In that moment, I wanted Ifrahim beside me more than anything, Ifrahim who had tasted a thousand dishes in a hundred different port towns. *Ale, hacer de tripas corazón.*

I opened my eyes. I'd give them their fine food. I'd drown the pale, bland chicken on their plates with flavours of Andalucía, spike their wine sauces with spices. It would be a vagabond cuisine; beguiling, never quite one thing or another. That's what they wanted, these ex-patriots and exiles. That's what this city was.

When I told Bouzid what I would need, he frowned at the eccentricity of the ingredients.

'Monsieur Hubert—' he began.

'Monsieur Hubert was a fraud,' I said with as much arrogance as I could, 'and a drunk. I know what I am doing.'

He shrugged, and turned away.

'Where are you going?' I stepped after him like a child. I was afraid to be left alone there, in that carnival of new things.

'To hire a porter,' he said shortly. 'You can find your way back to Dar Portuna?'

'Of course,' I said, hiding my hands in my pockets. It was only then I felt the book. *The Gentleman's Guide*. The back of my neck prickled beneath my second-hand shirt.

If you're going to play the game, you have to learn the rules.

'Wait!' I called, stepping after Bouzid. 'I don't suppose you know a good tailor?'

It was easy enough to follow Bouzid's directions out of the socco, towards the Rue Siaghines where most of the tailors could be found. It was a harder matter to find one that suited me. I didn't want the clean, sober shops, where sallow Englishmen sweated into arrow collars. I needed something different.

I found it by wandering the nearby alleyways. No grand glass windows, no courteous mannequins, just a peeling sign.

Sastrería Issac Souissa

I pushed open the door. Inside, a man sat hunched, needle-blind, working at a piece of mending. When I greeted him, and asked about a suit, he looked at me as if I was a young thug, sent to press him for money.

'A suit?' he repeated. His face trembled between dubiousness and hope. 'Well . . .' He glanced at his shop, the shelves almost empty of goods.

'A suit,' I said, firmly. 'And shirts. Underwear. Socks. Anything else a gentleman might need.'

The tailor stood, fumbling a pair of spectacles on to his face, smoothing his wayward grey hair. 'Of course,' he said, ushering me closer, as if I might run out the door any moment. 'Of course, it would be my pleasure.' He held up a measuring tape, but hesitated. 'Only . . . I am sorry to ask, monsieur, but do you have the means to pay? You see, I cannot extend credit.'

He'd noticed my suit at last then. His tailor's eye had picked up its second-hand nature, the tiny holes where embroidery had been picked from the fabric. I gave him my best smile.

'You may send the bill to my employer, a Monsieur Arthur Langham, of Dar Portuna. He will pay it. He wishes me to be well dressed.'

'Dar Portuna?' The tailor scrawled a hasty note.

'That's correct.'

Play the game, learn the rules. There were a hundred rules in *The Gentleman's Guide* about how to dress. And if I was to be part of Langham's world, I had to look the part, didn't I? I swallowed and raised my chin, hoping I was right; that the book had been an invitation, of sorts. If not, I would have a lot of explaining to do. *Even if he kicks me out*, my old, thievish self thought, *at least I'll have a good suit.*

'Very well,' the tailor was saying, 'if you would please remove your jacket.'

'There is one more thing I require,' I said, stepping back.

I took the remaining five pesetas from my pocket, plus the coin the goat-eyed man had given me. My only money in the world. The tailor stared at it. It could keep his family fed for a week, I knew. It could buy him bottles to drown in, a dozen pipes to dull his misery.

'Yes?' he asked eagerly. 'What is it?'

I shifted my chest in the bindings and placed the money in his hand.

'Your silence.'

Tangier

July 1978

Outside, night fell as the man talked. He didn't switch on a light. *Better that way*, Sam thought. In the shadows he could imagine himself back there, to the Tangiers of fifty years before: a place of French champagne and Moroccan rosewater, Indian opium and cold, dry Plymouth gin.

He heard stories about parties and thrilling flights to Gibraltar, night cruises on the strait, where the lanterns and flares of smugglers lit up the three-mile limit. The man spoke of a city built from the materiel of the Great War – the bones of the old world wetted with the blood of the new. Sam gulped the man's words like the cocktail in his glass. If he'd been there, if he only could've been there . . . In that moment, he would have given anything.

Finally, when it was completely dark, the man stopped talking. Sam couldn't see his face; he could barely see his own hands that rested on the writing case.

There was a knock at the door. When neither of them answered, it creaked open, letting in a sliver of warm, yellow light and the smell of toasted spices.

'Dinner's ready,' the young woman said, breaking the web of words around them. 'Is he staying?'

The man said nothing, as if he had exhausted himself. Sam hesitated. He did want to stay for dinner. He wanted to desperately. And yet . . . His head was bursting with what he had heard. He needed to remember it, write it all down.

'No.' His voice sounded clumsy in the dark room. 'Thanks, but I've got to get back.' Too late he realized he hadn't actually been invited. 'Another time?'

'Another time,' the man murmured. 'Yes. Come back tomorrow, around five. Bring that old suitcase.' The chair creaked as he leaned back. 'Zahrah will show you out.'

Awkwardly, Sam put the glass down on a side table. He paused, the writing case in his hand. Should he give it back? The man hadn't asked for it. He decided not to.

'Thank you, Mr Langham,' he murmured.

He received no response.

In a daze, he followed the young woman back into the kitchen. On the table he saw a platter of meat scattered with pomegranate seeds and herbs; rounds of bread wrapped in cloths. He began to regret his decision not to stay.

She showed him out a different way, through the garden, where plants and vines dragged at his shoulders, releasing their scent. He caught a glimpse of water through the trees; a swimming pool, tiled blue and white. The stones around it were cracked but clean, as if still in use. Dar Portuna only pretended to be abandoned, he realized. Like a rich man dressed in pauper's clothes. But why?

'Tomorrow come this way,' the girl told him shortly. 'Don't use the front gate. It's always locked.'

'It wasn't today,' he said. 'I walked straight in.'

The girl made a noise. 'I forgot to lock it. I was distracted. Some idiot chased me through the medina.'

'Sorry.'

They'd reached the far end of the garden. Hidden behind a tree was a short flight of steps, and a second door, white-washed like the wall.

'Tomorrow, wait for the end of Asr, the call to afternoon prayer, then come here and knock. Don't let anyone see you. Don't be late. I won't wait around.' She turned away.

'Wait, Miss . . . is it Zahrah?' She nodded curtly. 'Listen, I'm not going to cause any trouble, I promise. I'm just a writer who wants to talk to your –' he hesitated '– grand-father? Uncle?'

The woman snorted and held open the gate. 'We're not related. Remember, be here, right after the call.'

Sam stepped through, and turned, meaning to apologize again, only to find himself facing a locked door. From this side, it blended almost imperceptibly with the wall, weathered dust-grey wood, tucked into an alcove. He looked up and found himself standing on a narrow, trash-strewn walkway below the Bab al-Bahr. Stone steps disappeared down into the darkness, hugging the curve of the old fortifications. He'd never seen them marked on any map.

An escape route, he realized. *But for who?*

That night, he wrote feverishly, trying to remember every sensation, every smell and sound of Dar Portuna. He wrote about the woman – Zahrah – and about the exquisite villa with its gentle decay. He wrote about the strange figure at the heart of it all, who had drawn him there.

He used the final piece of the writing paper, and had to scrabble about under the bed for the old, half-typed sheets he had discarded from the Hermes. First, he wrote on their backs. Then, when he ran out of space, he wrote around the letters that were already there, until they merged, ink on ink, new story on old, becoming something that was both, and neither. *Like the city*, he thought.

He didn't remember falling asleep, but when he awoke it was with ink-stained fingers and a page beneath his face, every inch covered with writing.

He didn't read it – worried it wouldn't make sense in daylight – only stacked it with the others. The pile was growing now. He laid a hand on top of them. As long as he could keep going, he was sure those pages could become something. A new start, perhaps.

There was now only one sheet of paper that remained almost blank. He lifted out the strange pencil-written note. Why hadn't he mentioned it to Langham?

A,
I am sorry.
One day, I hope you'll understand.

He sat back, uneasy. What did it mean, and why had it never been sent? Why had it remained, hidden in the writing case, when it was obviously so important?

I was there, the night it happened. I saw him. I saw them both.

Could he believe Lillian, old and ill as she was? Something had happened at the grand house, back in 1928, Sam was certain of that. His skin prickled. Alejandro del Potro's fate was still unknown. All Sam knew was that he had left a passport behind. What if Alejandro was A, and Langham had done something terrible?

Sighing, he slid the letter back into the writing case and closed the lid. He felt as if he was chasing phantoms around the city; A. L. had become Arthur Langham, the strange figure he had pursued through the medina had become a young woman. When would Alejandro del Potro reveal himself, step from the passport photograph into life?

He itched to get back to Dar Portuna. By two o'clock in the afternoon, he couldn't stand waiting any more, and headed towards the medina.

His feet took their usual route, past the pigeon-haunted wreck of the Cinema Rif, up towards the Place de France and the Gran Café. Outside the El Minzah, he stopped. Norton usually took a nap at his hotel before returning to work after lunch. Sam had hours yet to kill, and a cool drink in the bar wouldn't go amiss. Maybe he could even borrow a tie . . .

'Hack!' Norton exclaimed, striding from the elevators. 'What a nice surprise.' His face was puffy from sleep, eyes a little reddened. They widened at the sight of the suitcase in Sam's hand. 'Don't tell me you're leaving?'

Sam smiled. 'No. I'm just . . .' He hesitated. He hadn't told Norton about the suitcase yet, or what it contained.

'Does that belong to your old man?' Norton asked.

'Yeah. How'd you know?'

'Same leather, same initials.' Norton pointed at the top of the case. 'Obviously part of a set. You pick that up from your kif broker, too?'

Sam nodded slowly, unsure about why he was lying. It seemed easier than trying to explain the bizarre series of events at the Hotel Continental. That was *his* story, part of what he was writing, still private.

'Anything good inside?'

'Just clothes.' He tried to sound casual.

'And your old man wants them back?'

'It's sentimental, I think,' Sam said, turning away. 'Time for a quick drink?'

''Fraid not.' Norton looked towards the bar mournfully. 'But walk me to the office?'

They crossed the busy street and went along in silence for a while.

'This old chap,' Norton said. 'You met him then?'

Sam nodded. 'I worked out where he lived. A huge old place in the casbah called Dar Portuna. It looks abandoned, but it isn't.'

'And you're going to take that back to him?'

'Yes. This evening.' He walked on, thinking about it all again. Langham had talked for hours yesterday, but he hadn't actually *answered* anything. Was he hiding something? Was there another way to find out?

'You all right?' Norton said, when they arrived outside a modern-looking building near the American Embassy. 'You've hardly said a word.'

Sam nodded vaguely. 'I was just thinking . . . how long has there been an Interpress office here in Tangier? Do you know?'

Norton chucked the end of his cigarette into the gutter. 'I do, in fact. We've been here since nineteen twenty-one, venerable establishment that we are. They told me that at orientation last week. Don't say I never listen.'

1921. Sam tried to keep the excitement from his voice, but it was no good. 'Do you have archives, in there? You must, right?'

'Of course, in the basement.' Norton narrowed his eyes. 'Why, what are you after?'

Sam felt as if his skin was fizzing. If something had happened at Dar Portuna back in July 1928, there was every chance it might have made the papers, especially in a town like Tangier.

'I don't know. I've been writing about the twenties, right? Nineteen twenty-eight. Is there any way I could look through your archives?'

'They're off-limits to civilians, staff members only, I'm afraid.' Norton paused. 'I mean, *I* could look for you, if it was for something specific.'

'You could? Today? That would be—'

Norton cut him off with a snort. 'Not today. I do actually have to work sometimes. It'd take me an age to trawl through a whole year's worth of papers.' Sam's disappointment must have shown, because Norton sighed. 'Look, if you could narrow it down to a particular week, it would be easier. And if I knew what to keep an eye out for . . .'

Sam was barely listening. His mind was flying back to his room at Madame Sarah's, where he'd left the writing case and the strange, undelivered letter.

I am sorry.

'What about a date? An exact date?'

Norton raised his eyebrows.

'28th July 1928,' Sam said quickly, the date escaping his lips before he could stop it. He felt as if he was spilling a secret, but he wasn't, was he? He hadn't really said anything.

'I'm guessing you want me to look now,' Norton said, 'before you see your old man?'

Sam swallowed. 'If you could. I'm due there at five.'

'All right, I'll do my best.' Norton looked down at the suitcase. 'Want to leave that here for a few hours, rather than dragging it around? I can ask them to keep it behind reception, if you like. Don't want it getting nicked.'

Sam followed Norton through the glass doors, his mind jumping, trying to ignore a vague sense of guilt.

28th July. The date at the top of that desperate letter; perhaps the date when everything changed.

One day, I hope you'll understand.

CORPSE REVIVER NO. 1

Take a pony of Italian vermouth and a pony of Calvados. Add a jigger of Cognac. Shake well with lump ice and strain into a cocktail glass. Drink before eleven a.m. to awake the dead.

Back then, it was impossible to tell what was real. We all of us had our masks, servant and lord, demimonde and diplomat. No matter that some of the masks were made from silk and diamonds, and others from sack and tailor's chalk. They all worked the same. They all hid as much as they revealed.

The crowd at Dar Portuna was no exception. Lady Bailey's mask was made from thin clouds of opium smoke, Bouzid's from calm and stony silence. As for Langham . . . I couldn't see his so clearly. After the gift of the book, I thought he might have sought me out for another conference. But one day became two, became three, and I barely saw him.

Often he was gone very early, where I didn't know. Sometimes, he would appear on the landing upstairs when I could have sworn he was out. At other times, I would hear the gramophone playing in his study and peer through the window to find the room deserted.

There was no one I could question. Apart from Bouzid and me – and the women who came early in the mornings to clean – Langham kept no other staff. It seemed strange: according to *The Gentleman's Guide* wealthy men were supposed to employ a household. There were whole chapters on how to get the best out of one's valet, but Langham didn't employ one of those either.

At the inn, people gave themselves away by their actions, by their words, by their tongues soaked in sangria. I saw none of that from Langham. And so, although I tried to wait and listen patiently, curiosity soon got the better of me.

It was my fifth day at the house, and I was beginning to find my stride in the kitchen, feel some tiny glimmer of security in my little servant's bedroom. That morning, Lady Bailey went out on a call and Bouzid left to see to some business in town for an hour. Monsieur Langham, I had been informed, would not be back until evening. Evidently, they had decided I was trustworthy enough to leave alone. For the first time, Dar Portuna was mine, and I intended to take full advantage.

A minute after Bouzid closed the gate, I crept from the kitchen to the bottom of the stairs. My chest felt tighter than ever beneath the bindings, my ears straining for any sound of life. I hesitated, one foot raised. I had no reason to go up there; as at the inn, my room and my work were on the ground floor. Upstairs was a different realm. One that might spell trouble. The step creaked as I set my weight upon it.

'Hello?' I called, into the silence. Nothing. I took a breath and walked carefully up the stairs, until I stood, nerves twitching, on the landing. The room to the right was Lady Bailey's; I could see a chaos of strewn clothes and stockings through the open door. And to the left . . .

'Hello?' I murmured again, though I had no idea what I would say if anyone answered. Silence. Before I could think about it, I walked quickly along the corridor, reached for a handle, and opened the door to what I thought must be Langham's bedroom.

It was the finest room in the house. Windows opened on two sides, one on to the greenness of the garden, the other on to endless blue: the Mediterranean – my first love – throwing herself into the embrace of the Atlantic. Had I been Langham I would have lain in bed all day and drowned myself in that blue. The thought gave me shivers. His bed stood against one wall, the mosquito net tied back, the cotton sheets pale and smooth. I lowered my palm to the pillow, and was overtaken by an image of my own head resting there.

I snatched my hand away, but it was no use, an aching heat was pulsing through me, spreading through my body. I clenched my fingers, trying to will it away. I'd felt it sometimes at the inn. A few years ago, there had been a young gitano who had kissed me in the darkness of the stable, and put his hand between my legs. But I had shoved him away and run for the kitchen. It was too dangerous for me to feel anything like that, to be a woman who could be had. If I had allowed Morales, or anyone else to think of me as a woman, to remember that I was a virgin in a whorehouse, she might have weighed my value differently, and tried to sell me again, as she had done all those years ago.

But Langham was not like the Señor; he was not like any man I had ever met, not even Ifrahim. I let my hand drop, still staring at the bed, not knowing if it was the room

I was aching for, with its quiet luxury, or the man who inhabited it.

Distracted, I went to the wardrobe and pulled it open, as if I'd find the answer there. The scent of sandalwood and musk enveloped me. Here were his suits, a dozen of them, and shelves of neatly folded shirts. Here were stacks of clean, silk underwear, finely woven, and a whole rack of ties. One in particular took my liking, a deep, secretive green; the same colour as Dar Portuna's gate. It slid from the rack like a whisper. Slowly, I looped it around my neck, feeling its coolness against the hot skin of my throat. My hand lingered on the fabric, hanging above my bound breasts . . .

A terrible jangling broke the silence, made my bones leap in my skin and my heart blunder into panic. It was the bell, I realized, the bell at the gate. People hardly ever rang it. Bouzid usually knew who was coming and when. The tie slithered through my fingers. As I stooped for it, I saw something crammed into the bottom of the wardrobe.

Had it not been for the colour, it wouldn't have caught my eye, but that shade of cream linen was lodged in my memory for ever. It was the suit Langham had worn the first day I saw him, in his shining car. Despite my fear, I reached down and tugged out the jacket. It was in a terrible state; it made me angry to see it so ill treated. I began to shake it, wondering if anything could be done, only to stop. One sleeve was stained, spattered cuff to elbow with something dark and rust-coloured.

Dried blood.

The bell jangled again, for longer this time, and I shoved the jacket back into the wardrobe, slung the tie over the rack and ran from the room, slamming the door behind me, my heart pounding down the stairs before I had reached the landing.

What had happened to the suit? I frantically tried to smooth my face, so that whoever was at the gate would not see the guilt or the blood spatters in my eyes.

I needn't have bothered. It was only a small boy, perhaps seven or eight years old. He stared up at me from behind a huge, flat box.

'For Señor del Potro from Señor Souissa,' he told me gravely.

Souissa . . . my mind scrambled before I recognized the name of the tailor.

'Is he your papa?' I asked.

The boy nodded with such wide eyes that I wondered whether his papa had spilled my secret.

As soon as I got the package inside, I forgot all about the tailor's son. In the safety of my locked room, I loosened the string around the box, my hands clammy with anticipation. I'd requested a British-style suit – Langham was British after all – and for a moment, I was afraid that the tailor might not have been up to the job. But as soon as I lifted the tissue paper, I knew I had chosen well, for here it was: a suit of pale tan flannel, as unobtrusive as fine leather. A jacket with notched lapels, a single-breast waistcoat, wider cut trousers that hugged the waist. Three ties, deep red, pale gold and cocoa brown, and shirts, gloriously smooth and unstained. Underwear too, and socks in black and tan. I didn't want to think about how much it would all cost. When the bill arrived, perhaps Langham would summon me into his office to explain myself. Perhaps he would close the door, leaving the two of us alone . . .

I stroked the unblemished sleeve of the new suit. Where had they come from, those bloodstains upstairs? Langham wasn't injured, I was sure of that. And if it was simply an accident, why hadn't he ordered the suit cleaned?

Lifting the clothes aside, I saw something else in the bottom of the box. It was individually wrapped, with a note pinned to the paper.

> *I have listed this on your bill under 'sundries'. I am no expert in these matters, but my daughter advises me that it should suffice. Issac Souissa.*

Inside was a garment made from heavy cotton. From the front it looked like a simple vest, apart from a wide elastic panel, and flat laces on either side to pull it in tight. I struggled out of my jacket, smiling at the memory of old Souissa's horrified expression when I had told him my secret, why I was paying for his silence. He hadn't been happy, but as soon as I had suggested I would take my business elsewhere, his face had changed. He'd swallowed and adjusted his glasses and said, *I'm sure I can accommodate you, monsieur.*

My hands were trembling as I drew on the new clothes: the clean underthings, the brassiere that laced in tight to flatten my chest – no awkward bandages threatening to slip or unravel – the crisp shirt, the beautiful trousers.

It all fit better than a dream, and when I looked into the mirror, I could scarcely believe what I saw. I was exactly what *The Gentleman's Guide* said I should be: neat and elegant without fuss. The pale brown of the suit contrasted with my black hair, the deep red of the tie was a splash of colour, just a hint of excitement. There was a straw hat to go with the suit, trimmed with a brown band. When I put it on, I had to blink hard to stop tears from falling on that perfect cloth. No one would have recognized me as the person I was before, the scruffy, frightened kitchen girl of the Hostería del Potro. Here was my new face. Here was freedom.

I'm afraid I grew rather vain, and forgot all about Langham, and about lunch as I tried to style my hair exactly the way he did, swept back, using a few drops of olive oil in place of pomade. I posed before the mirror, hands in my pockets, leaning as any young, handsome troublemaker might. I was so preoccupied, I didn't even realize anyone had returned, until Bouzid came looking for me.

When I opened the door, my face flushed, he paused before speaking, his eyes taking in the fine, new suit.

'Lady Bailey has asked for an aperitif,' he told me eventually. 'She is beside the pool.' He glanced at me a moment longer before striding away. I smiled to myself as I closed the door. It was as close to surprised as I had yet seen him.

Pernod, with very cold water, that was Lady Bailey's afternoon habit. Her slim figure was not a fashion statement, I knew now, but a consequence of her devotion to her pipe. Most days, I would sneak extra things on to the tray with her drink: a bowl of salted almonds, or clean, brined olives, or tiny triangles of fresh baked bread from the casbah ovens. Sometimes she would eat it. Often not. That day, I loaded up the tray with whatever I could find, my new, fine clothes making me feel generous towards her. Since my arrival she had been distinctly cool towards me. Perhaps I would finally crack her exterior. It wasn't until I stepped on to the terrace that I saw she was not alone.

Langham was kneeling beside her, one hand touching her arm. Where on earth had he come from? I hadn't heard the car in the road, hadn't heard the front gate open at all. My neck prickled. How long had he been back? Had I replaced everything properly in his wardrobe?

I was still standing there when he looked up. For a second, I couldn't hide anything, not my surprise at seeing him, or my guilt at discovering the bloodstained suit. Hurriedly, I looked away.

'Del Potro,' he said.

Two words had never held so much meaning to me before. Were they a statement, a dare, a question? I said nothing. The silence bloomed between us.

'Is that my drink?' Lady Bailey's voice was sharp.

'Yes, madame,' I murmured. Cheeks burning, I set the tray down beside her.

She said nothing more, only stared at me with her eyes shaded and her lips tight. I knew I should turn away, knew I shouldn't look at Langham again, but it was impossible; it was as if my eyes were being pulled on a wire towards him.

'You look very fine,' he said. I opened my mouth to respond, but stopped, for he had stepped forwards until he was only a hand's breadth away. 'Though I'm afraid your tie is a little crooked.'

It was a lie: my tie was perfect. It was an excuse, a reason to come close.

'Here.' He pulled at the knot of the tie, to loosen the fabric. My heart was thundering and I knew he would see the pulse in my neck, feel my quickened breath on his skin. He smiled.

'The red suits you,' he murmured, hands still on my collar. 'Though I think you would look better in green.'

I couldn't move, I couldn't even swallow. In any other moment, that comment might have been a coincidence. Not then. He knew that I had been in his rooms, he knew what I found there . . .

'Where did you get those clothes?' Lady Bailey asked, her voice breaking the taut silence between us.

Langham stepped away. 'From a tailor, in the medina, madame,' I managed to say.

'And how did you pay for it?'

There was no pretence of politeness in her voice. She was suspicious.

Time to play my dangerous hand: 'Monsieur Langham was kind enough to pay for a new suit.' I glanced towards him. 'He said I should look more gentlemanly.'

Langham just watched me, with that half-smile, and didn't say a word.

'Go and fetch another glass,' Lady Bailey snapped. 'And ice. What you've brought is half melted already.'

I nodded and made my escape, staring at the paving stones so as not to see Langham's face. I should've gone straight to the kitchen, but I didn't. I couldn't. My whole body was trembling. Instead, I ducked beneath the fig tree's old branches and leaned my head against the trunk, trying to breathe, trying to slap out the heat that was threatening to burn me up.

The secrets we both held, they were like electric currents, charging us full of potential. What would happen if one of us was revealed? I squeezed my eyes tight. I had to be more careful.

'What are you doing?'

Lady Bailey's voice broke the quiet, and my eyes flew open. But she wasn't talking to me. Her voice was coming from the terrace. I stayed perfectly still, out of sight, listening.

'I don't know what you mean.' Langham's tone was light.

'You know exactly what I mean.' I heard the sound of Pernod being poured. When she spoke again, her voice was soft, almost pleading. 'We know nothing about the boy, Arthur. How do you know someone didn't send him here?'

'Oh Hilde.'

'And why not? For all we know someone picked him up in Gibraltar after the accident. And how did he even get to Tangiers? Don't you think it's odd?'

Silence. My heart felt as though it was trying to punch through the brassiere. Hilde was nearer the truth than I liked. Finally, Langham spoke.

'I left del Potro some money in Gibraltar. Along with the hat.'

'You did? Why on earth?'

The silence stretched. Ten seconds, twenty.

'I can't stop you,' Hilde murmured. 'But please, Arthur, be careful. He isn't who he says he is, I know it.'

Tangier

July 1978

Outside the Interpress building the day felt lazy; an after-school, honey-slow heat that was at odds with the fluttering in Sam's stomach. As he walked, he imagined Norton descending into the basement, pulling out files full of old newspapers, turning their thin, yellowed pages to find . . .

Norton would probably find nothing; he had to be prepared for that. Still, even the vague possibility of seeing Langham's name in fifty-year-old print made his fingers itch.

For the first time in days, his hands were empty. He'd left the writing case in his bedroom and the suitcase was safely lodged behind the reception desk at Interpress. Without it, he felt unanchored, like a piece of litter that might be whirled away on an air current at any moment.

There were a couple of hours to kill before he met Norton again. In the Grand Socco, the streets were filling up with people returning from early afternoon prayers, with boys standing on plastic crates, yelling out their stashes of contraband – sunglasses, radios, batteries, lipstick – with kids in the white uniforms of the French Catholic School, buying glasses of buttermilk.

He found Abdelhamid at the Café Tanger, amongst a group of men who were glued to a fuzzy black and white TV that was showing the football.

'Monsieur Hackett.' Abdel removed himself from the group to clasp Sam's hand. 'Where have you been? Writing your great book?'

Sam smiled back. 'I don't know about great, but yeah, I've been writing.'

Several of the men shifted their chairs to make room for him, without taking their eyes from the game.

'It's good you have come by today,' Abdel said over the noise. 'Mouad is here to visit.' He nodded towards a large man, hovering in his chair as a player approached the goal. 'We can ask him about the writing case, if you are still interested?'

'Yes.' Sam glanced over at Mouad. 'Yes, very interested.'

Abdel took out his sebsi pipe. Eventually a waiter came by, walking crab-wise, trying not to look away from the television. He nodded vaguely when Sam ordered coffee.

'I – have to tell you something,' Sam murmured, once the waiter had sidled away, 'about the case, and about those things I found, the tag and the key.' Abdelhamid nodded, working at the sebsi. 'I figured out what they were,' Sam said in a rush, feeling himself turn red. 'It was a tag for the cloakroom, at the Hotel Continental. So I went there and I asked them if they had any old luggage, and I found—'

The waiter returned, setting down two glasses of nus-nus. Sam stared into the soft, milky coffee. He didn't know how to go on, how to explain that his everyday reality had been altered, ever since he opened the writing case. How he felt possessed by the story; how writing about it was the best and most nerve-wracking thing he had ever done. How afraid he was that it would all amount to nothing.

Around him, the café let out a wail of frustration at a missed goal.

'You found a suitcase,' Abdelhamid said, when the hubbub died down. He lit his pipe, and drew on it a few times before looking at Sam, smiling. 'My friend's boy, Mohamed works there. He told me about a visit from a mad American, who said he was a writer.'

Sam grimaced. 'I'm sorry. I should have told you sooner.'

Abdelhamid waved his words away. 'I said to myself, if Hackett finds anything worth selling, he will bring it to me. If he does not . . .' He shrugged.

'Still, I should've told you.'

'You have told me now,' Abdel said, and drank his coffee.

Sam did the same. He began to feel at ease for the first time in days, the genial noise of the match, the kif and the coffee melting his tension like glue. He glanced over at Abdelhamid. The man was a bit of a crook, no doubt, but he was straightforward about it; he'd never tried to fleece Sam, always charged fair prices for kif. If anyone knew Tangier – as it was now – Abdelhamid did. Which meant he might know of Dar Portuna. Sam scraped the spoon through the coffee residue. Could he trust him? That whole world seemed so secretive; Dar Portuna, Langham, even the woman, Zahrah. He looked up to find Abdelhamid watching him, and swallowed. He had to be careful.

'Have you . . .' He cleared his throat. 'Have you ever heard of a house called Dar Portuna?'

Abdelhamid rubbed a hand across his greying stubble. 'Dar Portuna,' he repeated. 'No, I do not think so. Where is it? In the city?'

'Yes, up in the casbah, by the old walls. Near the Bab al-Bahr.' Abdel's face changed, recognition replacing thoughtfulness. 'You know it?' Sam asked.

'A big house, white walls all around?'

Sam nodded.

'I know the house.' Abdelhamid frowned. 'But not this name, Portuna. We have always called it Dar Nglîz. The English House.'

'Yes.' Sam gripped the coffee glass. 'It belongs to an Englishman. A man called Langham?'

'Langham.' Abdel shook his head. 'I don't know that name.' He cleared his throat. 'People always said Dar Nglîz was cursed. It's a good story.'

'Cursed?' In the noisy, sweat-thick café, the word seemed ridiculous. 'What do you mean?'

Abdel leaned forwards. 'Cursed by Aicha Kandicha. People say you can hear her voice, by the Bab al-Bahr. It is the sea gate, and the sea is hers.'

'Who's Aicha Kandicha?'

One of the other men turned around when he heard that, looked at Sam, and said something in Darija.

'He said,' Abdelhamid translated, 'that you should not say her name so loud, and never after dark, not anywhere in Tangier. Even Americans are not safe from her.' He smiled. 'Aicha is a djinn, a spirit. She will call your name in the night and if you turn around, you will see the most beautiful woman in the world. She likes to drive men mad. So, if someone calls your name near the Bab al-Bahr, do not turn.'

Sam tried to smile. 'I won't.'

'Ah.' Abdelhamid sat back, his voice matter-of-fact. 'The game is finished. Now we can ask Mouad.'

Mouad was an older, broader version of Abdelhamid, in his late sixties but still bulky with muscle, dressed in a sports jacket despite the heat. He had the same quick eyes as his brother, the same easy, mocking smile that widened when Abdel asked him about the writing case.

'You think I remember one bag?' he said. 'We had fifty, at the shop, a hundred!'

'But we had *this* one for a long time,' Abdel insisted, speaking English for Sam's benefit. 'A small case, with gold letters. We had it twenty years, perhaps. You brought it in, I am sure.'

'It belonged to an Englishman,' Sam added hopefully.

'English.' The crease between Mouad's eyebrows deepened. 'Maybe it came from the English police, then. When the station closed, we took many things from there.'

'What things?' The word *police* rang in Sam's ears.

Mouad shrugged. 'Just things. They had a lot. Bags, coats, shoes. Perhaps taken from a person who did a crime, or as evidence. I am not sure. But when the English police left in . . . the fifties?' He looked to Abdel for confirmation. 'They sold all these small things, cheap. I bought some. Maybe that is where the case came from.'

'Was that legal?' The minute Sam asked it, he felt stupid. The brothers laughed.

'They were not going to pay to send it back to England,' Mouad smiled. 'And anyway, no one cared. The crimes were old. The things didn't matter any more.'

Sam frowned. If the writing case had been taken as evidence, what did that mean for the suitcase, abandoned at the hotel, as if someone had just disappeared? What did it mean for Alejandro del Potro? He tried to pull his mind back to the café.

'And have you ever heard of a place called Dar Portuna?' he asked. 'Dar Nglîz, Abdel said it's sometimes called. An Englishman lives there.'

'Dar Nglîz.' Mouad nodded. 'Up by the wall, yes. You think the case came from there?' He glanced rapidly at Abdelhamid. Sam turned, trying to see the other man's face, only to find Abdel looking pointedly in the other direction. 'No Englishman has lived at Dar Nglîz for a long time,' Mouad continued slowly, still looking at his brother. 'Some others, maybe, but not an Englishman.'

'That's not true.' The words were out of Sam's mouth before he could stop them. 'His name is Langham, Arthur Langham.'

Mouad was shaking his head. 'There *was* an Englishman who lived there, many years ago. I was only a boy, but I remember the story. Shall I tell you?' Although the question was directed at Sam, he couldn't help but feel that Mouad was asking for permission. Out of the corner of his eye, Sam saw Abdelhamid give an almost imperceptible nod.

'Yes,' Sam said, watching both men. 'Please.'

'OK.' Mouad shifted, looking a little uncertain. 'They say that, one night, the Englishman heard Aicha Kandicha call his name from the strait. He took a boat out to look for her.' Mouad lowered his voice. 'Of course, the boat sank. They say there was a party that night, up at Dar Nglîz.

They say the man could see the lights of his house as he drowned.'

A shudder went down Sam's spine.

'That must have happened to someone else,' he heard himself saying. 'Not to Langham. I saw him. I spoke to him, just yesterday.'

He looked between the two brothers. This time, it was Abdelhamid who shook his head.

'There have been many rumours about the people who live at Dar Nglîz, but Mouad is right. There has not been an *Englishman* at the house since that day.' He looked at Sam over his coffee, a hint of a smile twitching the corner of his mouth. 'Whoever you spoke to, he must have been a ghost.'

TEMPTATION

Take a piece of orange peel and a piece of lemon peel and twist them together. Soak them in two dashes of Dubonnet Rouge, two dashes of absinthe and two dashes of Curaçao. Pour in a jigger of Canadian Club whisky and stir until inextricably mixed.

He isn't who he says he is.

Identity can be a slippery thing. It is easy to see a fine suit and a hat and say *gentleman* when you should be saying *stranger* or *thief* or *liar.* And yet, we are drawn to those in who we see ourselves, for better or for worse.

I was drawn to Langham, though I couldn't begin to untangle what my attraction consisted of. So I did as I had been brought up to do at the inn: to watch, to listen, to needle out the information I needed to ensure my safety. I began to linger in corridors and doorways obsessively, hoping to catch a fragment of conversation. I dropped whatever I was doing when the telephone rang, hoping to beat Bouzid to it and hear who was calling. I never did. He was too conscientious for that. It did not stop me from trying to wrangle information from him, especially when I found out that he – for all his stoicism – had a sweet tooth. After that, I bought the best sweet pastries from the medina in an attempt to win his trust.

Much good it did me. He told me some things, true; where to find the best olives, and who Lady Bailey paid for opium, which diplomats brought their mistresses to dinner rather than their wives and who could be relied upon to cause trouble at parties. But on the subject of Langham, he was resolutely and frustratingly silent. What was it, that made him dust the sugar from his hands and leave the kitchen, whenever I asked a question about the man we worked for? Had Langham also made him swear loyalty? Perhaps Bouzid had sworn and meant it, unlike me. I still did not know whether I was capable of loyalty.

Perhaps Lady Bailey's words had some impact on Langham after all, for I saw even less of him, and began to wonder if he was avoiding me. His absence affected me almost more than his presence. The heat from our encounter by the pool hadn't yet left my body, and no matter how hard I tried I couldn't ignore it.

Too dangerous, I thought, in an attempt to silence it. Langham thought I was a boy. If I went too far, if he found out the truth, what then? Every night, I found myself reliving the encounter on the terrace in my mind, until I had to open my eyes and read a chapter of *The Gentleman's Guide* to distract myself.

Finally, I couldn't stand it, and one day, having heard the gate close behind Langham, I crept up the stairs into his room. Even before I pulled the wardrobe door open, I knew what I would find. The bloodstained suit was gone. In its place, coiled like a snake, was the green silk tie. A taunt? An invitation? I took it up with shaking hands, and returned to the kitchen.

The days were beginning to turn hotter, as June wore on. That day was the hottest yet, a strange sea fret hanging over the city, turning the sun into a gelatinous orb behind the clouds, making the air cling like gum. Beneath my shirt, the tightly laced brassiere was soon soaked through with sweat, and I longed to rip it off and dive naked into the pool.

Sweat beaded my forehead and upper lip as I worked in the kitchen. It ran down my neck and collected in the hollow of my throat, beneath the collar, where Langham's hand had brushed my skin. I tried to concentrate. I couldn't.

That thick heat sent me into a sort of delirium. When Bouzid came at eleven to inform me there would be seven guests for dinner and to ask what I would need from the market, I gave him a list that might have come from a deranged person. Oysters, with the cool water of the port still in their shells, and honey and champagne, saffron and artichokes. Bouzid seemed on the verge of asking me if I was well, but he knew my ways by then, and only nodded, mopping his own brow. Perhaps he thought it didn't matter that I had lost my mind in the heat; everyone else was likely to be in the same state.

Later, when I looked down at that strange collection of ingredients, I felt the old kitchen-duende shiver rising in me. I had always tried to cook what I thought other people wanted, and yet, here were my own desires, laid out before me. I wanted the colour of the sea and the ochre sunsets seen from the best room in Dar Portuna. I wanted the sting of cold champagne on my tongue and the sear of spice from the medina street vendors. I wanted the perfume of dawn flowers and the must of unswept streets, the pungency of kif and the bitterness of hot coffee, served in a silver pot. I wanted to own the streets. I wanted to stride the world as Langham did. I wanted to be inside his skin.

My hand slipped on the oyster I was shucking, sending the knife slicing into my thumb. Blood welled, a droplet falling into the dish that held the liqueur. I watched it disappear.

I cooked for so long that day, I barely had time to run to my room, scrub the sweat from my neck and change into a fresh shirt. In the mirror I caught a glimpse of myself; it showed a black-haired young man, red high on his cheeks, perspiration shimmering at his temples. Slowly, I drew the green silk tie from my pocket and put it on. Was I making a wrong move? No way to tell, until I saw Langham's face.

I made my way to the lounge, tying the long, white serving apron about my waist. I already knew the drink that I wanted to mix that night. I had found it in *The Gentleman's Guide. Temptation*, it was called; orange and lemon skin entwined, both of them in fine spirits. When Langham stepped into the lounge with his first guest, I already had the drink waiting, and handed it to him before he could ask. His eyes travelled over my face and down to that green tie. Did I imagine it, or did he smile?

Now I have you, that look seemed to say.

A few minutes later, I escaped to the kitchen, leaving Bouzid to deal with the drinks, and the guests. I'd watched them with interest, trying to gauge their relationships with Langham. There was a man with watering eyes, who spoke no English, only French in a thick German accent. A tall, black American woman in a shimmering satin dress who sang a snatch of Italian opera. A florid Englishman in a striped waistcoat that broke every rule in *The Gentleman's Guide*.

I was lingering by the kitchen door, waiting for the signal that they had gone into dinner when I heard footsteps and Langham's hushed voice in the hall. I leaned closer.

'Any word from Cabrera?' he murmured.

'Not yet.' That was Bouzid.

Langham swore.

'Call down and see if there's trouble.'

'Of course.'

I ducked into the kitchen, and was back at the stove by the time Bouzid put his head around the door.

'They are going in to dine,' he told me, and hurried away. To call Cabrera, I supposed.

Trouble, Langham had said . . . I began to arrange the plates, my heart skipping a little. What did he mean? I'd never heard him sound agitated, never heard him swear in frustration like that. I tried to forget about it. It was probably just business, and I had my own to concentrate on, the heady, eccentric meal that had swallowed my day. First came the starter: poached artichoke hearts, each of them holding a single oyster, surrounded by its liqueur and a sauce made from champagne. It smelled earthy, of flesh and salt, like alcohol spilled on sea-wet limbs. I helped Bouzid carry in the plates, but I could not look at their faces, least of all Langham's.

Make them think of you as a kitchen-thing, a duende, a stove-spirit, then they will want you for your usefulness, and will leave you be. That wasn't what I was doing. I wasn't hiding behind a kitchen apron, or keeping to my place at the stove any more. I was out in the open, I was brazen. I watched through a crack in the door as Langham spooned up the oyster and tipped it whole into his mouth.

The next course was different. First, I sent out bowls of water scented with rose and orange blossom, to awaken their senses. Next came chicken, burnished with saffron and lemon, cinnamon, ginger and chilli. It was a dish to revive throats that had been burned by too many spirits, to quicken lips numbed by luxury, to entice them to eat and drink and talk and never stop talking.

During the meal I paced the kitchen like a cat locked in a room waiting for . . . I didn't know what. Something *had* to happen after a dinner like that, after the glances that Langham had given me. When Bouzid came in I almost grabbed him by the arm.

'Señor Cabrera has arrived,' he told me. How could he be so cool? 'Please make him up a plate. He is in the study with monsieur. The other guests will take their dessert on the veranda.'

I nodded. Had I not been so distracted, I might have proceeded with more caution. I might have tried to eavesdrop before approaching the study. As it was, I simply knocked and stepped through the door, thinking only of Langham's face.

'Excuse me,' I said, 'I have brought a plate for Señor—'

I froze. The goat-eyed man, Bautista's contact, was standing before me.

Look away, I screamed at myself, *turn your head*. But I couldn't and he met my gaze, his yellow eyes flat in the lamplight. For one, desperate moment, I hoped he wouldn't recognize me. Then his eyebrows were twitching into a frown, and I knew it was too late.

'Gracias,' he said, staring hard. 'How kind.'

I had to step past him to put the tray on a side table. He watched me do it. I could feel his eyes on the nape of my neck and thought wildly of the Señor.

'Will there be anything else?' I murmured to the rug, wanting to run from the room, wanting to vomit up the crushing fear in my stomach. I didn't want to look at

Langham, not with Cabrera watching me, but when there was no answer, I had to raise my eyes.

Langham's face was unreadable as stone.

'No,' he said coldly, 'now leave us.'

I had to lock myself in the bathroom after that, and tell Bouzid through the door that the heat had made me sick. I was terrified, and furious with myself for being so. I never wanted to feel that way again, as I had been at the inn, voiceless, exposed . . .

I forced myself to think. So what if Cabrera knew me? I had done one job for him, that was all. He could only know what Bautista might have told him: I was a young man who had arrived in La Atunara with no papers and had paid for some new ones. He knew nothing that could hurt me, I told myself.

But Langham had seen the recognition pass between Cabrera and me. He was no fool, and would have guessed in that second that my past was murkier than I had let on. It went the other way too. Langham *knew* Cabrera. Knew him well enough to telephone him, to be concerned with 'trouble'. What was Langham's business?

When I finally emerged from the bathroom, I knew what I would find. Bouzid was waiting in the kitchen, his face as calm as ever. He had served the dessert of iced apricots and candied rose petals without me.

'Monsieur Langham,' he said, 'is in the lounge.'

I nodded. Silently, I shed the apron and pulled on my jacket. Words and excuses crowded to the front of my mind, ready to come spilling out. They would do me no good; Langham had asked for loyalty and now he had found out that I had given him less than the truth.

I opened the door of the lounge without knocking. It was dark in there, as always, lit only by candles and the lamplight that crept from the veranda. I could hear the guests out there, Lady Bailey and the other woman laughing softly, could smell their bitter smoke and kif.

'Monsieur?' My voice was barely audible.

Langham was standing at the piano, turned away, his hands clasped behind his back. He was twisting the ring on his little finger around and around. I had never seen him do that before.

'Why are you here?' His voice drifted to me, like the smoke.

'To be your cook, monsieur.'

He didn't turn around.

'Are you working for someone? I will find out if you are lying.'

Any excuses dried on my lips. We had been spinning such brilliant, unspoken truths between us, he would know a lie in an instant. I clenched my hands behind my back.

'I don't work for Cabrera, if that's what you're asking.'

He turned his head a fraction. 'But you admit that you know him?'

A bloodstained jacket. *And you?* I wanted to ask.

'I don't know him. I only met him once.' I took a step forwards. 'I carried a bag here for a man in La Atunara, named Bautista, in exchange for new papers. Cabrera was the man I delivered it to. I haven't seen him since and I've no wish to again.'

Let that be enough. I stared at the edge of Langham's cheek, at his sharp jawline, at the shadow of stubble beginning to show. *Be satisfied. I did it to get to you.*

'Why would you tell me that?' His voice was soft.

'Because you asked me to,' I said. Langham's face was half hidden in shadow, but his eyes found mine. 'Because I promised you loyalty. Because I want—' My words ran out, replaced by smoke-filled air. *Because I want to crack you open and see what's inside. Because I want to know you.*

'Because you want what?' He stepped towards me, raising a hand to touch my chin.

A knock on the door, as loud as thunder and I stumbled away, tripping on the edge of the rug. Langham moved back too. His face was tight, as if we'd been caught in the act. Nothing had happened, but my whole body was buzzing as if it had.

'What is it?' Langham called impatiently.

The door creaked open. Was it a trick of the shadows, or did Bouzid's eyes flick to where I stood trembling, for one brief second? 'A telegram, monsieur. It is marked urgent. I thought you should know.'

'Fine, I'll be there shortly.'

Bouzid shut the door. For one uncertain moment, Langham looked at me, his lips parted.

'Alejandro—' he began, but the rest was lost in a tumult of voices and laughter as the guests called Langham's name from the veranda, demanding more music, more drinks.

I turned and fled, the danger of it all burning on my lips.

Tangier

July 1978

There have been many rumours about the people who live at Dar Nglîz, but Mouad is right. Whoever you spoke to, he must have been a ghost.

Abdelhamid's words were in Sam's head as he hurried back towards the Interpress building. The late afternoon light was playing tricks, throwing angled shadows everywhere. In their depths, he thought he felt someone watching, a figure whose eyes were moonlight on water and whose breath held the rank, mineral sweetness of the sea as she called his name . . .

He shook his head. It was idle café chatter, the gossip of radio medina, passing from one tea glass to another, that was all. A story told around the sebsi, a tale for dark nights in the casbah, a warning that even foreigners weren't immune to the hidden magic of the city.

He strode across the busy Place de France, the sun in his eyes, not caring about the taxis that blared their horns at him. Mouad and Abdelhamid were wrong, he told himself; Langham was alive and well and living in Dar Portuna, as he had been for years. He was just private, that was all, intensely private.

Still, it was obvious that Abdelhamid knew more than he was letting on. When Sam had tried to press him about the 'rumours' that surrounded Dar Nglîz, Abdel had become strangely vague, before quickly taking his leave. Why didn't he want to talk? Sam's neck kept prickling as if someone was breathing on it, thoughts of drowned men and old crimes filling his head as he ran up the steps of the Inter-press building. Before, he'd been praying that Norton would find something. But now . . .

'Sam Hackett,' he gasped to the woman on reception. 'Here to see Ellis Norton, please.'

She put down her pen. 'He was here a little while ago waiting for you. I'll ring up and tell him you're here.'

He'd sat with Mouad and Abdelhamid for longer than he thought. He only had half an hour to get up to the Bab al-Bahr, to be at the gate just as the afternoon call to prayer ended. It felt like an age before the lift doors opened and Norton appeared.

'Sorry,' Sam rushed, stepping towards him. 'Sorry, I lost track of time, and now I've got to run—' He stopped. Norton was wearing a strange expression, his face flushed. Under his arm was a huge, leather-bound folder. Sam's stomach tightened. 'What is it? You didn't find something?'

'I did,' Norton said breathlessly. 'I bloody did, I hit the jackpot.' He heaved the binder open, balancing it on one arm. 'Look.'

He was pointing at the front page of an old newspaper, one of the dozens sewn into the binder. Sam had to blink hard in order to focus on the close-set type, his eyes still full of dust and sun and smoke.

THE TANGIER GAZETTE
Tuesday, 31 July 1928

31 July . . . Just three days after the mysterious letter. He skimmed over the tight columns, past news of the Summer Olympics in Amsterdam and communists arrested in Paris, to a short article below the fold. A column headed by four, impossible words:

ENGLISHMAN DROWNS IN STRAIT

Spanish police recovered a body yesterday from the western end of Plage Merkala. The body has been identified by personal effects as that of a Mr Arthur Langham, late of Dar Portuna, Tangier. Langham was last seen late on Saturday night, when he is believed to have sailed his yacht, Spindrift, out on to the strait while under the influence of alcohol. The yacht itself was discovered capsized and abandoned shortly after the discovery of the body on Monday afternoon. Investigations are ongoing.

'No.' Sam pushed the article away. 'No, it's a mistake. Or a misunderstanding. I've *seen* Langham. I've talked to him. I was with him last night.'

They say the man could see the lights of his house as he drowned.

'Don't you get it?' Norton was saying. 'Whoever you've been talking to isn't Langham.'

'What?'

'Look, "Investigations are ongoing".' Norton jabbed at the article. 'It means the death was suspicious.' He leaned closer, his voice low. 'Why would someone take a yacht out when they were drunk in the middle of the night? What if Langham did himself in? Or was done away with, for his money?'

Sam's mind was racing. At Dar Portuna, hadn't there been that trophy on the shelf, proclaiming Langham the winner of a sailing race, an experienced yachtsman? Why would he capsize on a summer's night in familiar waters? He shook his head. 'It doesn't make sense. I've been talking to . . . Who the hell is it if it isn't Langham?'

The minute he said it, a face came to mind, sullen, beneath a pale hat, and a name: Alejandro del Potro.

'That's what I'd like to know.' Norton's face was alive with interest. 'I think you might have stumbled across something here, Hackett. And *someone* wants to keep their identity quiet, hence the notes, the secrecy.'

Sam couldn't answer. The writing case had come from the police station, taken as evidence, or from a person who had committed a crime.

A, I am sorry. One day, I hope you'll understand.

'My god,' he heard himself murmuring.

'My god indeed.' Norton's eyes were bright. 'OK, here's what we do. You go back there tonight and act like nothing's happened. Plumb the old man for information, when he came there, what he does for money, all of that. Ask about the yacht if you can manage it in a roundabout way. Keep an ear out for anything suspicious, and don't let your guard down. I'm going to talk to editorial, phone around, see if I can find anything else about this Langham or his death—'

'No!' Sam stepped away from Norton. 'No, don't do anything, please. Just let me . . .' He tried to think. This was *his* story, and it was running away from him in Norton's hands. He had to get it back under control. 'Let me talk to the man first. We might be jumping to conclusions. There might be a simple explanation for all of this.'

Norton didn't answer.

'Ellis, please.' Sam took his shoulder. 'This is my discovery, after all.'

For a moment, he thought Norton would refuse but finally, he sighed. 'Fine. I won't mention it to anyone yet. I'm going to keep looking though, and I want to hear what happens as soon as you're out of there.' He checked his watch. 'Speaking of which, shouldn't you get going?'

Sam glanced at the clock. It was quarter to five. 'Damn!' He wheeled towards the door, only to stop. 'The suitcase! I need it!'

Norton was hurrying towards the reception. 'Jan,' he called to the receptionist, 'give Mr Hackett some petty cash for a taxi, will you?'

The receptionist frowned as Norton disappeared into the room behind her. A moment later she was taking a lockbox from under the desk and counting out a handful of coins. Sam checked the clock again. He felt sick. If he was late, would Zahrah be there to open the door? Or would he have missed his chance?

'There you go,' the receptionist said, pushing the money towards him.

'Taxis can get through as far as the Bab al-Bahr, can't they?' he babbled, fumbling the cash into his pocket.

'I think so,' she said, bewildered.

Then Norton was back, swinging the suitcase over the reception desk.

'Thanks.' Sam grabbed it. 'I don't know if I can pay—'

'Don't worry, call it an advance. Now go!'

Sam barrelled out of the Interpress doors, almost knocking down a man on the other side. He made for the line of grand taxis that waited by the kerb at the edge of the Place de France. Unlike the cheap, petit taxis that zipped about, crammed with people on different journeys, these cars were almost always empty, reserved for rich people, for long trips. He'd never had the cash to take one before.

'Bab al-Bahr,' he gasped to the first man in the line. 'Please, quickly!'

The taxi driver waved his hand. 'Not far enough,' he said, flicking ash from his cigarette. 'Take a petit.'

'Here.' Sam shoved the pocketful of dirhams at him. 'I'll pay you that, just get me there as fast as you can.'

The man's eyes widened in surprise. A moment later, he threw away his cigarette and was climbing into the car, motioning for Sam to get in. Then, they were speeding into the traffic, almost blindsiding a motorbike.

'When's the call to prayer?' Sam yelled over the man's radio, blaring out a French rock song.

'For Asr?' The man checked his watch. 'Soon.'

'How soon? I need to be there before it ends!'

'Vale!' The driver put his foot down, cutting off another taxi.

As they turned on to the Rue d'Italie, Sam heard the first crackle of static. The muezzin's voice began to echo from somewhere above them, competing with the noise of the traffic. *Come on*, Sam begged silently.

The driver slammed his palm to the car's horn, trying to ram his way through the crowds of people spilling from the medina on to the street. They ignored him, for the most part. Finally a gap opened, and he sped forwards. Sam was thrown back in the seat as they raced up the steep road, the taxi's engine whirring and struggling. The call followed them, taken up by one loudspeaker after another until Sam felt as if they were racing it to the top.

With a final rev, the taxi screeched around a corner, beneath an archway and into a ramshackle square. Ahead, the Bab al-Bahr loomed. It was as far as they could go; the streets of the casbah were too winding, too narrow for cars. The taxi driver stomped on the brake just as the muezzin's voice began to fade.

Shoving his way out of the car, Sam gasped a few words of thanks before setting off at a run, the suitcase clutched in his arms, towards the old sea gate.

Please be there, he thought, as he ran down the steps on to the perilously narrow walkway, collapsing against the wooden door with a *thud*. Almost instantly, it creaked open an inch to reveal the young woman. She took in Sam's sweaty face, his heaving chest.

'What's wrong with you?' she said.

'Nothing. I just . . . ran . . . to get here on . . . time.'

She looked at the suitcase in his hands.

'Come in then.' Her voice was quiet.

They walked through the overgrown gardens. With every step, the city outside the walls receded; the fumes and radio fuzz and traffic became a distant memory.

'You look strange,' the woman said, frowning at him as they approached the back door.

Sam realized he'd been staring fixedly at the house. 'I'm fine,' he said, though he knew he wasn't. There was sweat coating his back that had nothing to do with the heat. Who was waiting for him inside? 'Could I have a glass of water?' he asked.

She shrugged and poured one from a jug on the sideboard, where a lace handkerchief kept off the flies.

He drank slowly, trying to calm himself.

'Thank you,' he said, handing the glass back. 'It's Zahrah, isn't it? Your name?'

She nodded briefly. Today she was wearing denim shorts, a faded blue t-shirt. Her nails were stained yellow, as if she'd dipped her fingers into pollen.

'Is Mr Langham . . .' The words from the newspaper article nagged at him, like someone whispering in his ear, even as he tried to speak. 'Is he your employer? Do you work for him?'

She half smiled. 'Something like that.'

'For how long?' he pressed, his voice low. 'I mean, how long have you worked here?'

'About five years.' Somewhere in the house, a door creaked. 'Go on,' she said, motioning to the corridor. 'You're expected.'

Sam hesitated. She seemed like a bridge between times, this woman; a real person in a place of shifting, unreal things. *How did you come to be here?* he wanted to ask. *Who are you? Do you live here? What do you know about all of this?* But she had turned her back and was clattering at the sink. She wouldn't talk to him, he sensed, until he'd spoken to the person waiting in the study.

The man was standing at the window looking out on to the garden, his hands behind his back, twisting a ring on his middle finger around and around. For a long time, Sam just stood in the doorway, unable to speak.

The body has been identified by personal effects as that of a Mr Arthur Langham.

'Did you bring it?' a low voice asked.

'Yes.' Sam's throat was dry, despite the water. 'Yes, it's here.'

He took a step into the room, then another. Finally, the man turned.

'Good.' His eyes flicked to the case. 'A drink first?'

'Yes,' Sam said automatically before remembering Norton's words about staying on guard. 'I mean, no thanks, not just now.' His face was burning, and he knew he must look awkward. Somehow, he couldn't remember how to act normally. All he could think about was Mouad's story and the words *Englishman Drowns in Strait*.

The man frowned at him. 'You're different today,' he said. 'Yesterday you were so full of questions. What's changed?'

'Nothing,' Sam said quickly. 'I mean, I'm just trying to get my head around all of this, you know, first the writing case, then you and this house . . .' He trailed off, knowing he sounded false. 'Here,' he said, holding out the suitcase. 'Don't you want to see it?'

'Of course I do.' The man had a drink in his hand, and was moving stiffly towards his chair. 'Of course. But you must understand, Mr Hackett, that you are bringing me the past, things which have lain undisturbed for a long time. A rusty knife can still be dangerous.' He took a sip of the drink, and motioned to the case. 'Show me,' he said.

Hands trembling, Sam knelt down on the sun-faded rug and pressed the clasps of the suitcase.

'It was locked when I found it,' he murmured. 'I opened it with the key that was hidden in the writing case.' The man said nothing, his worn fingers gripping the glass tightly. With a breath, Sam pushed the lid open.

The case was in disarray. The linens and collars were jumbled together, the suit trousers balled up, the jacket half-inside out. The book had been shoved clumsily into one corner, its cover bent, the bottles and packets ripped from their holders. Sam stared at it all, horrified. He'd packed it carefully, just the way he'd found it, except for the passport, which he'd slid down one side.

Frantically, he began to search through the muddled clothes. It was not a big case; it should have been impossible to miss that smooth, green card. When his fingernails found only the suitcase's lining, he felt a stab of panic. Had he left it in his room? No, he remembered packing it. The old man knew something was wrong, he was leaning forwards, the drink forgotten.

'What is it?' he demanded.

'The passport.' Sam forced himself to look up. 'It's gone.'

The man's eyes were hard. 'What are you talking about?'

'The passport, belonging to Alejandro del Potro,' Sam said, pushing hopelessly at the clothes. 'I don't understand, I put it in myself, this afternoon. I haven't—'

I haven't taken my eyes off it, he was going to say, but that wasn't true. He had. He'd left it at Interpress, and Norton had been the one to fetch it from the back room . . . He let out a noise of frustration. 'That bastard, he took it.'

'Who?' The man leaned forward.

'Ellis Norton, a journalist from Interpress.'

'A journalist.' The man's face was tightening with anger. 'What have you told him about me? What do you know?'

'What could I have told him?' Sam shoved himself to his feet, his temper flaring, kindled by Norton's actions, by the way his story was being twisted into something rotten. 'I don't even know who you are! Arthur Langham has been dead for fifty years. That's why Norton took the passport. He wants to know who you are and what you had to do with Langham's death. And so do I.'

The man stared. 'I never said I was Langham,' he spoke slowly.

'But you let me believe it.'

'Yes.'

'Why?' Sam swallowed, trying to tamp down the anger. 'So I would give you the case? It never even belonged to you.'

The man didn't answer. He just stood, staring down at the suitcase, with its old, jumbled possessions.

'What will he write about me,' he said, eventually, 'this journalist? How much information does he have?'

Sam sagged a little. 'I don't know. He wanted to talk to his bosses, start digging for more information about Langham. I asked him to wait until I'd spoken to you, but obviously . . .' Sam shook his head. Despite everything, he felt guilty. 'He thinks that Langham's death wasn't an accident. He thinks it might have been suicide. Or – or murder.' He glanced at the man. For all he knew, Norton was right, and he was talking to a killer. 'He probably thinks it will make a great story, get him the front page.'

The old man shook his head. 'Why did you have to stir this up? You don't know what you've done.'

'Then *tell* me. Tell me what really happened, who you are, and maybe I can stop him. Please.'

For a long moment, the man held his gaze. There was defiance in that expression, and anger, and something else as well; a hint of resignation.

'There's brandy on the bar,' he said.

Sam knew an instruction when he heard one. He went to fetch it, searching through the forest of bottles until he found one marked *Fundador*.

He turned to find that the man had pulled the case towards him. He was holding the book, *The Gentleman's Guide*. Sam watched as it fell open.

'If you want to play the game,' the man said softly, 'you have to learn the rules.'

Sam almost took a step back. The man's voice had changed completely. It was lighter, softer, an accent replacing the clipped British tones.

'Who are you?' he asked. 'Are you A—'

'Yes.' The stranger looked up at him with a twisted smile. 'For this story, I am Alejandro del Potro.'

SANGAREE

Take a jigger of Old Tom gin and two teaspoons of sugar syrup. Shake with ice and strain into a chilled glass. Slowly pour over a pony of port wine so that it sinks, like blood in water.

My life at Dar Portuna began to change the night I dreamed about the Señor.

I dreamed that I stood beside his corpse, laid out on a slab as he had been on the floor of Elena's room, the pink rug still stained beneath him. His head was tipped back; the ragged wound through which his life had escaped was dark as a wolf's mouth. I approached, a step at a time, to peer into his still face, to touch his cheek and make sure he was dead. Only then did I realize something was wrong. His neck was still bleeding, a slow ooze at first, then more, welling up, splashing to the plinth, scattering droplets across my suit. The stench of Scotch came with it and I let out a cry but hands were seizing me from the darkness . . .

I opened my eyes. I was in my little room at Dar Portuna, pale light filtering through the window. A dream. Nothing but a dream. Nevertheless, the memory of blood remained, the faint scent of it. I stumbled from bed to push open the shutters and let the morning in.

The air was damp, filled with sea mist, not yet burned off by day. It clung to the roses that surrounded my ground-floor window. I breathed in deeply, and caught the smell of petroleum. Had Langham ordered the car already? Thinking about the previous night made my skin tingle with nerves. What would have happened between us, if Bouzid had not knocked on the door? What did I want to happen? Langham wanted me, I was sure, but as Alejandro. Would it be different if he knew the truth? And say *I* wanted *him* in the same way, say I allowed things to happen – what would that make me? Cook or servant or whore? Despite myself, my hand strayed down my body, past my waist, to touch the silk underwear.

My fingers came away tacky with blood.

I froze in utter horror. Then, in a rush, I realized what was happening. It was my course, my damn monthly course; the one thing I had forgotten about in my preoccupation. I swore and swore again, my eyes burning. The underwear was stained, my thighs streaked with dull red. I pulled back the sheet and saw a small rust-coloured splotch, soaked into the cotton. I ripped away the bedding and bundled it up. I would have to get rid of it, or sneak it into the laundry hamper, so the laundresses assumed that it was Lady Bailey's.

Grabbing out a handkerchief, I wet it from the pitcher and began to scrub at myself frantically. At the inn I had been surrounded by other women, by their cramps and cravings, their drawers full of rags and lint, their belts and pins and girdles to deal with a monthly flow. Here, I had nothing.

I forced myself to breathe, to think calmly. I had to hide it. I couldn't just stay in my room and feign illness until it passed. What if they sent for a doctor?

I found some of the old bandage I had once used to bind my chest and wadded it up, winding the rest around the tops of my legs and my waist. It wouldn't do for long. I needed sanitary napkins, and pins, and for those I would have to go to town, into one of the Spanish farmacias. A young man, asking for such things . . . Would they even sell them to me? Perhaps I could say they were for Lady Bailey.

Lady Bailey. *She* would have something to deal with this. Her room was always in a state of chaos; she might not even notice that anything was missing. It was risky, but what choice did I have?

By the time I made it to the kitchen, dressed and wrapped in the kitchen apron, I felt as if I was going to vomit. Bouzid came in to tell me that madame would take some coffee in the garden. I nodded, and if he noticed that I was pale and sweating, he didn't comment.

The fact that Lady Bailey was in the garden was good. She often sat out for a long time before it got too hot, listening to the birds, smoking endless cigarettes. Her room would be empty.

She was in her usual place, the bench by the lilies. I greeted her quietly, setting the tray down beside her. Between my legs I could feel a creeping dampness and I prayed to any god who was listening that I had tied the bandages well enough, that nothing would stain my beautiful suit.

'He's gone away,' she said, opening one eye to look at me. 'Left a note.' She picked something up from the bench beside her. 'Listen to this. "Gone to Gib. Taken the boat. Back soon." Why would he go off to Gibraltar just like that? We usually go together.'

My hands were clammy in the warm air. Could he have gone to check up on my story?

'I don't know,' I said.

'Did something happen, last night? He was odd after dinner.'

'Isn't that his business?' I bit back the words as soon as I said them, too late. Lady Bailey's face had hardened.

'Do not presume to tell me what is and isn't my business.'

'Of course,' I murmured. 'I am sorry, madame. If you'll excuse me.'

With every step towards the house my heart began to beat faster. She was more alert than I would like, her eyes had none of their usual torpor. I couldn't help that. Surreptitiously, I made a circuit of the house. Bouzid was in the study; I saw him through the window, frowning over something on Langham's desk. I let myself in through the lounge, and crept into the hallway. It was now or never.

Up the stairs, two at a time, thankful for the carpeted runner that dampened my steps. Lady Bailey's door was open, as always. I slipped inside and shut it behind me, just in case Bouzid should pass. I could barely breathe in the perfumed air, especially with the tight brassiere squeezing my chest, but I forced myself to look about carefully. The wardrobe was a mess, silk and lace and linen garments sagging out of it. I checked the shelves in there, searching through bundles of stockings and garters and suspender belts. I tried the dresser next, listening for any sound outside.

I found what I needed at the back of the bottom drawer, shoved into a corner. A whole pile of padded white napkins, a jumble of safety pins, a garter to keep everything in place. I had to stifle a noise of relief as I scooped them up and stuffed them into my jacket.

I was about to push the drawer shut when I saw it: something made of smooth cardboard, stamped with red, hidden beneath the napkins. Whatever it was, I was almost certain it didn't belong in a lady's dresser. I couldn't help myself. With one rapid glance over my shoulder, I pulled it out.

It was a file, covered in official-looking stamps. They were Italian, of which I didn't speak much, but enough to recognize the word *segretissimo*.

Inside were dozens of typewritten pages. I flipped through them, trying to find something to tell me what this file was about; why it was in Lady Bailey's possession. Finally, I found a page covered in drawings, strange angular parts, labelled with tiny numbers and letters. My eyes widened. It was something to do with the military.

I didn't hear her footsteps until it was too late.

Lady Bailey stepped into the room. Her tanned face drained of its colour when she saw me holding those papers.

'I knew it.' Her voice was thick with shock. 'I knew it.'

'Wait.' I dropped the file, holding my jacket closed with one hand, concealing the napkins beneath. 'Wait, it is not what you think.'

'Who are you?' She was frightened, backing towards the door. 'Who sent you here?'

'No one.' I took a step towards her. 'Please, I can explain—'

'Help!' she cried, whirling around. 'Bouzid!'

I threw myself after her, dragging her back with one hand, shoving the door closed and turning the key with the other. In the confusion, the bundle of napkins and pins fell from my jacket, scattering across the floor. She was struggling, shouting for Bouzid even as I tried to cover her mouth, shaking with panic.

'Listen!' I begged, over her shouts. 'Please listen, I'm not – I'm a woman!' I grabbed at her face, trying to meet her eyes. 'I'm a woman. Look!' I gestured at the floor.

For a long moment she only stared at me, breathing hard. Then her eyes flicked to the pins and napkins scattered about our feet. I was about to take my hand away when there was a hammering at the door.

'Madame Hilde?' Bouzid sounded alarmed. 'Madame, are you all right?'

I looked into her eyes. *Please*, I mouthed, and released my grip.

'I am fine, Bouzid,' she said, her voice trembling. 'Fine. I thought I saw a scorpion but it was only an old stocking.'

Through the door I could hear Bouzid's breathing. He must have run up the stairs.

'Are you sure, madame?' he asked after a moment.

'Quite sure, thank you.'

There was a pause. 'Madame, I do not wish to trouble you, but I cannot find del Potro. I did not see him leave the house. Monsieur Langham was very clear that he—'

'I sent del Potro to town.' Our eyes locked as she spoke. 'He is running an errand for me.'

'Very well, madame.' The reply sounded reluctant.

'Thank you, Bouzid.'

Neither of us moved until we heard his footsteps retreat down the stairs. Then Hilde pushed me away. Her eyes were clear, her expression icy.

'Explain.'

I swallowed down nausea.

'I'm a woman.' I forced the words out. 'And I needed . . .' I gestured at the sanitary napkins, my cheeks burning.

Her face didn't change. If anything, it grew colder. 'A fine story,' she said. 'If you've taken any papers, I suggest you give them back, now. You will not get another chance.'

I gaped at her. I'd confessed my secret and here she was, unmoved. 'I don't know anything about papers!' She was turning towards the door again. 'All right,' I rushed, 'I saw the papers, but I don't know what they are. I don't read Italian. I only looked at them because—' The words stuck on my tongue. *Because I want to know what I did for Cabrera. I want to know what you and Langham are involved in*. 'Because I was curious,' I finished, knowing it sounded pathetic.

Her lip curled. 'You expect me to believe that?'

Anger rushed through me, adding its heat to my face, to my stinging eyes. She had no idea, this woman with her fine clothes and her idle life. She didn't know what I'd seen, what I'd done just to be here, just to wait on her and cook her food. Furiously, I shrugged out the jacket and threw it to the floor.

'What are you doing?' she demanded.

I didn't wait, but dragged the shirt from my waistband and hauled it up to my chin.

'There,' I spat. 'Do you believe me now?'

Her eyes were fixed on the brassiere, her mouth open. Then, out of nowhere, she made a noise that was almost a laugh.

'My god. So, in Gibraltar . . .' She met my eyes. 'Does he know?' she asked suddenly. 'Arthur? Does he know about you?'

I let the shirt drop, my anger receding. 'No.' I paused. 'Will you tell him?'

'I don't know.' She crossed the room and sank on to the bed. 'God, I have no idea.' When she looked up at me again, some of the hostility had left her face. 'There's a bottle on the bureau. Bring it here, would you? And the glass?'

It was gin, half empty. She poured out a measure, splashing her fingers as she did, and drank it down.

'This still doesn't explain why you followed us here,' she said huskily, pouring another measure. 'I need to know why you did that.' She swallowed again, before grimacing and shoving the bottle in my direction. 'Here, drink if you need it. But talk.'

In that cluttered bedroom, with the curtains billowing at the open windows, I told her a story. It held some of the ingredients of my own, only measured and mixed differently. In it, Elena and I became the same person. The Señor became a rich man who had made promises of love to me, only to break them and grow violent; the murder became an attack, which I had fled, in fear of my life. I became a terrified woman, alone on the streets, who had sought safety in men's clothing.

'I had nowhere to go, no friends, no money,' I told her, the gin stinging my dry throat. 'You and Monsieur Langham were so kind to me that day. I thought, perhaps, you would be kind to me again. And I couldn't stay in Spain. I was too afraid that he . . . that the man I mentioned would find me, and drag me back. I couldn't let that happen.'

I risked a glance at her. She was staring at her hands, at the faint stripe where a wedding ring had once been.

'Yes,' she said slowly. 'But you could have told us this. And there are ladies who wear men's suits, you know – I wear trousers, quite often. If you did nothing wrong, why keep pretending to be someone you're not?'

I couldn't keep down a laugh at that. 'They're rich aren't they, your ladies who wear men's clothes?'

'Well,' Hilde said, 'I suppose they are.'

'Then they have a choice.' I met her eyes. 'Would Monsieur Langham have listened to me, that night of the party, if I had come here as a woman? Would he have given me a job, a room, safety? Would you? Or would you have seen me as trouble, as a foolish girl who had gotten herself into a mess, and turned me away, told me to go and find my work on the streets?'

Her face was red. 'It is not that simple.'

I shook my head at her. 'I thought you of all people would understand.'

'Why do you say that?' Her voice was sharp again, but unsteady.

I hesitated. I had to win her trust, if I was to stay in the house. I pointed to her ring finger. 'You're running from something. If you weren't, you wouldn't be here, in Tangiers, with a man who isn't your husband. You wouldn't be smoking as much as you do, and drinking, if you weren't trying to forget.'

On the floor near by was her tray, with its opium pipe and lamp, its little tweezers and pots. For a moment, her face was pinched and I thought she would be angry. Then, she sagged and reached for the bottle again.

'Am I that obvious?' she asked, and there were tears in her voice, like the air before it rains.

Over the next hour she told me about herself, between sips of gin. I drank too, to seem companionable, and as the liqueur disappeared she grew warmer with me, as if confiding to a friend. I believe she forgot all about the papers in the drawer, about my revelation. She was caught in the pattern of her own past, in the aching relief of confession.

Her story began with a marriage to a wealthy Italian businessman, followed by an idyllic honeymoon that went sour the moment they arrived back at his family home in Milan.

'He turned overbearing, controlling, none of the things he had been when we were courting. He wouldn't let me see my friends. He said they were offensive, though before he had spent nearly every day in their company. And his business –' she laughed, tears wetting her eyelashes, loosened by the gin '– I had never asked much, you see, before the wedding. I knew he owned factories that made parts. I thought the details too dull to bother with.' She drank. 'But then the conferences began, the dinners, and I saw the sorts of people who attended, I heard them talk, discussing armaments and weaponry as if they were sweets.'

She looked at me. 'A British wife with government connections is a useful thing in the arms trade. That's how he saw me, a tool in his negotiations. I couldn't stand it. Finally, I told him I was leaving.' She drained the glass. 'He disagreed. He tricked me into going to our country house, in the middle of nowhere, and locked me up there until he was sure I was with child.'

She held her hand out for the box of cigarettes on the dresser, and I handed them to her, helped her light one. 'He thought that would stop me, you see,' she said. 'He was wrong. One night he left me alone, and I ran. I caught a train to the nearest town and I fixed the little problem he had given me. You can do that, you know, with enough money, even in places like Italy.'

Her hand was trembling as she took a drag on the cigarette.

'Then I did exactly the same as you. I got out of the country. I knew he'd never agree to a divorce, and that I wouldn't be safe, once he discovered what I'd done.'

'Where did you go?' I asked it quietly.

'France,' she said, ignoring the cigarette ash that fell on to the sheets. 'Back to the Riviera. I had friends there. I thought about going home to England, but I was scared my family might intervene, send me back to Francesco. So I floated between Antibes and Nice, keeping as quiet as I could. That's where I met Arthur, a year ago, at the Beau Rivage.'

There was something in the way she said it, softly, quite different from the terrible matter-of-fact way she'd discussed her marriage.

'Were you and he . . . ?' I felt my cheeks burn. Had he looked at her, the way he looked at me, in the shadows of the lounge? I shifted on the bed, trying to seem casual. It was no use. She knew.

'Yes,' she said. 'Yes, we were lovers.' She smiled and took another drag of her cigarette. 'For a little while anyway. But the thought of it all growing hateful and burning out, it was too much for me. Arthur felt the same. He has so many other concerns. We soon realized we were much better suited as companions.'

I looked down at the floor, more confused than ever. Beside the bed were the papers, spilled from their file. Had she drunk enough to talk about them?

She followed my gaze, and sighed. 'Insurance, against my husband,' she said, stirring the papers with a bare toe. 'They're blueprints. Original copies. I stole them when I left, and told Francesco that unless he leaves me alone, they will find their way into the hands of every foreign military attaché I can think of.' She smiled. 'It is the only language he understands.'

'I'm sorry,' I told her.

'So am I. But we're here now, aren't we?'

Sitting on that rumpled bed, we looked at each other.

'I won't tell Arthur,' she said abruptly, stubbing her cigarette in an overflowing ashtray on the bedside table. 'But you will have to.'

My stomach tightened with nerves. 'What will he do?'

'Honestly?' Her eyes travelled over my suit, my tie, my reddened face. 'I have no idea.' After another moment she smiled, like the sun through cloud. She was looking at the napkins on the floor. 'Do you really need those?'

When I grimaced and nodded, she let out a laugh.

'Go and use my bathroom, then. You don't want Bouzid walking in and surprising you.'

I found myself smiling at that, as I collected them up. 'He's suspicious enough already.'

'Oh, he knows something's up with you, just as I did.' She laughed again. 'Poor Bouzid, when he finds out.'

I made for the bathroom door, my head swimming from the gin and the smoke and the knowledge that someone at Dar Portuna could see beneath my mask.

'Alejandro.' Hilde's voice stopped me. 'Tell Arthur soon. He is not a man to keep things from.'

Tangier

July 1978

Birdsong, that was what he heard, sweet and scattered and echoing back from high walls.

Sam opened his eyes. Sunlight was spilling past the heavy velvet curtains, revealing a blaze of greenery beyond. He blinked hard, and a low bronze table came into focus, covered in empty glasses and plates and oil-slicked dishes. Dar Portuna, he realized. He was still at Dar Portuna, waking on one of the old, sagging sofas.

He pushed himself up to sitting, massaging his stiff neck, and a thin embroidered blanket fell to the floor. Someone must have covered him with it in the night. He had no memory of falling asleep. He remembered talking until very late – or rather listening – to a story of another time. He'd drunk brandy at the border of Gibraltar, starving and sun-struck. He'd been a terrified smuggler's accomplice, then a fierce young cook trawling the markets of the medina, spinning truth potions out of spice and liqueur. He'd met Langham all over again, this time through Alejandro's eyes. He'd fought to build a new life amongst the splendour and squalor of this city.

Of all the Tangiers tales he'd heard, it was the best.

But now, his head was pounding as he eyed the empty glasses on the table. It had all been too much, a wild concoction, as many flavours as words. He rubbed at his eyes, trying to remember the last thing he heard before he fell asleep. Something about a discovery, two women seeing each other clearly for the first time. He clambered to his feet, swaying, and made for the garden door.

The sun made his eyes water, but the air was a balm, each tree clinging to a faint halo of coolness. Water droplets still lingered in the shade. He was brushing his hands through them when a figure emerged at the other end of the veranda.

It was Zahrah. She was scattering handfuls of crumbs out into the garden. A little brown bird flew down and started to peck up the bits of bread.

'Hello,' he called, his throat dry. 'I – fell asleep.'

'I know.' She dusted off her hands as the bird flew away and, for the first time, looked at him with something like a smile.

'We talked all night,' Sam said, embarrassed, walking across the cracked tiles. He glanced up at the house. 'Is . . . ?' He still wasn't sure what to call the person he'd spent so many hours listening to.

'Ale's asleep,' Zahrah said, turning away. 'Will be for a few hours yet.'

Ale. Sam tested the name . . . Alejandro. Alejandra.

'You must have thought I was pretty stupid,' he said, remembering his demands to see 'Langham', his insistence on talking to the 'old man'.

She shrugged. 'People see what they want to see. You came here with an expectation.'

He winced. 'That's true.'

She smiled a little more. 'Ale has fooled smarter people than you, Mr Hackett.'

He didn't take offence. He deserved it. 'It's Sam,' he said, closing one eye, as his headache surfaced again.

'I know.' She jerked her chin at the kitchen. 'Do you want some breakfast?'

At the huge old table, she set him to picking mint leaves from the stems while she made coffee. He watched her move around the kitchen, easily, quickly, a little carelessly. She was in control here, he realized. Ale had talked last night of the safety that could be found in kitchens, the power and control that came with feeding people. Had this young woman learned the same?

For all her new friendliness, Zahrah didn't look at him again. By the time he'd got through half the mint stems, she'd shoved a basket of bread and a jar of honey on to the table, a bowl of plums and a dish of what looked like soft, white cheese, drizzled in oil and fresh herbs. Last came the coffee, very strong, poured into tiny, chipped cups.

She dropped on to a stool opposite him and didn't wait, but scooped up a bit of cheese with a wedge of bread. Foggy-headed, he did the same.

'So,' she said as she chewed, spooning out some honey. 'How are you going to fix the mess you've made?'

Sam almost choked on the bread. 'What?'

'The mess you have made with the journalist,' she said. 'Telling him about this place, letting him think that there is some scandal to be dug up about Langham and Ale.' She looked him in the eye. 'What are you going to do about it?'

His stomach twisted with guilt all over again. She must have eavesdropped on the conversation, or else Ale must have told her. 'I don't know,' he said. 'First I'll go and find Norton, try to persuade him to drop it.'

'You have to do better than try.' Her face was serious. 'Listen, there's a reason why we are so private. No one, apart from a few trusted people, knows that this is where Ale lives.' She twisted her coffee cup around, obviously wondering how much to tell him. 'Ale has had an ... interesting career. And the name Alejandro del Potro is linked to certain kinds of trouble. If the authorities found out about this place, they would come and look for Ale, search the house at the very least. And if they thought they could tie Ale to a murder, however long ago it happened,' she shook her head, 'they'd use it as an excuse for an arrest, an investigation. You understand?'

He blinked, trying to process it all. 'I think so.' He looked at her, but she was stirring sugar into her coffee, avoiding his gaze. What did she mean, *certain kinds of trouble?* He remembered Abdelhamid's furtive glance at Mouad. Both of them knew something of Tangier's underbelly. Had they heard of Ale? Not for the first time, he felt as if there was a whole other world he couldn't see, operating in plain sight. 'You know I'm writing about Langham and Ale and this house too, don't you?' he asked cautiously. 'Not an article, a book. A novel, maybe.'

She took a piece of bread. 'That's different.'

'Why?'

'Because it's fiction.' She smiled at him then, in a way he couldn't quite decipher. He opened his mouth to ask her what she meant, but she was pulling the bowl of fruit towards her. 'Anyway, that doesn't matter. What matters is that you stop this newspaperman from letting half the world know where to find Ale. Can you do it, Sam?'

It was the first time she had said his name. He fought the urge to smile stupidly.

'I'll try everything I can, I promise.'

She nodded, and carried on eating.

They were both silent as they worked their way through the bread and fruit. Sam couldn't stop himself from sneaking glances at Zahrah's face, and eventually, she caught his eye. He looked back to his plate hurriedly. Another mystery to unravel.

He made short work of the food, despite the rich meal he had eaten with Ale the night before. There had been bowls of olives marinated in herbs, a rich potato tortilla, a dish of softly stewed aubergines and pomegranate that he couldn't get enough of.

'The food last night,' he said, breaking the silence. 'Did you make it?'

'Of course.'

'It was wonderful.'

A hint of a smile returned to her face. 'Ale always says that food is important, that if you can cook, you can discover what people want, and then, you can know them for what they are.'

Sam stopped, in the middle of mopping up all the traces of oil and soft cheese from the bowl with his finger, and swallowed, wondering what she thought he was.

Together, they tidied up, putting the plates into the huge chipped sink. Maybe it was the food, but Sam felt a glow of warmth, completing that simple chore alongside Zahrah. Abruptly, he wanted to stay, wanted to ask if she would teach him how to cook something, so that he could remain in her company in that bright, worn kitchen.

But eventually they were done, and she was stepping into a pair of sandals, taking a djellaba down from a hook behind the door and dragging it over her head, to cover her faded t-shirt and shorts. 'Ready to go?' she asked.

She was the mysterious figure again, the one he had first seen, emerging from the Gran Café de Paris.

'You don't need your disguise, there won't be any letters today,' he said.

She gave him a sarcastic smile in return. 'You try being a woman and walking around this city in shorts.'

She was right, he thought, as he followed her out of the kitchen door. He'd never considered how Tangier might be a different city for her than it was for him – another experience, a different face. One that was less permissive, less open. Just as the streets of La Atunara had been for Ale, without a man's suit.

'Ale wants you to come back,' Zahrah said, as they crossed the garden. 'Later, after you have spoken to the journalist.'

The thought of confronting Norton made Sam feel sick. But Zahrah was right. It *was* his fault; he had to try and fix it.

They used the front gate this time. He held aside the fall of jasmine while Zahrah unlocked it with a huge, old key.

'Not the most convenient entrance, is it?' he said.

'I told you, we don't want people to know about this place.' She locked the gate behind her. 'It's Ale's safe haven.'

They stopped on the nearest corner.

'Well.' For the first time, Zahrah seemed awkward. 'I will see you later.'

'Wait!' he called before she had even taken a step. 'Can I walk with you, for a while? Where are you headed?'

'To the library.' She glanced at his face. 'It's not on your way, but you can walk, if you like.'

They set off together. Abruptly, Sam felt more real than he had for weeks. The sun that shone into his eyes and made his headache worse was *today*'s sun, not yesterday's, not the sun of five deçades ago. He glanced over at Zahrah, smiling foolishly. She caught his look.

'Now what?' she asked, as they passed into the shade of an alleyway.

'Nothing. I was just wondering whether you are as secretive as Ale.'

'I'm not secretive,' she said coolly. 'What do you want to know?'

'Have you always lived here?'

She shook her head. 'I was born in Melilla. You know where that is?'

'Isn't that a Spanish city, down the coast?'

'An enclave, yes.' She quickened her step as they passed a group of men who sat smoking on a doorstep. 'My father was Spanish. He was a soldier in the Legion.'

'And your mother?' He had to hurry to keep up with her.

'She was from the Rif. They were not married.'

'Oh.' He glanced at her, but her face was unreadable as she navigated her way out of the casbah. 'Where are they now?'

She shrugged. 'My father is probably back in Spain. I'm not even sure of his name. My mother couldn't read or write. She left me at a mission when I was a baby. That's all I know.'

He shook his head, his cheeks burning.

'It must have been hard,' he said, idiotically.

She let out a breath of laughter. 'Being on my own was harder. I left the mission when I was sixteen. They found me a job as a child-minder in Tetouan. It didn't work out.' She looked away from him, into the bustle of the medina. 'So I came here. I thought there'd be more work. But I didn't know anyone, and my Darija wasn't very good.'

The market was in full swing, not only with its fruit and spice and food, but with people at the fringes scraping money from stolen goods and scavenged items, with children who watched and hustled for cash, with women who never moved from one spot all day, too tired to lift their hands from their laps. Abruptly, he remembered what Abdelhamid had once said – that there was always more money for an American like him. He hadn't meant physical cash, Sam realized, but the presence of safety. Even when he *claimed* to have nothing, there had always been that ticket back to the States, where four walls and a bed and a meal on the table would be waiting. However hard he found it at home, however much he tried to outrun it, it *was* safety.

'I'm sorry,' he muttered to Zahrah.

She only shook her head at him, knowing, as he did, that the apology was of no use.

'So when did you meet Ale?' he asked, trying to push away the feeling of guilt.

She smiled at that. 'In a café in the Petit Socco, one night about five years ago. I thought I saw an old foreign man, an easy mark. Eventually I realized my mistake, but we were talking by then. Ale spoke English and Spanish and somehow, I ended up spilling everything. Then, Ale bought me a glass of tea and offered me a deal.' She stopped at the edge of the medina. 'I could live and work at Dar Portuna. In exchange, Ale would teach me things, help me study. I only had to promise one thing.'

'What was that?'

She looked at him, her face serious.

'Loyalty.'

NONE BUT THE BRAVE

Take a jigger of brandy and half a pony of Pimento Dram. Add a dash of Jamaica ginger, a dash of fresh lemon juice and a dash of powdered sugar. Shake with ice and strain into a cocktail glass. A drink with a lasting and bitter allure.

Were we brave, back then? Hilde and I had raised our masks a little, and glimpsed each other's real faces. There was a bravery in that, I suppose. The hours that followed our talk passed in a sort of heady gladness. For the first time since Ifrahim died, I had made the first steps towards what might be a friendship with another person. But soon, the gin wore off and I was left with reality: Langham would return, and I would have to face him, I would have to tell a truth that might mean the end of my time at Dar Portuna.

I tried to rehearse my confession, whispering to the fruit I cut for Hilde's supper. I even tried to say it to the mirror, imagining that he was my reflection. I watched my lips part, my lungs fill with breath, but every time I tried to speak, the words turned to dust in my mouth.

'Did Monsieur Langham say when he would be back?' I asked Bouzid, as we drank glasses of tea by the kitchen door, trying to catch the breeze. I resisted the urge to press the hot glass to my cramping belly.

Bouzid took a slow sip. 'No. Monsieur is often away on business.'

His manner was cooler than usual; a few times during the day I had caught his eyes on me. If Langham *did* check on my story while he was in Gibraltar, what would he learn? He knew Cabrera; it followed that he knew Bautista too, however dubious company the smuggler seemed for someone as fine as Langham. Bautista knew nothing about me, I reminded myself; he'd confirm my story, and I would be safe. I was a young man from nowhere, with a few pesetas in his pocket. That was all.

The next day dawned sweltering and muggy, and the hours heaved their way past. I didn't leave Dar Portuna; I was still too nervous about the napkins hidden beneath my trousers, covered by three pairs of underwear. They were hot and uncomfortable, clinging around my sweat-damp legs. Luckily, we had no guests, so there was not too much for me to do. I made small, light meals for Hilde, to try and tempt her, despite her lack of appetite. I made more rustic dishes for Bouzid and me to eat at the kitchen table. When Hilde rang the bell on the second day of Langham's absence, and Bouzid told me to take her some refreshment, I welcomed the distraction.

Perhaps she was bored too, for she beckoned me over to the rug where she lay. The room was dim, shuttered against the heat and I saw that she had been at her pipe, though not enough to put her in a stupor.

'Take that away,' she said, pushing at the pipe with her bare foot. 'Sit and talk with me for a while, so I won't smoke any more.'

I did so, and instead poured seltzer water with ice and mint and made her a drink. She took it, rolling the cool glass against her forehead.

'I won't do it for ever you know,' she said. 'I'll stop, some time. I just need it now. While I'm renovating myself.' She smiled up at me, with her lovely, sad grey eyes. 'I'm trying to outgrow her, Mrs Francesco de Luca. You understand.'

I thought of the woman I had outgrown, hiding beneath her stained apron, looking at the world with her head lowered, like a dog expecting to be kicked.

'Yes,' I said. 'I understand.'

That day passed, quiet and drowsy, and then another. I kept myself busy taking inventories of the bar and pantry, with polishing pans and brining olives. Although none of us said anything, it was obvious we were all anxious for Langham's return.

Hilde was the one to break the unspoken vigil. On the fourth day she emerged at noon, looking clear-eyed and impatient. I was feeling better too, more my usual self. My course seemed to have finished, and my body no longer felt swollen, my breasts had stopped their aches and protests beneath the tight brassiere.

'Bouzid,' I heard Hilde calling, 'telephone Mademoiselle Alisée, tell her that I will come this evening after all. Oh, and could you send my blue gown to be pressed? It is on the table here.'

She came into the kitchen after that, ostensibly to ask for some lunch.

'I can't stand this waiting,' she whispered to me, 'and I don't want to be here when he gets back. I can't lie to him, he'll know something has changed the minute he sees me.'

She stepped away abruptly as Bouzid came in. 'No need to make me supper, del Potro,' she said crisply, 'I shall be dining out this evening.'

So she did, breezing from the house in a cloud of powder and scent and tinkling jewellery as evening began to blossom in the sky above the casbah. In truth, I was pleased to see her out and about again, though the thought of facing Langham alone made me more nervous than ever. Bouzid too told me that he had business in town to attend to, and would not require any supper.

'And Monsieur Langham . . . ?' I asked.

'Will be back tomorrow morning, no doubt,' he said smoothly, before taking his leave.

Alone in the house once more. First I tried the study, but found it locked. Bouzid had taken the key with him, meticulous and mistrustful as always. But Langham's bedroom was open, as clean and cool as it always was. At his dresser I sat and opened his pot of hair pomade, smoothed a little of it over my own short black curls. The scent lingered; wax and attar of roses. It smelled like him. I closed my eyes and breathed it in.

Sunset was orange and ochre, casting a spectacular mural of light on to the white bedroom wall. I stood, staring out at the sea and sky and boats, drifting through colour. It was as if Dar Portuna was a tower at the edge of the world. Slowly, the room turned old gold, then shadowy violet. I sat on the bed and lay my cheek on the crisp cotton pillow, thinking of how different this wide room was to my cramped, creaking cot next to the stove at the inn, with my coverlet of flea-bitten cats, and the rats running across the floor, their claws like the tapping of rain . . .

⋆

I opened my eyes to pitch darkness. For a second, I had no idea where I was, though I could smell roses and the earthy-salt scent of rain on the sea. I could hear wind, mouthing at the walls, sticking its tongues through the gaps in the carved shutters. I pushed myself to my elbows in horror. I was in Langham's room, had fallen asleep, where anyone might have found me.

Eyes wide, I listened. Everything was quiet in the house, only the sound of drenching summer rain and wind, throwing a tantrum-like squall to break the endless, sticky days. I got to my feet, feeling my way in the darkness towards the window. There was a little light from a drowning moon, and I closed the shutters, hoping none of the rain had found its way inside. Out in the corridor, I tried to remember where the switch for the light was. I found it eventually, sending a sickly, yellow glow down the stairs. It flickered as the wind blew the wires and I shivered, more from unease than cold.

No one had returned. I was the sole guardian of Dar Portuna. The house had an abandoned feel to it, as if its doors had been left open to the wind and weather for years as I slept.

In the kitchen I splashed myself a tumbler of cooking wine and sat down at the table, to wait out the loneliness, and the storm. I was nearing the bottom of the glass when I saw something through the window: a flicker in the darkness of the garden, like a firefly tossed between wet leaves. I stopped, the wine halfway to my mouth, sour on my tongue. There, again, a spark, moving in a strange, weaving pattern. Despite the humid air, my body turned cold. It was torchlight. Someone was out there.

Carefully, I set down the glass, keeping my eyes fixed on the light as it swayed closer to the house. Whoever it was, they hadn't come through the front gate: I would have heard. They had come in another way, as I once had, illicitly, like a thief.

I stood, careful not to let the chair squeak on the tiles. There was a knife on the table, the long serrated one for cutting bread, crumbs clinging to the blade. It would have to do. I crept to the back door, keeping to the shadows. The torchlight was nearer now, and I could hear footsteps, the thrash of wet leaves on fabric. When it was within spitting distance I couldn't stand it any more. I shoved the door wide open, the knife clenched in my hand.

'Who's there?' I yelled, as harshly as I could.

The torchlight stopped, not eight feet away. In the rain, I could see a shimmer of drenched fabric, a pair of dark, wet shoes. Whoever held the torch was keeping it away from their face.

'Who's there?' I called again, shifting my grip on the knife. 'If you don't—'

Torchlight dazzled me, shining straight into my eyes; feet were rushing forwards. I yelled and struck out with the knife.

'Del Potro, it's me! It's me, damn you!'

Wet fingers were gripping my wrist. I blinked hard.

'Monsieur?'

With a rush of breath, Langham released me. 'Who else? Put that knife away, for god's sake.'

Stunned, I backed into the kitchen and placed it on the counter. Langham was drenched, not only with rain. As he walked across the kitchen, he left traces of wet sand on the tiles. I had never seen him so dishevelled. He leaned against the kitchen table, his jaw tight, his shining hair matted.

'Monsieur,' I asked, stepping closer, 'are you all right?'

He didn't answer. I saw then that one hand was clasped around his sleeve, blood oozing through his fingers. I made a noise and reached out, but he jerked away.

'Is Hilde in?' His voice was taut.

'No. She is out with Mademoiselle Alisée.'

'Good.' He released a breath. 'That's good.'

'Monsieur,' I said, for he was pushing himself away from the table, walking towards the door, 'shall I call someone? Bouzid, or a doctor?'

'No. No doctors. And Bouzid will not be able to come, he is with the boat.' He paused and looked to where I stood. 'You can help me, del Potro.'

The danger had passed, so why wasn't my heart slowing down?

'Of course.'

'There's a medicine chest beneath the sink. Bring it up, with a bottle of brandy.' His eyes flicked to the darkness outside. 'And lock that door.'

It should have only taken me moments to grab the medicine chest, with its painted red cross, and a bottle of brandy from the pantry, but my hands seemed incapable of doing anything properly. I kept fumbling things. Finally, I made it to the top of the stairs.

Langham had switched off the electric lights. The dim glow of an oil lamp was coming from his room, along with a hissing sound that I had never heard before. I stepped inside, hoping that I had not left the shape of my cheek on his pillow.

The bedroom was empty. Langham had not stopped to sit down. Instead, his clothes were strewn in a trail across the floor, towards his private bathroom. His dark jacket, torn across the sleeve, a sodden tie, gritty shoes and the salt-stained trousers, and finally, a shirt, its cotton pink with blood.

I forgot how to do anything except walk. The bathroom door was open, the soft, flickering light reflecting back from the tiles. I stepped inside.

The hissing sound was that of the shower above the bath tub. Langham stood beneath it, his head tipped back, his eyes closed. The water cascaded over his naked body, across tanned shoulders and down his torso, across his hips, his buttocks, his slim legs, the hair bleached gold by the sun. As I stood there, he raised his arm and blood joined the flow of the water, spiralling from a long cut above his elbow.

A second later, he slicked the water from his face and looked at me.

'Did you bring the brandy?' His voice was low. I nodded, and held out the bottle.

He pulled the cork and drank, his throat funnelling the liqueur into his belly. My eyes strayed downwards, until – face flaming – I had to turn away.

'I'll get some bandages.' My voice sounded odd, echoing. I opened the chest and stared at the items. Finally, I made sense of them, and found a bottle labelled *iodine*. Behind me, the water was shut off with a squeak. I heard Langham sigh, and step from the tub. 'Here,' I said, holding up the bottle. 'This should . . .'

A touch on my shoulder, and I looked up into the mirror. Langham was standing behind me, but in that misted surface, I wasn't certain which was his face and which was my own.

'Leave it,' he said.

I could feel the heat of his naked body through my clothes. His hand moved from my shoulder to my chin.

'Alejandro.' His fingers brushed my lips. 'Why can't I trust you?'

'You can.' I hardly knew what I was saying. His other hand found the side of my leg, my thigh, moving upwards. 'You can trust me.'

The bottle of iodine fell into the box as his fingers trailed from my lip, to loosen my tie, to release the top button of my shirt.

I froze. A second later I was pushing myself away.

'I can't.' I scrabbled for the shirt's button. 'You don't know—'

'Don't know what?' He came forwards, naked still, to grip my arms. 'Tell me.'

He would hate me; he would sneer at me in disgust. He would hide his nakedness from me as if it were something shameful and tell me coldly to avert my gaze, to leave his house.

His eyes were inches from mine. They were so beautiful, golden-brown ringed with black, impatient, searching. 'Alejandro,' he said.

A noise broke from me, a half-strangled sob. 'I'm not what you think.'

His expression changed, turning hard with distrust, and I had to look away.

'I'm a woman,' I whispered bitterly.

When I finally looked back, he was staring at me, his face unchanged. I couldn't stand for him not to believe me, the way Hilde hadn't, and before I knew what I was doing, I was grabbing his hand and pressing it to my chest, so he could feel the brassiere. 'You see?' I was desperate. 'It's true.'

For a long moment he didn't move, only stood there, silent, one hand against my breast. Then, suddenly, he let out a laugh.

'You fool,' he said, leaning close. 'You think I care what you are?'

His mouth met mine, urgent, hungry. My hands found his face, his shoulders, the muscles of his naked back and finally, I was dragging him to me, our bodies were crushing together, as if we wanted nothing more than to be pressed, moulded into one being.

Tangier

July 1978

Loyalty.

Sam sat on the edge of his narrow bed, staring at the writing case and the stack of pages next to it: a story half told. It was a story that had resurrected the past, that had dragged it from a forgotten basement, from beneath dusty piles of wares in a casbah junk shop out into the hot light of the present. *He'd* done that. He had been following this story as if he owned it, as if it was in his control.

But of course, it wasn't. He had barged into a series of events that had begun fifty years ago, and hadn't yet finished. And now there was a chance that someone could be hurt.

If the authorities thought they could tie Ale to a murder, however long ago it happened, they'd use it as an excuse for an arrest, an investigation.

He had to take Zahrah's word for that, but it didn't matter either way. He'd promised.

He hurried down the stairs, the writing case gripped in one hand. What on earth was Ale involved with? If the authorities were a threat, then it must be serious. Part of him felt uneasy, wondering whether he should report

Alejandro del Potro himself. He knew he'd never do that, but what if Norton was *right* to be asking questions? Sam had only Ale and Zahrah's words to go on, and there was still so much he didn't know. Not least that note.

I am sorry.

He screwed his eyes shut.

'Monsieur Hackett!'

Madame Sarah was standing in the kitchen doorway.

'Sorry,' he said, flushing. 'I – what is it?'

Her lips were pressed tight, as if she was working up to something. 'Monsieur Hackett, if you want to stay after this week, you must pay me in advance. I cannot allow any more late rent.'

He stared at her, trying to haul his mind into the present. 'In advance? But . . .' He'd just about been managing to pay a week in arrears. 'Can't we just carry on as normal? I won't be late with it, I promise.'

In truth, he wasn't entirely sure how much money he had left. Most of the cash from the typewriter had gone on rent, the rest on kif and a supply of paper, new ink and coffee and beers.

Madame Sarah looked unhappy. 'My sister says I should not let you stay here unless you pay in advance. Last night, when you did not come back, I thought you might have run off without—'

'I'd never do that! Last night I was with a . . . a friend.' He sounded so guilty. No wonder she was frowning at him. 'OK, I'll pay a week in advance, I swear. As soon as I get back later.'

She looked unconvinced. Not for the first time, Sam wished he was a better tenant. Or a better liar. Behind her shoulder, the clock was pointing at two. He'd have to run if he wanted to catch Norton before he got back to the office.

'Here.' Impulsively, he held out the writing case. 'This is incredibly important to me. Keep it as a security deposit. Tomorrow I'll give you the rent, I promise.' Perhaps he could borrow a few dirhams from Ale.

Madame Sarah frowned at the leather case, with its scuffed corners. 'All right,' she said quietly, taking it. 'But tomorrow, please.'

Sam's hands felt empty as he hurried through the casbah. He stuck them in his pockets, full of kif dust and rolling papers and small change. Facing Norton would be easier in a suit like Ale's, something smart and elegant, rather than his usual scrubby jeans. He straightened his shirt as much as he could before stepping into the El Minzah.

He needn't have bothered. Norton wasn't there. The desk clerk, side-eyeing Sam's attire, told him coolly that Mr Norton had not returned at all that day. Grimly, Sam strode out into the street and started in the direction of the new town. Was Norton putting in extra hours to dig around the archives, looking for information about Langham? He walked as rapidly as he could through the sweltering afternoon, until he saw the brown glass windows of the Interpress building glinting up ahead.

He stopped in the middle of the street, staring at the lobby. What the hell was he going to say? Norton might be a bastard, but he was on the right track, there *was* a scandal to be uncovered, Sam was sure of it. How was he going to convince Norton otherwise? He swallowed hard, and walked towards the building.

The reception was hot, a couple of fans shunting cigarette smoke about the place. The woman from the day before was pushing typewriter keys one at a time, struggling to stay awake.

'Hello,' Sam said, clearing his throat. 'I'm here to see Ellis Norton.'

The receptionist blinked at him. 'Mr Norton? I'm afraid he just went out.'

Sam hesitated. He'd come here ready for an argument. Did this mean he'd have to sit and wait like an idiot until Norton returned? Frustrated, he nodded and turned away, gritting his teeth when he pictured how Norton must have swiped the passport . . .

Sam stopped. The passport. Norton had taken it for a reason. It was proof, he realized, the only concrete bit of evidence Norton had that someone else might have been involved in Langham's death: the only thing that named Alejandro del Potro. If he could get the passport back, Norton would have nothing, just speculation, rumours. No editor would accept an article without verifiable evidence.

Quickly, he searched through his jeans pockets until he found what he was looking for. A business card, crumpled and a little grubby:

ELLIS NORTON
JUNIOR FOREIGN CORRESPONDENT
INTERPRESS

'Actually, do you mind if I wait for him upstairs?' Sam waved the card at the receptionist. 'Ellis and I are working on a story together. I was here yesterday, remember? You gave me some money for a taxi.' He felt as though his smile was creaking.

'That's right,' the woman said, stifling a yawn. 'You were in a rush.'

'I'll go wait at his desk, then.' He moved towards the elevator, his heart beating faster.

'Wait!' The receptionist's voice stopped him. She was leaning over the edge of the counter, holding a pen. 'You need to sign in first.'

Trying to steady his hand, he took the pen and wrote a name in the register.

'Thanks, Mr –' she glanced down '– Langham. You want the second floor. I'll tell Mr Norton you're here as soon as he arrives.'

Sam nodded, and made for the elevator. He'd have to be fast.

The second floor turned out to be a messy open office space, blinds pulled down over the windows to keep out the fierce sun. He expected someone to stop him at the door and ask what he was doing, but no one did. He passed one man snoozing behind a huge stack of files, a woman who was working at a typewriter, her glasses sliding down her nose with perspiration.

'Excuse me,' he asked her. 'Which is Ellis Norton's desk? I'm meant to wait for him and—'

'Who?' she asked, not looking up from her typing.

'Norton, Ellis Norton, he's a junior correspondent.'

The woman tutted over a typo and pushed her glasses up her nose. 'Corner desk.' She jerked her head towards the windows. 'Next to metro.'

Sam had no idea what that meant, but he walked confidently in that direction, until he saw a piece of paper pinned to a cubicle divider that read *E NORTON*.

He was sweating now. So was everyone else in the room, though he wagered they were sweating from the heat rather than nerves. He lowered himself into the chair at Norton's desk, ducking behind the divider.

The workspace was cluttered, carbon copies strewn around a typewriter, newspapers in French and English piled up next to it. This could have been his own life, Sam realized, with a bizarre rush of clarity. If he had followed a different path, if he had studied harder at college and made the right connections, he might have been sitting at one of these desks working, rather than skulking like a thief. He wasn't sure which was worse.

Quickly, he began to search. No one seemed to be looking his way. The only man within eyeshot was smoking and reading a copy of *Al-Alam*. He found a handwritten note and snatched it up only to discover that it was all in shorthand, like a taunt. *Think*. The passport was Norton's proof. He wouldn't just leave it lying about in the open.

Beneath the desk was a squat metal filing cabinet. The top drawer opened with a metallic squeal, and the man opposite gave him half a glance. Sam smiled back. *Be calm*, he told himself.

The drawer was full of cardboard files, all the same shade of beige. The passport could be in any one of them. He started to lift covers at random, peering at the papers inside. They were full of cuttings, edited notes, picture references. He began to scrabble through them faster. It would make him look suspicious, but he didn't care; he didn't know how much longer his nerves would hold out. He opened the fourth file down and felt smooth card beneath his fingers, thicker than carbon copy. He yanked it out.

PASAPORTE.

Thank god.

The photo of Alejandro looked up at him, defiant and sullen. He recognized Ale now, so young, and felt his chest tighten with sympathy, with admiration. What had happened, during those dark, hot days of July 1928? He still didn't know.

Englishman Drowns in Strait.

Skin prickling, Sam shoved the passport into his back pocket. He was reaching down to close the drawer when something else caught his eye, a photograph of a familiar location. He pulled it out.

The picture was black and white and grainy, as if taken in low light, but he could tell it showed the entrance of The Hold. Two blurred figures were standing by the door. He squinted, trying to make them out. Only when he saw the shape of a cigar did he realize that one of the figures was Bet. Bet and Kline, his head near hers, as if in quiet conversation. Sam's fingers tightened on the print. What the hell was Norton playing at? Abruptly, he remembered the intent way the journalist had stared at Bet across the bar, the way he'd feigned drunkenness as he declared, *I've just been hearing the most marvellous stories from Giles. He said that you were a smuggler!*

'Bastard,' Sam hissed.

'Hackett!'

He shot up from the chair, the picture still clutched in his hand. Norton was striding across the office, pale beneath his sunburn. 'What in god's name are you doing?'

People were looking now, but Sam didn't care.

'What in god's name are *you* doing?' he said. 'What the hell is this?'

He threw the photograph at Norton, who barely managed to catch it. When he saw what it was, his face went even paler.

'It's my job,' he said, with deliberate control. 'I'm doing my job, Hack, investigating what I think needs to be reported. This isn't personal.'

'Yeah, right.' People were standing now, craning to see what was going on. *Let them*, Sam thought recklessly. 'Stalking isn't doing a job. Neither is stealing from my suitcase. It's theft.'

'That suitcase wasn't yours,' Norton snapped. 'And that passport is a fake. I called the consulate, they have no record of any Alejandro del Potro—'

'I asked you to wait.' Sam stepped towards Norton. 'There are people who could be hurt by what you're doing!'

'People who deserve it.' Norton shook his head, as if Sam were a child, throwing a tantrum. 'You have no idea, do you, the kind of people you're dealing with? I found Langham's record. He was a crook, just like this del Potro character, or whoever it is living in that house.'

'You don't understand!' He was shouting.

'No, you don't. You're so bloody naive. That lot at The Hold, Bet, Kline, all of them, they're *criminals*. They've charmed you with their stories, flattered you into thinking you're special, but I'm not fooled, I can see them for the scum they are—'

Before he could think twice, he raised his arm and punched Norton square in the face.

BETWEEN THE SHEETS

Take three quarters of a pony each of brandy, Cointreau and white rum. Add just a dash of lemon juice, shake well and strain into a glass. How you drink it is nobody's business.

June slid into July like butter on a hot plate. I was used to Andalucían summers; the fierce sun and the darkness of shuttered rooms, the constant thirst of those who cannot escape the city for mountain or coast, who only emerge in the greyness of dawn to crawl to mass and pray for rain. But Tangiers heat was different. It was the heat of the desert, come to try its luck by the sea. It was an old god, one who laughed to see us sweat and swoon. It found me wild with anxiety and joy and fear and desire shaken up together.

The night with Langham turned into another, then another. My morning meetings with him – ostensibly to discuss the day's menu – would more often than not descend into a frenzy of fingers on buttons and loosened garments, up against the locked door. There was no hiding it from Bouzid, of course, or Hilde. Early one morning she had walked into Langham's room and found me there, in my strange collection of male underwear and the tight brassiere. She had laughed, and I felt a huge wave of relief. I wanted her for my friend.

'I see he took your news well then,' she said, helping herself to a cigarette from the box on his dresser. By the time Langham emerged from the bathroom, Hilde and I were standing at the wardrobe, holding up suits, trying on hats, Hilde with a cravat looped about her neck.

'What's this?' he said, with his secretive half-smile. 'A pantomime?'

'Tell del Potro,' Hilde said around her cigarette, 'that a gentleman *must* have a flannel suit for days like this. A gorgeous, white flannel suit, with –' she rifled through the shelves '– a pale green shirt, or a rose pink.' She held one up beneath my chin. 'Yes! Just like that. You'll look a dream. And a sprig of jasmine at the lapel. The ladies won't be able to keep their eyes off you. Or the men,' she added slyly.

'No, no.' Langham came forwards, his robe brushing against me, his hair still gleaming with water. 'A gentleman is never ostentatious.' He was quoting from *The Gentleman's Guide*, and I smiled at him. 'He does not covet attention but attracts it by way of an engaging ensemble.' He pulled out a saffron-coloured shirt and held it up to my chest, with his arms around me. 'One that defies analysis,' he finished, his eyes on mine in the mirror.

Smiling, I took the shirt, and slid my arms into it. Langham followed every movement. 'This one,' he murmured, pulling a suit from the rows that hung there. 'Try this.'

It was white flannel, just as Hilde had suggested. I pulled the trousers over my legs, felt a rush of delight as I adjusted the waistcoat and settled the jacket over my shoulders.

She clapped when I was dressed.

'Perfect. Just perfect.'

Langham was smiling. 'Hilde's right. How fine you look. You must get one of your own.'

We were almost of a height, he and I, and though the suit was too big across my shoulders and around the waist, it wasn't a bad fit. He ran his hands through my hair, combing it back from my forehead, like his own. Quietly, Hilde let herself out.

'There,' Langham murmured when he was done. Our faces were next to each other, his flushed from washing, mine from his touch. 'We could almost be the same man.'

I turned to find his mouth, the hangers in the wardrobe clattering as we leaned back against it.

Later that day, I slipped outside the back gate for the first time in days, and beckoned to one of the children who were always lingering near the Bab al-Bahr, on the make. A boy came running over. He wore rope sandals, his hands quick and grubby, his eyes appraising of my fine suit.

'Yes señor, monsieur, yes?' he asked.

'You know Souissa, the tailor down near the Petit Socco?' I asked.

He nodded rapidly, answered *sí sí*, his eyes on my pocket as I took out a handful of centimes. 'Take this down to him right away.' I handed over an envelope, one from Langham's personalized leather case. 'Tell him to send the bill as usual. You can remember that?'

The boy snatched the letter from my hand before I finished speaking. 'Sí, señor, claro,' he smiled, holding out his hand for his payment.

I watched him run off with a smile, picturing Souissa's face when he opened the letter and found my order for a white flannel suit, and a shirt of palest saffron gold, just like Langham's.

As I turned back towards the house my neck prickled, despite the heat. I looked about, searching for the eyes I was sure were watching me, but all I saw was a flash of movement as someone disappeared around the corner of the Bab al-Bahr.

In those hot weeks, Langham did not go out as much as he usually did. Perhaps he was feeling on edge too, or perhaps we were simply being gluttons, revelling in each other's company. We hadn't spoken about the night he had returned, sea-drenched and bleeding from what looked like a knife wound to the arm. Indeed, though I began to know every centimetre of his body, from the jut of his hip and the smooth gold-brown hair of his thighs, there were multiple scars across his back and chest and now his arm that eluded definition. I asked him about the wound only once on that first night, as we lay tangled in clothes and bedsheets. He had only looked at me, and smiled. 'A scuffle, that's all.'

Whether that 'scuffle' was the cause of his lapse in business, his increased presence in the house, I didn't know. Bouzid knew, I was sure. He'd been 'with the boat' on the night it happened. On a few occasions I saw them together, talking in hushed voices, but I could never get close enough to hear.

I tried to forget about it, basking in my new life at Dar Portuna, in the delicious, decadent freedom. I slipped from being domestic help to lover, friend. I knew things had changed for good when Langham caught my hand and asked me to eat supper with him and Hilde as they lay on the veranda, rather than in the kitchen. I still cooked, still served food, but that was my power: something neither of them possessed. I shared it with affection and was proud.

For two weeks, the outside world did not exist. It was as if the three of us – Hilde, Langham and I – had signed a pact to be idle for a time, to take joy in each other. Bouzid did not break the hierarchy as I had. Sometimes, he could be compelled to join us on the veranda for tea, during the afternoons that seemed to last a century. Mostly though, he left us to our revels.

We soon lost all notion of *should* and *ought*. I began to leave off the tight brassiere, certain that Bouzid now knew my secret, and would keep it. Every day I sent orders to town for ice, more ice; ice to chill melon to tooth-stinging coldness, ice to mix drinks powerful enough to make us forget the heat, until we rolled on the hot tiles of the poolside, laughing as freezing gin slid across our cheeks. One afternoon Hilde produced a lump of hashish and told me, looking like a child who has raided the pantry, to 'do something nice with it'.

Exactly what she meant, I didn't know. It took several plates of briwats and wondering aloud whether I was meant to bake it before Bouzid relented and impatiently explained how to make mahjoun – his grandmother's recipe, he said.

That afternoon, I worked at the stove, grinding the hash, melting butter, dicing nuts and dried fruit, mixing spices and honey and rosewater until I had a sticky, delicious mass. Bouzid had gone out, so I couldn't ask him if it was right. *Only one way to find out*, I thought with a smirk.

That afternoon, the whole world was as soft as cinnamon.

'We should serve this at a party,' Hilde said, licking mahjoun from her fingers. 'Send the stuck-up old diplomats wild.' She'd left off smoking her pipe so much over the past few weeks, and she looked bronze and healthy in the sun. Langham too, seemed freer than I had ever seen him, especially when Bouzid was not around.

'A party,' he said, leaning back on a lounger, naked except for a pair of sunglasses. 'Yes, we should.' I was watching the way the sun licked at his hair, bringing out its gold lights. 'How about it, del Potro?' he said, glancing to where I stood, mixing drinks in my shirt and underwear. 'Shall we give the Tangerines a show?'

I tried to smile into the melting ice. I didn't want a party. During those glorious, honeyed days, the rules of society had melted away, until all that mattered was the next moment, breath and skin and hunger, not names or rank. I didn't want to step back into my old position. I didn't want to see Langham flirt with young men and rich ladies and watch it all from behind a tray. I wanted to be there beside him.

I shrugged. 'If you want.'

'That settles it then. We'll have one on Saturday.' I couldn't see his eyes behind his sunglasses as I handed him the drink, though I knew he was looking at me. 'Got to keep up appearances,' he said softly.

I should have told him then that it was a bad idea. I should have argued that no good could come of a party when the whole city was broiling in the heat. I should have leaned in close and asked him who he was keeping up appearances for, when he so clearly didn't give a damn about society.

But I forgot Ifrahim's advice about watching and listening, and instead shut my eyes to my anxieties, and when Langham and I were alone, I kissed him all the harder.

The party would be white and red, Hilde declared, like strawberries and cream, like the St George's cross, like fire and ice. Slumped in the shade of the lounge we went through *The Gentleman's Guide* together, laughing at its tips for greeting ladies and how to tip a hat. She picked out cocktails she liked the sound of, Ruby Fizzes and Gin Rickeys, and Champagne Juleps.

'Blood and Sand,' she murmured when she reached the page. I had stared at it so often, it had taken to falling open on its own. 'What a name. Let's try.' She thrust the book at me. 'Can you make it?'

I knew the recipe by heart. But make it? I forced a smile. I was Alejandro del Potro now. The past, with its bloody prints, belonged to someone else.

'Of course.'

It wasn't hard. Orange juice from the kitchen, a search through the bar for some cherry-flavoured stuff. I poured it all into the mixing glass before reaching for the Scotch. And though I tilted my head away, and tried to shut off my nostrils, it was no use. The smell took me back; it reached up and clawed at me, mingling with the cloying sweetness of juice and cherry, like cheap perfume and blood on a pink flowered rug, and I dropped the bottle with a clatter.

'Alejandro?' Hilde looked up. 'Are you all right?'

I nodded, swallowing bile. 'It's nothing. I just need a moment.'

I fled into the corridor, where the air was clean and scented with sandalwood and distant spices from the kitchen. There, I leaned against the whitewashed wall, wiping my streaming eyes, trying to regain control of my untrustworthy body.

'. . . wise at the present time . . .' I lifted my head a little. That was Bouzid's voice, coming from Langham's study. 'Until we are sure that—'

'Bouzid, it's not without reason. A party will ensure that everyone has enough to talk about. Someone is guaranteed to do something absurd and the whole city will gossip about it for a month. It'll distract them from other rumours.' There was a thud, a desk drawer being closed.

'And del Potro? If people talk?'

My face burned against the cool wall.

'All the better.' Langham sounded impatient. 'Another distraction.'

'But we still cannot be sure if—'

'We can be sure enough. Bautista confirmed del Potro's story and in this instance, I believe the old bastard.' A pause. 'Del Potro promised me loyalty, Bouzid. And more besides.'

There was silence, as if the two men were staring at each other. Finally, I heard Bouzid let out a sort of sigh. 'Very well.'

It curdled with the Blood and Sand, that conversation, until I wasn't certain which had affected me more. For the rest of the day, it nagged at me, alongside memories of the night at the inn, until all my muscles were filled with jumping, anxious energy. Perhaps Langham was feeling the same way, for that evening he asked Hilde to bring down her pipe – something he rarely indulged in – and the three of us sat on the lounge floor, cushioned by pillows, hiding our fears behind a veil of smoke.

Friday came, and with it a constant ringing of the bell at the gate. Barrows of fruit and vegetables from the market, baskets of nuts, sacks of sugar and flour. Bouzid was the king of operations, and between us we carried box after box through to the kitchen. None of the delivery people were allowed within the walls of Dar Portuna. Not even the woman who brought the flowers – blood-red roses and pale lilies, voluptuous hibiscus and dreaming jasmine. Even the eccentric French decorator was allowed in only on the condition he remained with Hilde at all times. Such caution would've seemed extreme to me, had it not been for the conversation I had overheard the night before, the fact that Langham was clearly preoccupied with something.

When the bell rang for the twelfth time, I was ready to take a hammer to it. I yanked the gate open, ready to receive whatever crate of booze or ice or frivolity had been ordered, only to find Souissa's little boy, his eyes huge as always.

'Hola, Daniel,' I told him wearily. 'Have you brought my suit?' In truth, I had almost forgotten about it in my worry.

But the child's arms were empty. 'No,' he whispered to my shoes. 'Papa asked if you might come to the shop. He needs to check the fit on you, señor.'

I couldn't keep down a noise of frustration. Perhaps I had been wrong to entrust an expensive suit of white flannel to Souissa, who probably did not have occasion to make many of them.

'All right,' I told Daniel, a little irritably, 'tell your father I will be there in half an hour. I need the suit ready by tomorrow.' I knew Langham would think it the perfect thing for the party.

The boy was nodding, backing away into the dusty street. I let him go, and went to struggle into the brassiere, and find my hat. Hilde was deep in conversation with the decorator, Bouzid and Langham shut up in the study. The thought of knocking on the door and hearing their voices cut off, knowing he was keeping secrets from me, was too much for my strained nerves. Instead, I scrawled a note on a piece of brown paper and left it on the kitchen table.

Gone to tailor, back soon. A.

I walked the alleyways of the casbah, moving to the side to make way for a lady with two brimming buckets of water. I tipped my hat to Hilde's friend Mademoiselle Alisée, who sat outside the Café Central sipping Pernod with her florid gentleman. I strolled freely, just a young man about his business, without worrying for my safety, without cringing at stares or catcalls; finally, I felt the streets were mine.

With a light heart, I pushed open Souissa's door.

'Hola, friend,' I called, 'I hear you are having some trouble—'

Something smashed into the back of my head, driving the sense from me. I staggered and tried to turn but hands were seizing my jacket, throwing me on to the dusty, pin-strewn floor.

My ears were ringing, eyes flooding, but still I heard the door being slammed and locked. Panic shot through my body. I knew I should run, should shout or scream but I was winded, my lungs like useless scraps of cloth. From the corner of my eye, I saw a boot, drawn back to strike and I closed my eyes in terror.

'Enough,' someone said.

One heave, two and my lungs filled at last. Gasping, I looked up.

Two eyes, yellow as a goat's, stared back at me.

'Hola, del Potro,' said Cabrera.

He was sitting on the little tailor's stool, elbows on his knees. Souissa was nowhere to be seen.

I struggled to hide my fear.

'What do you want?' I coughed, wiping my lips on my sleeve, trying to make my voice as gruff as possible. How much did he know?

Cabrera leaned back. 'You were more courteous the other night. That food, by the way.' He looked heavenward. 'I haven't eaten so well in years. It was like being back home, in Andalucía.'

He smiled, and a wave of fear escaped my control. If Souissa had talked . . . I tried to look about me for some way to defend myself, some way to escape. My knife. But I didn't have it. Dar Portuna had made me forget the lessons I had learned so hard from Morales. I felt something trickle on to my collar and reached up to find my scalp wet with blood. It was Márquez who had hit me, I realized, looking up into the gloom, Márquez with his terrible breath.

'Where's the tailor?' I demanded.

'He is in the back.' Cabrera was still watching me. 'The new suit looks marvellous by the way.'

'The bastard can keep it.'

'Ah,' Cabrera clucked his tongue. 'Don't blame Souissa for your own foolishness, chico.' He threw a piece of paper at me. I recognized it immediately; stationery from Langham's writing case, covered with my own writing, ordering the white flannel suit. 'You shouldn't entrust such letters to street rats.'

He must have been watching the house ever since he visited, I realized, waiting for an opportunity, like the one I had stupidly handed him.

'Get on with it. What do you want?' Despite my efforts, there was a tremor in my voice.

Cabrera shook his head at me. 'I have to say I am impressed. Getting yourself employed by Langham like that. That took cojones.' He looked deliberately at the crotch of my trousers. 'Perhaps when all this is over, we can work together.'

'I'd rather eat shit.'

A blow between my shoulder blades sent me sprawling again. This time it was Cabrera himself who pulled me to my knees.

'Easy,' he said to Márquez. 'Not where it shows.' He sat back and looked into my face. His smile was turning down at the edges. 'Monsieur Langham and I have had a disagreement which needs to be resolved. He refuses to meet with me himself, so you are going to help me set up a little rendezvous.'

I stared at him, the blood pounding in my head.

'No.' I hated how my voice shook.

Cabrera leaned forwards. 'You don't have a choice, Alejandra.'

That name . . . There was nothing I could do to stop the horror that flooded across my face. How did he know?

'It's all right.' Cabrera was still too close, I could smell his stale sweat, his pungent cologne. 'Souissa's given us all the details.' He flicked a hand towards my chest and laughed when I recoiled. 'I admit, I was surprised. I'd never have guessed. You make a better man than you did a whore, I'll wager.'

He took a case of cigarettes from his pocket, and offered me one. I didn't move. I was imagining smashing them into his face.

'But you should've chosen a better name. *Del Potro.* Anyone from Andalucía who moves in certain circles knows the Hostería.' He lit a cigarette. 'It was all over the Spanish papers, you know, for a while. The Córdoban Murderess, the puta cook turned killer, vanished in the night, last seen heading south.' He laughed out some smoke.

In that moment, I would have gladly become the murderer everyone said I was and taken a bottle to his throat.

'All right,' I spat. 'Name your price.'

Cabrera smiled. 'Good girl. Let's talk business.'

Tangier

July 1978

Sam had heard many stories about wild times on the road during his travels; run-ins with border police in Spain and train cops in France and narcos in Italy. They were one thing. Actually waking up after a night in a Moroccan jail was quite another.

Idiot. He sat up from the thin mat, his neck cricked out of shape. *Goddam idiot.*

His knuckles still ached a little from the impact with Norton's chin. Or was it from the wall he'd collided with, as the security guard shoved him down the stairs? He didn't remember. It was all so messy. Norton had yelled about police, sure, but Sam hadn't thought he was serious until the security guard had dumped him in front of two bored-looking Moroccan cops.

When trying to explain didn't work, he'd handed over all the money he had on him, in the hope they'd let him go. For a minute, it looked like they would. Then, one of them had pulled the old forged passport from his pocket and their expressions had changed. They'd looked at each other, and shrugged, had hauled him off to the lock-up instead.

They'd given him one phone call, like they did in the movies. His fingers had hovered above the smeared digits. He couldn't phone his parents, anyway, the police would never allow him an international call. Not the American embassy – that would mean expulsion from Tangier. As far as he knew Abdelhamid didn't have a phone. So he did the only thing he could think of: dialled the operator and asked, in bad French, to be put through to Dar Portuna.

The operator paused when she heard that. A moment later she told him that there was no such place. Of course. In the end, out of options, he had asked to be put through to The Hold.

Thankfully, Roger answered. He said he'd tell Bet and the others as soon as he could, that they'd all do their best to help. And if they didn't, or couldn't? Sam didn't want to think about it.

The other men in the cell were waking up now, wincing and yawning. There were four of them, all Moroccan, Sam guessed. Three had been there when he arrived, one had been shunted in during the night, a young man with long hair, wearing jeans and a ripped t-shirt. His nose was swollen and crusted with dried blood. When he saw Sam was awake, he half smiled and nodded.

'*Hola*,' he said, and pointed to himself. 'Amir.'

'Sam.' He shook the man's hand. Was he meant to do that? He had no idea about prison etiquette.

'American?' the young man asked.

Sam nodded, rubbing at his face. His eyes felt gritty, face caked in sweat and grime from the sweltering room.

'¿Por qué . . . ?' Amir gestured around the cell, looking incredulous.

'A fight.' Sam held up his bruised knuckles. 'You?'

Amir shook his head, as if he didn't understand. One of the older Moroccan men said something, and the others laughed sourly.

The young man kept his gaze on the floor after that. Eventually, he took some tobacco out of his jeans pocket.

'Do you have papers?' Sam asked, feeling in his own pockets.

The kif dust he shook from the lining was negligible, but Amir's face lit up when he saw it. Carefully, they rolled it into a cigarette. One of the other men hammered on the door. A heated negotiation went on, until finally, a guard was passed the joint to light. After taking the first few puffs for himself, he passed it back into the cell.

Amir smoked, then passed it to Sam. He took a drag, trying to figure out what he was going to do. What if he was deported, before he had a chance to go back to Dar Portuna, to see Ale and Zahrah and explain? It was unthinkable. He coughed out a little smoke, and passed the joint back to Amir, who passed it on to the next man.

He shouldn't have let himself get so angry, he thought, watching as one of the other men accepted the joint with a nod of thanks. And the stupid thing about it all was that Norton had been right. Crimes *had* been committed in the past, and in the present too, most likely, whether he ignored them or not. He *had* been charmed by Ale's tale. He had wanted stories full of glamour and danger, rather than the grim reality of the present.

He was about to try and ask the men what would happen to them all next, when the door clanged again, and the guard stuck his head inside.

'Vamos,' he said to Sam.

Amir smiled and gestured as if to say *there, you see*. Sam didn't know what it meant, whether he'd be thrown back again in five minutes; nevertheless, he leaned down and shook the young man's hand. Then, because it seemed rude not to, he shook the hands of the other three men in the room, who looked up at him with varying degrees of amusement and confusion.

Out in the lobby, beneath the sluggish ceiling fan, a familiar figure was waiting.

'Bet!' He rushed forwards to hug her, though he knew he must have smelled terrible. 'Thank god, thank you so much for coming.'

She pushed him back a little, patting his arm. He hardly recognized her. She was dressed in a prim tweed skirt suit, a scarf tied around her head, like a little British grandmother. Holding on to his arm, she turned and asked the officer at the desk something in Darija. The policeman began to root around beneath the counter. Finally, he came up with the passport.

'That's—' Sam started to say, but Bet cut him off, taking the document with a tight smile and tucking it into her handbag. Then she was steering Sam towards the door, her grip like iron.

'Wait,' he said, glancing over his shoulder. There had been no paperwork, no release forms, nothing. 'What's going on?'

'Shut up and walk.'

He'd never been so glad to smell the traffic fumes outside, to feel the morning sun prickle across his scalp. Bet kept marching him along the road until they turned the corner and emerged on to the Place de France. Only then did she loosen her grip, and look up at him.

'Brawling, Samuel?' she said with a sigh. 'I thought you were smarter than that.'

'So did I.' He blinked at her. 'Bet, I can't thank you enough. How did . . .' He waved a hand at the police station.

The sun caught on the dull gold of a tooth. 'The station chief is a dear friend. He was very understanding. Hot-blooded young men get into scraps every day. And as for this –' she peered down at the passport as they walked towards the Gran Café '– that took a little more explaining. I told him that you were a writer, with a predictable penchant for old things, and that you had probably picked it up at a junk shop. Why on earth were you carrying it around?'

He groaned. 'It's a long story.'

They must have made an absurd-looking pair, Bet in her tweed, he more grubby and rumpled than ever. Wearily, he told her what had happened. How he'd located Dar Portuna, and met the person who lived there. How he'd ill-advisedly asked Norton to check the archives, only to come up with Langham's suspicious death. How Zahrah had warned him that the authorities would descend on Dar Portuna if they found out it was Ale's secret address. How he'd been trying to shut Norton up.

The smoke spiralled around them, mingling with the smell of fresh coffee and morning pastries. Only when he started talking about the fight did he remember what he'd found in Norton's desk.

'Bet,' he said, hastily wiping pastry crumbs from his mouth, 'Norton had pictures of you in his desk, with another person, Kline I think it was, taken outside The Hold. It's part of what made me so mad. He's obviously been sniffing about, trying to dig up dirt on you too.'

For a moment, Bet's blue eyes were sharp. 'Photos? What were we doing in them?'

'Talking, that's all, from what I could see.'

Bet grunted. 'I'll have to have a chat with Mister Norton some time. He's quite the annoyance.'

She reached down for her handbag and took out a newspaper. He recognized it as *Tangier Today*, one of the cheaper English-language titles. 'Here,' she said. 'Yesterday's evening edition. He managed to get page five, above the fold.'

BACK FROM THE GRAVE?
MYSTERY OF DROWNED
MAN RESURFACES
AFTER FIFTY YEARS

Sam felt sick. He heard Zahrah's voice again saying, *You have to do better than try.* He had promised he would try to keep Ale from danger, and here it was: proof of his failure. He didn't want to look at the paper, every part of him wanted to hurl it across the room, but he didn't. He had to see what the damage was. It was his responsibility, after all.

It was a dreadful article. Norton's suppositions had been written up in lurid detail. The passport was made much of: the mysterious Alejandro del Potro who existed in no records, but who was undoubtedly linked to an underworld smuggling ring, and to Langham's disappearance. Sam forced himself to read on.

> *Whilst the closure of British institutions in Morocco makes it difficult to obtain accurate police reports from the era, an inside source from the embassy – who did not want to be named – revealed that before his untimely death, Mr Arthur Langham may have been wanted by the British authorities on serious charges, in an investigation which was never fully concluded. This new information regarding Alejandro del Potro's connection to Langham and possible involvement in his murder, as well as the location and existence to this day of a mansion safehouse in the casbah named 'Dar Portuna' – which was discovered by Interpress journalist Ellis Norton – has now been shared with Moroccan and Spanish authorities, as well as customs officials. It is* Tangier Today*'s understanding that the police will use the information in their ongoing efforts to apprehend and prosecute the individual known as 'Alejandro del Potro' for contravention of customs law.*

'The bastard,' Sam muttered, his throat tight. 'Why did he have to do it?'

'He's trying to write himself out of here,' Bet said, looking down her nose at the paper. 'Making the news, so that he can report it.'

Sam stared down at the article, wishing he could scrub the words out of existence. 'Zahrah, the woman I told you about who lives at Dar Portuna, she said something like this could put Ale – Alejandro – in danger. Do you think it will? Do you think the authorities will act upon it?' He shoved the paper away. 'It's all my fault.'

'No denying you had a role to play.' Bet's blue eyes were kind. 'But you didn't publish it, did you? I'll hazard a guess that *your* version would be a bit more nuanced.'

He just shook his head. She let him sit in silence for a while, before tapping the paper.

'Norton's "embassy source" is old Giles, I'd bet my hat on it. I saw the pair of them in the El Minzah the other night, getting cosy over the Benedictine.' She smiled darkly. 'I'll have to have a chat with him, too.'

Sam folded the paper over, not wanting to look at it any more. 'What if Norton tries to use those photos of you?' he asked quietly. 'What if he writes something about your . . . past?'

'About me?' Bet raised her eyebrows. 'What could he possibly write? I'm just a pensioner, spinning out her retirement in a nice warm country. And anyway –' she slid him a look '– he'd never be able to prove a thing.'

Outside in the street, she re-tied the scarf over her cropped grey hair, becoming a little old woman once more.

'Well?' she asked briskly. 'What are you going to do? I'd suggest a bath, for starters.'

He tried to smile. 'I have to go to Dar Portuna to tell them about all this, try to apologize and hope that Ale can stay out of trouble. Then . . .' He looked around at the heedless, blistering city. 'I guess there's no point in me staying. If I'd gone home a month ago, like my parents wanted me to, none of this would have happened.'

Bet patted his arm. 'Well, be sure to come and say cheerio to all of us at The Hold.'

She didn't sound overly concerned. *She must have met hundreds of people like me*, Sam thought bitterly, *seen us all give up and go home.*

'Thank you, Bet,' he said. 'For everything.'

She smirked. 'Give an old lady a kiss.'

He finally managed a weak laugh, and leaned down to kiss her weathered cheek. Before he could pull away she grabbed his collar.

'That newspaper's a rag, Sammy,' she whispered rapidly in his ear. 'Don't let it get you down. Hacer de tripas corazón, as my old friend always says.'

She released him and he stepped back in surprise, trying to see her face, but she was already walking away, stomping through the traffic with practised ease. He watched her disappear around a corner, half stunned, wondering whether he'd imagined what she'd said. Only then did he realize she hadn't given him back the passport.

He rubbed at his eyes. *You're not to be trusted with anything.* Still, he was sure she'd keep it safe. He was so tired, beat down by the long night and the awful newspaper article, he couldn't think any more, could barely look where he was going. When he stepped into Madame Sarah's cool hallway, it was with relief. All he wanted to do was wash and sleep, but he knew he wouldn't be able to. He had to get to Dar Portuna and face what he had done.

The moment he set foot on the stairs, there was a shout from the kitchen and Madame Sarah appeared, pushed aside by her sister, a formidable woman in a bright orange headscarf.

'Monsieur Hackett?' she said.

'Yes?' he answered wearily. He dug his hands into his pockets, ready to give up however many dirhams he had left, only to stop – all of his money had gone to pay off the police. He felt himself turning red. 'Ah, about the rent. I just need an hour or two before—'

'No.' The sister glared from the doorway. 'Two nights you stay out, you don't pay, and now you bring *women* into the house.' She raised her chin. 'This is a respectable place. We will not have it.'

'I'm sorry, I'm—' Her words caught up with him. 'What do you mean, women? I've never brought anyone here.'

She let out a disbelieving laugh. 'You tell us that, when there is one upstairs right now, one who is rude, who came in here without—'

He didn't wait to hear more. He ran up the stairs two at a time, racing for his top floor room, knowing it could only be one person.

Zahrah was standing by the window, wearing her old djellaba. Her short hair was messy, as if she'd been running her hands through it.

'I'm sorry,' he gasped, stepping through the door. 'I'm so sorry, I tried everything. You won't believe the night—'

She turned to face him. Her eyes were reddened, swollen from crying. The guilt froze solid in his chest.

'What's happened?'

She said nothing. A moment later, her face collapsed and he knew. She stepped towards him; instinctively he put his arms around her, as her breath turned into a sob.

'Ale's gone.'

SCOFFLAW

Take one dash of orange bitters, three quarters of a pony of Canadian Club whisky, the same of French vermouth, a tablespoon of lemon juice and a tablespoon of imported grenadine. Shake well and strain into a cocktail glass. Drink fast, before it catches up with you.

All things come at a price.

I'd grown up around swindlers and thieves – I should have remembered not to trust anything that seemed too good to be true. I should have realized that the diamond walls of my world could turn to glass and crack; that the elegant fabrics could rip and unravel, that my saint's gold could peel away like cheap gilding on a false coin. But I didn't. Not until it was too late.

Bouzid found me at the gate of Dar Portuna, bracing myself against the wall, my eyes screwed closed against the awful, dull throbbing in my head. The wound had stopped bleeding now, but I could feel it, flaking and tacky at the base of my skull. Bouzid was angrier than I had ever seen him. He grabbed my jacket, the way he had all those weeks ago when I had first trespassed into the gardens, and dragged me into the house, unheeding of my protests.

He didn't stop until we reached the study.

Hilde was perched on the edge of the desk, her face strained, chewing at her nails. And Langham . . . when he looked at me, his eyes were like flint.

'Where did you go?' he demanded.

I couldn't think straight; the pain was muddled together with the memory of Cabrera saying my real name, with the fear of what he might do if I didn't comply. 'I went to the tailor's.' My voice sounded vague. 'I left a note.'

'The truth, del Potro.' Langham's hand was beneath his desk, in one of the drawers. 'I need to know where . . .'

I didn't hear the rest. The throbbing grew worse, blue and yellow lights filling my vision. The next thing I knew I was on my knees, staring at the rug, hearing Hilde's panicked voice.

'Arthur!'

She was at my side. I could smell her scent: powder and lilies and the clinging bittersweet tang of smoke. Coolness touched my skin, her fingers, exploring the back of my neck. 'My god,' she murmured, when she found the crusted blood. 'Who did this to you?'

I forced my eyes open. Langham was staring down at me, his face taut. I couldn't betray him, I realized. Not now. I met his eyes.

'Cabrera.'

Bouzid was dispatched to fetch ice, Hilde the medical chest. For a moment, it was only Langham and I in the room.

'Cabrera knows about me,' I said, hauling myself up using the edge of the desk. 'He knows what I am and he wants me to set you up. He said you have unfinished business.'

Langham's shoulders dropped. 'Alejandro.' He was stepping close, taking my face in his hands. 'I'll kill the bastard for hurting you. Did they . . . ?' His hands tightened.

'No.' I closed my eyes, unable to focus on him. 'No. He didn't want anyone to think anything was wrong. He needed me to be able to pretend everything was normal.' I reached for the back of my head. 'I don't think Márquez was supposed to hit me so hard.'

Langham produced a bottle of brandy and pushed a glass into my hand. I sat on the floor cushions in the lounge and sipped at it while Hilde swabbed at the back of my head. More nauseous than ever, I told them what had happened, how Cabrera had intercepted my note to Souissa and sent the tailor's son to lure me there.

'They must have been watching the house,' I said, looking up. My eyes were swimming with the sting of alcohol, but even so, I saw the look that passed between Bouzid and Langham.

When Hilde had finished, she made me lean back against the sofa. Langham came to sit opposite me, his face serious.

'What information does Cabrera have on you?'

'He knows I'm a woman,' I murmured. 'He knows my real name.' I gripped the glass of brandy, its amber colour all too similar to Scotch. 'He knows I'm wanted by the police in Spain, and that if I'm caught I'll be garrotted for murder.' I glanced up at them. 'I didn't do it, but that won't matter. There are people who will swear I did.'

Langham was very still. His eyes never left my face, but I could tell he was thinking hard, trying to decide what to believe of me, whether I was capable of killing a man, what it meant that I had lied about it. Would things ever be the same between us, now? He had asked me not to bring trouble into his house, and that is exactly what I had done. There was no sympathy in his look, or anger. Part of me wished he would react: shout and swear at me, or take my hand, but he did neither and I had to look away.

Hilde was frowning at me too, worrying at her lip. Her trust in me had been based on the story I had told; a story so like her own. Now she knew that I had lied – would she understand?

Finally, Langham blinked. 'What exactly did Cabrera want you to do?' he said slowly. 'Use his exact words if you can.'

I closed my eyes. I didn't want to remember it; the stench of Márquez at my back, the awful closeness of Cabrera's face as he spelled out his demands.

'He wants me to report everything to him. Who telephones, who comes to the house, what Bouzid does. He knows about the party tomorrow night. He wants to set up the rendezvous for then, he said it would be the perfect cover.' I forced myself to look up at them all. 'He wants me to get into your study and take some papers from your desk, from any green file he said, and place them secretly in your coat or bag so that you carry them to the meeting.' I could feel my face growing hot, ashamed of my own foolishness. 'He said that would be enough.'

To my surprise, Langham was nodding. 'What about Hilde? Did he mention her?'

Hilde's face was curiously pale, her eyes fixed on Langham.

'No,' I stammered, looking between them. 'No, he didn't mention Hilde at all. He said that I should stay here during the rendezvous. He said that some other people might come to search the house, and that I should let them in.'

'Other people – did he say who?'

'No. He said I'd be able to tell when they arrived, though.'

'And that was all? You're sure?'

I nodded my throbbing head. 'Yes. I swear.'

Abruptly, Langham's flint-like expression softened. He reached over and squeezed my shoulder, before looking up at Bouzid.

'It's the British. I'm sure of it.'

The other man grunted. 'Would they trust Cabrera?'

'They'd trust a mule if it trotted up to them with a promise in its mouth.' Langham's voice was filled with contempt. 'Cabrera must've done a deal with them. No doubt they are offering him ample reward for ensuring I am caught red-handed.'

I stared at the side of his face, his smooth skin, the fine lines about his eyes. 'I don't understand,' I murmured. 'The British authorities? What do they want with you?'

Langham looked over at me then, with a soft, half-pitying smile.

'Same as the Spanish want with you. They want to hang me, chico.'

'Arthur!' Hilde started up, glancing at me.

'No,' he stopped her. 'If we are all to get out of this, Hilde, Alejandro needs to understand.' He focused on me again. 'Bautista and his crew are small fry, when it comes to contraband. The real business isn't in booze or tobacco, but in information.' He raised an eyebrow. 'The sort of thing you delivered to Cabrera.'

'The suitcase full of papers?' I asked slowly. 'What were they?'

Langham smiled humourlessly. 'I'm afraid I have no idea. You were lucky not to be caught, though. Cabrera's obviously been double-crossing us.' He looked a little thoughtful. 'You didn't catch any glimpse of what the papers were? Any stamps or letters?'

I shook my head.

'Pity,' he murmured.

'But,' I shifted to look at Bouzid, at Hilde, 'smuggling isn't a hanging offence, is it? They'd have to hang the whole of La Atunara, and half of Tangiers, if it was.'

Langham laughed a little, and drank his brandy. 'No, smuggling isn't a hanging offence. Treason is, though. And murder.'

I stared into his eyes, trying to see the man I thought I knew, but all I saw was my own reflection.

Later, as afternoon became evening, we sat at the kitchen table – all four of us – our elbows resting on the scrubbed wood, drinking tumblers of wine and picking at food. We had never sat and eaten like that before. *We are in this together*, that meal said. We had to work and act as equals, if we were to get out of it. At another time, Bouzid's lack of formality would have made me glad. But in that moment, all I could think was that everything was changing.

'What's important is that they are not connecting you to anything,' Langham said to Hilde. 'They see you as a socialite, nothing more. That makes you a safe pair of hands.'

She nodded, and shifted in her chair. She had lied to me then, about her knowledge of Langham's activities.

'What about the party?' I asked. 'It can't go ahead, now, surely?'

'On the contrary, it must.' Langham was twisting the ring around and around on his little finger. 'If we call it off, Cabrera will know that you've told me everything. Then we lose the upper hand.' He looked at me, eyes travelling over my hair, my collar. 'Alejandro,' he said softly. 'The suit you ordered from the tailor, it was the one we talked about?'

For some reason, a shiver ran down my neck. 'Yes. White flannel. And a shirt of saffron gold, just like yours.'

'Will it be ready by tomorrow?'

I nodded, feeling queasy. 'Cabrera said so. He told me it would be delivered in the morning, with a note inside about the rendezvous. I'm to send information back with the delivery boy.' I swallowed. 'They will be watching the house.'

'Good,' Langham said. He looked away and stood up and I was left feeling cold, as if someone had closed the door of a stove. 'Bouzid,' he said, 'come with me. We have a lot to do.'

Despite the heat of the day and the brandy I had drunk, I could not stop shivering. Langham and Bouzid left Dar Portuna by the secret back gate, where to I didn't know. Hilde and I did what we could to distract ourselves, decorating the lounge for a party that none of us wanted. We arranged glasses and chose platters. Once or twice we tried to talk of what had happened, what was to come, only to find we couldn't; the words turned to ash in our mouths. Finally, we parted, Hilde to her pipe, I to the privacy of Langham's bathroom.

In the shower, I tried to sluice away the fear and anxiety, wincing at the sting of water on the back of my head. I tried to forget that there was a world outside the house. I wanted to sever Dar Portuna from Tangiers, wanted to untie all of the strings that tethered us to the past and send us drifting away into the world, untouchable.

Later, wrapped in Langham's robe, I sat on the tiny roof terrace above the bedrooms, trying to catch a breeze off the strait. It was like a nest up there, the highest spot in the house, from which I could see everything. The edge of the casbah and beams of motorcars on the beach road, the ships on the strait, the vastness of a continent behind me of which I still knew nothing. I stared into the darkness, trying to imagine what life lay ahead for me, tomorrow, next week. I found that I couldn't.

'Here you are.' It was Langham, emerging from the stairs. 'I've been looking for you.'

He came and stood behind me, his arms encircling my chest, careful not to touch my bruised head.

'I don't even know your name.' I murmured it to the night. I wasn't sure where the words came from, only that they were truth.

For a moment, he stiffened. Then, I felt him relax, leaning closer. 'I could say the same for you,' he whispered. 'Why don't you choose us another one?'

'What do you mean?'

'I've been thinking.' His breath was warm on my cheek. 'If it happens that I have to leave Tangiers, would you go with me?'

Leave Tangiers, Dar Portuna? 'And go where?'

'Anywhere. Argentina, Shanghai. The other side of the world, where no one knows us.'

Those places, I knew them from Ifrahim's stories, but they'd always seemed like a fantasy; impossible to reach for someone like me.

'You mean travel together?' I leaned my head against his, closing my eyes. I could see us now, two gentlemen standing at the railing of a ship, smoking and laughing, playing cards with ladies in cocktail lounges, idly reading newspapers over breakfast, sharing a cabin, where we could shed our disguises and be together, breath and skin, upon a vast ocean.

'Of course together.' His lips touched the side of my head. 'With you as my wife—'

I opened my eyes, as if someone had stuck me with a pin.

'Your wife?'

'Yes. They will be looking for us, after all, for Langham and del Potro. But as a gentleman and a lady we could slip past. Mr and Mrs Porter, of Gibraltar, maybe. You could borrow a few of Hilde's dresses, perhaps a wig, until your hair grows out.' He ran his hand through my short curls and I jerked away, my guts knotting.

He frowned. 'What is it?'

He reached for me again, but I shrugged out of his grip. I couldn't explain it. Langham's wife . . . to be with him, openly, in public. Wasn't that what I wanted?

'No,' I told him shakily. 'I can't.'

'Ale, as my wife, you'd have protection.'

I turned to face him. 'I don't want to be protected, to need protection. I don't want to be a wife.' I searched for his eyes in the darkness. 'I want what you have. I want to be like you, to be free.'

There was silence between us for a long time. I couldn't see his face clearly, only the outline of his features. Then, his chest jerked and I saw a glint on his skin. It was a tear, I realized.

'To be like me,' he said, his voice soft with dismay. 'No, Ale, I couldn't wish that on you.'

I pulled him into my arms. His tears were warm and slick as lamp oil on my cheek as I kissed him, feeling my own eyes sting. We clung to each other, there on that rooftop, like two people about to fall from the edge of the world.

Tangier

July 1978

Sam stood motionless, one arm around Zahrah. She was fighting not to cry; he could feel the hitch of tears in her chest, barely contained.

Gone.

'What happened? Tell me.'

She looked up at him, and for a moment there was such recrimination in her face he thought he wouldn't be able to stand it.

'We waited for you,' she sniffed, wiping her nose on her sleeve. 'Last night, we waited up but you didn't come. In the end, Ale sent me out to get the evening papers . . . You promised,' she said fiercely, stepping away from him. 'You promised you'd stop it.'

'I tried!' He was too ashamed to meet her gaze. 'I went to Norton's office, I got Ale's old passport back, I *tried* to make him leave the story alone, but . . .' His voice trailed off and he gave a dull laugh. 'I spent the night in jail. That's why I didn't come.'

'In jail?' Zahrah looked alarmed. 'Why?'

He rubbed his eyes. 'I got into a fight, with Norton.' It sounded so ridiculous. 'Everything would've been fine, but the police found the passport and decided they didn't know what to do with me. So they threw me in the lock-up. I'd probably still be there if my friend Bet hadn't bailed me out.' After a moment's silence, he looked up at her. 'Please,' he begged. 'Zahrah, tell me what's happened to Ale.'

Her shoulders dropped. 'Last night, we read that article of Norton's,' she said, sitting wearily on the edge of the bed. 'Ale saw the bit about Langham, and Dar Portuna, and the authorities, and didn't say a word, just locked the door of the study and didn't come out all night.' Zahrah was worrying her hands, red with nail marks. 'This morning, early, Ale came to the kitchen and asked me to go and buy the morning papers. Neither of us had slept, I could tell.' She swallowed a sort of laugh. 'It was just an excuse to get me out of the house . . . By the time I got back, everything was quiet. There was no sign of Ale. Nothing except for this.'

She reached into her bag and pulled out a thick envelope. There was writing on the front, addressed to him. He took it.

Dear Sam,
Don't blame yourself. Some stories are beyond our control.
A

'But – this doesn't mean anything,' he said, gripping the envelope. 'Ale could have just . . . left town for a while, or something, until this blows over. You don't know for certain that it's *for ever*.'

He looked across at Zahrah. This time, there was no anger in her face, only sadness as she shook her head.

'There was a letter for me too.' She took a second envelope from the bag and held it in her lap. It was thick, containing many more pages than the one left for Sam. He caught a glimpse of writing on the front, the words *Dearest Zahrah*.

'There's a will inside,' she said softly. 'Ale has left me everything. Including Dar Portuna.'

'Is there anywhere else Ale could have gone?' Sam asked desperately. 'A hotel, another house, friends?' His voice ran out. Zahrah was shaking her head.

'No,' she whispered. 'No one would leave a will unless they meant it. Unless they never intended to come back.' She looked across at him. 'In the letter Ale said I should come and find you right away, that we should read what's in there together.' She nodded at the envelope in Sam's hands, the one addressed to him.

He couldn't believe it. Dazedly, he turned over the envelope and broke its seal. Inside were ten written pages, all in the same restless, dashing hand. He leafed through them, before turning back to the beginning, looking for a note, an explanation, anything.

'"Shanghai",' he read, and glanced down the page. 'I don't understand.'

'Keep reading.' Zahrah leaned closer to see the letter, her arm brushing against his.

He blinked hard, and cleared his throat.

SHANGHAI

Take two dashes of imported grenadine, one and a half tablespoons of lemon juice, half a tablespoon of anisette and a pony of Jamaica rum. Shake well, strain into a cocktail glass, and drink to what's behind you.

The day before the party passed like a speeding automobile; even as I tried to seize on details, they were whisked away, leaving me with streaming eyes. The details I do recall are scattered. The smell of coffee in the kitchen, the quiet breakfast Hilde and Langham and I took together in the garden, my aching head, the purple bruise around the wrist of the tailor's son, who would not meet my eyes. The beautiful new suit hiding a message from Cabrera and a forged telegram from 'Colonel Mayer', an old associate of Langham's, begging his presence at an urgent meeting that night. I showed it to him in the safety of his study, and he had studied it hard, before burning it up in his ashtray, his hand on my shoulder.

Langham did not mention marriage again, though during the night he had asked me once more to go away with him. His manner all that day was odd, sometimes distant and formal, at other times fraught, passionate. He would send me away with an order, only to catch me and pull me to him in the shadow of the door. Finally, I agreed to accompany him, on the condition that it was not as a woman, not as his wife. He seemed so relieved, and held me, whispering about what we would do, how we would lay low in some quiet port town, drinking and listening to the wireless, until Hilde sent us the all-clear. I felt a rush of exhilaration at the knowledge I held some power over him: that he wanted me so.

Even so, I was far from easy. *Why can't I trust you?* he'd whispered to me, that first night in the bathroom. And though it pained me to the pit of my stomach, I found myself thinking the same.

For one thing, the party itself was a masterpiece of cunning. Langham understood how to manipulate people with food, too, I realized, how drinks could be used to charm people, to undo them, to make them malleable. I wondered whether that was what he saw in me, my first night at Dar Portuna.

Between us, we plotted every detail, as if planning an assault. The food was to be light, nothing to soak up the forceful cocktails we planned to serve. Ajoblanco, I suggested, oysters on ice, blanched almonds rolled in salt to make people thirsty and drink more, crystallized rose petals, raspberry jellies laced with liqueur, for those who tried to be abstemious. Mahjoun, too, a mountain of it, made with a block of hash the size of a small melon.

'Good,' Langham murmured, watching me roll the balls of it in powdered sugar, to fool people with its sweetness, to compel them to eat more than they should. 'Make sure this goes around all evening.' He picked up a piece, only to put it back on the tray. 'Be generous with the spirit measures, too.'

I nodded, though my throat was tight, stuck with floating sugar. If it all went to plan, the guests would be reeling, roaring drunk or lost in a haze of hash and smoke, and no one would be able to remember a single reliable thing.

'It's time,' Langham murmured to me, when the hall clock struck seven. 'Go and pack, then come upstairs.' He ran a hand through my hair, careful of my bruised skull. 'I want us to dress together.'

I was shaking as I closed the door to my room, that modest, little space that meant so much to me. Waiting on the bed was a suitcase of Langham's; pale, buttery leather, embossed with his initials. *A. L.* It gave me pause. For all its beauty, I didn't like the idea of placing my belongings into a case emblazoned with his name.

It's just a bag, I told myself, *what difference does it make?*

Rapidly, I packed cologne and pomade, put on a robe so I could pack my fawn-brown jacket and trousers, my fine underwear and socks, and *The Gentleman's Guide*, my first gift from Langham. The new, white flannel suit was waiting on its hanger. It was beautiful. Despite – or perhaps because of – Cabrera's intervention, Souissa had outdone himself. And yet, there was something unsettling about it. It was white as bones are white, bleached by the sun. Clean as flesh when drained of blood. It had no place in a kitchen, and part of me felt uneasy about wearing it.

Soon, Bouzid was knocking on the door. He looked wonderful, wearing a magnificent brocade djellaba. When I looked down, however, I noticed a glimpse of plain, dark trousers protruding from the hem.

'You are finished?' he asked, pointing to the suitcase. I assumed he was going to hide our bags somewhere, the car perhaps, so that it would not seem suspicious.

'Yes,' I said, retrieving the precious passport and sliding it into a side pocket. 'But I don't have the key.'

Bouzid came forwards and closed the lid, picked up the case. 'Mr Langham has the key. He will lock it now. Shall I take your suit up to the dressing room, too?'

He had unhooked the suit before I could answer. Why did it make me so anxious, to see my possessions being borne away?

'Bouzid!' I called. He turned around. I wanted to ask how long it would be before I saw him again after tonight, what he would do while Langham and I were away, but I couldn't.

His face flickered. 'He is waiting for you,' he said.

I met Hilde coming out of Langham's room. She was carrying a curling iron.

'He's done,' she said, and tried to smile. 'You should have heard him fussing over his hair. Vain as a debutante.'

For a long moment we just looked at each other. Then, we stepped forwards and held each other tight.

'I'm frightened,' she whispered in my ear. 'I've never seen him like this before. What if . . .' She pulled back. 'What if it goes wrong? I couldn't bear it.'

'It will be fine.' I told her what we both wanted to believe. 'You'll see. We'll be back in a month or two, maybe sooner if things have calmed down.'

'And what if they don't?' She was too clever for my placating words. 'What if you can't come back?'

'Then we'll send for you,' I said, putting my hand to her cheek. 'We'll send word and you can lock up the house and join us, and we'll sun ourselves on a yacht in Algeria, or take tea in Ceylon.'

She tried to laugh, but it was more of a ragged breath. 'You sound like him,' she said. As I stepped away, she held on to my sleeve. 'Please, Alejandro,' she whispered.

Langham stood at the window of his room, looking out. Beyond him, the water of the strait was pearl violet with evening. I stared at the back of his head, wanting to fix it in my mind like a painting, a moment I could always return to.

When he turned, and met my eyes, I knew he was thinking the same.

'Well?' he said, raising his hands towards his hair. 'I think it is ridiculous, but Hilde says it will serve.'

Earlier that day, he had washed his hair with dye to darken it, and now, curled by Hilde, it looked almost like my own. He'd darkened his eyes too, with a smudge of kohl, shaded his cheekbones to make them more like mine. It changed his face, made it seem less formal, less English. Looking at him, I managed a smile. Was that how he saw me?

'What will your guests say?' I asked, touching his cheek. 'Won't they think it strange?'

'Strange?' He snorted. 'Everyone is strange in this city.' He smiled a little. 'If anyone asks, I shall tell them it is part of our party theme. A good, white English suit, hiding a red-blooded Andalucían.' He reached out, and slid the robe from my shoulder. 'Shall we?' he murmured.

Article by article, we dressed. I smoothed silk underwear over his hips, he pulled the brassiere down over my head and laced it tight. Face to face, we fastened each other's shirts, finding excuses to touch, to linger. When it came to the trousers, I thought we should never manage to dress each other, but eventually, we did, settling the white flannel creases in place. Jackets, ties; his fingers took their time straightening my collar, brushing against my neck. Finally, I sat before the mirror and he dressed my hair, his face serious with concentration. When he'd finished, he let the comb fall to the table, and sat down beside me.

We were reflected, shoulder to shoulder, cheek to cheek. The same suits, the same hair, the same sober, watchful expression. The same man, almost. Enough to fool a casual glance.

'You said you wanted to be like me,' he whispered into the glass.

Eventually, he stood up. 'Here,' he said, 'the final touch, for later.' From the bottom of the wardrobe, he took two hatboxes. Inside each was a hat, two identical straw boaters, each with a wide red ribbon. 'It should be your size,' he said, and placed it on my head.

At any other time, Hilde would have clapped and laughed to see us walking down the stairs, hand in hand, the spitting image of each other. As it was, she only watched us solemnly, as if we were descending into the trenches.

'This is it, then?' she asked, as she fixed a hibiscus flower into each of our lapels. She too was wearing white. Her eyes looked heavy with make-up, and from whatever she had taken, for courage.

Langham squeezed my shoulder once, and let go. 'This is it,' he said, and nodded to Bouzid, who threw open the front doors.

Soon, the house began to rattle with laughter and music and the boisterousness of those who were the first to arrive. I stood behind the bar, my outfit hidden by a long white server's jacket and apron. The drinks I made were strong and cold and perfect for throats parched with road dust. I watched as they were thrown back, one after another.

Langham seemed to be everywhere, during those first hours; smoking on the veranda with gentlemen, winding up the gramophone, allowing ladies to exclaim and touch his curled hair and try to win the hibiscus from his lapel. Everyone wanted to be near him. I, on the other hand – who could have been his twin – was invisible behind my tray. The apron and serving jacket relegated me to a piece of furniture, beneath notice. Only those who had been at Langham's party the night of my arrival glanced my way, some – men and women both – with curiosity.

By the time the clock struck eleven, the party was in full, wild swing. Hilde was pale under her powder, her smile painted on. Langham too had started to sweat in the hot night – unusual for him.

I knew why. 'Colonel Mayer' had asked to meet Langham at the far end of the port at one o'clock. Of course, we all knew who would truly be waiting there. Whenever I thought about it, I felt sick.

'What will you do to Cabrera?' I had whispered earlier, in the safety of the study. 'Will you kill him?'

Langham had turned away.

'It's better you don't know.'

'I have to know.' I moved until I could look into his eyes. 'Cabrera is the only one who can connect me to the Señor's murder. He could hold that over me, for years. He could use it to blackmail me again . . .'

Langham put his hand against my cheek. 'He won't do anything, after tonight.'

Hearing that cold promise, I shivered. I wanted Cabrera silenced. I wanted him gone. Langham would do that for me.

When it was nearing midnight, he sought me out, under the pretence of giving orders. 'The mahjoun,' he muttered. 'Go and get more, for god's sake. They're far too sober yet. This is like trying to drown fish.'

It was true. Tangerines, for the most part, could hold their liqueur. They were no match for the mahjoun though, which they gobbled like candy, their lips powdered with white. I exchanged a look with Bouzid, who was circling like a shark, keeping every glass filled to the brim. Slowly, the party began to grow more riotous. I saw one woman pour a bottle of champagne over a man's head, while two others sprawled unconscious on the cushions of the veranda. Still more were at drunken business with each other in the shadows, trying to stifle gasps and moans. Finally, there was a great splash and a chorus of laughter as one man went careering into the pool.

Half past midnight. It was time. I raced back to the kitchen, my heart hammering, my mouth dry with nerves. After a minute, Langham appeared, locking the kitchen door behind him.

'Ready?' he asked, retrieving my suit jacket from its hanger behind the door.

I nodded, trying to be fast, my fingers slipping on the gilded buttons of the server's jacket. He helped me to pull it from my shoulders, and within moments, we had swapped. He now wore the apron and the serving uniform. I was the one resplendent in white flannel. Last, he took out his pocket watch, and hooked it into my own waistcoat.

'Remember, keep your head down, and don't let anyone get too close,' he said. 'They have to believe I'm you, Ale, if I'm to have an alibi.'

I nodded again, unable to speak, and caught him by the arms.

'An hour and a half, by the Hotel Continental,' he said rapidly. 'Then we'll be away from here. At two o'clock. You hear me?'

We kissed, once, and too soon he was turning, picking up the tray of mahjoun, his head lowered.

'Arthur!' My cry stopped him by the door, and he looked back. His posture had already changed, his expression, his whole demeanour. It was as if I was looking at a stranger.

Then he was gone, slipping through the shadows towards the back gate where Bouzid would be waiting. I grabbed the boater hat from the kitchen table and made for the lounge, keeping to the shadows.

For forty-five, dreadful minutes I flitted through the rooms, lingered beneath tree branches and in doorways, careful to be seen only in glimpses by the guests who stumbled across the veranda and down the paths.

When the clock in the lounge struck quarter past one, I almost sobbed with relief and made for the stairs, half running in case anyone should try to stop me. Finally, I reached the safety of the roof terrace with its locked door, and sagged against it, breathing hard, trying to stay calm. This was the part I didn't like. Everyone at the party had to see me; they had to swear that Langham had been present all night, especially between one o'clock and half past.

Was a murder happening even now? I thought feverishly, peering out across at the city. Was Cabrera dead, lying crumpled in some alleyway, or face down with a bullet in his back? How had Langham done it?

I knelt down behind the parapet, wiping sweat from my upper lip, and checked the pocket watch. Twenty past one. I took the box of matches from my pocket, snapping three before I finally managed to light one and touch it to the waiting fuse. Then, I backed away to the farthest corner, watching it burn down, knowing that from this point on, there would be no return.

The firework exploded into the night, red and gold and white. I stepped to the edge of the roof terrace and threw my arms wide, knowing my figure would be illuminated, in its distinctive white suit. Below in the gardens, people began to cheer and *aah*, pointing up at me and clapping, yelling, *Arthur darling, don't fall off!*

Done, I ducked back down. I had to hurry.

At the bottom of the stairs from the terrace, I ran straight into Hilde.

'People are coming up,' she said breathlessly. 'Quick.'

She hustled me into Langham's room and locked the door behind her, just as voices echoed in the corridor.

'Langham,' a man bellowed, hammering on the door, 'come out and settle a bet!'

'I think he's busy,' a woman's voice slurred, 'or didn't you notice the bus boy was missing?'

There were sniggers and Hilde threw a look at me. They were too close to the truth. Suddenly, she was kicking off her shoes, pulling the dress over her head. 'Hold this,' she hissed. I threw off the hat, ruffled my hair and turned my back to the door just as she opened it, wearing only her slip.

The sniggers ceased.

'If you'll excuse us,' she said, her voice low. 'Mr Langham and I are enjoying a private conversation. We'll re-join you in a moment.'

She slammed the door and locked it. We didn't move, listening to the laughter on the other side.

'They're at it again,' the woman crowed, as they stumbled away back down the hall. 'Who'd have thought! So much for the cook!'

Hilde was dressing rapidly. 'It's nearly quarter to two,' I told her, my pulse racing. 'I have to get to the Continental. Hilde, what if he—'

'Don't.' She looked at me, her face set. 'For god's sake, don't talk about it any more.'

She went ahead of me to make sure the way was clear. Before the front doors, we stopped, only for someone to yell my – Langham's – name. We had only seconds. Hilde leaned in and kissed me on the mouth.

'Go,' she whispered, tears in her voice. 'Just go.'

I turned and fled. Behind me, I heard Hilde's voice, falsely bright. 'Oh, don't try and stop him. He has some mad idea about taking out the yacht. *I* certainly can't dissuade him . . .'

Ten to two. I slipped through the gates of Dar Portuna, the scent of jasmine catching at my jacket like the hand of a lover. In the dark, dusty street, I swiped tears from my face.

Don't think, I told myself savagely. *Hacer de tripas corazón.*

I reached the Hotel Continental in record time, with minutes to spare. I had almost run through the dark streets and was breathing hard, my chest constricted by the brassiere. The wound on the back of my head had started to throb again, tiredness and anxiety making me sick. Would Langham arrive with blood on his hands, staining his fine, white sleeves? With Cabrera dead, would I finally be free from my past?

The illuminated sign of the Hotel Continental cast pools of red and green light on to the street. I edged into it, for comfort, glancing at the pocket watch. Three minutes to two.

From the terrace above, I could hear the sound of gentle conversation, smell wafts of tobacco. I wished I was one of those guests; tipsy and oblivious to everything except the warm darkness and the ship lights that twinkled on the strait. When a figure in white stepped to the edge of the terrace, I almost cried out, but it was only a waiter in a neat serving jacket, clearing one of the tables. He saw me, though, and seemed to hesitate. Then he was gone.

It didn't make my nerves any better. I had made up my mind to walk to the other side of the dark street, to listen for footsteps when a door creaked open in the lower part of the hotel terrace, and the waiter emerged.

'Monsieur Langham?' he called. The green and red glow didn't make it easy to see. 'Are you there? It is Monsieur Langham, isn't it?'

My skin prickled. Was this part of the plan he hadn't told me?

'Yes,' I said, keeping my voice low, doing my best impersonation of Langham's familiar, clipped accent.

The waiter came forwards. I tipped my hat even lower, pretending to look at the watch.

'Here it is, monsieur. As you asked.'

He was holding something out towards me. For a moment, I almost told him he was mistaken, until I realized what it was. It was Langham's writing case, personalized, stamped with those two, golden letters.

Slowly, I took it. *When did he leave it here?* I wanted to cry. *What did he ask? Why was he here at all?* But I couldn't, the waiter would think I was mad, asking those questions about myself.

'Thank you,' I muttered.

'De rien, monsieur.' He lingered, hoping for a tip. When I didn't move, he gave up and disappeared back into the building.

What was going on? Maybe Langham had been early, I thought rapidly; maybe he'd left our bags here, so as not to be suspicious. I flipped the latch of the writing case, thinking he might have left some note for me inside.

But before I could open it, I heard scuffling, the sound of feet trying to walk quietly on the gritty stones. Two o'clock exactly. My heart leapt as I latched the case and stuck it beneath my arm, moving quickly to the corner.

'I'm here,' I called softly. 'Is it—?'

Light flared, blinding me. I threw up my arms, the case thudding to the dirt. Suddenly, I was surrounded, voices were shouting, hands were swarming out of nowhere to grip my arms and shoulders, shoving me face first to the ground. I screamed in panic but my mouth was full of dust, and I choked. Someone was pulling at my jacket. That sent me crazed, and I lashed out, clawing, kicking, thrashing at anyone within reach. It didn't stop them. One man – I could smell it was a man – kicked me, before leaning all his weight on to my back, ripping Langham's watch from my waistcoat, scrabbling through my pockets.

Thieves, I thought wildly. I tried to yell for them to take what they wanted and leave me alone, but my voice wouldn't work, all I could do was wheeze with pain and fear.

But a pair of shoes were stepping into the light, and they didn't look like they belonged to a thief. They were good shoes of black leather, below black suit trousers. I struggled, craning my neck until I could look up. A man was holding my passport in his hand, shining a torch down on to it. They had pulled it from my pocket, which I didn't understand, because I had put my passport in the suitcase, hadn't I?

Then, through streaming eyes, I saw: it wasn't my passport at all.

Every knot of bravery I had tied around my heart unravelled when I realized what was happening.

'It's him,' the man with the torch called in English, before looking down at me. 'Arthur Langham, I am arresting you in the name of Her Majesty's Service for the crime of treason against your country . . .'

Tangier

July 1978

Sam fell silent, staring down at the letter.

'He betrayed Ale.' Zahrah's voice was soft, calling them both back to the present. 'After everything they had been through, he did that, *knowing* the danger.'

'Maybe that's not what happened.' Sam swallowed. 'Maybe there was some kind of mix-up, or Langham was double-crossed himself before he could get there, or—'

Abruptly, his mind went back to the strange, brief letter he'd found in the writing case. He squeezed his eyes closed.

'Why are you defending him?' Zahrah demanded. 'Can't you see he planned it? Ale was a *decoy* not an alibi—'

Silently, Sam stood up and went to his own pile of papers. There, sitting on top was the pencil scrawled note.

A,
I am sorry.
One day, I hope you'll understand.

'He must have left this in the writing case for Ale to find,' he said, handing it over to Zahrah. 'He must have dumped the suitcase at the Continental, and hidden the note and the key in the writing case just in case Ale got away. But Ale never saw it. And I never mentioned it either . . .' He trailed off. 'Langham died that night,' he forced himself to say. 'His body washed up two days later, on one of the beaches.'

Zahrah shook her head. 'Maybe whatever happened with Cabrera went bad. Maybe there was a fight. Or—'

'Maybe he ended it himself.' Sam looked down at the letter.

Silence stretched between them.

'What about Ale?' he asked suddenly. 'What happened after the arrest, back in nineteen twenty-eight? Do you know?'

'I'm not sure.' Zahrah leafed through the pages that had been addressed to Sam, detailing what had happened, the night of the party. 'Wait, it carries on, look.'

'Thank god.' He leaned in to see, close enough that Zahrah's shoulder brushed against his. She smelled of the kitchen, warm oil and faint spices.

But before he read a word, there were footsteps in the corridor, raised voices and the door was shoved open, without so much as a knock. Madame Sarah's sister stood there.

'You see!' she said, pointing to Zahrah.

Sam jumped up from the bed. 'It's not like—' he started, holding up his hands.

'This is no good.' The woman was incensed. 'My sister will not stand for this in her house.'

'We were just reading.' Zahrah sounded indignant.

The woman made a derisive sound, eyeing Zahrah's cropped hair, her bare legs and sandalled feet beneath the djellaba, before rounding on Sam. 'You want to stay? Then she leaves. And you pay what you owe. Now.'

Madame Sarah came hurrying on to the landing, her face bright red. 'I am sorry, Mr Hackett,' she said, 'but . . .'

He looked away. This was her house after all; she shouldn't be the one apologizing. Zahrah stood up from the bed, staring at Madame Sarah's sister with obvious dislike.

'It's fine,' she snapped. 'I'll go.'

'No.' He shook his head. None of this was Zahrah's fault. Or Madame Sarah's. He met his landlady's eyes. 'It's OK. I know I've been a terrible lodger. You deserve better.' He gathered up the few remaining coins on the bedside table. 'I can't pay in advance for another week anyway. Here, this is all I have.' He straightened up, looking around at his few scattered possessions. 'I'll be gone as soon as I've packed and tidied up. I don't think it'll take me very long.'

Zahrah stood behind him, holding the papers.

'Can my friend wait with me?' he asked. 'Then we'll go.'

'Yes,' Madame Sarah said, interrupting her sister's refusal. She hesitated, before holding something out to him. It was the writing case. 'This is yours.'

He smiled as he took it, and she gave him a small smile in return. Then she was taking her sister's arm and steering her towards the stairs, ignoring her furious whispers.

'I'm sorry about that,' Sam muttered, once they were gone. 'Do you mind waiting? I'll be as quick as I can.'

He began to stride around the room, grabbing odds and ends. A creased paperback, a useless sock, his other shirt, left on the floor. He dragged his duffel bag out and began to shove things in haphazardly.

'Was that the truth?' Zahrah asked, watching him. 'About the money?'

He nodded, face burning to the tips of his ears. 'I gave everything I had to the police as a bribe. Didn't work.'

'Then what are you going to do?'

'Honestly?' He stuffed a t-shirt into the bag. 'I have no idea. My parents said they would pay for a one-way ticket home. I guess it's time for me to telephone them.'

'But you said you had no money, so how can you telephone?'

Was that a hint of mockery in her voice? He carried on packing, not looking at her.

'I'll ask my friend Abdelhamid,' he said quickly. 'I sold him my typewriter. He might be able to get me a phone call. Or maybe I could sell back . . .' He stopped, looking down at the writing case. The police must have seized it when Ale was arrested, he realized. They must have filed it away as evidence, left it forgotten on a shelf for thirty years, until the building was emptied, until Mouad bought it and took it back to the shop, where it had sat, waiting for him.

He held it out. 'You should have this,' he told Zahrah. 'It was never really mine.'

She took it, and slowly opened the lid. The smell of the past was released into the room once more, drowning them, taking them back.

She lifted the thick envelope that Alejandro had addressed to her – the one Sam presumed contained the will – and placed it gently inside. He wanted to ask what else Ale had written on all those pages, but they were Zahrah's after all, and she didn't seem inclined to tell him. She closed the case with a snap.

'Come on,' she said, standing up decisively. 'Let's go.'

'Go where? I told you—'

She cut him off with an impatient noise. 'Sam Hackett, there is an entire house standing empty, just a few minutes away. You can stay with me.'

'What about the police?' The threat had been enough to drive Ale away. 'What if they come to raid the place?'

Zahrah raised her head. 'Let them. They won't find Ale. And since Dar Portuna now belongs to me, they'll have to leave well enough alone, eventually.' She raised an eyebrow at him. 'So are you coming? Or do you want to sleep on the streets? I have to tell you, I don't think you'd last a minute.'

He didn't know what to say. Despite his guilt and shame and uncertainty, a kind of thrill rose in his chest at being allowed to stay at Dar Portuna; even if it was for what might be his final few nights in Tangier.

'Thank you,' he said, hoping she knew how much he meant it.

She just nodded and stepped towards the door.

'Wait.'

Hurriedly, he shuffled together the scrappy, mismatched papers on the bedside table.

'Is that . . . ?'

'My book. Yeah.' He shook his head. 'If I hadn't been so obsessed with my own damn writing, none of this would have happened.' His fingers tightened on the old paper, on the new sheets. 'I should burn these,' he said. 'It's not my story. I've already caused enough trouble—'

Zahrah took hold of one side of the manuscript. 'Don't you dare. Ale told you this story for a reason. And anyway –' she gave him a half-smile '– I might want to read it.'

With the duffel bag over his shoulder, the manuscript carefully wedged within, he made a penitent farewell to Madame Sarah and received a ferocious, thoroughly undeserved hug about the knees from Aziz. Then, they were out on the street, bustling hot at noon.

They didn't speak, just walked rapidly uphill, towards Dar Portuna, towards the rest of the story. After checking to see if anyone might be lurking, spying on the place, they brushed the jasmine aside, and slipped in through the old gate. In bright sunlight, the house seemed more unreal than ever, as though at any minute it might flicker and disappear from the surface of the world. They stepped through the front doors, into the faded, echoing hallway.

'It feels so strange without Ale,' Zahrah whispered. When her fingers brushed his, he took her hand, squeezing it tight.

Together, they walked slowly through the entrance hall, towards the quiet, dust-filled rooms. Sam peered up the stairs as they passed, his skin prickling all over. He almost expected to hear footsteps, to see a young Alejandro come running down, hear the warble of a gramophone and Hilde calling out from the veranda, to see Langham look up from the desk as they stepped into the study.

'This is where I found the envelopes,' Zahrah said.

There was a strange smell in the room. Something sharp, at odds with the old leather and worm-eaten wood. Smoke, Sam realized; smoke and burned paper. In the grate, a huge pile of ash had been pushed to one side. Dropping his bag, he knelt and picked out a fragment of dull green cardboard that might have belonged to a file.

'Ale spent all night in here.' Zahrah was standing over him. 'All the drawers and ledgers are empty. Everything was burned, I think, except for what she left me. And what she left you.'

Reaching into his bag, he pulled out the envelope with his name on, and shook out the pages. The rest of Ale's story, unfinished. He sank into the creaking armchair, déjà vu shimmering across his mind.

'Go on,' Zahrah said. 'Read it.'

Blinking hard, he turned the pages until he found where they'd left off.

'"Old—"' he began and stopped.

'What is it?'

'"Old Pal",' he said, disbelieving. '"Take a pony of Canadian whisky, a pony of Campari and a pony of French vermouth" . . . for god's sake.'

Zahrah laughed, though her eyes were bright with tears. 'That's so like Ale,' she said. 'What does the rest say?'

He had to clear his throat before continuing. '"Stir into a cocktail glass and drink to friends, absent, old and new."'

Zahrah wiped at her face. 'I think we had better do as we're told.'

Together, they hunted through the dozens of bottles on the bar, some of which looked decades old, perhaps even from Langham's day, their labels torn, containing nothing but sticky residue.

Sam found himself glancing over at Zahrah. What was he doing here? A few hours before he'd been slammed in a cell, and now here he was, in a decaying villa, making drinks with a woman who . . . He looked down rapidly at the bottles.

Don't go there. You have to go home.

Finally, they had two glasses of liqueur before them, glowing in the afternoon sun.

'To friends,' Zahrah said. 'Absent, old and new.'

They touched glasses, and drank. It was incredibly strong.

'Ready?' Zahrah asked, glancing at the pages.

He swallowed down the taste of the past, of what might be his last drink in Tangier.

'Ready.'

OLD PAL

Take a pony of Canadian whisky, a pony of Campari and a pony of French vermouth. Stir into a cocktail glass and drink to friends, absent, old and new.

I have cared for many people in my life, whether I have wanted to or not. That's the trick of friendship. You can lock your doors, board up your gate, and still, some soul will find a way in, slipping through your shutters, creeping over your walls, tripping and falling face first into your life and there is nothing you can do to stop it.

I class you as a friend, Samuel, though a new one. Zahrah too, now more like family to me. Both of you came uninvited, trespassers into my life. But I am glad of it. Once, I was the person who climbed the wall. I was the one who crashed into a life unasked for. Should I have been surprised then, by what Langham did to me? Perhaps not.

But at the time . . . I felt as if someone had reached into my chest and ripped the insides from me, guts and heart and all. I was wretched. I was terrified. And most of all, I was furious with myself.

At the inn, I'd watched people deceive themselves over and over; the girls, the clients, Elena, even Morales. I had thought I was above it all. But of course, I was not. I had spun myself falsehoods out of jasmine and smoke, bound my hands with white flannel and silk and stepped smiling into a trap of my own making.

Langham had shown me over and again what he was – traitor, liar, charlatan – and I had chosen not to see it. *I wouldn't wish that on you*, he had told me, when I said I wanted to be like him. But I hadn't listened, and as a result I found myself in danger, facing what could have been the Spanish police, extradition, and the end.

Could have been, but wasn't. I avoided that fate not through luck or cunning or trickery, but through friendship.

As ignorant as the British police were, it did not take them long to realize their mistake. I still remember their pink faces, pale beneath their sunburn when I told them for the last time that I was not Langham and finally proved it. If I hadn't been so frightened, I would have laughed.

They were incensed by their mistake, and declared that, whoever I was, I must be involved with Langham's criminal activities, seeing as I was dressed like him and carrying his papers, his pocket watch, his writing case. I had to think faster than I ever had before.

It wasn't hard to make myself cry – for I was terrified – and through the tears I told them that I worked in Langham's house as a cook and that it was his particular perversion to have me dress up in his clothes. The passport I couldn't explain. I supposed, between sobs, that he must have left it in his jacket. Eventually, they came to the obvious, and correct, conclusion: Langham had used his silly, trusting domestic as a decoy, in order to secure his escape from Tangiers.

By this point, the clock on the police station wall read a quarter past five. Langham had won himself over three hours' head-start. More than enough for a man like him.

The police knew it, and they vented their frustration on me. They grilled me for hours. What had Langham done in the days prior? Who did he talk to? Who visited the house? Again and again, I pleaded ignorance. I was just the cook, a poor girl Langham had taken a fancy to, who he liked to see dressed up in men's clothes. I didn't know about his business, I was always in the kitchen.

I knew they were getting desperate when they asked me about Cabrera.

You won't see him again, I almost said. But I didn't. Instead, I gambled that Cabrera had kept the information about me to himself, for future use. I told the police that a man of that name had once come to dinner, that was all.

I told them my name was Alejandra del Potro, praying they wouldn't check it with the consulate. *I'm just a poor silly girl*, I tried to make my demeanour cry, *taken in by her corrupt employer*. Of course, they wanted my papers; they wanted proof of who I was. My story would have unravelled then, and I would have found myself headed for a Spanish jail and the garrotte, had it not been for the cool, familiar voice that rang out beyond the cell door.

Hilde. It was Hilde. And though I could hear the panic in her voice, she was strong enough and smart enough to hide it from them. In icy British tones, I heard her complain of the police tramping through her bedroom all night. I heard her declare that she had no notion of where Mr Langham might be – though she was sure he would return in a day or two – and that in the meantime, she would like her cook released, since she, Lady de Luca Bailey, couldn't so much as boil an egg on her own.

She vouched for my story. She dismissed their charges of impersonation and immorality with a haughty laugh and a casual reference to her solicitor. She paid the desk clerk to discharge me, took me by the arm and swept me from the station towards Langham's car, which stood, gleaming in the first light of day.

Only when we pulled away from the station did I see how much her hands were shaking, how she had started to cry, every breath turning into a sob.

'My god,' she said as she raced through the deserted streets, half-blinded by tears. 'My god, Alejandro, what has he done?'

I couldn't answer, slumped in the passenger seat in my beautiful, crumpled suit. In that moment, it was too much. I had envied Langham his wealth and freedom; I had wished for all the things he had, everything that been denied me as a poor woman without family or name. And now here I was, sitting in the front seat of an expensive motorcar, being driven around by a Lady in an evening gown. I almost let out a bitter laugh. As twisted as it was, I had been granted my wish.

Dar Portuna had been ransacked. No one had cleaned up after the party, and the tiled floors were scuffed with boot prints, with spilled drinks.

'Bouzid?' I asked, already knowing the answer.

Hilde shook her head. Like Langham, he had vanished.

'The police came through,' she told me as she looked around, her make-up smudged from crying. 'They took everything they could find from the study, all of Arthur's papers. Except . . .'

I followed her to her bedroom, where she pulled open the bottom dresser drawer. There, hidden in the lining, beneath a layer of sanitary napkins and knickers and stockings, she revealed a dozen green cardboard files, stashed alongside her own, secret Italian ones.

'I wagered they'd be too squeamish to look closely at a lady's necessities,' she said, with a bleak smile. 'I don't know what else they got, but I think these are the most important. As soon as I heard hammering at the gate, I knew something had gone wrong. I went and snatched these up from the study, just in case.' She sank on to the edge of the bed. 'I was so frightened. I hoped both of you might have got away, but then the police told me that they had arrested you, in place of him and I . . .' She trailed off, tears on her face.

Clumsily, I pulled out a file. It was filled with papers written in French. There was another entirely in German. I saw addresses in Marseille and Tripoli, Cape Town, and Trieste, shipping manifests and pages of drawings, like Hilde's prototypes, photographs of buildings and people who stared darkly from the paper, lists of names written beneath them. Whatever the documents were, I had no doubt that in connection to Langham, they were incriminating.

'Maybe he thought they'd let me go, once they realized their mistake.' My voice sounded hollow. I didn't have it in me to believe my own excuses any more.

Hilde sniffed, and pushed back her hair. 'Even if that's true, he knew what you were running from. He knew all it would take was for the British police to liaise with the Spanish, and then . . .' She looked at me. 'I'm so sorry, Alejandro. I never dreamed.'

I went to her, and we held each other tight, until our tears subsided and we were able to turn our burning eyes to the mess before us.

The days that followed were terrible. We leapt every time the telephone rang; we broke into cold sweats when a fist hammered on the gate. Police came at any hour of the day, not just the British, but gendarmes, guardia, polizei, even. It was clear that Langham's activities stretched far, far further than any of us had imagined.

Cabrera had thought of Langham as an easy catch; he obviously had no idea what kind of person he was dealing with.

Then came the news of Langham's boat, abandoned on the strait, and a call from the station, a few hours later, to say that a body had been recovered. Hilde was the one to identify it. She came back shaken and pale, but strangely excited.

The corpse was almost unrecognizable, she said, battered by the rocks. Most of the hair was gone, as well as the eyes. But it was wearing the remains of Langham's clothes, the white flannel suit, the saffron shirt, torn and spoiled, his gold ring, which for some reason was jammed above the knuckle, as if the fingers had swelled.

Neither of us said what we were thinking: that it didn't matter at all whether the body was Langham's or that of a man with yellow, goat-like eyes. In that moment, we made a silent pact to keep it a secret, to never mention his name to anyone. Even if somewhere in the world, someone was walking around wearing his face, the man we had known as Arthur Langham – the man we had loved – was dead to us. Our silence would ensure he stayed that way.

Langham had been clever in some ways, and rather stupid in others. He had left Hilde in charge of Dar Portuna, counting on her loyalty, perhaps intending to reclaim it from her one day, when the British had moved on to other targets, and her anger had faded enough to forgive him. A mistake. The very day Hilde returned from the coroner's office, we set about securing our future. We made a good team, Lady Bailey and I; she beyond reproach with her title and fine manners, me with my knowledge of the streets and petty scams.

It didn't take us long to hack out a will on Langham's typewriter, even less time for me to dress up in one of his suits and find some poor backstreet notaire half-blind with opium withdrawal to witness the document, no questions asked. If he noticed that the will was dated June, rather than July, he didn't say a word, just took the generous fee and shook my hand and murmured, *Merci, Monsieur Langham*.

A week later the formalities were concluded. Lady Hilde Bailey became the legal owner of Dar Portuna. Immediately, without a second thought, she had a new deed drawn up, and gave half of the house to me. We both knew then that, whatever happened, we would always have a place of safety and sanctuary. A home.

I had never had a true friend, apart from Ifrahim. That is what Hilde became, the closest and dearest person to me. And if Tangiers society whispered about us, so what? We could close the doors of Dar Portuna and let jasmine grow over the gate and not bother with them in the least, until the world had moved on, and forgotten both of our names.

Two months became six, and the phone calls from the police stopped. Six months became a year and mutterings of a financial crash began to reach us. A year became two, and Italy was hit hard and Hilde's extortion of her ex-husband was no longer viable. So, we found new ways to live, using some of Langham's old contacts. Tangiers has always been a flexible city, and in times of economic depression, *other* markets tend to thrive . . .

When you arrived at my house, Sam, I could have told you that story. It's a tale of how an Englishwoman and a Spanish orphan made their fortunes on the tip of Africa. I could have told you how they made friends and lovers and enemies. How they built up an empire of their own, one to rival Langham's, by employing people they trusted: women like them, who wanted to live by their own terms, secretaries and cooks and captains with gold teeth, who knew when to keep their silence . . .

It's a story of how those women evaded capture by being smart and fast and quiet, taking new names when they needed them, disappearing into their secret haven – known only to a few close friends – whenever they sensed they were in danger. For many years, until she died, that Englishwoman and I lived and loved and cultivated the one thing both of us wanted more than anything else: freedom.

All stories must come to an end. Hilde is gone, Zahrah has learned all I can share, and it seems the authorities might have found my doorstep at last. And so I find myself wondering whether Dar Portuna has become a cage, rather than a haven; whether freedom might better be found out in the world. Whether, by breaking my silence about Langham, I might finally be able to shake off the past, and begin a new story, even at my age.

The thought is irresistible.

But, I didn't tell you that story. I'm telling you this one, and it is almost finished. Hold out your glass and I will pour the very last drop.

It tastes of a foggy morning in March 1932, when a letter arrived at the gate of Dar Portuna, postmarked Shanghai. For long minutes it sat damp with rain on the kitchen table, while Hilde and I stared, trying to decide what to do. Then, as the coffee pot began to whistle, we met each other's eyes, picked it up, and dropped it into the stove. For a moment, the whole kitchen seemed to smell of wax and musk and rose-scented pomade.

Not for long. By the time it had crumpled to ash we were sat on the veranda, talking and drinking coffee and listening to the rain, falling over the strait of Tangiers.

Epilogue

Tangier 1988

LAST WORD

Take a pony of dry gin, three quarters of a pony of Chartreuse Verte, three quarters of a pony of Maraschino liqueur and the same of fresh lime. Shake well with ice and strain into a cocktail glass. A drink to cleanse the palate, when the day is done.

Le Mal de Tanger.

Tangier Sickness, it's the excuse people give, the reason why they remain in this city. I already had it bad, back then. Now I'm incurable. I'm a true Tangerine, like the best and the worst of them.

Of course, Tangier – *my* Tangier – is gone. It changed around me, even as I walked the streets, just as it had for Ale, for Hilde, for Arthur Langham.

Still, I see that lost city every day. To live in Tangier is to live in a dozen versions of the same place, to walk with one eye filled with ghosts. I see it in the faded advertisements on the medina walls. I see it in Abdelhamid's shop, which hasn't changed a bit. I see it in the old, flamboyant characters, clasping their fraying masks to their faces, taking the same seats in the Café Central that they did fifty years ago, sullenly sipping tea where once they drank down Fundador.

I see it every time I walk past the Bab al-Bahr, and the white walls of Dar Portuna rise up before me. A few times, I have almost forgotten myself and turned the corner, almost raised a hand to brush aside a fall of jasmine that is no longer there.

Dar Portuna doesn't belong to me, any more. It really never did. Zahrah chose to sell, just after we were married. The authorities didn't like that – they were still turning up every so often, looking for Ale – but they couldn't do a thing. Ale's will was watertight. So we had our wedding there, a final party attended by our friends in the city: by Abdelhamid and Mouad and their families, by Bet and the crew from The Hold, who had known all along that I would never leave, by my bemused parents and siblings and a few people we later found out were never invited at all. For one last evening, champagne flowed and music tangled in the old fig tree and I'm sure the lights could be seen from the darkness of the strait.

Then, Bet helped us sell the place to a contact of hers, a foreign gentleman investor whose name I never quite caught. Zahrah used the money to start her own business. We had a future to build, not a past to languish in. Dar Portuna is a hotel now, an exclusive one, where they serve cocktails on the terrace and cook English-style breakfasts for those that want them. It seems fitting. Sometimes, Zahrah and I joke that we'll spend the night there for our anniversary, but we never have.

We live in the new town, in a flat that overlooks the strait with its eerie blue colour, its constant mix of two waters, tumbling together. My writing desk is by the window, and on good days, after a coffee at the Gran Café de Paris, I stare out at the smudge of Spain on the horizon and hack out a few chapters, before picking up the girls from school.

Zahrah often works until late. Her business – imports and exports – is going from strength to strength. Sometimes I think about the envelope that Ale left, addressed to her: thick with papers that she has never let me read, surely containing more than a simple will. Sometimes, I ask if I can help. But my wife only smiles at me, and says I wouldn't like all of the details. These days her personalized briefcase is full of papers in English, Spanish, French, even Russian.

As for me, it took two years to knock that first, scrappy manuscript into shape, another year to find an agent in London willing to take a punt, and another before I was finally holding a finished copy of the book in my hands. *Last Drink in Tangiers*. It did OK, for a debut. Sure, there were some critics who said it was far-fetched, but my editor told me to ignore them; she said that as long as there are readers, there will always be appetite for a good story.

I guess she's right, because my books have sold pretty well since then. They're crime novels mostly, tales of smuggling and glamour and adventure, all set in a past age. Bet helps me when I'm stuck for ideas, says she has more tall tales than she knows what to do with.

But recently I've been thinking of writing something different, a particular story that has been nagging at me for a long time. I know how it begins. I was reminded of it just the other day, when my daily walk took me past the ragged old Hotel Continental. When I glanced up at the terrace, I swear I saw two elderly gentlemen sitting there, wearing beautiful white flannel suits. They stuck in my mind, so I decided to turn around, to take a closer look.

By the time I jogged up the steps, they were gone, leaving nothing but a pair of empty cocktail glasses. I asked the waiter if the old men were lodging at the hotel, but he didn't seem to know what I was talking about.

Of course, I could have tried to find them. I could have tracked them down and asked where they had come from, where they were heading, Marrakech, Paris, Shanghai? I could have asked whether they were old friends who had previously lost touch, but who now, in their autumn years, saw each other clearly for the first time.

I could have told them they reminded me of people in a story I once heard. I could have asked whether that drink on the terrace of the Hotel Continental was the first or the last of many . . .

I could have, but I didn't. Instead, I went home, sat down at my desk, and began to write.

Acknowledgements

Writing this book has been an adventure in more ways than one. Thanks must be mixed and measured according to equal parts, as follows:

To my dad, for his stories of camels and kif, travelling and trouble, airmail letters, near-arrests and Pete the Squeak.

To my mum, for her endless support and encouragement, and for helping me to find my own freedom.

To my sister, fellow traveller.

To the Coppells, for aiding and abetting.

To Grandma Iris and Pat, who can spin any yarn over a drink.

To Ed, for the Negronis.

To Darcy, for helping to shake up the good parts and strain out the bad.

To all at Transworld, for their work behind the scenes.

To Gareth, for giving this book its own recipe.

To Zahrah, for her spirit, and the use of her name.

To everyone at La Tangerina, Tangier, for the food, tea and welcome.

To Abdullah, for the tall tales.

To Charlie, Tim and Louis, for always opening the door, no matter how late.

To Alashiya, Maartje and Emma: partners in crime.

To Becky, for propping up the bar and listening to the same old woes.

To Nick, for being there at the end of the night and the beginning of the next day.

The Secrets Between Us

Laura Madeleine

A gripping mystery with a heart-breaking revelation, *The Secrets Between Us* is a deeply moving story of lost love, betrayal and the dangers of war.

High in the mountains in the South of France, eighteen-year-old Ceci Corvin is trying hard to carry on as normal. But in 1943, there is no such thing as normal; especially not for a young woman in love with the wrong person. Scandal, it would seem, can be more dangerous than war.

Fifty years later, Annie is looking for her long-lost grandmother. Armed with nothing more than a sheaf of papers, she travels from England to Paris in pursuit of the truth. But as she traces her grandmother's story, Annie uncovers something she wasn't expecting, something that changes everything she knew about her family – and everything she thought she knew about herself . . .

Where The Wild Cherries Grow

Laura Madeleine

I closed my eyes as I tried to pick apart every flavour, because nothing had ever tasted so good before. It was love and it could not be hidden.

It is 1919 and the end of the war has not brought peace for Emeline Vane. Lost in grief, she is suddenly alone at the heart of a depleted family. She can no longer cope. Just as everything seems to be slipping beyond her control, in a moment of desperation, she boards a train and runs away.

Fifty years later, a young solicitor on his first case finds Emeline's diary. Bill Perch is eager to prove himself but what he learns from the tattered pages of neat script goes against everything he has been told. He begins to trace a story of love and betrayal that will send him on a journey to discover the truth.

What really happened to Emeline all those years ago?